~ A ~
COLDNESS
IN THE
BLOOD

Fred Saberhagen

TOR®

A TOM DOHERTY ASSOCIATES BOOK
NEW YORK

A COLDNESS IN THE BLOOD

Copyright © 2002 by Fred Saberhagen

A Tor Book
Published by Tom Doherty Associates, LLC
175 Fifth Avenue
New York, NY 10010

www.tor.com

Tor® is a registered trademark of Tom Doherty Associates, LLC.

ISBN: 0-765-34011-9
Library of Congress Catalog Card Number: 200202471

First edition: October 2002
First mass market edition: October 2003

Printed in the United States of America

0 9 8 7 6 5 4 3 2 1

Dramatis Personae

MATTHEW MAULE—has lived and gone to his grave in other centuries, under other names, most notably VLAD DRACULA. Currently Maule is developing a theory in which vampires, the *nosferatu*, form a distinct subspecies: *Homo dirus,* or man inspiring dread. Few are going to argue the point with him.

JOE KEOGH—a generation ago, as a young Chicago cop, Joe married into the Southerland family. Ever since he has been bound to them, and to Maule, by ties of loyalty and money, blood and love, horror and secrecy. Now Joe is worried about his son, Andy.

ANDY KEOGH—a few weeks past his nineteenth birthday, he had no idea that vampires were real. The facts of life, Southerland family style, would come as a great revelation.

DOLORES FLAMEL—her grandfather was a great magician who left young Dolly a puzzling legacy, plus a warning about certain of his associates. When she came to the big city, she thought it wise to bring along a sawed-off shotgun.

SOBEK—was something both more and less than human. In ancient Egypt, he had been offered the sacrifice and worship due the god of crocodiles. In twenty-first-century America, he intends to accept no less, from breathers or vampires.

CONSTANTIA—almost as old in the ways of the *nosferatu* as Matthew Maule himself, she is still as young and beautiful as the day she turned eighteen—and very little wiser.

DICKON—probably the oldest vampire Mr. Maule has ever met—but even more frightened than frightening. Centuries of being terrified have made Dickon very good at sheer survival, and he can be extremely dangerous when cornered.

LAMBERT—quite young for a vampire, and exceptionally violent. He was fascinated by the rumors of a magnificent magician's treasure, a Stone that gave all wealth and power to its possessor. Lambert fears neither Maule nor monster.

~ A ~
COLDNESS
IN THE
BLOOD

~ Prologue ~

*I*t was smuggling that got the stuff out of Egypt, Dolly. A crooked operation. Crooked as all hell."

The speaker's voice was faint and wheezing, a crippled, dying sound, issuing from a shrunken figure in an old hospital bed tucked away in one corner of a wide corridor in a timeworn building. Crowding being what it was these days here at County, the corridor was doing duty as a ward.

A window nearby was propped open a few inches, letting in the smells of dust and warmth and weeds, automobiles and pavement. Beyond heavy screening and thick dirty glass, the city lay in a summer afternoon's warm blur of sights and sounds.

The young woman in sole attendance on the old man leaned a little closer in her chair. She had the look of one grown accustomed to bewilderment, and her appearance suggested she had been summoned to this bedside without much time for preparation. Her youthful face, and her outfit of old jeans, old sneakers, and a new pullover shirt with the initials of Thomas More University emblazoned on the front, strongly suggested the beginning college student.

In soft, weary tones she said: "Take it easy, Gramp. It's all right if you don't tell me. Everything will work out."

Wrinkled eyelids opened in a jaundiced face. Where once had grown a neat theatrical beard, carefully trimmed and tended, now showed only irregular gray stubble. The gray head on the clean pillow shook back and forth, slowly but vehemently. The exhausted voice rose louder. "Got to tell you, Dolly . . . the whole secret . . . worth a fortune. More . . ."

Words faded in a breathless mumble, but the anxiety on the old man's face was plain. It had been building for several hours.

Dolly had been treated to this suggestion of a fortune several times in those several hours, since the beginning of her day's bedside vigil, otherwise pretty much a repeat of yesterday's. Once before, about two hours ago, her grandfather had spoken incoherently about smuggling, and Egypt. But so far there was no evidence the talk was anything but delirium.

Still, the young woman wanted to be sure, and she wanted to be fair, and by nature she was kind. "All right, Gramp. Tell me if you have to, whatever it is. Take it slow, easy. I'm right here. I'm listening."

The gasping voice slowly became intelligible again. ". . . little statues . . ."

" 'Statues,' Gramp?"

". . . once they were in this country, got stolen again, y'see. By some stupid bastards, didn't even know they were antiquities. Sold 'em off any way they could. . . ."

A nurse came by, practical heels soft on the worn

hard floor. She smiled impersonally at the young woman as she felt briefly at the old man's wrist, before moving on to the next bed, a few yards down the corridor. There was still a small bandage on the back of the old man's hand, where the IV had been disconnected an hour ago.

Keeping quiet while the nurse was near had given him a chance to store up a little breath. When her firm step had passed, he went on, a little more strongly.

"I went through all kinds of hell, Dolly, to get a list of names, final purchasers. You wouldn't believe . . . but you find it, and it's all yours. I'm done for. Don't tell Tamarack, or Dickon. They're . . . no good. Neither of 'em. Cheat you blind."

The old man frowned and shook his head and closed his eyes. "Project I've been trying to do with them . . . won't work. I never should've . . . but I wasn't altogether crazy. Real secret . . . is here." He gestured feebly toward his tiny bedside table. At the moment the tabletop held nothing at all except a half-filled carafe of water capped with an inverted plastic tumbler, and a thick paperback novel, looking tired and worn enough to have been borrowed from the hospital library. To Dolly the faded, creased cover suggested some kind of historical romance. The author's name was not one she recognized.

"Sure, Gramp. Lie back, take it easy."

But Gramp was ignoring orders, reaching out for the tattered paperback. His trembling fingers snatched from it a scrap of paper that had been doing duty as a bookmark. This he held out to his granddaughter.

"S'good way t' hide things . . . in plain sight." The old man lay back wearily, seeming well satisfied at having managed one last successful deception.

Accepting the scrap of paper, Dolly stared at it, still not comprehending. One side was blank. The small space available on the other side was crowded with four names, four corresponding addresses, cities and streets and house numbers, all hand-printed in small, neat characters. She could recognize Gramp's script, as it had been before his body had finally betrayed him. One of the addresses was right here in Chicago, the others scattered across the western United States. It was possible, she thought, that her grandfather had once had a connection with someone in Carmel, California—she seemed to remember that Clint Eastwood had once been mayor there.

"What are these, Gramp? Names of people who bought the statues you were telling me about?"

There was no answer.

"Gramp? You said there were six statues? There are only four names on this list."

"Tamarack," breathed the old man in the bed, "has one statue." At least those were the enigmatic words the single listener thought she heard. Glancing at the scrap of paper, she saw that, sure enough, the name "Tamarack" was there, right next to the Chicago address.

Gramp was going on, though Dolly couldn't tell which of her questions he was trying to answer, if any.

"Tamarack doesn't know yet why it's important," the old voice rasped. "But I think I do . . . one of the six has to have the stone inside. . . ."

"The stone, Gramp? What stone?"

"Dreams confirm it." (That was the puzzling statement young Dolly seemed to hear.) "But I don't know . . . which one. Before I could start to check 'em out . . . got sick."

"Dreams? Did you say 'dreams,' Gramp?"

"Dolly, what I should have told you is . . ." The vague triumph that had been growing in the old man's face now faded suddenly, to be replaced by a look of deep concern.

"Listen . . . could be dangerous for you . . . you'll need some real help . . . wish I could've . . ."

The nurse was back. Giving the old man a single professional glance, she stood looking down at the young woman with compassion. "Is there anyone else you should be calling?" the nurse asked quietly.

As soon as the nurse came back, the man in the bed fell silent once again. Outsiders ought not hear any of his secrets. His eyes had closed, and now his breathing was starting to grow harsh.

Dolly shook her head. "I guess his girlfriend's not going to show up. I'm his only relative."

After a pause she added: "He was a great magician."

~ 1 ~

The adventure began for Mr. Maule in the fading daylight of a long June evening in Chicago, with the racket made by a terrified vampire pounding on his door.

The intrusion caught Maule at an awkward time, snug in his high apartment, with his vision focused on a glowing screen, his attention deeply absorbed in the material he was trying to learn. Just the sheer noise was jarring, apart from whatever might be the reason for it. More than nine hundred feet above Michigan Avenue, the soothing quiet that Maule preferred was the rule rather than the exception.

Even through the thickness of hidden armor reinforcing the wooden panels of the door, Mr. Maule could tell that his caller, alternating blows of an inhumanly powerful fist with pushes on the doorchime button, was, like Mr. Maule himself, one of the blood-drinking *nosferatu*. The delicacy of Mr. Maule's own vampirish senses allowed him to hear the murmured pleading through the solid barrier, and he recognized the voice.

The sole other occupant of the interestingly decorated living room where Maule was sitting was a breathing youth, only a few weeks past his nineteenth birthday. Young Andy Keogh had no idea that vampires were real, and so far he was paying no attention to the racket. Lank hair of sandy color, parted in the middle, framed a blue-eyed, sharp-chinned, clean-shaven face, at the moment vacuous with concentration. Wearing baggy jeans and a lurid T-shirt, Andy slumped in his chair, toes clenched in scruffy sandals, fingers poised like nervous claws above a keyboard. He seemed oblivious to the discomforts of this position, which allowed him to see both the large monitor screen of a very late model desktop Macintosh, and the even larger screen of a new television. The two machines were wired together, and at the moment the magic casements of both screens stood open on the enchanted seas of cyberspace, displaying complementary images.

The youth's ears were not blessed with anything like the sensitivity of Mr. Matthew Maule's, a deficiency having nothing to do with the fact that one of Andy's lobes was pierced with a bright narrow ring, a mutilation that irritated Maule, though so far he had been too polite to mention it. So the young man could hardly have heard the voice out in the public corridor, pleading for sanctuary. But the pounding on the door and the repeated chime were loud enough to force their way into his consciousness, even half-entranced as he was.

"Someone's at the door, Uncle Matt." The words were uttered dreamily, and with no sense of urgency. A mighty spell was on the youth, but it was no doing of Mr. Maule's—not directly anyway. What gripped Andy was the self-induced enchantment of the creative artist, brought on by what the glowing screens were telling him—which was considerably more than they were telling Mr. Maule.

Annoyed at being interrupted in what he considered his important studies, the man addressed as Uncle Matt rose from his chair.

"Indeed, someone is. I shall return in a moment." Maule's deep voice measured out the English words with only a trace of middle-European accent. He noted as he got to his feet that the room was growing dim, the midsummer sun having at last fallen below the northwestern horizon, and he opened draperies and switched on a single lamp in passing as he moved lithely toward the door. He was sharp-featured, dark-haired, moderately tall, informally but elegantly dressed. A casual observer would probably have put his age at forty.

The room had an unusual number of bookshelves, but enough wall space had been reserved to display several examples of European Renaissance painting. There was also a crossed pair of wooden spears, vaguely resembling harpoons, as decoration.

On reaching the front door Maule made no move to open it, but instead pressed a switch nearby on the wall, and studied the image that sprang instantly to life in the adjoining screen.

"What is it, Dickon? Who is that with you?" He kept his voice very low, knowing that at least one of those outside could hear it, even without the amplification afforded by the intercom.

Out in the hallway stood two figures, the one nearest to the door pausing with right fist upraised to pound again. Dickon's posture might have been described as menacing, but his face was anything but. Dickon was a gray-haired vampire, of a little below average size for adult male humanity. Like Maule and the great majority of their kind, he showed no obvious grotesqueries of fangs or pallor. Closed-circuit video accurately displayed Dickon's Caucasian coloring, cheeks slightly red as if from healthy exercise. He could easily pass unnoticed in a Chicago crowd. In his left hand he gripped the neck of what appeared to be a simple cloth laundry bag. Below that effortless grip the fabric was bulging unevenly, straining with some substantial load.

Dickon's companion was shorter, thinner, and even less remarkable in appearance. His tousled hair was such a mousy gray as to suggest invisibility, and the hue of his skin was not much different. His contracted posture and the quick, darting movements of his eyes expressed deep, quiet fear. Both men were dressed in clothing so dull and drab it almost defied description.

Dickon slowly lowered his raised fist. Gazing beseechingly up into the camera's eye above the door, he poured out anguished words in a language older than any form of English. "I pray you, Lord Tepes, allow me to come in. Let us both in!"

The response of the master of the house came in the same tongue, and it was icy. "No one in this dwelling answers to that name. You are assaulting the door of Mr. Matthew Maule."

"Mr. Maule, then. Please!" Dickon had switched to modern English, which he spoke with something of a mid-Atlantic accent, in tones that unintentionally suggested the late Boris Karloff. Recently paying more attention to television than had been his wont, Maule had become something of a closet fan of vintage Hollywood monster movies. He had found it a seductive way of wasting time when he really ought to have been study-ing.

Dickon was babbling on. Something had upset him so badly that he was virtually incoherent. Knowing the elder vampire as he did, Maule was not particularly sur-prised; Boris Karloff could have terrified Dickon without half trying.

Now the vampire outside the door was saying: "My associate here is Mr. Tamarack, and he is every bit as harmless as he looks. We beg you! It is a matter of life and death."

Studying the video image of Mr. Tamarack, Maule felt ninety-nine percent certain that Dickon's companion was no vampire. Considering the company that Tama-rack was in, Maule would have been willing to wager he was not your ordinary breather either; but perhaps that was irrelevant. Certainly the fellow gave no impression of menace.

Still Maule hesitated, his long, pale, sharp-nailed fingers drumming briefly on the wall beside the screen. Dickon had never been invited into Maule's house, not into this one anyway, and in the case of a vampire the invitation once extended tended to become permanent. Maule would have preferred to keep the importunate one out on the doorstep while they talked, but he thought Dickon in his present mood would not stand for that. Driving him away would probably require a serious ef-fort, and might create more of a problem than letting him in. Living nine hundred feet above the middle of a huge city had advantages, particularly when one could fly; but there were drawbacks to dwelling in any apart-ment, including the fact that invariably some neighbors were nearby.

Maule sighed, a habit that had outlasted by centuries his biological need to breathe. To the supplicants on his doorstep he declared: "Very well, then. But I warn you that the young man you will see here is a—distant relative of mine, and to be respected as such. He is perfectly mundane. You will both conduct yourselves accordingly."

"Of course, Mr. Maule, of course!" Dickon was almost slobbering in his gratitude.

Mr. Tamarack still said nothing. If his fear had been much relieved by being granted sanctuary, he gave no sign of it. Possibly he had not even understood the English words. Quietness and unobtrusiveness seemed to be Tamarack's game, as if he might be willing to disappear from the universe altogether if that were possible. Also he was now swaying on his feet, as if on his last legs, though whether his condition was due to drugs, illness, injury, or simple exhaustion was more than Maule cared to try to determine at the moment.

The door opened briefly and quickly closed again, all three men now inside. Dickon, enormously reassured just by having been allowed to cross the threshold, was already peering with curiosity from the small entry into the living room.

His whisper was almost inaudible, even to Maule. "What is he doing?"

Young Andy Keogh's face was still turned away from the men in the entryway, toward the two glowing screens. He was totally absorbed in his craft, hands on the computer keyboard, and at a distance of fifteen feet or so he could not have heard the tiny whisper anyway. But Maule's response was just as quiet.

"Among other things, my relative is helping me prepare to establish a web site. He should be departing soon—probably within the hour. Then we will talk."

"Web site." Dickon echoed the words without inflection, without any suggestion that he understood them. It was as if the only web sites he had ever heard of were those occupied by spiders. Much the same would have been true of Mr. Maule until quite recently. As for the silent Mr. Tamarack, if he had ever heard the phrase before, he gave no sign.

Young Andy barely looked up from his keyboard and his screens as Dickon and his silent companion, the former still lugging the weighty laundry bag, were conducted past him through the living room and on down the short hallway leading to the three bedrooms.

The chamber into which Maule led his visitors, switching on lights as he entered, was one of his spares, used now and then by breathing or unbreathing guests, neatly furnished but as bland and undistinguished as a hotel room. Once Mr. Tamarack found himself in a private and enclosed place, with two closed doors between him and the outer world, he slumped into a chair beside the bed. If he did not exactly fall asleep the instant he sat down, he did give the impression that mental oblivion might claim him at any moment.

Dickon had immediately gone to the window to make sure the drapes were closed as tightly as possible; that anyone or anything who might come flying by out there could not see in.

Turning back to meet Maule's inquiring look, the gray-haired one sighed. Twice he began what must have been an explanation, and twice fell silent before he had really said anything at all.

On his third attempt he got out a wrenching cry: "My eternal gratitude, dear Mr. Maule! You in turn are welcome in any residence of mine, whenever you choose to honor me!"

"Try to calm yourself, Dickon." Maule was leaning with his back against the door, arms folded. "Just what is so frightful this time?" The last time had been a year and a half ago, when an encounter with a group of Christmas carolers, of all things, had brought on a serious panic attack, though not as bad as this one seemed to be.

"We are being hunted," said Dickon simply. "Stalked. Our lives have been attempted." With a minimal gesture he indicated that he meant Tamarack and himself.

"Hunted by whom? Not carolers again?"

The elder's cheeks grew redder at the suggestion. "No. I said I was sorry about that."

"So you did. Then what is it? Some breathing fan of vampire novels is ready to believe in you? You have been threatened with crucifixes, caught a whiff of garlic, heard enemies sharpening their wooden stakes? Bah! Surely in almost a thousand years you have learned ways to deal with that sort of thing?" Dickon was not only the most cowardly vampire Maule had ever met, but probably the oldest, though Maule suspected that a few even more ancient could be somewhere in the world.

Dickon looked pained. He assured his host that this time there was much more to the matter than overexcited fans of horror being carried away by their own enthusiasm.

"Then what?"

The old one was trying to summon up his dignity. "Really, Mr. Maule, it is Mr. Tamarack's story, and I feel he should be the one to tell you."

Both men glanced at their silent companion, but he

seemed to have fallen thoroughly out of touch, head nodding as he sank gradually deeper into his chair, giving way to what looked like a sleep of absolute exhaustion. The regular rise and fall of chest and shoulders showed that he was indeed a breather.

"Does he speak English?" Maule wondered aloud.

"Of course. And many other languages. He is a true adept."

"A true *what*?"

Dickon looked uncomfortable. He seemed unable to come up with an answer.

Maule was nodding. His voice and manner were sardonic. "I know the type who usually claim that title. Usually a true 'inept' would be more like it. Pining to belong to some ultimate inner circle of secret knowledge and ancient wisdom. Master of many languages, or so he claims, but at the moment nothing at all to say . . . so, it is up to you to tell me something about this terrifying threat."

Dickon swallowed. "An hour ago, Tamarack and I were in Old Town. Are you familiar—?"

"With Old Town? Of course. The neighborhood about a mile north of here. Go on."

The old one made a spasmodic gesture with both hands, elegantly conveying the idea of chaos. "There was—destruction, that barely missed us. Only by a miracle did we escape with our lives! I had to abandon my car."

Maule raised an eyebrow. "Car? You are no longer living in that recreational vehicle, like a turtle in its shell?" Last year Dickon had inhabited a kind of house on wheels, taking comfort from the fact that so long as he stayed inside his dwelling, other vampires, lacking an invitation to come in, would be unable to attack him. The brilliance of this arrangement was somewhat dimmed by the fact that, as far as Maule knew, the poor wretch had no real enemies, *nosferatu* or otherwise.

"No, I had to give that up. It was too—conspicuous. And the parking often impossible. And the license—"

"Yes, yes. Never mind. Tell me of this 'destruction' that has sent you fleeing. Exactly what was destroyed in Old Town?"

Gasping like a breather, Dickon took in air to speak. "A whole building, our home and our place of work. Gone, ruined, within seconds after Tamarack and I were out the door."

"A building destroyed. Do you mean by fire?"

"Fire and destruction, certainly. And worse. Violence. Death."

"Whose death?"

Dickon hesitated. "Perhaps not death, but very nearly. It all happened in broad daylight, so I could not change form. Or even reach my car, it was parked too near . . . we came here in Tamarack's vehicle."

"You are gibbering. If you cannot control yourself, you will have to leave."

The threat had the desired calming effect. Relapsing into the ancient tongue, the elder asked: "Vlad Tepes, what do you know of the Great Work?"

Maule had to stop and think for a moment before he could fit the words into a sensible context. Then the answer seemed to shape itself more naturally in Latin. "*Opus magnum?* Are you asking me about alchemy?"

When Dickon nodded tensely, Maule went on: "I know about as much as I find useful: which is that the great majority of the practitioners are idiots." Suddenly a dark eyebrow went up, and he chuckled, reverting to modern English. "Don't tell me a gang of alchemists are after you? A posse of inepts. They've decided that powdered vampire is really the Philosopher's Stone?"

Dickon shuddered and closed his eyes. Now he was shaking his head sadly.

"You may think less of me, Lord—Mr. Maule, when I admit that I myself have lately become an active alchemist."

Maule gave a noncommittal grunt. He could hardly find it possible to think less of Dickon and still think of him at all.

"But, lord, I swear to you that we, my two partners and my humble self, were on the very brink of success!" Dickon seemed to gather himself for a substantial effort, as if what he was about to divulge would not be easy. "You speak of the Philosopher's Stone. Dear Mr. Maule, I swear to you that the goal of every master of the art—*yes, I mean the very Stone itself*—was practically within our grasp! If we had been allowed another few hours, perhaps, or even a few minutes . . ." He raised both arms, and let them shake. In his long, long life he had acquired a strange repertoire of gestures.

"So, who attacked you?"

The answer was so low that Maule could barely hear it. "I fear that our most deadly enemy is a god."

"Bah! One need not possess even a spark of divinity to start a fire." Now Maule felt truly though quietly angry. He shook his head. "There is but one God, Dickon, that anyone need fear. Were you never baptized?"

"Baptized, my lord? Oh, several times. Truthfully, more than several. Twice by total immersion." He rushed on. "No, my lord, I assure you it is no joke that brings us here, no mere religious quarrel . . . if I may use your telephone? My cell phone's back there in my automobile, and I must somehow reach Flamel to warn him. If it is not too late."

Suddenly Maule was more attentive. "Flamel? Just who is that?"

"Our third partner in the Great Work."

"I knew a man of that name, decades ago." Maule was shaking his head. In his experience, almost none of Dickon's alarms were ever to be taken seriously. "We shall see about the phone. What are you carrying in that bag?"

"Oh! Allow me to show you. I will have no secrets from you, Lord, ah, Mr. Maule. And it will perhaps make explanation easier." On entering the room, Dickon had tossed his weighty cloth bag on the bed. Now he reached into it and began to remove its contents, item by item. There were about a dozen things in all, each individually swathed, some in paper, some in plastic sandwich bags, some in bubble-wrap held on with rubber bands.

"I hope you are not unpacking for a lengthy stay."

"Oh, no, Mr. Maule! Nothing like that, I assure you. Only a few objects that I managed to save . . . and some that were in Tamarack's car already."

Leaning against the doorjamb, Maule watched, frowning, as bits and pieces of what looked like alchemical equipment made their appearance, a couple of small flasks, a metal clamp, little tubes of twisted glass. There were two books, one of them looking really ancient.

Now Dickon dumped out the last of the contents, all carelessly unwrapped, consisting of a few common items, spare men's shirts and underwear, aspirin and over-the-counter vitamins, a cheap safety razor. Giving the empty bag a shake, he cast it aside, with an air of one who had revealed all his secrets.

All in all, Maule considered, it had been a strange speech, a strange performance, even coming from Dickon. For a few moments Maule stood frowning at the incomprehensible display scattered across the bed. At last, with a foreboding that he would soon regret his curiosity, he simply asked, politely: "May I?"

"Of course."

Lifting one at a time some of the more interesting objects in their little cocoons of bubble-wrap or crumpled newspaper, partially unwrapping a few of them in turn, Maule conducted an examination, probing with his mind as much as with his fingers.

One item in the trove was a panel of thin wood, approximately a foot square, painted in brilliant colors in a way that suggested a miniature door. The little door was skillfully decorated with what Maule, who was no expert in the field, took to be Egyptian hieroglyphics. There were also neatly, brightly painted images of small animals, predominantly beetles.

At last setting the panel gently down, Maule picked up the next piece, a package the size of a thin man's forearm. His frown deepening, Maule held it in his hand longer than any of the others. Inside clear plastic was what appeared to be quite a simple small statue, carved or molded in whitish material that felt like plaster, of no particular artistic merit. The slender figure, whether animal or human was hard to tell, was very slightly chipped in a couple of places. It stood on two small feet on a narrow plaster base. The arms, or forelimbs, swathed in concealing drapery, hung straight at the sides. The face unpleasantly combined a pug nose with a long jaw and a suggestion of large teeth.

Maule weighed the statue thoughtfully in his hand; it did not seem quite heavy enough for solid plaster. He noted that Dickon was now watching him with a faint smirk of satisfaction, as if to say: *Yes, that is it. I felt confident that you would pick out the most important thing*.

Something about the object curiously jogged Maule's memory—surely at some point in more than a half-millennium of life he had encountered another relic very much like this one. And not in any museum, either, but in some more memorable environment, amid circumstances that ought to have made the encounter hard to forget. But where had it been, and when?

Finally he challenged Dickon, pushing the thing at him: "Just what is this?"

Dickon put both hands behind his back, as if he feared Maule had some ulterior motive in thrusting the grotesque artifact upon him. His answer came reluctantly: "A very old statue, lord."

"I can see that."

The other writhed as with internal discomfort. "I have—have been given reason to believe that it will be of enormous value to us in completing the Great Work. As to just how . . ." He shrugged.

"As to just how, you wish to keep that secret."

"No, lord!" There had been no threat in Maule's words, but Dickon could not keep from cringing. "I meant what I said, to have no secrets from you. This has a secret we do not yet know!"

"Very well." Maule shrugged, and tossed the package back on the bed. "Where did you get it?"

"That is a long story, Mr. Maule, and very complicated. Lord Tepes, in even discussing this with you I am trusting you with the heart, the key, of our secret of success. Tamarack says we only need—"

"Yes, it is always the same story with the inepts.

Always just one more secret ingredient, one slight improvement in the mystic incantation, one delicate adjustment in our laboratory techniques, and our success is guaranteed. When we have the Philosopher's Stone we shall be able to know all things and do all things. Common matter will be turned into gold, and our own evil hearts transformed. . . ."

Maule let his words trail off. A memory had stirred, one he could almost grasp—but not quite.

Except for the two items he had examined carefully, the things in Dickon's collection were all completely innocent of occult power, as far as Maule could tell. The painted door and the little statue were special cases, artifacts of such formidable antiquity, both thousands of years old. As usual, extreme age in itself lent a tinge of the supernatural to human handiwork. But Maule doubted that a real magician would consider any of this stuff worth fighting and killing for.

Instinctively dusting off his fingers, though they had had but little contact with anything but modern wrappings, Maule asked: "So, what we have is this: there was a fire in Old Town that destroyed a building, and also prevented your moving your parked car? And the two of you fled the scene, because you think some kind of god is chasing you?"

A measure of Dickon's recent fear returned to his ruddy face. "I fear it may be so. At least someone armed with truly godlike powers."

"And you have come to me for protection."

"Dear Mr. Maule, we both know of many individuals, humans as well as—as certain others—who would be perfectly ready to persecute me. For one unjust reason or another. But who, on the other hand, would never dream of—of—"

"Of even irritating me. Yes, I take your point. It will be a brave caroler or alchemist—or would-be god—who tries to set fire to my apartment."

Dickon managed a smile. "And, because I am sure we are confronted by a being far mightier than any ordinary human, I would much prefer that you rather than I should attempt such, ah, negotiations as may become necessary." Basking in his present feeling of relative safety as in grateful warmth, Dickon seemed inclined to become secretive again.

"I am honored by your confidence," said Maule dryly. Faintly from the living room there sounded a rapid-fire burst of keyboard clicks—young Andy had emerged from another period of deliberation, and was issuing commands to his machines.

Inwardly Maule had now relaxed almost completely. But he thought that, just to be on the safe side, when his young instructor in the arcane arts of software and the Internet shortly took his leave, he, Maule, would ride with him in the elevator down to the garage, there to see him safely into a cab and on his way back to his own apartment. Andy's parents lived in the suburbs, while the young man shared student quarters on a crowded city street, within walking distance of Thomas More University. Though his family was indeed well off, he owned no car. He had come here today by cab, at Maule's invitation and expense.

"Wait in this room," he cautioned his two unexpected visitors. At the same time he was wondering if he might be under some kind of curse that denied him the peace required for study and contemplation.

Dickon nodded.

Closing the bedroom door on the pair of refugees,

Maule followed the short hallway back to the dusky living room where two glass screens and one floor lamp were glowing. Beyond the open drapes, the lights of the city had now come fully alive, a million sparks making a thousand patterns across square miles of darkness, clear out to the murky Chicago horizon. The blurry line between earth and sunset sky was notched by only one or two other towers of height comparable to this one.

Maule paused to briefly admire the dark and splendid view, familiar as it was. Then he turned back to business. He would just sit down and review with Andy the material they had covered in this evening's session. Maule noted as he resumed his seat that both screens were showing the same image. He sat back in his chair and started to relax, thinking this one was a strange image indeed. . . .

. . . *yes, strange images indeed, to form the contents of a dream. Someone, a young man, was running through an unfamiliar city, and he, Maule, the dreamer, was unexpectedly drifting away among these visions. They glowed sharper and brighter than anything encountered by a vampire in his customary daytime trance.*

Maule wondered, without being able to generate any urgency about the question, just what was going on. This was diametrically the wrong time of day for Vlad Tepes, Prince Drakulya of Wallachia, to be going into trance. This was nightfall rather than dawn, the timing twelve hours out of phase. . . .

A violent crashing noise, as of a human body falling to the floor, seemed to reach Maule from a great distance, but it could not break him free of this—this unprecedented, almost indescribable, state in which he found himself. And somewhere men were shouting. . . .

Yes, certainly he *was* dreaming. What was happening to him now could not, *could* not, be any part of waking life. Not even for a vampire.

In his dream he was a different person altogether.

The body that he now inhabited was male, but otherwise totally unfamiliar, and so young as to be not quite fully grown. Looking down at himself, he saw a network of wiry muscles working swiftly under a brownish skin, clad in nothing but a kind of whitish kilt. Certainly this body was not *nosferatu,* for it gasped for breath, in urgent need of oxygen. He gasped because he was running, racing at a frantic speed, bruising his shoeless feet on the hot stones of streets and alleys, under a cloudless sky.

The city around him had an ancient look, with beasts of burden moving in the streets, and the time was late afternoon. Or possibly, despite the heat, just early morning—in any case the sun was very low in a flawless sky. Breathing was all the harder because he was carrying a hard, egg-sized lump of something in his mouth, holding it there because it was absolutely necessary to keep his hands free for climbing, vaulting, the walls and fences that sometimes threatened to box him in.

In the perverse and illogical way of dreams, the dreamer now felt the beginnings of a numbing cold inside the mouth of his dream-self. In the midst of the surrounding heat, it was a welcome mystery.

But this strange oral burden had its drawbacks too. It aggravated his desperate need for air. It jarred and scraped against his teeth. The chill of it was so intense it almost burnt his tongue and the inside of his cheeks, yet there was some overwhelming reason why he must not spit it out.

The air that seared his panting lungs was very hot and dry. The memory of what it had felt like to be terribly afraid, back in the years of the vampire's own breathing boyhood, was suddenly keen and clear.

Here loomed another wall, threateningly high, blocking his way, and he leaped for his life, clawing desperately with both hands to get a grip on the wall's top. Shooting a quick glance over his shoulder as he straddled the barrier, he saw, as his borrowed self had both feared and expected, that a small group of brown-skinned men ran behind him in fanatical pursuit. They too were clad scantily in white, and they waved an assortment of edged weapons and uttered savage outcries.

The pursuers vanished from the climber's view as he dropped into a courtyard on the wall's far side. In three directions loomed darkly magnificent doorways, each presenting an unknown choice. He immediately chose one of these—on what basis Maule could not have said—and darted into its shelter.

Three or four steps into shadow, he had to pause to let his eyes recover from the glaring sun. The hard, mysterious burden in his mouth still interfered with his breathing, yet he dared not spit it out. His gasping filled his lungs with strong smells, bitter and ominous, of decay and chemicals.

In a moment his eyes had begun adapting to the change, enough to let him see where he was going. A long room, low and narrow, stretched before him, and he went running through it toward a brilliant blur of sunlight at the far end. But somewhere near the halfway point, Maule's dream-body came to an abrupt stop. Now he had noticed that a single shelf of dark stone was built into the walls on either side of him, at about shoulder height.

And each of these two shelves held three little white

statues, lined up in a straight row. The plaster of which they were formed still glistened wet, fresh from some kind of molding process, so it seemed evident they had been set out in this shaded place to dry. The pale and slender figures were practically identical, no more than about a foot high, and each looked very much like the statue Maule had just seen and handled in waking life.

~ 2 ~

An alarm was sounding stridently, not in any of the rooms of Maule's high condominium but in the hypnotically darkened caverns of his mind. What he had just experienced had been no natural vampire-sleep, no routine daytime trance transposed into the evening. A dreaming trance, a near-oblivion not far from the true death, had been imposed upon him by someone—or something—that was no friend of Matthew Maule.

He had been overcome by some form of hypnosis, inflicted on him with fiendish stealth, devilish power and skill. The attack had taken him totally by surprise but, now that it had happened, it was all too easy to believe. He knew that when he could be caught unawares, his susceptibility to such a mesmeric assault was, if anything, greater than that of the average breathing man.

Slowly the mercilessly effective grip that held Maule's mind prisoner was being loosened. He could tell that soon he would be free. Evidently, whatever power had forced him into temporary mental bondage did not desire his destruction. To that nameless power Vlad Tepes, Prince Dracula, was no enemy—but only because it did not consider him important enough to be awarded that status. Instead, he and the defenses of his apartment were only a curiosity, deserving no more than a brief and casual inspection before being violated and cast aside.

He thought it had invaded his house for reasons having nothing directly to do with him. Its business had been with the people and objects newly installed in his third bedroom. Now Maule remembered the crashing noise, the shouting that had not been part of any dream.

Meanwhile, he could take some comfort in having escaped the unreal predicament of the dream. Men with knives and swords were not really chasing him through the dry heat of some ancient city. But even as that scene dissolved, Maule realized that what he discovered on waking might be worse.

He was no longer running for his life beneath a blinding sun, scrambling through stifling, cavelike buildings. In truth he was still sitting in the twenty-first-century air-conditioning of his familiar apartment high above Michigan Avenue. But his foreboding had been correct: plenty of trouble, all too real, waited to greet him on his waking.

An unaccustomed stiffness had seized the vampire's body. Something was indeed terribly wrong. With a groan he sat up straight in his chair. It was very late at night—or early in the morning. His wristwatch and the small clock in the corner of his computer screen agreed that the time was just three-thirty. At this time of year, that meant that the hours of darkness were swiftly running out. One lamp was still turned on in his large living room. Two screens still glowed, one now showing a television test pattern, the other displaying a computer screen saver.

Soon the merciless dawn would be here to further sap his energy. It was sickening to realize that he had lain in his chair for something like six hours as helpless as a baby, while his home, what Maule had thought was a practically impregnable stronghold, was violated. The sense of ruthless, callous encroachment was very strong.

As soon as Maule's eyes were fully open he turned them on Andy Keogh. The young man was still slumped in his chair, in almost the same uncomfortable-looking position as before, but now his eyes were closed and his arms hung loosely at his sides. Andy's chest rose and fell as if in normal breathing sleep, and he showed no obvious sign of injury. But Maule was sure that all was not entirely well with Andy Keogh.

The vampire struggled to his feet, muscles stiff, body swaying dizzily, trying to free himself by sheer willpower from the lingering effects of unnatural trance. Lurching to the young man's side, Maule bent over him, shaking him to no avail. "Andy? Andy!"

Still no response; but, thank God, the basic signs of life seemed almost normal.

Now Maule straightened fully—it cost him a mighty effort. He took a staggering step or two, almost losing his balance. He was sure that at sunset his front door had been tightly closed and manifoldly locked, as usual. But now he could see it standing ajar, the city dweller's usual paraphernalia of extra bolts and chains projecting in air or dangling uselessly. Someone had neatly unlocked and unbolted all the fastenings and then had left the door in that condition. Damn Dickon! He must have opened it from the inside, and fled in a blind panic.

Having himself had intimate experience of the intruder, Maule could hardly blame the timid one.

Or could it possibly have been the stranger, Tamarack, who left the door in that condition? Dickon in ordinary circumstances would never have dared do such a thing; but Dickon, confronted with the same intruder who had taken Maule by surprise and overcome him, might have done almost anything at all.

Having staggered to his front door, Maule stood there, clinging to the jamb to keep from falling, trying to marshal his confused thoughts. He took a quick look out into the public hallway. At this ungodly and vampirish hour the passage was deserted, and he could hear no sounds of movement anywhere, no elevator hum or feet on stairs.

Closing the front door solidly and shooting one simple bolt to hold it shut, he went reeling and stumbling back across his living room, to the wall where the wooden spears hung in the form of a diagonal cross. He snatched one from its brackets, and with this weapon in hand went down his apartment's interior hallway to the end, where the door of the third bedroom was also standing open.

Evidently it was not Mr. Tamarack who had forgotten to close the front door on his way out. For only his spirit had departed. Tamarack's body was sprawled on the floor, and it needed no careful look to be sure that he was dead. The ugly wounds had been inflicted by no ordinary weapon, and strongly suggested the tearing of claws rather than the carving of a blade. Involuntarily Maule looked at his own fingernails, at the moment very human in appearance, to make sure they were clean. There were no great pools of blood, but some had been spattered around the room, on walls and furniture and carpeting. The maculations were sheer carrion, hours dried and already decaying, red-brownish scum that aroused not hunger but nausea, like rotten food to a breather.

As Maule had expected, Dickon was nowhere to be seen. The baggage from the elder vampire's laundry bag had been scattered. Some things, the spare shirts and aspirin tablets, along with the bag itself, were now lying on the floor. The little white statue had been torn out of its plastic wrap and smashed to powder and small fragments, which lay scattered mostly over the bed. Mingled with fragments of ivory-colored plaster was a small mass of dark and crumbly stuff that seemed to have been somehow encased inside the plaster shell.

A New Testament quotation regarding whited sepulchers ran through Maule's mind, but at the moment it was of no help. He saw that the little painted panel of thin wood had also been torn out of its wrappings, but was not damaged. It too remained on the bed, but was now standing on edge, propped against the headboard.

A swift inspection proved that no one, no human being, god, or monster, was hiding in the closet, or under the bed.

Maule's dizziness persisted, and he swayed on his feet. *Mammalian blood. He badly needed fresh blood, to strengthen him.*

On his way to the kitchen he detoured to make another quick check on Andy's condition; there seemed to be no change.

The freezer offered Maule what he needed, in the form of raw young beef liver; the microwave swiftly brought it to a palatable temperature. Leaning over the stainless steel sink he sucked out liquid nourishment, fastidiously using a paper towel to dab small blood spots from his lips.

Returning strength, increasing clarity of thought, brought no relief of mental pain, but only growing rage. Now he thought he could understand how the victim of a rape must feel. Murder and robbery had been committed, *and right here in his own home*. His territory, his castle in this later age, had been savagely, ruthlessly defiled.

How *dare* they—how dare anyone—lay hands on, let alone murder, a visitor Vlad Drakulya had admitted under his protection?

Could Dickon have been the killer, after all? No, no, surely not. Any vampire would have the physical strength to mangle a breather, but the cowardly one would never in a million years have dared to play a trick like that on Maule. Besides, Dickon's faults did not include a tendency to sudden violence.

Now he, Vlad Drakulya, was again in deep trouble, and without quite realizing just how he had got there. It was a situation in which he had found himself in the past, more times than he liked to count. Certainly more often than the laws of probability ought to allow, even in a lifetime of more than five hundred years. It was a familiar but discouraging problem, all the more discouraging for being so familiar. Over the last century he had begun to hope that he might someday succeed in avoiding this kind of thing.

Stop and think. How had the intruder, or intruders, entered? If *nosferatu*, then someone inside the apartment, inside Maule's home, must have invited them to come in.

Dickon? Dickon was going to have to answer many questions.

At last feeling himself fully awake, Maule, still in the kitchen where Andy could not possibly see him, endeavored to change his body into a nonhuman shape. He was eager to sharpen his senses, to discover if any attacker might still be on the scene, lurking in some room he had not yet inspected.

But on making the attempt to change, he discovered that he had been even more drastically affected than he had first thought. He found himself starting to change into something lizardlike, almost a giant serpent, rather than the inconspicuous bat he had been trying to become.

Attempting to resume man-form, he succeeded with a great shudder of relief. Walking solidly on two legs, he quickly returned to the living room; he found Andy still in a daze in front of his two electronic screens, both still glowing with letters, numbers, jargon, and symbols almost meaningless to Maule. But now the youth's eyes occasionally flickered open, as if he could still be studying the images on the screens before him. Perhaps he found amusement in whatever he thought he saw, for he began to gently giggle.

Effortlessly Maule lifted the large young man from his chair and stretched him at full length on a sofa. Switching on more lights, he felt Andy's relaxed limbs, checked his pulse, lifted an eyelid to peer as nearly as possible into his brain. Quickly he examined the youth's neck, then loosened his clothing to look at other areas, for evidence of pinprick biting. To his great relief, he could find none.

So, things might have been even worse.

For all that he could tell right now, the sole purpose of the violent intrusion had been to dispose of Tamarack. Maule had no idea why anyone should want to do that. But it did not seem as strange as the only other reason that suggested itself: that the intruder's goal had been merely to shatter a small plaster statue, exposing the dark rubbish inside.

Maule spent the next minute in a methodically thorough search of his apartment, which turned up no more surprises. No further trace of any intruder, nor any sign at all of Dickon.

When I get my hands on him, thought Maule, *he may wish that he had stayed in the burning building in Old Town.*

But the thought had no real urgency behind it. In his heart he realized that it was pointless to blame Dickon, who after all had tried, at least halfheartedly, to warn his host. Instead he must inescapably blame himself, for negligence and carelessness.

And when he had discovered the identity of the intruder, as he eventually would—then judgment, the assignment of blame, would take on hard substance.

The next step was grimly distasteful, but duty and honor alike forbade him to delay it any longer. After considering and rejecting one or two more exotic methods of communication, Maule reached for the phone.

No need to look up the number he needed, for he had used it recently, only a few days ago. That was when he had made what now seemed an ill-starred decision, to begin a serious study of the Internet and related matters, and had started looking for a tutor. What more logical than that he should turn for guidance to the breathing folk he knew best in this region of the world?

Maule's hand slowed as he pressed buttons. He would have to explain to Andy's father—or worse, to his mother—what had happened to their son here in Maule's domain, when the tornado of murderous force, part occult and part physical, swept through.

"Yeah." The answering voice was sleepy but coherent, that of a man not entirely unused to being awakened at all hours by the telephone. No doubt that attitude was a residual benefit of years spent on the Chicago police force. Maule silently offered thanks that it was Joe who had answered and not Kate.

"Joseph, it is I. Your Uncle Matthew." A trace of irony in the last words.

He could hear Joe Keogh breathing in his distant house, Joseph needing the space of a breath or two to pull himself together. Then he was ready for business. "What's going on?"

"I regret the necessity of waking you at this hour. Andy, your son, is here in my apartment. He has not been harmed, as far as I can tell, at least not seriously, and at the moment is peacefully asleep. But—there have been certain strange events. You had better come, with all deliberate haste. When you are here we will talk."

There was hesitation at the other end, but only briefly, as several natural questions were framed and then postponed. Then Joe Keogh repeated: "Strange events."

"Indeed."

"Your condo on Michigan Avenue."

"That is correct."

"All right. I'm on my way."

"Good." Then Maule added, as an afterthought: "Arrange for John to come as well, if that is feasible." Joe's brother-in-law, John Southerland, had also served in the past as a capable and knowing ally.

Having made all the speed he reasonably could to get here from his suburban home, Joe arrived at Maule's apartment about daybreak, which came very early in the morning at this time of year.

Joe Keogh hadn't smoked for more than twenty years, but there were moments when he still felt the urge, and on entering Maule's building from its underground garage he experienced one of them. The place held frightening memories.

Joe was fifty now, but he looked somewhat younger, sandy hair turned half-gray, cut short over a tough-looking face. Eyeglasses added a scholarly touch. Of average size, and sparely muscular, so far resisting the tendency to put on weight, he was casually dressed today, tieless, his lightweight sport coat worn unbuttoned. He looked respectable and inconspicuous, as was appropriate for the head of a small but successful company specializing in the more unusual kinds of private investigation.

Maule had just finished a routine closing of all the drapes, against the burning of the day's new sun outside, when the doorchime sounded. His last squint out at the fast-brightening world showed him a lone canoeist, starting downstream, heading inland from the locked junction of the Chicago River and Lake Michigan. It was unlikely but possible that the voyager was commencing a voyage to unknown lands, down the Mississippi as far as the Gulf of Mexico.

Something rippled in the water, not far from the canoe. Since the river's restoration to good health, only a few years ago, there might be bigger fish in it than anyone imagined.

When Maule answered the door he was still gripping a wooden spear in his hand. He used it to beckon his visitor inside, then in the next moment turned, and in a spasm of impotent anger, flung the weapon like a harpoon at the wall across the room, where it stuck quivering with the brutal force of impact. "Violated! Like some helpless maiden!"

Before trying to come up with a reply to that, Joe took two steps inside the apartment and stopped, visibly relieved at the sight of Andy sleeping peacefully.

In a calmer voice, Maule said: "My home was invaded last night—by exactly what, or who, I am not yet sure—and we were both put to sleep. Another who was here fared worse."

Joe shot him a questioning look. Then he went to sit on the sofa beside his son, took his arm and shook it lightly. "Hey, guy. You sound asleep, or what?"

This time Andy's eyes stayed open. "Guess I crashed." The realization seemed to utterly astonish him, in a dazed and lowkey way. Another long moment passed before the fact of his father's presence fully registered. Then Andy sat up abruptly, rubbing his face and eyes. "What time is it? Dad? What the heck you doing here?"

"Going for an early walk. Doing my aerobics. How you feel?"

Andy considered. "Okay, I guess. What is this? Did I sleep all night?" Turning around slowly, he got his feet on the floor. He raised both hands and began to rub his neck, as if it had gone stiff.

Joe stood up from the couch and turned to Maule. His voice was grim, but still respectful. "What happened, Uncle Matt?"

The vampire made an economical gesture in the direction of the kitchen. "I have made coffee, and there is food available. I assume you have not breakfasted."

Joe sighed. "You're right, I haven't. Thanks. Andy, how about some chow?"

"Sure." And Andy got to his feet, where he seemed to wobble for just a moment. "Be with you in a minute." He started for the small bathroom just off the entryway.

Keeping an eye on the youth to make sure he did not wander down the bedroom hallway, Maule relaxed a little. That Andy was hungry seemed a healthy sign.

When Andy returned from the bathroom and walked into the kitchen to join his father and their friend at the small table, the young man was the calm one, still seeming utterly unaware that anything really bizarre had taken place. His dazed condition had somehow kept him from noticing, while passing through the living room, the spear with its hardened wooden point still deeply embedded in plasterboard, its point well into the sterner stuff of the building's wall beneath.

On entering the kitchen, Andy paused to remark to his father: "You know, that's a funny mirror in there. In the bathroom. I just noticed."

"Not really a mirror," his father told him shortly. Joe had visited that lavatory some years ago. Now he was puttering around in search of food, while Maule sat motionless at the table with no plate or cup before him. This was only what Joe had expected. Keogh caught a glimpse, in the sink, of a small plastic dish that had recently held something bloody. Resolutely he refused to be distracted.

"It looks," his son was telling him, "like a closed-circuit TV screen."

"That's what it is," Joe informed his son. He glanced

at Maule, who was paying no attention to the exchange. "Some people like them better than mirrors."

"Wow."

A glass of orange juice tasted good to Joe. The refrigerator held bacon and eggs, in unopened but freshly dated packages, as if in anticipation of breathing guests who preferred a diet of solid food. But Joe wasn't going to bother with anything that elaborate just now. He settled for a bagel and cream cheese to go with the excellent coffee.

"Any interesting dreams in your long sleep?" Maule was asking Joe Keogh's son, in a casual tone.

Andy thought about it. "No." He seemed not totally clearheaded yet, still recovering slowly from whatever had put him out for the night. "At least I don't remember dreaming anything."

"Perhaps you will recall something later." Maule waited until the youth's gaze rose to meet his own, then added, firmly: "You can try."

Andy nodded absently. He had poured himself coffee, and was munching on a piece of toast, but his responses were still slow. Obviously he was not yet completely right. He seemed not to notice the fact that while in their company Uncle Matthew neither ate nor drank.

While Andy helped himself to a second bowl of cereal, Maule rose, and with a slight motion of his head signaled Joe alone out of the kitchen and down the bedroom hallway.

At the end of the short hall he stopped, before a door now firmly closed. Turning the knob, he whispered: "Andy has not seen this, and knows nothing about it. I, unhappily, know very little more."

Joe took in the scene of death and destruction with

the professional gaze of a former cop. His face changed only slightly; obviously, having been called here in the middle of the night, he had been bracing himself for something of the kind.

Under his breath, Joe Keogh murmured an obscenity, words he rarely used. Then he added: "Who is he?"

"Someone called Tamarack. That name is almost the only thing I know of him."

"Who did it?"

"That remains to be discovered, and I intend to do so."

Joe was pointing, without touching them, at fragments of the shattered statue, an outer layer of whitish ceramic, now mixed with what had evidently been its hidden contents. "What's this?"

"Last night, when still intact, it was a small, white statue. I do not know the nature of the dark material now revealed to be inside, but it is very old, and at least partially organic."

Keogh grunted. "Weird. I wonder."

"Yes?"

"Well, two days ago I was in the Field Museum, looking at their Egyptian exhibit. I don't remember any little white statues, but in one of the cases there was a little panel, very much like that one on the bed. The label on it said . . . what did it say?" Joe ran strong fingers through his sandy hair. "Yeah. A 'false door,' that was it."

Maule was intrigued. "You were at the Field in a professional capacity? Perhaps regarding theft?"

"Professional, yes. But they haven't had anything stolen, it's just that their alarm systems are acting up. A couple of times they've shown evidence of intrusion, but when their people go to check it out, there's never an intruder. I've been called in to consult."

"Complications, complications." Maule was frowning. "I wish to retain possession of this panel for a time. But it might be well for you to photograph it, and show the picture to your contact at the Field."

Joe nodded. "All right." He rubbed his hands together and looked around. Knowing Maule as he did, it had not even occurred to him to ask if cops were going to be called in. "Lots to be done. But before anything else I want to get my kid out of here. Thanks for calling me."

"I entirely agree, Andy should be removed at once. I must apologize for his accidental involvement in this—this monstrous invasion of my home." Maule's thin-lipped mouth was twisted.

Joe seemed torn between anger and relief. Then he managed a brief grin. "We've been through even worse than this."

Maule nodded grimly.

"After I take Andy home I'll come back and help. I expect you can use some help?" The question was calm and businesslike.

"Your offer is gratefully accepted, Joseph. I expected nothing less. But do not come back here today—I plan to be elsewhere."

The doorchime sounded.

Andy had risen from his kitchen chair and started toward the front door, but somehow, without seeming to make any special effort, Maule managed to traverse the bedroom hallway and get there two steps ahead of him. As soon as he arrived, he relaxed. The face on the screen was that of John Southerland, Joe's brother-in-law and Andy's uncle. Maule let him in.

John came in warily, face unshaven, clothes rumpled, as if he had thrown them on before he was fully awake. Then he relaxed. "Hi, Joe, Andy. Hi, Uncle Matthew." He looked around. "What's up?" John Southerland was about the same size as Joe, a little under six feet, and younger by twelve or thirteen years. In his high school days John had been quite an amateur wrestler. He was strong-jawed and sturdy, light brown hair now graying at the temples and showing a tendency to curl.

Three minutes later, father and son were in the kitchen, while Maule was busy acquainting John with the contents of the third bedroom. The doorchime sounded again.

This time Joe Keogh was first to reach the little entryway. He recognized the young woman shown in close-up on the video screen near the entry, but before he could respond to her presence in any way Maule was at his elbow. The effect of nearly instantaneous movement was so strange that this time Joe had to fight back an impulse to giggle.

Maule looked at the screen, grunted something, and relaxed. When he opened the door, the woman in the corridor gazed at him blankly with her wide, dark eyes, and smiled winningly with cheerfully painted lips. Her voice was light and musical. An indeterminate faint accent came and went. "Mr. Maule? I have come to your door to sell you a magazine subscription. You may win a gr-reat prize in our contest!"

Maule shook his head, frowning. "Come in, Constantia. No need to play games. I believe you have met Joseph Keogh, and John Southerland."

The dark eyes flashed at each man in turn. "Ah yes! Regrettably only a brief encounter in each case. But for years dear Vlad has been telling me marvelous things about both of you. Ah, Johnnee, your poor hands, both little fingers missing—how could one ever forget the story of your bravery?"

John murmured something in response. The fingers had been gone for more than twenty years, and few people even noticed. It was hard to believe the woman before him was almost as old as Maule, but he knew it to be true. Connie looked wide-eyed and innocent, prim and ladylike, though she was not dressed to fit that role, wearing tight pants and some kind of high-heeled sandals showing bright red toenails. Dark curly hair and heavy silver earrings contributed to a gypsy look. An entrancing wave of subtle perfume entered with her.

She turned as Andy emerged from the kitchen, coffee cup still in hand. Her red lips shaped briefly into a perfect O. "And here, the handsome young one with the nice new beard could he possibly be Kate's son? I see something of her in his eyes—how is your lovely wife, by the way? And Judy?"

"Kate's fine," Joe Keogh said abstractedly. "She's home. Judy's traveling in Europe this summer, along with Andy's sister."

Constantia turned back to Joe. "How fortunate for you to have married into the Southerlands, for they are of Mina Harker's blood. And so they are dear Vlad's—excuse me, Mr. Maule's—favorite breathing family—and have been for a long time now—my goodness, it must be more than a hundred years!" She marveled prettily.

Joe cast a sharp glance at his son. The bit about a hundred years of blood-related friendship, if it had registered with Andy, ought to just about sink any possibility that the Family Secret could be kept from the younger generation much longer. But the kid still looked somewhat dazed. So far he was still ignoring the spear stuck in the wall.

"Who are Vlad and Mina?" Andy asked, frowning. He was making a game effort to follow the conversation, though much of it was going past him.

Connie's gaze came back to the youth, and she murmured: "Pretty earring!" and smiled at him fondly—a tentative movement of her small pink hand toward the ear in question earned her a warning glance from Mr. Maule. The movement came to an abrupt halt.

For a moment there was silence. Then John cleared his throat and said quietly to Maule: "Uncle Matt? I can start that job for you now, if you like. The cleanup in there." He moved his head just slightly in the direction of the rear hallway.

"Not just yet, but soon," said Maule, and nodded gratefully. "Thank you."

Andy asked: "What cleanup?" No one answered. He turned back to the kitchen. "I'm having some more coffee."

Maule was looking thoughtfully at Connie. "What brings you here?" he asked in a low voice.

"I have just been talking to our mutual friend," Connie reported. "I mean, of course, the old one, Dickon."

Maule grunted. "Friend or not, I was reasonably sure he had survived. He is actually very good at survival, though not at much else. Where is he now? He must tell me everything that happened here."

"He asked me to intercede for him with you, dear Vlad. I am here as his surrogate—is that the right word?—to beg forgiveness for his running away last night. He didn't tell me much, but I got the feeling some very bad things must have happened . . . Vlad, you won't be mean to him, will you? He says to tell you that he intended no harm, it's just that he was very much afraid."

"Abject terror is Dickon's normal state. Where is he now?"

"I don't know, honestly! I can only tell you where he said he was going."

"Constantia—"

"All right, all right! He told me he would be hiding out on the roof of the main public library. At no great distance from here, on the street called State, just north of Congress."

"I know where it is. But on the roof..." Maule seemed to find the answer utterly bewildering.

"That's what he said."

"But it is broad daylight, early in the morning." Maule squinted toward the windows, where brutal sunlight burned around the margin of closed drapes.

"You are right as always."

Maule shook his head. "The day promises to be sunny, and there cannot be much shadow there ... he might find it rather awkward."

Constantia shrugged, dismissing Dickon and whatever problems he might have. "Now that I am here, how can I be of service?"

Maule considered. "Did you notice as you approached, whether anyone was watching the building—? No, I suppose you would not have noticed. Probably your most useful function will be to carry a message from me to Dickon."

"Have you tried to phone him?" Connie asked.

Maule pressed his fingers to his head. "Was Dickon carrying a cell phone—? No, not when he was here. Because he said something about wanting to use mine."

"And what is the message, dear Vlad?" Constantia now seemed to be working at an imitation of an efficient secretary.

"I want to give him a conditional reassurance, that if he helps me now, tells me all he knows, holding back nothing, he will not be punished."

The secretary approved. "You are not going to try to hunt him down?"

"Certainly not now. I have more important things to do than haunt the roof of the public library."

The prospect of carrying her message to that exposed environment in daylight did not seem to worry Connie—taking note of this, Maule surmised that perhaps she really had no intention of going there at all. Well, for the time being he would be content to have her out of his way.

Evidently wishing to speak with Vlad Tepes privately, she switched to another language, sibilant, not quite as old as Dickon's native tongue. "Are you going to be very angry with him, Vlad?" she persisted. When he did not answer at once, Connie looked at him closely. "I see you are. Oh, how unpleasant!"

Maule answered in English. "The sooner I can talk to him, the better. You must try to convince him of that. Tell him I admit that what happened in my house is at least partly my own fault. I am ready to listen to Dickon now, and if he will tell me the absolute truth, the unpleasantness will be minimized."

"Then—if no one is going to tell me exactly what happened here last night—?"

"No one is going to tell you now."

"Then I will be on my way." To Maule's relief, she took her departure in a conventional manner, protected behind dark sunglasses and a broad-brimmed hat. To make sure, he listened until he could hear her boarding an elevator. He would not have put it past her to try climbing down the building's shaded outside wall.

~ 3 ~

Maule felt a strong impulse to begin a personal search for Dickon without delay, to get his hands on the elder one as soon as possible and question him, intensively if necessary. But regretfully he decided that it was necessary to deal with certain other matters first. And it would be not only dangerous, but probably unprofitable, to spend valuable time on the roof of the public library.

Again he was struck by what a bizarre hiding place that was for any vampire to choose. Maybe Dickon had been lying to Constantia. Or maybe the old one had in mind some particular hidey-hole on the roof. Eight or more hours of unshielded summer daylight, even at Chicago's relatively northern latitude, would be more than enough to kill any vampire. Having visited the library on occasion, Maule was able to recall some structural details. The old coward, if he was really there, would almost certainly be somewhere in among the folds of the molded decorative draperies whose shapes on the high roof suggested gargoyles, or to some less imaginative minds, gigantic flowers. These were made of some artificial material, plastic or fiberglass the grayish green of weathered bronze, and when seen from street level gave the building a look of having been infested by monsters. Maule supposed the one advantage of such a hiding place would be that no one would ever think of looking there—which, come to think of it, might well outweigh the shortcomings.

He roused himself to pay attention to Joe Keogh, who was coming up with some practical questions. The two of them were in the kitchen again, while out in the living room John was keeping Andy's attention focused on the computer.

The things Joe wanted to know had nothing to do with the Internet. "Did this Tamarack and the other fella arrive together? And were they driving, or—?"

Maule had the unfamiliar feeling that his memory was shaky. He pressed the fingers of both hands to his temples. "They did arrive at my door together. What did Dickon tell me? That they walked from Old Town? No, he said they drove, in a vehicle belonging to Tamarack."

Maule now repeated, as best he could, Dickon's vague but suggestive report of a fire and worse, that had driven him and Tamarack to look for sanctuary. Dickon had also said something about being forced to abandon his car, and that they had come in Tamarack's.

Joe Keogh, easing comfortably into the role of investigating officer, nodded. "So the vehicle belonging to the late Mr. Tamarack is probably still down in the garage, unless this Dickon drove it away. Is he—?"

"Dickon, *nosferatu*? Yes. The other one—" Maule indicated the back bedroom with a nod "—was not."

"Didn't think so. Let's go take another look at him. And I want a picture of that little panel. And some of that other stuff, before it gets cleaned up." From a side pocket of his sport coat, Joe pulled a camera, very small. To Maule it looked extremely modern and efficient. He didn't know whether he ought to find that reassuring or not.

In a minute the two of them were back in the third bedroom, where Joe photographed the panel while it remained propped against the head of the bed.

There remained the question of the significance of the shattered statue.

"Dickon told me it was very valuable, important in his work. But he would not or could not tell me how."

"If it was worth a lot, why smash it? Sheer vandalism?"

"Or perhaps to get at something inside. It was hollow, as we can see, and contained a dark organic substance, which must be as old as the statue itself. But very little of that material could have been taken."

Joe dutifully snapped a couple of pictures of a few handfuls of dust and broken plaster.

When he had done so, Maule pointed out a detail that was just visible when keen eyes looked carefully. In the dark debris that had spilled from inside the statue, there were bits of what looked like narrow cloth tape, suggesting ancient bandages.

Joe took what seemed a long time, looking, then snapped another close-up. "Know what this suggests to me? Some kind of mummy wrappings. It couldn't have been the body of an infant, could it?"

Maule shook his head. "The statue was too thin. No human infant, I think, nor even a late-term fetus, could have been squeezed inside. But I believe small animals were sometimes mummified in Egypt. Perhaps this was a snake? Or . . ."

"I can show these pictures to my contact at the Field." Joe knelt beside the mess and from somewhere in his pockets produced a tweezers and an envelope. "And maybe I can get him to look at a sample of this tape, or whatever the hell it is. Also I can ask if they're missing any little white statues."

When the tape sample had been secured, the two men turned their attention to the murder victim. There would be no need of forensic science to determine the cause of Tamarack's death.

Looks like the work of a strong vampire in a destructive mode, thought Joe. But he didn't see any need to make that comment aloud.

"Want a picture of him?" he asked. Maule shook his head.

Maule now made his first close examination of the corpse. There were no rings or other jewelry on Tamarack's hands or head or neck, no evidence of pinprick biting in any of the traditional vampire places—although of course such traces on the head and neck might have been obliterated by the greater damage.

A quick, efficient search of Tamarack's pockets produced an assortment of odds and ends, entirely unremarkable. These included about fifty dollars in cash, and a simple keychain, one of whose keys bore the symbol of a prominent automotive manufacturer. Another pocket held a parking ticket issued by the machine in the garage beneath Maule's building.

Maule separated the automobile key. "Our next step should probably be to examine this vehicle."

*   *   *

Leaving John to keep Andy occupied and out of trouble, Maule and Joe Keogh set out for the garage. When they had the elevator to themselves, going down, Maule asked: "Is there something wrong, Joseph?"

"Not really." But still Keogh kept looking around him, involuntarily, nervously, at the door and the three enclosing walls. Just coming back to this building, riding again in these harmless elevators, brought back memories of terror now five years old, and made him edgy.

Well, they had won that battle five years ago, Maule and his breathing family working together, and they would win this one. But Joe still had to make an effort to concentrate on the current problem. "Did he tell you what model of car or truck they came in? There must be about a hundred vehicles parked down there."

Maule's thumb stroked the key. "Probably more than a hundred. But I will find it, if it is still there."

The garage was a busy place now, in the early morning rush hour. Maule and Keogh, two casually dressed reverse commuters getting ready to carpool to their jobs, moved along at a steady pace between the rows of numbered spaces.

Now and then Maule slowed, looking intently at one vehicle or another. Eventually, for no decisive reason that Joe could see, the vampire came to a stop. "This one."

The car was older than most of those surrounding it, and like the great majority of them, it carried an Illinois license.

Before Maule tried to use the key, he satisfied himself by sniffing, and by certain probings of an even more subtle nature, that no explosive devices had been installed. A bad experience in Arizona, some years ago, had made him very cautious in such matters.

"Let us first look in the trunk." After sniffing the air again, with a wolflike twitching of his neck, and listening carefully, Maule used the key.

The trunk contained a few strange artifacts, as well as the usual miscellany to be expected in an old car. Maule recognized an alembic of clear glass, tying in with Dickon's babble about alchemy. He had been half-expecting another white plaster statue, but in this he was disappointed. The glove compartment, and the various pockets in the car's interior, held only common, mundane odds and ends.

It was good that there was nothing out of the ordinary to draw attention to the undistinguished vehicle. Still, something would have to be done with it, and fairly soon.

Maule pointed out that whoever disposed of Tamarack's vehicle would have to take care to wipe his own fingerprints from it before abandoning it somewhere. "I suppose the possibility exists that it is stolen."

"I understand," said Joe patiently. "I can try to get a make on the license. Some of my police connections are still open."

Maule closed his eyes briefly. Joe saw a pale hand knot into a fist. "Forgive me, I am—upset. The intrusion into my home . . ."

"That's all right. John or I can take care of the car. There's something else that'll be harder to dispose of, and I'm not sure of the best way to handle that." Joe raised his eyes to the garage ceiling, as if he could see into a room some ninety stories above.

"Leave that to me. If the body were elsewhere, I would be, as usual, a good citizen and anonymously pass word to the authorities." Maule paused, shaking his head. "But because the wretch was murdered in my home—no. Good citizenship must wait. It has become a matter of personal honor." His voice became harder, clearer. Joe winced slightly, recognizing that inflexible tone. "Best that you look after your son, until we are sure he suffers no lingering posthypnotic effects. I shall be the one to dispose of the vehicle, and the remains of its owner."

Joe wasn't going to argue with either part of that.

Going up in the elevator again, they had to share the small space with other passengers during the first portion of the journey. Traversing the higher floors, they were alone. Curiosity finally got the better of Joe Keogh, and he had to ask: "What will you do with . . . ?"

"There is a certain place I know of—but you have been there too. Perhaps two hours' drive out of the city."

Joe stopped to think. "Oh. Yeah." He would never forget that place. A chunk of land too hilly for crops or even pasture, consisting largely of low wooded bluffs and ravines on the bank of the Sauk River, near the town of Frenchman's Bend.

Maule went on: "I have a slight acquaintance with the present owner."

Joe nodded. He had his suspicions about that owner's identity, but he didn't want to get into depths of craziness beyond where he already was. The subject made him feel inwardly dizzy, and he wasn't going to think about it unless he had to. It must be some old and very tolerant friend. He wasn't going to try to find out any more about him. Or her.

Joe Keogh could vividly remember the strange battle that had reached its climax near Frenchman's Bend— God, that was almost twenty years ago. After what he had seen then on the banks of the Sauk, he had no trouble at all believing that traces of grotesque enchantment still lingered there, like the residue of some vast chemical experiment, not necessarily harmful. For a few hours, some twenty years ago, that soil had been intensely cultivated by the greatest true magician in the world.

A few minutes later, Keogh and Maule were walking Andy between them to the elevator. All the way down to the garage the kid kept commenting on the fact that he had never before crashed the way he did last night—at least never without a strenuous interlude of partying first.

"But last night I didn't even have a beer," he complained for the second or third time. "I guess I just zonked out, huh?"

Maule said: "I confess that much the same thing happened to me last night, also without benefit of alcohol." He paused, then added: "I had a strange dream, sitting in my chair."

"Yeah?" Andy seemed to find that mildly interesting. "I didn't dream anything." Then he paused, frowning. "I did dream something . . . but I don't remember it. Dad, how come you were here when I woke up? Did Uncle Matt call you because of me?"

"Your father and I had some matters to discuss," Maule said dismissively. He was thinking he had better wait before trying to extract more information from Andy. There remained the possibility of deep hypnotic probing, but that drastic treatment sometimes produced unwelcome side effects, and the vampire preferred to save it as a last resort.

Andy seemed to be moving easily, talking almost

normally as they made their way from the elevator through the garage.

But not till he had a hand on the door of his father's car did Andy suddenly recall why he had come to this building in the first place. He turned back. "Uncle Matt, are we going on with your project? About getting you a web site and all? It was getting really interesting, with all that neat new hardware."

"Yes, eventually of course I mean to go on. But for a few days I shall be too busy with other matters."

With Andy in the car and out of earshot, the men held a final low-voiced consultation on whether they should return him to his own north-side apartment, which he shared with two other university students, or to his parents' home. Joe didn't need long to conclude that the latter seemed a safer bet.

"He comes home with me," Joe decided. "Either way I'll have to tell Kate what happened, and when she hears about it she's going to murder us both." Joe made a gesture to show that "us" meant the vampire and himself. "I'm the one who suggested . . ."

"That your son should be my tutor and spend time in my apartment. Yes. Presumably Kate knows where you are now?"

"Hell yes. When I dash out in the middle of the night—thank God I don't very often any more—she knows where I'm going. That reminds me, I'd better call home, let her know Andy's basically all right. As far as we can tell." He felt at his belt for his cell phone, giving Maule a brief glimpse of the shoulder holster under the open sport coat. Maule had no doubt that today Joe's revolver was loaded with wooden bullets, the only kind effective against the *nosferatu*.

Maule said: "Indeed, I share your apprehension re-

garding Kate's reaction." He looked morose, then brightened slightly. "Fortunately your son's condition was
never serious, and is steadily improving."

"You think so?" Joe poked at his phone, held it to
his ear, and frowned. "Busy. I'll try again in a few
minutes."

"There are certain subtle signs. And it is common
enough for a youth of Andy's age to appear slightly
dazed, even—or especially—to those who know him
best."

"I hope you're right. You probably are." But Joe
sounded not entirely convinced.

The car doors were closed and the engine started
when Maule had a last-minute thought, and tapped on
a window. Joe rolled it down.

But it was Andy who got Maule's question.

"You are a student at the university of Thomas
More."

"On summer break right now, but yeah."

"Was not that institution at one time deeply engaged
in studies of ancient Egypt?"

"Ancient Egypt?" Again Andy sounded a little anxious, as if wondering whether he might again have
missed whole paragraphs of conversation.

"Yes. I should very much like to talk to someone
having expertise in such matters. As soon as possible.
But do not give anyone the impression of an emergency."

Even as Maule spoke, a new memory returned to
him, and he looked at Joe. "Did I tell you that last night
I heard Dickon mention someone named Flamel, describ-
ing him as his partner in an ambitious project? An unusual name, I think."

Joe frowned. "Eff-el-ay-em-ee-el?"

"That sounds likely. I have no certain knowledge of

the spelling. But some decades ago, in Europe, I had a breathing friend who bore that name. He might still be alive. If you can come up with any information—?"

Keogh nodded. "I'll see what I can do."

"I'll try to find out," Andy added. "How much TMU was into the Egypt thing. Maybe they still are," he added slowly. "But I don't know."

"I would appreciate your doing so."

By the time Joe's car had pulled up and out of the spacious underground garage, Wednesday morning's rush hour was over.

It was very inefficient, this repeated riding up and down, but this morning Maule did not see how it could be avoided. Ascending once more to his apartment, he meditated on the subject of mummified small animals, and pondered why certain folk among the ancients, presumably Egyptians, might have sealed them into plaster statues. His meditations made very little progress.

Nor had he yet been able to think of any reason why a small, mummified creature should provoke murder, but it certainly suggested a connection with ancient Egypt—and the fact that the scene in Maule's own visionary dream had been set in some hot, dry land was too apposite to be ignored.

"It would be folly to consider that a mere coincidence," he said to himself aloud. The woman with whom he was sharing the elevator at the moment looked at him nervously, and he gave her a reassuring smile.

Back in his apartment, entering the ravaged spare room, he noted with approval that John Southerland had already made a good start on the job of cleaning up. The young man had located the utility closet and laundry tub, and had fitted himself with an apron and a pair of rubber gloves, as well as a disposable paper mask of the type used by breathers to filter out particles of sanded paint and sawdust.

Now John was armed with several kinds of detergent, a pail and scrub-brush, which he was applying energetically to walls and furniture. The defiled spots on the carpet had been sprayed with cleansing foam. The bed had been stripped of all its covers, and in the utility room at the far end of the apartment a washing machine could be heard churning through its cycle.

Of course the major piece of debris had yet to be removed; Maule had reserved that detail for himself. Actually he would have preferred to do the entire cleanup with his own hands, and would have done so had he the time. His mental image of himself was much more a soldier than an aristocrat, and menial tasks were inescapably part of the life of any soldier in the field.

Besides, he was quite accustomed to performing for himself the humble chores of daily life. One of the drawbacks of vampire life down through the ages was the extreme difficulty of obtaining and keeping reliable household help. Over the past five hundred years, Maule's strong, pale hands had scrubbed an incredible number of floors, and he could have written a monograph on the best techniques to use in cleaning everything from ancient stone to twenty-first-century imitation wood. Nor was scrubbing floors the meanest task he had performed.

Joe Keogh, now well along in the process of driving his son home, was just turning off his cell phone after a brief and (he hoped) reassuring talk with Kate.

He turned to glance at Andy, riding in the passenger seat beside him. "Just thought I'd let your mother know you look okay," Joe told him.

"Uh-huh." Andy still didn't seem totally connected with his surroundings.

Now Joe mentally reviewed the horrible situation in Maule's building. Evidently you had to expect this kind of thing from time to time, if you were on close terms with a vampire. Joe had realized long ago that he was never going to completely understand the old friend of the family and his ways—nor would he ever want to. Joe was convinced that life would be easier and everyone would be better off if certain facts just never came to light—for example, the real name of the man whom he had had known first as Dr. Emile Corday.

Once more Joe looked sideways at Andy. "How you doing, kid?"

"Fine." But Andy's eyes still looked a little glazed, watching scenery glide by as the highway carried them toward their suburb. So far he hadn't commented on the evident fact that he was being driven home, not back to his own apartment.

Joe said: "Some day you and I have to have a talk about Uncle Matt. You know he's not a—a *blood* relation."

Andy looked at him, and his voice took on the tone of a child being patient with a parent. "Yes, I know that, Dad. I've known that for a long time."

"But—in some ways, he's closer to us than some of our blood relations are."

"Yeah." It was a noncommittal acknowledgment.

Having got that far, Joe stalled. Obviously now was not the time to explain anything complicated to his son. And an ancient proverb, popping up from somewhere, kept running through his mind: *A secret that is known by three, soon will not a secret be.* But he was going to argue with the proverb. The fact was that more than three in the family already knew the great secret of Matthew Maule: Joe himself, John, Kate, Joe's absent sister Judy. And of course Angie, John's wife, knew the facts as well as anyone—her introduction to the family, coinciding with the gruesome affair of Valentine Kaiser, had been spectacular indeed.

Joe could foresee the kind of conversation he would have with his kids, Andy and his sister Nell, when the time arrived for him to try to tell them about the reality of vampires, and just how close to home the subject came. It wasn't a discussion Joe looked forward to. In a way, it was probably going to be bizarrely like explaining about Santa Claus, or sex—though when those subjects had come up, he had soon discovered that the kids already knew the fundamentals almost as well as he did. That wouldn't happen in this case; Uncle Matt had a reality that Santa Claus was never going to achieve.

Maybe, Joe Keogh told himself hopefully, maybe the discussion could still be postponed until some future year. It wasn't like any of the family, including Joe, saw Uncle Matthew frequently—in fact, Joe realized now that years had gone by since their last meeting. The old people, Kate's parents, had rarely met Maule, and never dreamt of the truth about him, let alone Maule's nineteenth-century relationship with Mina Harker, their own great-grandmother. Chances were they never would. But the equally mundane youngest members of the family were in a somewhat different situation. Sooner or later, they were bound to notice that their "uncle" didn't age—at least not in any sane, linear way, like people were supposed to.

The trouble was, he didn't know whether Andy and his sister could be relied on to keep it quiet. Well, suppose they didn't . . . probably, Joe wanted to believe, *probably* all that would happen would be that "Uncle Matthew" would permanently drop out of all their lives. What would it feel like, Joe wondered, to know that the friendly old vampire was permanently gone? Trying to picture the departure, he experienced a strange mixture of relief and loss.

After being acquainted with the old man for more than twenty years, Joe would not have been at all surprised to learn that Maule had another identity or two in reserve, just waiting to be stepped into, like a spare pair of shoes. In five hundred years and more, a clever man would be able to come up with an awful lot of tricks to help him make his way in the world.

Andy was still gazing out the car window, apparently lost in thought.

Joe Keogh, having met a few vampires over the last few decades, had no particular liking for them as a group. But when he owed another man his life—in this case a lot more than his own life—then whether that man was a vampire or not, when he in turn stood in need of help, Joe was going to be there, and not picky about fine points of law.

Besides—and this trumped everything else—now Andy had somehow (accidentally, Joe was sure) become involved with the darker side of the *nosferatu* world. Joe could hope and pray that his son had had only glancing contact with that mode of existence. That Andy had only touched it and bounced away, so to speak, and that he was going to keep on getting farther and farther away as time went by.

Now Joe was inwardly angry with himself for suggesting Andy when Maule had called to say he needed a tutor in the arcane subjects of computers and the Internet. Even though Joe trusted Maule implicitly, at least where the safety of family members was concerned, still it hadn't worked out.

But, damn it (he could already hear in his mind the argument he was going to have with Kate), teaching someone about computers and the Internet had just sounded so harmless and innocent. So it would have been, Joe supposed, but something unforeseen had interrupted.

Besides, the kid was practically grown up now. Hell, he was grown up, old enough to join the army if his inclination had taken him that way. Soon Andy would be sinking or swimming in the world entirely on his own.

But whatever he told Andy would have to wait, at least until he was sure the kid was over this latest episode and thinking straight. Then, sooner or later, Joe and his offspring were going to have to have a serious talk.

Shaking his head, he resumed the imagined conversation: *You don't realize it, guys, a lot of it happened before you were born, but the man we call Uncle Matt has done more for us, for me and your mother and others in our family, than we can ever repay.* (Here he would pause to make sure his kids were listening.) *The thing is, a lot of the time he just doesn't live in the same world we do.*

By that time Andy and Nell would be looking at him incredulously. *Dad, are you trying to tell us Uncle Matt is gay? Or he does drugs? I don't think so.*

Joe didn't think so either. Uncle Matthew's unconformities were nowhere near that easy to explain. Well, the difference did have something to do with sex. All right, it had a lot to do with sex.

Does Uncle Matt like girls?

Does he ever. But talk about alternate lifestyles.

There had been a period, fortunately brief, when Joe was firmly convinced that this old friend of the family was a homicidal lunatic—that mistake, thank God, had been cleared up years ago. Maule lived in a very strange world, but he dealt with it sanely, honorably, and realistically. And, as Joe had gradually come to realize, Maule's world was part of the same universe that everyone else had to share. Which made the whole thing very weird.

Over the past twenty years John Southerland had also learned something about vampires, and he was intimately aware of the family relationship with this one. He could feel himself going a little pale as he began the cleanup job in the bedroom, but not because of the mere presence of a murder victim. He was trying not to notice his mute companion, but the real problem was that, like his brother-in-law, John was being unhappily reminded of the affair of Valentine Kaiser.

Vampire trouble again, John Southerland was thinking with an inward sigh as he peered in through the open door of the last bedroom at the end of the hall. He had finished the job and put away his tools, and now he was ready to leave, but he just wanted to check once more on the thoroughness of his cleanup. Entering, he went over the room methodically for the last time, making sure he hadn't missed any spots.

Just damned bad luck that the kid had happened to be here in Uncle Matt's place when, apparently, another delegation of the old vampire's enemies arrived on the scene. It seemed to John that Maule's enemies tended to show up at unpredictable intervals, like earthquakes, or killer tidal waves. Maybe it was just the normal thing for a *nosferatu* of Matthew Maule's age to have accumulated a set of deranged acquaintances, most of them also non-breathing. Trouble was, whenever these incursions happened, members of the extended Southerland family seemed to get caught up in them. Well, it might be worse—so far, trouble had struck only a few times in a generation.

John thought of Angie and his own two kids at home, and was beginning to be worried about them. Angie was as well acquainted with the truth about Mr. Maule as was John himself, and it was good for him to have someone he could talk to on the subject.

Now that the situation here seemed to be well in hand, for the time being at least, John decided that the time had come for him to call home and set his wife's mind at rest. Angie had been very worried when John told her where he had been summoned; but she hadn't tried to stop him.

The phone was answered on the first ring. John hastened to be reassuring. "Everything's under control here. For the moment, anyway."

"Fine." Angie wasn't going to ask, on the phone, for any details. "How soon are you coming home?"

"Looks like I'm almost out the door. How are the kids?"

"They're fine." Then her voice faded as she had to turn away to deal briefly with a questioning child. In a moment she was back. "Your son always looks forward to a chance to talk to Daddy on the phone."

"That's great, but tell him it'll have to be next time. See you in a couple of hours. Probably."

As John hung up the phone, Uncle Matt appeared in the bedroom doorway, looking thoughtful. Ignoring the corpse, he gazed absently at the telephone. "Ah, dear Angie. I trust she and the children are well?"

"Quite well, thanks." It came as no surprise to John Southerland that Uncle Matt did not regard the presence of Tamarack's dead body in his apartment as a serious difficulty—only another chore, bothersome and time-consuming. John began a routine reassurance that everyone in his own family was fine, but Maule interrupted, carrying on his own train of thought.

"John, are you a student of taxonomy?"

"I'm sorry?" Wondering if he had heard correctly, John shot a bewildered glance toward the corpse.

Maule showed some teeth in a thin-lipped grin. "Taxonomy, my young friend, not taxidermy. I do not plan to have Mr. Tamarack stuffed and mounted. Instead I make reference to the science of naming and classifying living organisms."

"Ah, no sir, I wouldn't say that I know anything about that."

"Nor do I—not much, that is—but I intend to learn." Looking at the body, Maule added: "I do not know if the creature or creatures I am seeking are human or not. If human—I would say certainly of the subspecies *Homo dirus*."

"I'm sorry?"

"There is no need for sorrow on your part. I have come to hold the opinion that we *nosferatu* form a subspecies of modern humanity—we are not precisely *Homo sapiens*, or thinking man, but *Homo dirus*, 'man inspiring dread.'"

"I guess I'm the wrong one to be asking about that."

But Uncle Matt had turned away. Moments later, in his own room, he was putting a few clean clothes and other items into a small traveling bag, obviously getting ready to head out. "Now, for my part of the cleanup." He smiled. "I shall probably not return until some time late tonight, or tomorrow."

John cleared his throat, and looked at Maule uncertainly. "How will you—? I mean, you're just going to—carry—?"

Maule smiled. "No one will pay much heed to a man carrying, among other things, a large plastic bag. To casual observers it will not appear heavy enough to hold a body."

He did not mention to his breathing ally the slight possibility that he might amend that plan, decide to retain the corpse somewhere on the banks of the Sauk for additional study.

It crossed Maule's mind, in the form of one more irritation, that now all of his electronic concerns, including the possibility of a *Homo dirus* web site, would simply have to wait.

Going into another room, he obtained from an inconspicuous storage place a suitably large, opaque, heavyweight plastic bag. It was one of those items that a well-run household rarely required, but whose unavailability when needed could result in serious inconvenience.

Taking a last look at Tamarack's blank face, drained of blood and life, Maule said to John: "Beyond the fact that this one, like the missing Flamel, was Dickon's partner, I know almost nothing about him."

"Partner in what?" John asked. "Or shouldn't I ask?"

Maule shrugged. "Some effort in alchemy, as I understand it." The vampire sighed faintly, seeing the blank look on John's face. "An attempt to turn lead into gold. That is a fool's project, and few in these days can take it seriously. But somehow it seems to have earned him a terrible enemy." He fell silent, brooding.

John glanced for the last time at the dead face and cleared his throat. "Can you tell me this much? Has all this anything to do with—things that happened that last time? Five years ago, Valentine Kaiser? Right here in this building?"

"I do not see how there could be any connection. That chapter is closed."

"That's a relief." One that he could feel in his gut. "Joe'll be relieved too."

Maule opened the plastic bag and, treating the deceased without either reverence or rancor, nudged the body's sprawling arms and legs into a more compact configuration, to make packaging easier.

John kept his back turned, worrying at a couple of practically invisible spots, while the encapsulation was in progress.

Still, Maule reflected that the situation, awkward as it was, might have been worse. He had a feeling, an instinct, about Tamarack: that whatever else the man might have been, he was an otherworldly wanderer with no close family to be concerned about his fate.

Now Maule considered whether he should dispose of Tamarack's bits and pieces of alchemical paraphernalia, along with his body; and soon decided that would probably be an excellent idea. He moved about the room doing a thorough pickup. Spare shirts, aspirin tablets, all went into the big bag.

At Maule's request, John had already repackaged in plastic wrap the dusty remnants of the shattered statue and its peculiar contents, then put the package in one of the drawers. He had handled the debris with gloves, and refrained from unnecessary breathing of the dust.

Maule had warned him: "Not that I have any specific reason to believe it dangerous, but—"

"Just to be on the safe side. Right."

Looking at the drawers now, Maule could tell, though his eyes could discern no visible mark, into which one John had dropped the package. He pulled the drawer open and there it was. He had a strong feeling that the little broken statue was, somehow, the key to the whole situation.

Instinct told him that the strange wooden panel was important too, and that feeling had kept him from sending it away with Joe. But now a strongly contrary premonition, that Maule did not stop to try to analyze, made him decide to rid himself of it, and he shoved the foot-square painted tablet decisively back into the bag holding the dead body. Away with it!

If, despite his intuition, the panel should turn out to be vitally important, he would know where to go to recover it again.

Thanking John again for his cleanup efforts, Maule casually hoisted his burden and was off, thinking he might take the service elevator this time. As an afterthought he returned to the living room, to take down the remaining wooden spear from its wall mounting—he supposed the point had probably been dulled on the one stuck in the wall. In the remote years of his early breathing life, he had on occasion used primitive firearms, but had never felt entirely at home with them.

He left his apartment carrying the spear and his small traveling bag containing clean clothes, along with not one but two plastic bags.

One of the bags was only lightly loaded, with dry and crumbling earth—he would probably, now that he thought about it, be prolonging his visit overday, and being able to rest on some of his native soil would afford him a comfortable trance.

~ 4 ~

Sliding into the driver's seat of Mr. Tamarack's vehicle, with all that was mortal of the late owner
neatly bagged up in the trunk, Mr. Maule applied
the ignition key, and began very skillfully to drive. Because of the length of his wooden spear, it had to ride in
the passenger cabin, rather like an old-fashioned fishing
pole, angled from low in the right front seat to high in
the left rear. But it was not fish that he had in mind.

Full daylight hit him with its expected shock as soon
as he pulled up and out of the subterranean garage, but
on he went, squinting through dark sunglasses at sun-
drenched pavement and the lancing reflections from
other vehicles. Sooner or later he would have to get out
of the car and face the sun. A broad-brimmed straw hat
lay on the passenger seat beside him, and he was wearing a long-sleeved shirt. In the trunk were his two plastic
bags, the smaller one long and flat, of the size to contain
a suit.

Tamarack's auto was not new, but it handled well.

Presently Maule was swooping north on Lake Shore Drive, looking for a turnoff that would lead him handily to the Kennedy Expressway.

Maule's destination today was a place he had not visited for several years. He was fully aware that drastic changes in appearance might have taken place, but he thought it highly unlikely that anything essential would be greatly altered. Too much magic had been applied, quite recently as time regarding such things was measured, and much of it must still be permeating the very earth, making several acres of black and fertile Illinois soil into something like a military minefield, pocked with possible surprises. Of course, in contrast to the minefield, not all the surprises would be nasty. Since Maule had been the great magician's ally, this water and land ought to be still hospitable to him in many ways. This would be by far the safest, most propitious locale for him to dispose of an unwanted car and corpse. He thought he could depend upon the river to engulf his discards in its muddy coils like some great enchanted serpent, and never give them up.

In another hour the four-lane highway had given way to a narrower one, and suburbs to early summer crops and pastures, interspersed with almost-European hedgerows and ravines too steep-sided to be anything but small preserves for wildlife.

Soon it became possible to see in the distance, when the road topped certain gentle hills, a fold of the broad, winding Sauk.

It was still a little before noon when he came to the re-membered, unmarked turnoff from the highway. Gratefully he observed that a large summer thundercloud had materialized to give him some relief from the sun's relentless hammering through the lightly tinted glass of the car windows.

The building now looked rather like a farmhouse, though somewhat oversized. The last time Maule had visited this site, it had supported a real castle, utterly incongruous in Illinois, imported decades ago from Europe by a means no more magical than money.

When he made the proper mental effort, Maule could still see, faintly against the sky, the outline of the castle, alternating with the image of a huge Gothic farmhouse. To see either one properly required concentration on his part; Maule himself had never been a truly fine magician—few vampires were—and he had almost resigned himself to the fact that he never would be.

Some more shingles were missing from the farmhouse roof since the last time he had been here. As he drew nearer, the structure regained, in his perceptive gaze, the dominant appearance of a castle. Now there were stone walls and a hint of battlement. Maule suspected that the several acres of land surrounding formed the remnant of some much larger holding, established more than a century ago.

Maule was surprised to see that this summer one side of the property was being encroached on by a vast field of tall summer corn, separated from enchantment by a prosaic fence, and well cultivated by some neighbor who evidently hoped for a high price per bushel in the fall. At one point the tall stalks were no more than about forty yards from the house. Maule wondered what a farmer in the cornfield would see, looking toward the house, or castle. Quite possibly the vision of a mundane breather would now see no building there at all, but only an inland view of trees growing thickly along the top of the riverside bluff.

The lowering thundercloud had begun to fulfill its promise, right when a brisk shower could be most helpful. Maule would have no need to be mindful of what sort of tire tracks he might be leaving on this land, for they were all going to be washed away.

He drove a little closer, then parked his car and got out, sniffing the air. The enigmatic building was now plainly no more than an abandoned farmhouse that seemed to grow a little smaller the nearer he approached.

Even before disposing of the burden in the trunk, Maule, out of curiosity and in search of the best place to sleep, entered the building. He had been invited into this dwelling years ago, and needed no renewed invitation.

Almost as soon as Maule stepped out of Tamarack's car, the urge for sleep, for near-oblivion, was very strong. But he steeled himself to fight it off a short time longer.

Struck by a strong intuition, or inspiration, of a kind he had learned centuries ago not to ignore, he climbed a shadowy spiral of stairs, seemingly compounded equally of stone and darkness. Moments later, standing on a flat and solid-feeling castle roof, he yielded to a sudden inspiration and erected his spear like a lightning rod, point upward, propping the weapon in place with balks of wood that he found lying providentially at hand. Dark clouds were swirling overhead in a most satisfactory manner, promising some summer pyrotechnics soon.

"Like Ahab, I will charge my weapon with the lightning," Maule murmured to himself, as a few heavy drops of rain came spattering. He suspected he might be facing a monster every bit as powerful as Moby Dick.

Now the restful delights of deep trance beckoned, and today they also promised information; but before he could allow his mind to be engulfed, there were the details of a more or less routine task to be completed. This meant disposing of the car, which had borne Tamarack's body in life, and held it still in death. Along with the car must go that very body, which had served as vehicle for his soul.

Back in the castle courtyard (if he tilted his head slightly, he saw instead the front yard of the farmhouse) Maule opened the trunk. He needed to make sure the larger of his plastic bags was still where he had put it, and that the contents were unchanged; he had now entered a domain where certain transformations unthinkable in mundane time and space could not entirely be ruled out.

It still seemed to him a good idea that master and machine should disappear from human sight together, going deep into a swampy pool between two jutting shoulders of limestone, just where the broad river curved at its nearest to the high-perched house. It cost the visitor a few grunts of moderate exertion to maneuver the heavy automobile into the right position atop the crag, and after a few more muttered words he sent it on its way. The effort of course left tire tracks and other marks on the high land; but he thought these would not long endure.

As soon as that task was accomplished, he reentered the castle. He thought he could detect a faint, comforting glow of welcome, from the walls around him and the land beneath.

Now he could almost fully relax. The distilled experience of half a millennium had refined his instincts until he thought they could—almost—always be trusted.

As a preliminary to restful trance, Maule turned off his own cell phone. Any incoming calls would have to wait, and the device would be of no help in an interior communication with his earlier self, which had now become his immediate goal.

For a time he continued to prowl restlessly through the dwelling, which continued its subtle alterations around him as he moved. He was intent on selecting the precisely best spot to settle in for peaceful sleep. The maximum possible shielding from sunlight was desirable. Meanwhile he continued his interior preparations, which he hoped would allow him to proceed with his research whilst he was asleep. Long experience had proven that this was the most effective way for him to search the more remote corridors of his own memory.

When he had made his selection, he spread out the garment bag containing some of his native earth, and stretched himself out on it with a sigh.

Maule had achieved the peaceful, dreaming trance he sought.

He intended to use a form of self-hypnosis to track down and extract the memory that was nagging at him—exactly where and when had he earlier encountered something very similar to the crushed white statue and its repulsive contents?

And when he had successfully attained the proper kind of trance, it came to him.

No sooner had the dream begun than he recognized the setting, and the time. On some level it seemed he already knew what was going to happen, but having come this far, he wanted to see all the details play out.

The time was a warm day in the early autumn of a year before the middle of the nineteenth century, long before he had thought of calling himself Matthew Maule. The place was a bedroom in a certain French château. There had been no intruding monster on that day—unless one could describe a jealous husband in those terms. And that the vampire had had any problem at all was really his own fault, for having the effrontery to persist in a risky assignation in broad daylight.

To state the case more precisely, the man who would one day be known as Matthew Maule, then well over a century younger and a hundred years less wise, had been overtaken by the rising sun in a room where he should not have been, occupying a bed in which he should never have fallen asleep. Yes, he had foolishly lingered on even past sunrise. No good berating his past self on that score now; he knew he ought to have known better.

The onset of daylight of course froze him in manform. Who can say why he overslept that day? But that morning the burning light outside somehow lured him into perversely dozing. The doze could never have turned into a restful sleep, of course—not in that bed, which lacked any trace of his native earth. Still his eyes were closed and his consciousness drifting. The sudden thunder of horses' hooves, startlingly close outside the window, took him unpleasantly by surprise.

Madame de Ferret beside him had also been shocked to wakefulness, and her voice was thick with quiet terror. "It is the count, my husband! My God, I had thought him in his room and fast asleep!"

Madame was thrown at once into a state of absolute terror, but she proved equal to the occasion.

And now, swift eager feet in heavy boots were thudding along the stone-floored corridor at ground level outside the bedroom. There were the windows, to be sure, offering a possible way out, but the unhappy vampire felt himself trapped by the searing rays of direct sunlight, as a lesser being might have been caught in the steel jaws of some great trap. But short of confronting the husband, and getting past him by force or guile, there was simply no means of escape available.

Given the circumstances, any attempt to prevail by guile seemed unlikely to succeed.

Casting a hasty squint at a curtained window, the tardy lover saw to his displeasure that the day was promising to be bright. Any long exposure to even intermittent sunlight would be uncomfortable at best, and might prove fatal. Even if he could manage to get out of the house without a hue and cry of pursuit close on his heels, the best he could expect would be long hours of a bitter ordeal, trying to find shade and shelter in the nearby woods.

No doubt the count (if in truth the man had any real right to such a title; twenty-first-century Maule still had his doubts) had been given reason to be suspicious of his wife's behavior, long before her most recent lover came on the scene. Neither could it be denied that the husband in this case was justified in taking a certain measure of offense at his rival's behavior—but like other creatures who are too proud for their true station in life, he carried his reaction to extremes.

By the time the jealous husband actually entered the room, the vampire, who could move very fast, was in milady's closet, every stitch of his clothing bundled under one arm, and with the door closed after him. Actually his own preference would have been to leave open the closet door, since it posed no real barrier to his discovery. Leave it open, and trust to the shelter of a small angled recess inside, just because an open door so strongly suggests that there is nothing and no one behind it worth covering up. But Madame had sprung out of bed almost as quickly as her lover. She pulled on a wrapper as she rose, and with an extension of the same movement pushed the door shut after him. If her husband was not in time to actually observe her in the act of doing so, he saw her turning away from the closet in an attitude strongly suggesting what she had just done.

But the lady's nerves were very good, so far. "You are very late," she said to him. "Or is it very early?"

Schedules were not what the husband had on his mind at that moment. "Madame, there is someone in your closet." His tones were hoarse, and coldly furious rather than excited. The man in the closet felt his heart sink at the prospect of having to do the poor fool harm, should a personal contest between them become inevitable. Strange, irrational schemes danced through the vampire's mind: Maybe he could arrange a challenge to a duel, and bear without wincing the brief and harmless pain of a leaden bullet in his heart. After that, he should have no trouble convincing a nineteenth-century physician that he was dead. At the moment, deliberately losing a duel was about the happiest outcome of the situation that he could foresee.

"No sir." Madame's courage and determination vibrated in her firm voice. The heart of the listening vampire sank even further as he contemplated what steps he might have to take to shield her from the consequences of his own folly in oversleeping.

In the next moment, it seemed that the Count had paused, rethinking his first impulse to yank it open. "If I open the closet door then, either way, our union is at an end."

The wife began a murmured protest, which the husband soon cut short. "Hear me, I know how pure you are at heart, and that your life is a holy one. You would not commit a mortal sin to save your life. Here, take your crucifix." There had of course been a rather ornate and valuable one, hanging on the wall. "Swear to me before God, on your crucifix, that there is no one in there; I will believe you, I will never open that door."

At the moment, the chances of a peaceful, outcome seemed too small to be worth estimating. Monsieur the count, if such he truly was, had murder in his heart.

Solemnly the wife let her pale hand rest upon the crucifix; in his mind's eye the vampire could see it, shaking slightly. Her voice at least was steady: "I swear to you that there is no one in my closet."

"Very well." There was silence for a few seconds, and then the husband, speaking in a different voice, turned to the maid, Rosalie, who had come in after him, and ordered: "Fetch Goron."

On hearing those words, the first impulse of the man in the closet was to relax just a trifle, for the count's tone suggested that he might be summoning a dog. In all his centuries since becoming *nosferatu,* the man in the closet had never encountered a four-legged watchdog, however fierce or strangely named, that he could not charm quickly into sleeping, or at least adopting an attitude of tolerance.

A few minutes passed in hopeful silence. But when Goron arrived, he came striding on two heavy and very human feet. In another minute, the directions that Monsieur began to give him were not reassuring. The fellow was directed to get his barrow, and bring here, into the bedroom, materials left over from a recent construction project at the other end of the house. Goron, whatever his usual job, was being assigned a project for a stone-mason.

Fortunately—or unfortunately, depending on one's point of view—some building materials, left over from a recent addition on the other end of the house, happened to be readily available—probably their presence had even inspired the count with his plan. Rosalie was directed to fetch water, required for mixing mortar.

Had that particular vampire been at all susceptible to fear, he would have begun to feel it then. Oh, not for his personal safety—no pair of clumsy breathers were at all likely to hurt him much, unless they came armed with wooden arrows, spears, or bullets, or with certain exotic poisons, and took him completely unawares. But he foresaw unpleasant complications. Surely the lady would soon be forced to give way in this war of wills and words that she was having with her husband.

But Madame showed no sign of yielding. *This,* the intruder thought, *is getting interesting*.

Rosalie was soon back, lugging two full buckets. Interpreting bits of dialogue being exchanged out in the bedroom, the hidden listener soon understood that Goron the stonemason had for some time been hoping to marry Rosalie the maid, and that only financial difficulties had held them back. Now the count in a few terse words was promising to provide the hopeful couple with money to set themselves up in style, most likely in another country, if they carried out his orders now and ever afterward kept quiet about the whole affair.

There was the repeated trundling back and forth of a handy wheelbarrow, whose iron wheel must have damaged stone and tile floors, though today nobody was protesting. By this means, the assembly of materials took only a few minutes. Then, briskly, without a word of explanation as to why he might want such alteration in the architecture, the count gave his workman orders that at this point came as no surprise to anyone. He was to brick up the closet door. "Be sure you make it solid and thick. There is to be no opening. If there should be, say, a fly trapped in there, he must never be able to get out."

The work began at once, while the master of the house stood by and watched.

Each of the four people in Madame's room knew what the certain effect of such a construction must be, on any being who happened to be trapped behind it. The stone wall of the old house must have been at least five or six feet thick at that point on the ground level, the closet a mere niche carved from its depth. There were designed tombs and mausoleums whose walls were more yielding and enclosed more airspace.

But of course the fourth listener, the man in the closet, knew something of great importance that remained unknown to any of the others. A certain vital fact about himself: once the sun was down, he needed no wide doorways; he would be able to pass freely through crevices so small they would screen out the smallest fly.

When Madame understood that her husband was deadly serious in what he meant to do, she still did not yield in an honest confession. Instead she took the easier way out of her dilemma and fell down in an equally honest faint. The vampire in her closet was listening carefully, waiting patiently with folded arms, leaning against the wall in his little alcove. He could tell that her swoon was genuine, from the changed sound of her breathing and the soft crumpling of her fall.

The vampire felt sorry for the lady, who, he was sure, had no understanding of her secret lover's true nature, his extraordinary powers. (In the half-conscious mind of Matthew Maule, now luxuriating in his twenty-first-century trance, there followed a learned discussion, in which he took both parts, on the proper taxonomy of the subspecies *Homo dirus*—it seemed arguable that the correct name should be *Homo sapiens dirus*. Maule in his dreaming trance could not decide. He would have to ask some expert at the Field, or perhaps at one of the universities.)

—but of course such a discussion would have meant nothing to Madame. Listening to the slight clues of her inward struggle, the man in the closet was touched, choosing to think that her terror and shock were on his account, the wretch about to be walled up alive, and not for herself. In sympathy the vampire vowed to himself that he would try to do his best for her in turn.

As soon as the lady fainted, the maid rushed to her aid, while the murderously angry husband did not stir a step. For the moment he was quiet, except for his rather heavy breathing, but the concealed listener could picture him standing there, arms folded and frowning like a betrayed monarch. The man in the closet could also visualize the build and movements of the sturdy bricklayer, without ever having seen the man. The rhythm of Goron's strong callused hands, applying bricks and mortar gracefully, did not falter for a moment as he kept on phlegmatically adding one more tier after another. He was one to follow orders, not asking a single question of his master.

The workman's breathing had grown rapid with his exercise. The hidden listener could not make up his mind whether the mason might be in poor physical condition, his body strained by the exertion of building a wall, or whether he was simply excited, probably more from the prospect of promised wealth than from having a hand in murder.

Soon the new barrier was high enough to prevent anyone suddenly entering the closet. Doing what little he could, under the circumstances, to ease the awkward position in which his lover found herself, the listener in the closet had been slowly and very quietly putting on his clothes. Having accomplished that, he found the situation almost boring—or would have, except that he was waiting to make certain that the wife was not going to be murdered. To prevent that, he meant to do everything . . . that could reasonably be expected of him.

The mason in his labors was necessarily making a certain amount of noise, enough that the intended victim decided there was little point in his maintaining *absolute* silence. No one was going to hear him if he moved about a little. So while waiting for the denouement of the little drama now playing itself out, he passed the time in examining the contents of the closet.

And here it was that Fate awarded him (and the dreaming, one-hundred-and-seventy-year-older Matthew Maule) with the object of his search.

In the closet there were some items of feminine clothing—no, more than *some*. Actually there were so many in the confined space that he had trouble turning around without entangling himself in sleeves and lace.

Here on a small shelf were more interesting items. Another crucifix, not as valuable as the one out in the bedroom—the vampire had no trouble picking it up for a closer inspection. Some superstitious folk who thought they knew him would have been astounded to see how casually, yet reverently, he did so.

Now he had put back the cross, and was toying with

an odd little figure he found toward the back of a dusty shelf—it was an item of ancient Egyptian origin, and had been brought back to France by one of the officers who had taken part in Napoleon's Egyptian expedition at the very end of the previous century.

At first he thought he had found a bizarre kind of doll, but in fact it was nothing of the kind. To the vampire's amazement and amusement, he was soon able to recognize it as an embalmed baby crocodile. Incredibly slender, doubtless having been disemboweled, and drained of its last drop of moisture, some thousands of years ago. Dark and faintly odorous, and threatening to crumble at the merest touch. The smell of it was very faint and vaguely pleasant, somewhere between dried flowers and old leather. It struck the visitor as odd, these Egyptian morsels in the middle of rural France—until he remembered that Napoleon Bonaparte had led a French army to the land of the pharaohs at the very close of the previous century, then only a few decades in the past.

Carefully he replaced the oddity on the obscure shelf, for it seemed to him that he had more important things to think about.

(And in the year of Our Lord Two Thousand and One, the dreaming vampire understood that a gutted, desiccated crocodile of such infantile stature would probably have fit very neatly into a certain small, thin-shelled white statue.)

Maybe, the hidden vampire thought, I should rehearse an explanation now, while I have the chance. It would be good to have one ready, just in case. Then I can at least say that I tried. *You see, Monsieur, in truth I have dropped in on your wife to admire her stuffed croc-*

odile. Not an easy sentence, perhaps, for even the advanced student of French to come up with on a moment's notice.

Had he been a breather, the dusty emission from his find would probably have forced him to sneeze, injecting a note of low bedroom farce into the potential impending tragedy.

So matters were going in the closet. Meanwhile, out in the charged atmosphere of the bedroom, the lady had revived from her faint, her maid had helped her to a chair, and the unhappy husband and wife were at least speaking to each other again. The start of reconciliation? No, not likely. The husband was adamantly refusing to hear any belated confession, or attempt at negotiation.

"You have sworn that there is no one there," he repeated several times. And that, it seemed, was going to be the end of that.

The concealed listener pondered: Would his dear companion of a few hours ago now have to present another serious sin to her confessor? It seemed to him a nice point for the theologians to wrangle about. She had taken a most solemn oath, swearing to what she was certain was a lie—although in objective fact it was essentially the truth. Once darkness fell again, stone walls would be no more obstacle to her secret lover than open windows.

It had become very dark inside the closet when the wall-building was complete at last, though in fact it was not yet the middle of the day. There were hours of daylight to be got through, but the man inside was very old, and he could be very patient.

Time passed. He had no trouble determining the exact moment when the shoulder of the spinning earth rose high enough against the sun to hide its radiance from central France. He could feel his powers returning promptly on schedule, as he had never doubted they would. From that moment, bricks and stones and mortar could hold him in no longer. A network of invisibly fine crevices existed in the thick outer wall, as they would in almost any barrier. Most of these defects were practically invisible, too thin to admit even a sharp knife blade, yet they easily sufficed to set him free.

Drifting in mist-form through the early twilight just outside the house, the vampire took thought regarding his next move. Given Madame's demonstrated concern for his welfare (she was still clinging to hopes that her husband would relax his vigilance long enough to permit her ordering the wall demolished and rebuilt, without his knowledge), it would have seemed very inconsiderate not to let her know that he had survived.

Everything was working out at least as well as he could possibly have expected—perhaps better.

He showed his face very briefly outside the parlor window, choosing a moment when his erstwhile companion happened to be looking in that direction, and her lord and master had his back turned. A smile, a wink, a slight wave of the raised hand to signify goodbye, and in the next instant the intruder was out of sight again.

Monsieur turned round on hearing the strange noise that his wife uttered in that moment, but she had been given the essential second or two in which to avert her face from the window and close her eyes.

The count was at bottom a very mundane fellow, and absolutely convinced that nothing could trump solid bricks and hardened mortar—except possibly money, gun-barrels, and his own warped conception of personal honor. By that last he chiefly meant that secretly and inwardly he lived in terror of being laughed at.

Later that night, when the lady tiptoed out of her room, where her husband currently was snoring—doubtless she had in mind some desperate plea to Goron—the vampire intercepted her. He had been waiting in a hallway, confident of his ability to melt into darkness if someone should come along.

Frozen in shock for a long moment at the sight of one she had seen so ruthlessly and horribly doomed, instead quite casually alive and well, she finally found the breath to demand in a fierce whisper: "How did you get out?"

"There are ways," he whispered in response. "The means of Mesmer." This was a marvelously irrelevant answer, but still the best he had been able to think up in the time available. France was still strongly under the influence of the great wave of enthusiasm for Anton Mesmer's hypnotic techniques, which had reached its peak a few decades back. It was an epoch when it seemed that the power of suggestion might be stretched to explain any marvel. By invoking Mesmer, he had given the lady a strange answer, but an enormously relieving one, so it was one she wanted to believe.

He went on, trying to be soothing. "So, you see, when you swore that mighty oath that there was no one in your closet—you were telling the exact truth."

"You mean that all the time Goron was building that wall—?" And Madame's pretty lips were soiled with an exotic oath. "I nearly died!"

"Be assured, Madame, that I did not."

The vampire did his best to confirm the lady in her swift-rising hope that she had committed no serious sin in answering her husband as she did. Having known several good Jesuits, each of them more skilled in debate than the others, he was certain any one of them could have made a powerful argument for that point of view. And he felt confident that the lady herself was sure to convince herself that his argument was correct, as soon as she had been given a little time to think about it.

The transformation did not take long. Even as the vampire watched, her life, her conscience, were visibly relieved of an enormous burden.

But she was still afraid, and would not want to be reminded of the close call. "You must go, we must never see each other again."

Her ex-lover sighed, gallantly, as if the prospect of such loss were well-nigh insupportable. "I fear that you are right. But first, one question, Madame, if I may?"

"What is it, then? In God's name, be quick!"

"There was a certain item in your closet that much intrigued me. I believe it to be actually the body of a small crocodile, dried out to the point of crumbling, mummified . . ."

Her mouth flew open. "Are you insane? What do you care about that trash? Fly for your life, before he comes!"

Once he was determined to find out something, he was not easily turned aside. "Nevertheless, I am intrigued. If you could just tell me—?"

She nodded at him, so frantically that ringlets of her hair went all askew. "It is some kind of mummified crocodile, the Egyptians find them in the Nile, and worship them. They say the hot sun breeds them from the mud. My father was with Bonaparte, and brought it back— are you satisfied now? Then, in God's name, flee!"

*   *   *

Years later, when both man and wife were either dead or too old to worry about it any more, the vampire heard, almost by chance and from another of his own subspecies, how the husband had spent the next two weeks in his wife's room, never letting her out of his sight for even a tenth of the time that would have been necessary to knock an escape hole in a wall of solid brick.

For a time he wondered what the sequel to the story might be: Did the lady eventually, at some time when her lord and master was out of the way, order the wall torn down, saying she was tired of being deprived of the use of her closet? Or might she have suddenly remembered that one of her favorite gowns or hats was in there?

Or was she never quite sure enough that she had really seen her endangered lover safe and free to risk any such bravado gesture?

Maule woke from his eidetic trance to the realization that he was still stretched out exactly where he had lain down, in a high room of what had once been a magic castle, established on a millionaire's strange whim in Illinois. The thunderstorm had passed; he had been aware only dimly of how it blessed his elevated spear. Now, small dust motes danced within a beam of restored sunlight, having that peculiar quality generally found in solar energy in late afternoon, slanting close above him as he lay.

The uncanny old house, and the strange land around it, were unnaturally quiet.

He was still alone—but he could feel that soon enough he would have company.

~ 5 ~

*I*t was midmorning when Joe Keogh finished the last leg of his drive home with Andy, cruising down the quiet, tree-shaded suburban street and turning into his curved driveway. Kate was there, actually standing in the driveway; she must have been keeping lookout from an upstairs window, and then run down to meet her returning menfolk. It was now more than twenty years since they'd first met, and Joe could tell from the angle of her slender shoulders, somewhat slumping, that she had been very worried but was now relieved.

The proud thought crossed his mind that she hadn't changed that much, in either face or figure, in twenty years. At least Joe couldn't see that she had changed. She was still pretty, and if a few gray hairs showed in the blond, well, he had more gray than she did. Which was only natural, being eight years older.

Kate clamped her son in a large hug as soon as Andy got out of the car, and then held him at arm's length, evidently to satisfy herself that he looked, sounded, and acted practically normal. For the moment she demanded no explanations.

After greeting his mother casually—as casually as he could in the midst of a bear hug—Andy said he was going to his room, and headed up the stairs. Joe noted with continuing relief that he was now walking quite steadily.

As soon as their son had disappeared, Kate turned to her husband. "What happened?"

Joe didn't answer until they had gone into the house, and he had sunk into a big chair in the living room and had taken off his shoes, letting them fall to the floor, one slow thump after another. Then he said: "To Andy, not much, thank God. He got put to sleep for most of the night. I think that's all it amounted to."

"But what—?"

"Uncle Matt says it was some kind of hypnosis, perpetrator unknown, and it hit him too. Knocked him right out."

"*Uncle Matt?*"

"Yep."

"That's all?"

"That's all that has anything to do with Andy. As far as I can tell."

A faint musical-mechanical note, a kind of electronic gong, came from upstairs: the sound of Andy's old computer, the one he'd left at home when he moved out, being turned on. Kate welcomed it as a sign of normalcy.

She found another chair and perched on the edge of its seat. Looking at her husband, who was not looking at her, she could see that there was much more to the affair than he had told her yet. Joe had his shoulder holster on, which was decidedly unusual, probably illegal, and he was making no effort to take it off.

Impulsively she said: "I wish you would stay out of it."

"Wish I could. But we both know I can't. I'll go back, after I get another hour or two of sleep."

"Did *he* ask you to help?"

"He wouldn't come right out and ask. But he expected help, and I don't blame him."

Old terrors and old excitements were drifting to the surface in Kate's mind. There were certain events of twenty years ago that she had imagined were forgotten, but now it turned out they were not. And of course there were certain other events she knew she would never be able to forget. "Who else was there? At his place?"

Joe frowned thoughtfully. For his wife's peace of mind, he decided not to mention Connie. "A man, a breather, named Tamarack—ever run into him, or hear of him?"

She shook her head.

"How about someone, man or woman, called Flamel?"

"No."

"You remember a man named Dickon?"

She shivered a little, then nodded. "Vaguely. He was one of Them, as I recall."

Joe nodded. "I didn't see him, but Maule said he was there last night. But I don't think Dickon was the hypnotist. Maule says he's a real coward. Something about how Dickon could manage to terrify himself by watching old movies about walking mummies."

Kate could no longer keep from pursuing it. "Just what all did happen last night?"

In response to that, her husband just looked at her, which was definitely a bad sign. Kate changed the subject slightly. "How about *him*? Is *he* all right?"

"I guess so. But actually Andy hasn't been to his place at all."

Kate blinked. "He hasn't?"

"Neither have I. No one you know has been up to his condo recently."

"Oh." There was a pause, in which Kate studied her husband's unexpressive face. "You're chewing gum. You only do that when you're trying hard not to go back to smoking."

"I'm chewing gum," Joe acknowledged at last. It was as far as he would go.

Taking off his coat but not his holster, stretching out on the sofa in his living room late on Wednesday morning, Joe managed to catch an hour and a half of sleep before lunch. It helped to make up for what he had lost.

Not that his nap was all that restful. One problem was that it included a strange dream, in which he found himself running through a hot and sunbaked street, while people were chasing him with knives. Rousing a little before noon, he considered what other pressing business affairs might have to be dealt with today.

Letting out a sigh, he looked at his watch and stirred as if he were going to get up. "I should have called the office."

Kate was sitting nearby, feet in house slippers up on a stool, thin portable computer unfolded on her lap. Joe supposed she would be working on the household accounts, or maybe on something for one of the charities with which she was involved. She said: "I already did. Told them something special had come up, and I didn't think you'd be in. They didn't seem all that worried, so you should get some rest."

"Thanks." He lay back on the sofa with another sigh,

a trifle uneasy that the office should be getting along so well without him. But soon he was going to have to get up anyway.

As if reluctantly, Kate spoke again. "Your client at the Field Museum called too. I got the impression it was moderately urgent."

Joe nodded. "Okay, I'll give him a ring. Actually there's something I want to ask him."

Going to the telephone in his home office, Joe recalled his own visit to the museum a few days earlier, his talk in the office of a worried-looking administrator.

Having settled into his office chair and put his feet up, he soon had the administrator's deputy on the phone.

So far her problems had nothing like the urgency of Maule's. "We had another event last night," her crisp voice reported. "But it's the same situation as before, no real intruders. The engineers have about ruled out any electronic problems."

Joe did his best to sound calm and capable and unsurprised. "I've been looking into a couple of things that might have a connection with your problem. I'd like to e-mail you something and get your opinion on it, if you don't mind."

Moments later, he was uploading into his computer the digital photo he had taken of the strange little wooden panel. Taking an on-screen look at the picture of the smashed statue, he decided against sending that to anyone; it would be hopeless to ask anybody to interpret that kind of mess. Maybe, the next time he went to the museum, he'd show them his sample of antique tape.

Once the photo of the panel was in the system, it was only the work of another minute to send it out by e-mail.

Just as it departed, Kate opened the door of his

study and put her head in. "Ready for some lunch?"

"Sounds good. Maybe a peanut butter sandwich."

"Have some soup too. Something hot will do you good."

"There's one more thing I ought to take care of first." In another minute he had called his office in downtown Chicago, getting one of his junior employees started at the task of finding out whatever she could about people named Flamel.

A few minutes later, Joe was at the kitchen table with his son, while Kate set out paper bowls of soup. The Keoghs were well able to afford regular household help, but so far Kate preferred to stick with only the cleaning ladies, who came in once a week. She also lacked enthusiasm for washing dishes.

"I'm going back in," Joe informed his wife, blowing on a hot spoonful. "There's a certain place in Old Town I want to take a look at. Some kind of a fire last night. Do we have a morning paper?"

Meanwhile, Andy had remained incurious about what his parents might be up to, an attitude they were ready to welcome as additional evidence of normalcy. Their son also seemed content to spend the remainder of the day loafing around the house. When Joe went out again, he did not ask Andy if he wanted a ride back to his own city apartment.

Maule had advised Joe Keogh not to return today to Maule's apartment, because Maule was planning to be elsewhere.

Joe had toyed with the idea of assigning some agent from his own office to bring him a report on the fire in

Old Town, and any out-of-the-ordinary events that might have happened at around the same time. But he hesitated, unwilling to risk the life of anyone who would undertake the job without a clue to what they might be up against. Quickly he decided that he would feel better about it if he undertook that investigation himself.

About an hour after leaving home, he was looking over the scene in Old Town.

There had been no trouble locating the burned-out building. It was surrounded by broad tapes of yellow plastic carrying stern warnings of DO NOT CROSS.

Originally it must have been a substantial and respectable house, or rather a typical small Chicago apartment building, undistinguished and rectangular, brick with a flat roof. Three stories high, it stood in the middle of a block, almost filling its narrow lot, half a block from the busy commercial thoroughfare, whose enterprises had spilled down this side street. Now, when Joe looked carefully, he could see that a part of the roof had indeed fallen in.

Beside one flank of the building was the mouth of a darkish alley, with a middle-aged auto parked in it at an angle.

Approaching the building, Joe stepped under the warning tape as if he had a perfect right to do so, thus practically guaranteeing that none of the passersby in the vicinity were going to pay him much attention.

Joe observed in the mud of the alley, right beside a manhole, a strange track—smear was more like it—such as might be left by the dragging of a large object. The alley was poorly drained behind the burned-out building, and the place had been drenched with fire hoses. The track must have been made after the firemen had rolled their hoses up.

The manhole cover was only a few feet in from the mouth of the alley, and the pavement immediately surrounding it was covered by a thin layer of drying mud. Marks in the mud suggested that the manhole cover had recently been displaced, pushed or dragged clear off its opening and then reclosed—but the closing had not quite been properly accomplished. Looking at the marks, Joe Keogh was eerily aware of the suggestion that something large, the size of a man or bigger, had come up from below, and then gone down again, seeking a wet refuge.

Well, if anyone was going to search the sewers on this case, it wasn't going to be Joe Keogh, or any of his employees. And any investigating he did was going to be done in daylight.

Raising his eyes, he took note of the fact that across the street, where the backyards of modest houses came up to the alley, a middle-aged man in a white-strapped undershirt stood leaning over a fence, intently watching what Joe was about.

Hands in pockets, Joe strolled in that direction. The man straightened up, but stayed right where he was. No doubt it was his own backyard.

As soon as he got into easy conversational range, Joe asked: "See anything really strange on the day they had the fire?"

"Just the usual stuff." The man sounded third- or fourth-generation Chicago-Polish. "Fire trucks, all that shit. You wanna hear strange, though?"

"Yeah, try me."

"Auto fix-it garage, two blocks over that way." He pointed with a stubby finger. "Had a big watchdog,

German shepherd. Later on that night, after the fire, something got in, through the barbed wire and all, and ate it. 'Bout half of it, anyway."

"Good lord. Ate a watchdog?"

" 'Bout half of it was gone. That's what I heard."

"Anyone call the cops?" That would seem inevitable, unless the dog had been guarding something less legal than autos and tools.

"You a cop?"

"No. Insurance." That was plausible, and, in a sense, was almost true.

The man shrugged. "Didn't call 'em. What good does it do? Crazy maniacs, running around—to do that to a dog."

After Joe went out in the afternoon, Kate managed to resist a certain impulse for almost twenty minutes. Then she gave in, and went to look in a certain upstairs drawer, where she found a certain spot quite empty. The shoulder holster had not been put away, which was not good news at all.

Oh God, she prayed silently, *let it not be starting all over again. Not the real bad stuff, you know what I mean, Lord.* Then she went to her own desk and sat down, determined to find something useful to fill the time and occupy her mind.

For the rest of Wednesday Andy played computer games, or sat around the house, leafing through books and magazines, sometimes staring at nothing. Once he came to his mother to ask her if they had any books on ancient Egypt.

Kate stared at him. "Didn't you do an on-line search?"

"Yeah, sure—only there's so much stuff."

She suggested he use the encyclopedia—which now, of course, was also to be found on the computer.

Around midafternoon her son uncharacteristically fell asleep on the sofa, but in an hour was up again, going back to the home computer, playing a couple of violent games with what appeared to be his normal skill.

On emerging slowly from his trance in the last minutes of Wednesday's daylight, Maule felt well rested. More importantly, he had gained what he thought might prove valuable information; he now felt instinctively sure that the mysterious, mangled contents of the little white statue in his apartment had once been a mummified small crocodile. How this would eventually help him to come to grips with the murderer who had invaded his home remained to be seen; but the gain of knowledge was an important start.

Maule's eyes were open for some time before he was able to see clearly and regain full awareness of his surroundings. Even before his eyesight became fully focused, his attention was drawn to certain muffled, puzzling sounds, originating perhaps a quarter of a mile away. Searching his centuries of memory, he could not quite match them with anything that he had ever heard before.

First was a great, belching, bubbling kind of splash, suggesting images of someone forcing an inverted bathtub under water and then breaking it apart, with the sounds of rending metal.

His eyes, as well as his inner sense of duration, told him that hours had passed since he lay down. The time was shortly before sunset, and he knew that he was lying in the old house that had once been a transplanted castle, on a bluff above the Sauk River, in northern Illinois.

For a brief time Maule remained motionless on his back, eyes dreamily following the golden beams of the sinking sun as their spots gradually crept upward along the stonework of an interior wall that sometimes still seemed to be made of medieval stone. His awareness persisted that he was not going to be alone for long, but the fact seemed to require no immediate action on his part.

Instead it seemed more important, at the moment, to think back over an extension of his meaningful Egyptian dream, with variations.

The sun was still not down when he rose lithely to his feet, then walked through the slanting beams where they entered his temporary bedchamber through a crevice in the wall.

For the time being, he left his thin mattress of plastic and native earth stretched on the floor. His next step was to climb once more to the roof of the castle to retrieve his spear—as soon as he laid his hand on it, he could feel that substantial power of some kind had been added. Taking the weapon in his right hand, where it rested lightly as a feathered dart, he noted that the point looked even sharper than it had back in Chicago. He brought his left hand over, intending to test the keenness with a finger, but at the last instant some instinct warned him not to do so. He would have to thank a certain legendary wizard when they next met.

Squinting occasionally in fading sunbeams, the vampire went out to see what he was going to get in the way of callers. Having taken certain other precautions of a more internal nature, he thought that this time he would be ready for an onslaught from any attacker, human or otherwise, who attempted to control his mind.

The walls of the ambiguous structure in which

Maule had enjoyed his dream seemed to have swelled up larger and thicker around him while he was entranced, almost as if they might be driven by some impulse to offer him protection.

He was pleased to note the sudden appearance of a door, placed very conveniently for his current use, in a section of wall that had been entirely smooth and solid when he entered the house. The new door, of thick oak with brassy hinges, swung open for him automatically as he approached. A moment later Maule was outside.

Now he knew he would not have long to wait to be confronted by a visitor, whoever or whatever it might be. Moving on with slow, deliberate strides, he passed close by a collapsed pit in the earth that not many years ago had been a modern swimming pool. A curved and rusted metal ladder still led down, burying itself pointlessly in mud or muddy water, as if it were a passage to some domain beneath the earth.

Someday, perhaps. But that was not going to be Maule's road this evening.

Shadows now covered almost the entire nearby surface of the earth, and avoiding direct sunlight was no problem. The fiery disk was just skimming lush distant treetops, more than a mile to the northwest, behind the green bluffs that confined the winding river.

Sometimes in the past it had pleased him to occupy his mind with trivia on the eve of battle. It amused Maule now to play another round of a mental game he had dallied with in the past. The game involved trying to decide how many sunsets he had ever seen, and into what categories, of clouds and skies and coloring, they could be divided. His most recent efforts at calculation had led to the conclusion that he must have witnessed that dramatic event some two hundred thousand times. He also supposed that no two of that number had been precisely alike.

Just beyond the rank weeds in the abandoned yard, in the direction of the steep slope that led down to the river, a certain something that had been drifting upslope from below, at first no more than an airy bulge of rising mist, was taking on a solid form. Was this meant as a distraction, while some greater threat took shape behind him? Looking around carefully, Maule decided not.

Maule saw it come drifting in mist-form up the hill from the riverbank. Had he not been watching intently for something of the kind, he might have missed it altogether. To Maule, the mere fact of shape-changing was routine. But in more than five hundred years of life, breathing and unbreathing, Vlad Drakulya had never seen the like of the shape that was now assuming a solid form in front of him.

~ 6 ~

The figure as it took on solid form was dripping wet, as if it had truly emerged only moments ago from the river or the swamp.

The first parts to assume a distinct structure were the feet, standing solidly on the ground, some ten yards in front of Maule. Of these there were only two, though of slightly more than human size, and looking more animal than human, tipped in the front with claws instead of human toes. Their coloring was a scaly, gangrenous green.

Then the shape abruptly wavered, taking on momentarily the aspect of a photographic negative. It was as if the creature's physical appearance might be only a projected image, created by some powerful radiant core at the center of its being.

Distantly the howl of some farmer's dog, a wolflike sound, came drifting to the vampire's ears. It seemed normal and wholesome, and even close to human, compared to the thing before him.

Maule continued to study the form, which had now completely materialized. Already he was certain that this was the invader of his apartment, Tamarack's murderer. Even to Maule's long and broad experience it was bizarre, outlandish, alien. This despite the fact that the shape was basically almost human, that of a man of indeterminate age, not especially tall. All his limbs were short and thick. Different branches of the breathing human race had widely varying standards of personal beauty, but this matched none that Maule had ever heard of. Broad shoulders and a flat chest suggested maleness. Scanty hair, mud-colored, lay plastered to the sides of a misshapen head. Dark-yellow eyes were almost grotesquely wide-spaced in a dark-skinned, thin-lipped face. The mouth and the beardless lower jaw protruded more than was proper for humanity, suggesting the face of the white statue in Maule's Egyptian dream. Several of the stubby fingers bore gleaming rings, suggesting power, as did the short, thick claws projecting from his fingers, where ordinary humans grew thin nails.

The ugly lips moved slowly, and understandable words came forth: "Try to run away, if you wish. I will find it easy enough to catch you." The language was some bastard form of Latin that Maule could barely understand, spoken with an accent that not even he could place. The voice was rough, uneven, tones almost stuttering, as if perpetually on the verge of breaking into humorless laughter.

If the thing was bothered at all by the invisible, residual glow of Merlin's magic, still faintly favorable to Maule though now a generation old, it betrayed no discomfort.

The calm assumption that he, Vlad Drakulya, must be struggling to keep from panicked flight, was a stinging insult. But the vampire chose not to let his feelings show just yet.

Maule replied, in his own version of the same language: "If I choose to turn and leave, I will not run. So, if at that moment you have the good fortune to be still alive, you might indeed be able to catch me." He paused momentarily before adding: "Even as you might catch a plague."

He might as well have been talking to the wind, for all the reaction he got from the monstrous creature before him. More evidence, Maule thought, that it was not human, despite its fluency in human speech. But whatever it was, it radiated a strange psychic power that set Maule on his guard, grimly determined to seek every possible advantage, so that when their deadly combat started, as he was sure it must, he could hope to survive.

Despite the summer's heat, his visitor's whole body down to the knees was covered in some kind of long-sleeved garment, something between a bulky sweater and a monk's habit, woven in an intricate pattern, with white, furlike tufts suggesting kingly ermine. Every time it opened its mouth to speak, Maule saw irregular teeth, more of them than he could quickly count, more than any human ought to have, and all sharply pointed in the way that might be expected of wild beasts and the aroused *nosferatu*.

Now it made a gesture of kingly arrogance, the right arm extended toward Maule, stubby, claw-tipped forefinger pointing at him—then that hand and finger pointed down. A command, silent but unmistakable, to make obeisance.

It pleased Maule to ignore it, as the beast had ignored what he had said to it. He stood leaning on his spear, its butt grounded in enchanted earth. He could feel a pleasant thrum of power, old Merlin's power, in the shaft. He hoped it would endure till it was needed.

If Maule's irreverent attitude aroused some emotion in the thing before him, it gave no sign. It simply let its extended arm fall to its side, and spoke again.

"You are the undead one who has been known as *tse-pesh*—but no more. I will change your name, when I have decided on a better one . . . soon you will become my slave, and will learn always to answer to your new name promptly . . . but what shall your new name be?" The speaker was obviously asking the question only of himself; he raised an ugly hand to his ugly chin, and stood there musing.

Maule offered his visitor a slight, mocking bow. His answer came in hard-edged American English.

"I, in turn, have thought of a few names for you. 'Slimy reptile' and 'murderer' are two which spring immediately to mind. Probably I shall use others as our talk proceeds. But let me offer you a choice. What name would you consider a most deadly insult?"

The creature was unruffled, and switched to English too, without apparent difficulty. "I am Sobek," it informed him absently, in its grating, coughing voice. And again there came that wavering in its appearance, a momentary reversal of light and dark, a startling, knife-sharp flash of red, leaving Maule with the feeling that he was looking at nothing more than a projected image.

The thing was going on: "There in the city you gave shelter in your den to the one calling himself Tamarack. Yet when I punished him for disobedience I spared you, because I saw in you the possibility of usefulness. You are quite strong, for a human variant, and also durable—I stunned you into dream-sleep, but here you are already moving about, when I had not thought your mind would yet be clear enough . . . did you understand what you were doing when you transported the portal here?"

Maule smiled, considering his reply. "The portal" certainly sounded like a reference to a door, and he had left Joe Keogh's false door, the strange little panel, inside Tamarack's body bag.

Less than a minute now, he thought, and the sun would be wholly behind those distant bluffs beyond the river. Maule had decided to retain man-form for the time being. He could feel how four of his teeth had involuntarily swollen and sharpened in this enemy's presence. The wooden spear, its butt-end still resting on the ground, the lightning-tempered point aloft, felt comfortable in his right hand.

He said: "I find this place restful and congenial, and came here because I thought it might afford me deep and soothing sleep, away from irritating, intrusive vermin like yourself. You were wise—prudent—to show such consideration, not to bother me while I was sleeping."

Still his words seemed only to go past their target, as if whatever he might say could not be worth the trouble of listening to. Now it mused: "On coming through the portal this time, I had thought to find myself again inside your dwelling-place."

The oddities of the thing's appearance were altering even as Maule watched, startling him so that he almost lost the thread of what he was about to say. Now, swiftly shedding the semblance of a crocodile, morphing even as it spoke into a shape more convincingly human, that of an Egyptian-looking man, it told Maule: "It will be easy to control your mind again, should I decide to do so."

"That we shall see."

Ignoring his response, it looked around, and seemed to give a condescending sniff. "There is a fair amount of human magic here. Probably you came to this place seeking protection from one greater than yourself. That was a foolish hope. No human works of enchantment can save you from the displeasure of a god. Nor will you be able to resist my teaching."

Maule looked around, as if seeking to discover some source of danger. He said: "So far I feel no need for protection."

His adversary maintained its air of unruffled patience. "Strange vampire, I could easily destroy you now, mind and body both. I have eaten the flesh of your kind before, and found it tasty. But I am still convinced you will eventually be useful, so I will not kill you yet."

"It might be helpful if I knew what sort of usefulness you have in mind?"

The creature looked at him in silence for a few moments before it answered. "For many centuries I have been curious about the object called by humans the Philosopher's Stone. It does exist, you know."

"There are those who say so. Tell me more."

The monster made a curious gesture with one stubby arm. "My curiosity on the subject has grown, until now I have begun to search for this Stone in earnest. So in a little while it must be mine. But I am impatient of delay. Therefore I tell you this: bring me the Stone, or show me accurately where it is, and I will reward you with some limited degree of freedom when you have become my slave."

Maule's eyes were glittering. He made a mocking little bow. "Such generosity is overwhelming."

Sobek accepted the tribute at face value, even with apparent grace. "It is a mark of my power."

Now Maule's dark eyes were glaring fiercely. What was in front of him had become undoubtedly a crocodile again, thought it still stood on two legs. Its eyes gazed back at him, the aim of their vertical, slit-shaped pupils not giving way before his stare, any more than two pieces of black rock might have done.

At last Maule said: "You must be aware that others besides Tamarack, others who are somewhat more human and less disgusting in their shape than you, are also intent on finding this famous Stone. If I am going to take part in this search, I must know all that you know regarding the location of the prize."

The crocodile said to Maule: "You have already experienced a dream, whose content should have revealed much to a relatively intelligent human. Thousands of years ago, the Stone was concealed, by the thief who stole it. In a moment of desperation, fearing he was about to be caught, he seized one of the small statues that had just been molded, encasing sacred animals, and forced the treasure deep into the wet plaster, hiding it from sight."

Maule's strong right hand played with the heavy spear. In the blink of an eyelid, if he so chose, he could twitch it into horizontal position and flick it like a dart at his chosen target. "You know some amusing stories. Tell me more."

It seemed that when the Crocodile chose to hear and understand him, it could do so with perfect ease. Now it was quite willing to provide its slave-to-be with useful information. "There were six such statues in the temple workshop. Six small dead reptiles, sacred to my name and worship, each sealed inside a plaster image of myself. On the right side of the dark room, three such statues were waiting on a shelf when the thief appeared. On the left side, three more stood on another shelf."

"And what happened to these grotesque and abhorrent statues? Perhaps they were used for target practice?" Maule waited ten seconds or so before he prodded: "If not, where are they now, these abominable statues so pregnant with possibility?"

Sobek's gaze jerked round at him. "That is what remains to be discovered. There exists, in the hands of one of those who dares to trifle with me, a list of names of humans who now possess the surviving statues. In one of those small figures—it is never given to the dreamer to see which—the thief sought to hide the perfect Stone, the matchless, supernatural treasure whose freezing cold burned at his mouth. The guards of my temple's workshop were closing in on him, as well as his original pursuers. He must have hoped to claim that he was innocent, if the treasure was not found in his possession when he was caught."

Sobek shook his ugly head, as if he might be marveling at the ancient robber's daring, or stupidity, or both. "As I have said, he pressed the Stone into the side of one statue, burying it out of sight in the wet plaster, and ran on, to meet his death only a few minutes later.

"A great search for the missing treasure must soon have followed, but none of the humans were bright enough to look in the right place. Some laborer in the workshop must have noticed that the surface of one statue was now marred by an unevenness, and smoothed it out, with annoyance but no understanding of its cause."

Maule could generate no sympathy for the thief whose dreams, through some quirk of magic, evidently kept getting projected forward several thousand years in time—a robber was, after all, one of the most detestable of humans, and in general those who took what was not theirs by right deserved whatever punishment fate might deal out to them.

"I begin to understand," he said. "And the intended purpose of those six statues was—?"

"In the beginning, they were meant to furnish the tomb of a certain priest, one who had faithfully served . . . served the great god Sobek." It was hard for Maule to read emotions on the inhuman face, but it seemed for a moment that the Crocodile had turned to introspection.

The thing talked on, disjointedly. It seemed that, down through the centuries, various people belonging to the brotherhood of alchemists—Maule caught hints that some of them had probably been vampires also—had searched intermittently for those little plastered mummies, even while trying to keep existence of the statues a well-guarded secret.

"One, who thought he was on the right track, was burned for witchcraft in Constantinople in 1353—but that has no present relevance.

"One statue I crushed in your apartment, and examined the debris. There was only one chance in six that it would hold the gem, and it did not. The remaining five are not so widely dispersed as you might think."

"Then you do have some idea of where they are. The names, locations, on this list you mentioned."

As their talk went on, the thing kept restlessly, slightly, changing shape—Maule got the impression that it could not really help itself, the alterations were to some degree involuntary. This was in addition to the occasional wave of near-transparency that seemed to suggest the presence of some inward fire. The vampire also noted that the direct light of the setting sun did not seem to bother his adversary at all, more evidence it was not *nosferatu*.

Now it was saying: "Have you any understanding, Vlad Tepes, of how much more valuable that jewel is than all other treasures that humans have ever pursued under the sun?"

"My understanding of this business of alchemy might surprise you." At various times, down through the centuries, a broadly representative assortment of adepts and inepts had discussed the Great Work with him, or in his hearing. Usually their voices had been filled with a sort of holy longing. Extravagant promises regarding the Stone were of the very essence of their business. Converting lead to gold was said to be the least of its powers.

"But," Maule assured the monster now, "I never believe all that I hear, regarding the magnitude of any treasure—evidently you are less skeptical.

"A little while ago I was almost sure that you were *nosferatu*, but now I see that is not correct. Vampirism, if you enjoyed its benefits, would be the least of your differences from *Homo sapiens sapiens*. Oh, it is only too obvious that you are not really human—or not entirely so. You simply must learn to deal with the fact that the difference is not at all in your favor."

The precise moment of local sunset had arrived at last. Without even turning to look, Vlad Drakulya knew to the fraction of a second when the great shoulder of the spinning Earth cut off the last direct rays from the spot where he and Sobek were standing.

A moment after the sun had gone below the horizon, he attempted to exert against Sobek the force by which he, Dracula, was usually able to control animals—but the touch was effortlessly repelled. The bulky figure before him did not move so much as one of its stubby fingers.

Maule gave no outward sign of his great psychic effort, or how discouraging he found its total failure.

He only said: "I hope, oh great and mighty and obscene reptile, that you will tell me—before anything happens to you that might render you unable to communicate—tell me just how did you get into my apartment? And what unfortunate impulse made you kill the one called Tamarack? He was no friend of mine, but he had become my guest, so your mistake was fatal. And now, before we have our test of combat, and while you still retain the power of speech, I would be interested in hearing from your own leprous lips just how you dared to do these things?"

His rage was building now, near to bursting out.

Sobek was grinning a crocodilian grin at him—as a man might find diversion in a snarling puppy. "The life or death of the one I killed is meaningless to you."

"Not when it happened in my home."

Sobek's amusement seemed to be gradually building, in step with the anger of the man before him. The monster spoke as one who tolerated an entertaining child. It was so amusing to see how the child refused to understand the obvious. "I owe you no explanations. I kill whom I choose, when and where I please."

Having remained utterly motionless for a minute, Maule made a sudden, catlike move, a sidestep that brought him no closer to Sobek and took him no farther away. He wanted to test the other's reaction.

"My very touch is death," the figure warned Maule, sounding only a little less amused. Its eyes had followed Maule as he moved, but that was all. Its large hands hung at its sides, holding no weapon but their own claws.

"Some would tell you that I am already dead!"

In the next instant Sobek made a sudden thrusting motion of his head and shoulders, intended to precipitate a victim into flight. Maule's own experience in the role of predator had taught him that an attacker was likely to have an easier conquest while dragging down his victim from behind than in a head-on confrontation.

But Maule showed no inclination to retreat. Having his spear in hand, he feigned a stabbing lunge toward the center of the monster's torso—not quite at the full speed he could command.

In response to the lunge, Sobek only moved back one step, magisterially. This time Maule was ready for the mesmeric surge that came as a riposte, and managed to fight it off. But it was disturbingly strong.

Now the self-proclaimed god of crocodiles repeated what he evidently considered a most generous offer: he, Dracula, might remain alive and even retain some measure of freedom, if he would cooperate from now on with Sobek in his ruthless quest for the Stone.

"I am certain that you would enjoy the rewards of power I sometimes grant to the most loyal of my servitors. You may have other humans, even *nosferatu*, below you, and utterly at your mercy."

Maule thought that not worthy of a response. After a moment of silence Sobek went on. "But there are, as you will see, yet others who oppose me. Most irritating are certain blood-drinkers of your own type, who are attempting now to find my statues, and the treasure that is in one of them. Should you bring me the heads of some of those human vermin, I will reward you, for they are an irritation, like sharp stones under my feet."

Maule's reply was very soft. "Perhaps those others, the blood-drinking human vermin as you call them, would give me a greater reward than you will. Supposing I brought them your ugly head, impaled on a sharp stick. Very probably on this." And very slightly he shook his spear.

It seemed impossible to ruffle the other's reptilian calm. For all that Maule could tell, Sobek was as fearless as Maule himself. He seemed the very archetype of a tolerant god, so high that no insult could reach him, willing to be patient in the face of human stupidity. "I am Sobek," he repeated now, "and many kneel to me as their god."

"Many?" Vlad Drakulya laughed, and it was not a pleasant sound. "No, I think no more than a few could be so foolish. A very few, and all of them deluded in their fear."

After considering him in silence for a time, at last it said: "I see that many humans fear you, Vlad Tepes, but that is nothing to me." That the smiling mouth should have so many teeth seemed to Maule particularly offensive, when even *Homo dirus* could be content with the usual human number.

The staccato voice barked on. "Remember that to me you are only an amusement, and cannot be a danger. Remember, Vlad Tepes, sooner or later, alive or dead, you will find yourself prostrate before me."

"Never! Not before any god as small as you, or with so many teeth." Maule roared a battle cry.

Then he swayed and groaned, as the surge of psychic power that he had been expecting struck at him, silent and invisible, and even faster and stronger than before.

Again he managed to fight off the enemy's psychic attack. But to his chagrin he was unable to do any serious damage thrusting with his spear. His enemy adroitly dodged, showing more speed than his looks suggested, and the spear-point only gouged out a few scales from Sobek's shoulder.

As far as Maule could tell, the disappearance of direct daylight had made little difference to Sobek, one way or another.

Again Sobek's image wavered, again taking on momentarily the aspect of a photographic negative, as if some powerful radiant core at the center of his being could be projecting an image that was his physical form.

And then, abruptly, the thing was gone.

Maule was left alone, staggering and stumbling in the dusk. To his amazement, it seemed that the struggle was over, for the time being at least. Certainly the monster had gone away.

What the outcome might have been if today's trial had been prolonged was more than Maule could say; but he had seen, heard, or felt nothing to inspire him with confidence of victory. Instead, the test had left his body slumped in physical weakness, sweating like a breather. If his lungs had needed air at all, he would have been gasping too.

Reflexively he growled at the world, and shook his spear. For a moment, in the hot aftermath of battle, he tried to tell himself that he had driven the other into flight, but in his heart he knew it was not so.

The struggle had left him slightly dizzy, and with a sensation of weakness that he had not known for many years. Moving carefully, on somewhat unsteady feet, he searched the ground where the clash had taken place.

To find a serious splash of blood would have been enormously cheering, but in that Maule was disappointed. After a minute's search he did find and pick up a single heavy, translucent scale, almost the size of his own palm, such as might have been gouged out of the hide of some legendary serpent or dragon. It was discouraging to realize that this had to be practically the full extent of the damage that he, with his best efforts, had been able to inflict.

But the find had its encouraging aspect, too. Juggling the fragment in his hand, he thought it might play an important role in their next meeting.

He looked around, probing the environment with inward and outward senses. Yes, for whatever reason, Sobek was truly gone. The monster had abruptly broken off this confrontation—as if listening to some distant call that somehow demanded his attention more strongly than this mere dallying to toy with a new slave.

Sitting down on the ground for a brief rest, Dracula replayed the incident, every detail that he could remember, in his mind. Inwardly he yearned to find some clue that would allow the hopeful possibility that he had driven his enemy from the field—but still he could not deceive himself to that extent.

Maule was not surprised that he had seen the retreating figure disappear in the direction of the riverside swamp, into which a few hours ago he had watched Tamarack's car sink out of sight. Of course it seemed only natural that a crocodile would turn toward a river. But of course the object Joe Keogh called a "false door" had been down there too.

"I wonder if the great beast took his portal with him this time?" Maule wondered if Sobek could pass like a ghost through a wooden panel, then bring the panel with him.

Still he could hardly believe that his enemy had so casually withdrawn. More than half-expecting some kind of stratagem, some trick, Maule patrolled the top of the little bluff for a little while, spear in hand. But as darkness deepened around him, and stars and moon made their appearance, he eventually abandoned his vigil, and decided he must return to the city.

Soon, he decided, he ought to call Joe Keogh on his cell phone, and inform his breathing ally of the most recent developments. But there was another matter to be decided first. Maule was tempted to reconsider his decision to drown the mysterious little wooden panel in the swamp. Such indecisiveness was highly unusual for him, and he took it as a worrisome result of his clash with the monster.

He spoke the words aloud: "The question is, should I bring it back to the city with me?"

Stripping off his clothes, he slid into the deep pool at one end of the swamp, where he had sunk the car. The lid of the trunk was open, now hanging only by one hinge, as if it had been burst open from inside with an explosive charge. The large plastic bag was still inside the trunk, but it too had been ripped open, and the dead body of Tamarack had been further damaged.

The little wooden panel was floating on the surface of the water, which was already invading the ancient, long-dried wood, causing it to swell. It seemed, then, that this was Sobek's portal. Could the monster indeed pass in and out of the solid wood like some ancient Egyptian ghost?

Back on dry land, and clad again, Maule considered trying to bring the panel back to Chicago with him. It was just about at the limiting size of objects that could, like clothing, routinely take part in the transformation of a vampire's body, when he or she assumed the form of animal or bat or a cloud of mist.

It even briefly crossed Maule's mind that he might try to use the panel in the same way Sobek had. He had no way of telling where it would bring him out—but it would be a bold way of seizing the initiative.

Or, perhaps, of landing himself in some disastrous fix. Nor was he at all sure such a mode of travel would even be possible for him. It would mean assuming mist-form first, and then . . .

Conceivably, using it would bring him out through the false door of some exhibit at the Field Museum!

Only belatedly did it occur to Maule to wonder how many false doors might currently exist in the Chicago area, and how many of those might Sobek be using to travel to and fro, perhaps to the far corners of the earth. But then he reminded himself that this strange mode of transporting himself was not the real key to the great Crocodile's nature. Maule decided he must not allow himself to be distracted by it.

Having determined not to try to use it, what good would it do him to have the portal, the false door, in his possession? None at all, Maule soon decided. Taking the panel in his two hands, he completed the ruin that muddy water had already begun, snapping the flat wood in two, then crushing each half in turn, reducing it all to fragments. His powerful fingers broke it easily, but he handled the splintering wood with appropriate respect; it was one of the few materials in the world whose sharp points or edges could do a vampire serious damage.

Now, he decided, it was time for him to return to Chicago. Moving quickly, Maule covered the first few miles running cross-country as a wolf. Then, when farm dogs began to pay undue attention, he altered his form again and flew on as a bat.

After traveling a few more miles, he paused, well concealed among the trees of an apple orchard, and briefly resumed his human shape, for the sake of possessing fingers, a voice, and a pair of trousers, one of whose pockets contained a small but efficient cell phone.

A few seconds later, he was calling Joe Keogh's house.

Before the third ring, a familiar voice came on. "Keogh here."

"I have met the intruder, Joseph, and I have survived."

Joe sounded relieved. "Good. What else?"

"Unhappily, he—or it—survived as well. He told me that his name is Sobek. I assure you that he is formidable indeed."

"*Nosferatu,* I presume."

"I think not. In my experience, to become a vampire one must first be unequivocally human. What I encountered today was something else, a type of being that I have never met before. He is at least my equal in many of the powers that we share, and I have no doubt he is my superior in others. He may also possess capabilities of which I am unaware."

Joe felt a chill, and for a full ten seconds he had nothing to say. The best he could come up with, finally, was the practical: "So what do we do?"

"I do not know." Maule sounded almost careless about the lack. "Oh, on one point I did gain some reassurance. It seems highly unlikely that Andy will ever again be bothered by the monster—as long as he keeps out of its way. In my opinion the young man should now return to his normal life."

"That's good news."

"Yes. Even Sobek's interest in me is apparently only incidental. I do not believe he takes me seriously as an enemy. His sole purpose in invading my apartment was to punish Mr. Tamarack, and examine a certain object in Tamarack's possession."

"The statue, like we thought. Why was it smashed?"

"In an attempt to discover whether the Philosopher's Stone was concealed inside it." Briefly Maule outlined what Sobek had told him about the ancient thief and his supposedly priceless loot.

Joe said: "Come to think of it, when I fell asleep this afternoon, I had a dream . . . about some situation like that. Running through the streets, someplace that was dry and hot, with people chasing me."

"I am not surprised."

"But the details are all fuzzy."

"Try to recall them, Joseph, if you can; they may eventually prove useful. But to return to Tamarack's statue—the Crocodile assured me that it held no treasure, and so the search goes on for the five remaining. Now I am invited to share the monster's labors."

"What do you mean?"

"It seems I am to become its slave."

Joe thought he had never met a less likely candidate for involuntary servitude. Now he truly didn't know what to say. Kate, standing only a few feet away, was looking at him anxiously, but he could only signal to her that he was at a loss.

At last Joe managed: "I take it you declined the job?"

It wasn't often that Joe had heard Maule laugh at anything. This time it was a surprisingly normal sound.

"Should I ever find my spirits flagging, Joseph, and myself in need of encouragement, I will come to you."

"I'm flattered. So, how're we going to take this guy if he's so tough? What else can you tell me about him?"

"Almost nothing."

"All right." Joe considered. "Let me tell you what I found out about the strange little wooden panel: My contact at the museum confirms what I told you. Of course he couldn't determine from the photo if our object is genuinely old, but he says it definitely looks like a magical device called a 'false door.'

"They were very common in ancient Egypt, but usually they were carved in stone, as part of the wall of a tomb. Seeing one on a wooden panel is odd but not unique. It was—how did he put it?" Keogh consulted his notebook. " 'A spirit-permeable membrane, separating the living world from the world of the dead.' The idea was that the relatives and friends of the deceased would leave offerings, food and so on, at the tomb. Then the occupant, or his spirit, was supposed to be able to get at the goodies by coming out through the false door."

Maule was staring gloomily into the dusk gathering around him, the litter of small green apples on the ground. "I wonder how frequently such traffic actually took place."

Joe hesitated. "I don't get what you mean."

"If there are false doors at the museum, then we have evidence to suggest that someone—or some thing—may be actually using them, from time to time. But the current user is not, I am reasonably sure, one whose convenience the doors were intended to serve."

Joe still hesitated. Maule went on: "Probably I should have given you my report first. I have now met my enemy face to face."

"What happened?"

The vampire made a low sound that might almost have been a laugh. "For now, I am well content merely to have survived." He went on to bring Joe Keogh up to date.

In the background Joe could see Andy still watching the movie, with some appearance of interest. The kid was used to his father getting business calls, sometimes very strange ones, and as a rule paid them no attention. Kate had drawn near to Joe and was listening. Joe gave her a smile meant to be reassuring. From where he was standing, phone in hand, he could still see the dusty Hollywood horror dragging itself painfully across the television screen.

Maule's voice on the phone said: "It will be easier, perhaps, to tell you more of what we discussed. We spoke of the Great Work and its object, and exchanged opinions about the value of crocodiles in the great scheme of things."

"Little dried-up crocodiles?"

Kate, who had been hearing only one side of the conversation, sure didn't know what to make of that. She seemed on the verge of giving up.

Maule said: "My enemy himself has something of that reptilian shape, and he is neither little nor dried up. When he broke off contact and moved away I was preparing an attempt to kill him. I doubt that I would have succeeded; I do not flatter myself that he was either frightened or forced into a retreat."

Next Maule explained to Joe what Sobek had said about the false door. "No doubt your client's difficulties at the museum can be explained by the monster's occasional coming and going there. But probably by now the great reptile has satisfied himself that what he seeks is not to be found in the Field. Of course he must have other means of travel available to him as well."

"So what should I be telling my client?"

"I believe you can offer reassurance. I hardly think the remaining statues are to be found at the Field, so its guards and administrators will probably not be much bothered in the future."

Joe went on to tell Maule about his afternoon visit to Old Town.

"The manhole cover had been moved. I see. Possibly significant. Probably I shall go there tonight and have a look around. Anything else?"

"A little. I started one of my people doing research on people named Flamel, and the first one she turned up was a recent death in County Hospital."

Joe passed on the few details his agent had so far found out. "This Nicolas Flamel was the third partner, with Dickon and Tamarack."

"That much I had heard."

"And he seems to have had a granddaughter, who came every day to see him in the hospital."

"That I did not know."

"They said the old man called her Dolly."

There was a pause. Then Maule asked: "How did he die?"

"Natural causes. My condolences, if he was your friend."

Maule sounded regretful. "Almost certainly it was he. Had I known of his reduced circumstances, I could have been of some help . . . but it is too late to worry about that."

Joe said: "The granddaughter claimed to be his only relative."

"Was she his only visitor as well?"

"As far as the hospital people could recall. Said she couldn't afford to claim the body, though."

"The Crocodile mentioned the existence of a list of names, but was very imprecise regarding who might have it. Very likely if it does exist it will be in the hands of this granddaughter."

When the call was over, Maule resumed his journey, proceeding by a bizarre form of hitchhiking he had perfected over recent decades. This involved remaining in manform, and on two legs jumping unseen aboard speeding trucks, or fast trains when that was more convenient. Another variation consisted in assuming bat-form, then matching speeds to get aboard one truck after another that seemed to be bound toward the city.

The straight-line distance from the center of the strange domain near Frenchman's Bend to the heart of the city was a little under a hundred miles. Maule's distance from Chicago speedily diminished. Gradually the massive sky-glow of cloud-reflected lights grew nearer.

By about three hours after sunset on Wednesday night, Maule was back in town. His first stop was at his own apartment. Everything seemed in order, and there was no sign that any further intrusion had taken place. He inspected the rooms carefully, making sure that the last traces of violence (except for the spear-hole in the wall) had been cleaned up, and that no telephone messages awaited him.

After that, he went out into the city streets. There were one or two things he wanted to look at.

The first was an investigation beneath the streets and alleys of Old Town. Maule located without trouble the manhole cover Joe Keogh had described, near the mouth of the alley beside the burned-out building. Sinking in mist-form into the subterranean darkness beneath the metal lid, Maule spent an hour in observation and contemplation before deciding there was no trail here that he could follow.

He wanted eventually to pay a visit to County Hospital, to learn what he could of the last hours of his old friend, and if possible pay his respects to the remains of Nicolas Flamel. But that could wait. Dawn came early at this season, and Maule had to decide how much he would attempt to rest, and where, during the daylight hours of Thursday. Obviously his apartment was no longer safe.

On Thursday morning the first brightening of the eastern sky found him in a remote portion of the Cook County Forest Preserves, a belt of largely undrained and muddy land that more or less ringed the city. Some years ago Maule had buried another cache of his native earth in this lonely spot, in anticipation of just some such emergency as this.

~ 7 ~

When Joe Keogh got home late Wednesday afternoon, following his explorations in Old Town, he was relieved to see that Andy seemed to have recovered completely from whatever might have happened to him at Uncle Matt's.

Joe had called home with the news that he was on his way, and dinner was almost ready when he arrived, featuring home-cooked hamburgers, and potato salad from the nearby suburban deli.

Conversation lagged. Joe wanted to tell Kate something about his experiences in Old Town, but it could wait, and with Andy present it was going to be impossible to discuss the possibilities of vampires. Someday soon, Joe thought, he would really have to get around to making revelations. But he also thought that today was not the day.

A somewhat awkward evening loomed. After looking through the cable listings, it fell to Andy to suggest what the family was going to do. His choice might have been

subconsciously affected by hearing his father offhand-
edly mention a recent business visit to the Field Museum.

"How about *The Mummy's Curse?*" Andy suggested.
Kate looked at Joe. "Why not?" he agreed.

A chiming phone interrupted the Keogh family at dinner.
Dark shadows, in which a mummy was lurking somewhere, filled the television screen. Joe pushed back his
chair. "I'll get it." In a moment he had picked up the
nearest receiver. "Keogh here."

"I have met the intruder, Joseph, and I have survived."

Joe felt relief at the sound of the familiar voice.
"Good. What else?"

"Unhappily, he—or it—survived as well."

When the long and somewhat unnerving phone call
was over, Joe gave his wife a vaguely reassuring smile,
the best he could manage at the moment. As soon as they
were alone, he would fill her in completely. Phone calls
about odd business were not uncommon in this house,
and Andy remained incurious about this one. He seemed
oblivious to the tension affecting his parents, while they
finished up their dinner and afterward.

The mummy in the movie had not begun life as a crocodile, Joe Keogh observed, but as a man. As a result of
a really nasty curse, the poor slob had been turned into
a shuffling monster muffled in bandages that after a few
thousand years were starting to come unwrapped. And
he was no longer a nice guy, if he ever had been. Joe
supposed the poor guy's grimness might be due in part
to the fact that he was so slow-moving. In his new career
as a monster, he had every reason to be discouraged. It

was a wonder he ever managed to catch up with any of
his victims.

That night Andy went to bed fairly early, in his old room,
and slept normally, except for another vaguely troubling
dream that he forgot almost as soon as he woke up.

It rained hard but sporadically during the night.
Early Thursday morning, the sun had burned its way
through the clouds, and was turning the wetness of the
city into steam. Andy was feeling fine, and when he announced that he was returning to his own apartment,
neither of his parents could see any reason to talk him
out of the idea.

Though Andy said nothing about it to his parents,
he was still bothered by his memory, or rather his lack
of memory, of what had happened on Tuesday evening.
Now he began to worry that he had somehow offended
Uncle Matt, who had been too polite to say so. Something
funny, in the sense of strange, must have happened
there, but he had somehow missed it. Had he been walking in his sleep? Not being given to useless fretting, he
soon ceased to worry about the possibility. When he saw
Uncle Matt again would be time enough to try to find
out.

Joe left the house a little after nine on Thursday morning, delaying his departure in hopes of avoiding the
worst of the rush-hour snarl. He offered Andy a ride back
to Andy's own apartment, and before he left he told Kate
as much as he thought practical regarding the next steps
he meant to take regarding the problems of Mr. Maule.

He had kissed her and turned and started away,
when Kate called him back, wanting to know when she
could expect to hear from her husband again.

"Soon. When I get a chance."

"And what if I don't hear from you?"

"You will. Can't tell you any more than that."

"I better hear from you, before too many hours have passed." Kate reached out with both arms. "Joe, come here a minute."

He went to her, and she held him, and he could feel her quivering.

"I have to go," he said. "It's broad daylight out there now, see? And I know what I'm doing."

"I know, I know. But things can happen in broad daylight too."

Just as he pulled out of his driveway, Joe asked his son: "Were you planning to see Uncle Matt again any time soon?"

"No. No, we didn't set anything up. Not that I can remember, anyway." Once more Andy frowned. He did remember promising Uncle Matt, just as they were leaving, that he'd try and find him the name of someone who might qualify as an expert on ancient Egypt. But his father wasn't asking about that.

"Maybe it would be best if you didn't bother him for a while. He seemed to have other things on his mind. I think he might be in the process of moving. Changing his address."

That was puzzling. "He didn't say anything about that. But okay. Sure."

Andy's father dropped him off right in front of his apartment, in the North Side neighborhood of Thomas More University, not far from Old Town. Not until Andy had let himself in through the building's small front lobby, and was climbing the stairs to the second floor, did he remember the name of the person that Uncle Matt, for whatever reason, was keen on finding: Flamel, that was it. He couldn't recall if Uncle Matt had said anything about male or female, or given a first name.

Well, Andy would see what he could do.

He'd only been away from the apartment a day and a half, but already the rooms had an unlived-in look and feel about them, despite the casual litter. Andy's two housemates, who were at least in theory equal payers of the rent, were away on summer visits to their respective families, and neither was expected back for several days. So there was no one to wonder where he had been. Andy stuck his head into his colleagues' rooms, looked for notes on the kitchen bulletin board, listened to two or three casual phone messages, thought them not worth saving, and wiped them out.

Next he looked to see if the refrigerator would be worth raiding, come lunchtime. The contents were minimal, consisting very largely of three-fourths of a large pizza that someone had providentially frozen a month or two ago. Right now the icy chunks didn't look all that appealing inside their plastic wrap.

His first act on reentering his private room was to turn on his computer. After checking for e-mail, and answering a few messages that seemed deserving of attention, he paused, trying to think of the most effective methods for searching the web for people's names. If he had somehow let Uncle Matt down Tuesday night, he would now try to do whatever he could to make amends.

And now, seemingly for no good reason, there popped up a sudden memory of something that he had dreamt during his strange sleep at Uncle Matt's. A dream of running, trying to escape pursuers, through a strange environment that now made Andy think of Egypt—a place that he had never visited.

The more he thought back to that Tuesday evening at Uncle Matt's, the stranger the whole scene grew in Andy's memory. It seemed that something very odd had happened, but nobody was going to tell him what.

Andy sat down on the edge of his bed. The more he thought about it, the more he realized that for most of his life he had been aware of some nagging oddity regarding the rarely seen presence in his life of the man named Matthew Maule. There was mystery, beyond the accepted fact that he was really no blood relative. As if there was something important and vaguely worrisome about him that neither Andy nor his sister had ever been told. Their parents knew all about the secret bit of business, whatever it might be, but the older generation, Lenore and Andrew, Kate's parents, probably did not.

He thought he could remember Dad telling him, years ago, that Uncle Matt had been a close friend of his, Andy's, great-grandmother Clarissa Harker. But that didn't make a whole lot of sense, for Uncle Matt couldn't be more than about forty, and Andy remembered hearing from the family that great-grandma Harker had died more than twenty years ago, back in 1979, before Andy was even born. People talked vaguely about the awful snowstorm of that year, which had come, like a bad omen, just at the darkest hour of family trouble.

That was also the time when, among other things, his Mom, Kate, had been mistakenly reported dead, her body in the morgue. And at the same time the kidnappers of teenaged Uncle John had torn a finger from each of his hands, as a demonstration that they really had him in their power.

But now, a generation later, with the world solidly into the twenty-first century, no one in the family ever talked much about those episodes of nightmare. At least no one spoke of them when Andy was around. Dad and Mom even seemed to have forgotten about the kidnappers—though as far as Andy knew, those dirty bastards had never been caught, or even accurately identified.

Nor did Andy's mom and dad ever have much to say about Uncle Matt, despite the fact that they were always willing to do anything they could to help him out.

But he'd worry about that later. Right now there was a little task, something possibly useful, to be done. If he could take care of one detail that Uncle Matt had asked him to look into, that might help straighten things out.

Flamel. All right. Probably it was spelled just like it sounded. Anyway, he'd try that spelling first.

Moving out to the kitchen, he tried the enormous Chicago phone book, which gave no help. Of course Uncle Matt would have thought of looking there himself.

He was back in his room now. There were a number of web sites connected in one way or another to the student organizations and clubs at TMU. If you knew how to look for things, it shouldn't take you long to find them; Andy thought he knew better than most. In this matter he was already a step ahead: last week he had had some fun figuring out, just for the hell of it, a way to get a look at the full roster of student and faculty names, all the addresses and home phone numbers that the university thought they were keeping confidential.

In just under a minute he had succeeded in calling

that privileged roster up again. Bingo! Right away, just as easy as that, he had discovered one, and only one, possibility: Flamel, Dolores, student. No e-mail address, but there was a phone number. She was listed as living in apartment 2A, at an address not many blocks from Andy's. It was an area where a lot of students lived.

Andy's next step was to see if, using her name, he could find her anywhere on the web. In that attempt he came up blank. He rocked back in his chair, whistling tunelessly between his teeth. What now? Call the unknown Dolores on the phone, just to see what she was like? But he had not the foggiest idea of what he ought to say to her, if anything. Of course he couldn't be sure that this was the right Flamel, and besides that he didn't know if Uncle Matt was trying to contact her or avoid her. Obviously his next move was to let Uncle Matt know what he had discovered.

The only response Andy got from Uncle Matt's number was an answering machine, his uncle's voice saying it was ready to accept messages for Matthew Maule. Andy dutifully delivered the name and address he'd discovered, adding a few words of explanation.

After that Andy scrounged in the refrigerator for lunch, still eschewing the frozen pizza, and just about wiping out the remaining possibilities, which consisted of stale bread, a small package of processed cheese, and a tired apple. Then, telling himself sternly he needed to get some studying done, in anticipation of next semester's intense demands, he regretfully put his computer to sleep.

Fortunately the books he had on hand provided some interesting content, and the hours went by rapidly as he read.

He had opened several windows, and by late afternoon a little breeze was blowing in, making the world feel more like spring than summer. Andy started to grow restless and went out for a walk.

Presently, remembering the apartment's notable lack of provisions, he treated himself to an early dinner at a hamburger joint whose chili and french fries he found somewhat above average. Coming out on the sidewalk again, into the slanting sunlight of late afternoon, he felt too restless to return immediately to his apartment, and decided to walk some more. It seemed like he'd been lying around a lot the past couple of days, sleeping too much.

When Andy realized that his feet were carrying him toward the address listed for Dolores Flamel, he yielded to the impulse and continued in that direction. He could simply walk past her building and look it over, with the vague idea of somehow picking up another morsel or two of information to pass on to Uncle Matt.

Her building turned out to be not much different from Andy's, or a thousand others in the city: three stories, brick, rectangular, and generally dull.

A vague impulse to seek excitement suggested that he ring Dolores's doorbell, just to see, if he could, what she looked like, or at least hear her voice. He envisioned, first, a slinky European-type woman whose age seemed as indeterminate as Uncle Matt's; next an old crone, whose relationship to Matthew Maule was hard to imagine; and then a sexy young secret agent, in the employ of some foreign government. But the closer he got to her building's front door, the more unwise seemed the idea of calling on her. Hell, though, he could at least take a look at the list of tenants' names sure to be posted in the lobby. From that he might be able to tell if anyone was sharing her apartment. That would provide another nugget of information for Uncle Matt.

As Andy approached the front entrance of the building, he noticed an older man, somewhat undersized, arrayed in dark glasses and a straw hat with a colorful band, loitering as if waiting for someone in one of the long, comfortable late-afternoon shadows cast by curbside trees. The man's arms, below the short sleeves of his sport shirt, gleamed pinkly as if they had been sunburned before being lathered with some kind of lotion or sunblock.

The fellow was red-cheeked, as if with excitement or embarrassment. He might not be waiting for anyone, Andy thought, but trying to get up the nerve to ring a doorbell.

The dark glasses seemed to focus on Andy as he approached, as if something about Andy made the man decide he was the one he had been waiting for.

Andy would have walked right past him, ignored the building, and gone right on down the street, but the man moved hesitantly into his way. The approach was almost cringing rather than aggressive, but the man making it seemed too well-dressed for a panhandler. And his first words had nothing to do with money.

His voice was soft and hesitant, touched with an accent that struck Andy as vaguely European-sounding. "Excuse me, sir, but if I am not mistaken, I believe I recognize you as a relative of Mr. Matthew Maule?"

That brought Andy to a surprised, reluctant halt. "Ahh, yes. I am."

"I thought so, I thought so." The soft voice sighed relief. "Oh, this is a happy discovery! You and I were both present Tuesday night in Mr. Maule's apartment. Perhaps he has mentioned me to you? My name is

Dickon?" The rising inflection seemed to make it a question. At the same time the speaker nodded encouragingly, like a salesman who dearly wanted the potential customer to agree with him.

"Mr. Dickon," said Andy, and stalled there, wondering what else to add. He didn't want to admit that much of Tuesday night was still a blur. And the more he looked at Mr. Dickon's face, the more he began to think he ought to recognize it—*had* anyone else been in Matthew Maule's apartment Tuesday night?

As soon as Andy asked himself the question, he remembered—sort of. Before falling asleep in front of the computer, he, Andy, had been deep in concentration, and Uncle Matt and one or two other people had walked by him, talking.

Had this man been one of them? Andy couldn't say; it was certainly not impossible.

Meanwhile Mr. Dickon continued to be the fawning salesman. "Were you—if it is not an imposition to ask—were you by any chance on your way to call on Ms. Flamel?" He inclined his head toward the apartment building.

"Well, ahh—"

It was evident that Mr. Dickon had some kind of problem, and whatever it was, it was making him very nervous. His jaw twitched, as if he wanted to ask more questions, but was afraid.

Something suddenly clicked in Andy's memory. He said: "This may not make much sense, but—I seem to remember someone in Uncle Matt's apartment, Wednesday morning, saying something about you—someone of your name—being on the roof of the public library? I'm sorry if that sounds crazy."

Mr. Dickon looked alarmed, then managed to recover. "No, no, just a little joke, I assure you." Now one of the questions he had been keeping back burst out. "And how is your—uncle?—today? That is, I believe, your exact relationship with Matthew Maule?"

"Yes, that's right." This didn't seem like the time to go into any involved explanations. "Far as I know, Uncle Matt's okay. He was fine Wednesday morning."

Dickon made a little moaning sound, hard to interpret. It might have expressed relief. He had clasped his hands in front of him. "I am glad to hear it. Did your esteemed uncle—did he say anything in particular about me?"

"Not that I remember." This fellow seemed harmless enough; maybe he could provide more information about Dolores Flamel.

Dickon seemed excruciatingly in need of more information himself, but for some reason just asking for it required all his courage. "I do not believe I caught your name?"

"Sorry. I'm Andy Keogh."

"Ahh." It was as if a sudden light had dawned. "Is it possible that Mr. Joseph Keogh is your relative—?"

"He's my dad. You know him?"

"Regrettably, not really. We may have met briefly, once, years ago. I trust that he is well? Excellent." Dickon clasped his hands prayerfully. "Tell me, Mr. Keogh, do you remember my companion, Mr. Tamarack, who was with me on Tuesday in the apartment of your uncle?"

"Tamarack. No. Sorry, I never heard of anyone by that name. I guess I was really concentrating on the computer thing that night."

"I see." Dickon nodded slowly. It was hard to tell if the information left him downcast or relieved; at least some of the tension had gone out of him.

~ 8 ~

Though Andy hadn't asked for any accounting, Dickon began a nervous explanation of his presence outside Miss Dolores Flamel's apartment building. It seemed that Dickon and her grandfather, Nicolas Flamel, were partners in a business arrangement of great importance. It was vital that he, Dickon, be able to talk to Miss Flamel, and soon, because it seemed that something bad must have happened to her grandfather.

"Sorry to hear that."

But, alas, he, Dickon, had never actually met the young lady. "We have conversed briefly on the phone, but that is all. It would be so helpful if you could introduce us. On the phone it is so hard to prove one's identity!"

Suddenly Andy was intrigued by the prospect of introducing to each other two people he had never met before—and, while he was at it, probably gaining some more information for Uncle Matt. "I can take a shot at it, if you like."

A few moments later, he and Dickon were standing

inside the narrow lobby. It reminded Andy strongly of his own building, with the two side walls lined with a score or more of inset mailboxes. The inner door, paneled entirely in small panes of glass, was locked, of course, a barrier to everyone but residents with keys. Looking over the rows of buttons next to the mailboxes, the visitors took note of the fact that number 2A had "Flamel" lettered in fresh-looking pencil on the paper insert just beside it. There was no other name.

Dickon's long-nailed, pointing finger hesitated, and it was Andy who finally pushed the button. In a moment a voice had answered over the scratchy intercom, sounding female, clear, and ready for business.

"Yes?"

The nervous one cleared his throat. "It is Mr. Dickon here, Ms. Flamel. It is urgent that we talk."

A moment later the doorlock buzzer sounded, granting visitors brief access. A minute after that, Andy (with Dickon sticking to him like chewing gum, murmuring encouragement) was knocking at the door of apartment 2A, and wondering exactly what he was going to say when it opened.

His first thought when the door did open was: She's much too young to be Uncle Matt's girlfriend.

Dolores Flamel's chin was up, and her demeanor wary. No slinky secret agent here, and certainly no crone. A little on the short side, and sturdy would be a better description than shapely—though definitely not fat. Andy thought her age must be very close to his own, maybe a year or two older. Clear skin showed a lot of established tan, as if she spent a lot of time outdoors. Wide-spaced hazel eyes, with the beginning of fine sun-wrinkles at the corners. A few locks of sun-bleached hair tried to escape from under a kind of turban improvised

from a faded towel. Besides the turban, she was wearing
jeans, gym shoes, and a fairly new-looking pullover shirt
emblazoned with the standard TMU emblem. Here was
a practical young woman, just interrupted in the midst
of some physical job, packing or housecleaning. Whatever was keeping her busy today, it had nothing to do
with trying to look glamorous.

The apartment behind and around Ms. Flamel had
an unsettled look, as if someone was in the process of
coming or going. Books and boxes were scattered about
on tables and the floor, and the walls were bare of decoration except for a couple of old posters. The faded and
undistinguished furnishings looked tired, as if accustomed to being rented with the rooms. A sink in the
background held a modest stack of dirty dishes.

Mr. Dickon spoke first, nervously introducing himself again. He seemed to have forgotten his earlier intention of having Andy perform that office for him.

Dolores Flamel examined the small man coolly.
"Come in, then. I wondered what had happened to you."
Opening the door wider and standing out of the way, she
addressed Andy. "I suppose you're Mr. Tamarack? I
thought you'd be older." Her voice was certainly not native Chicagoan—maybe, thought Andy, from somewhere
in the west.

He shook his head. "No, I'm not Tamarack. Things
are a little more complicated than that—my name's
Andy Keogh. Matthew Maule's my uncle." If Uncle Matt
knew this woman's name, he could hope that she knew
his, and that they were on favorable terms.

But the effect was not exactly what Andy hoped for.
For a moment Dolores looked elegantly dazed. "Really?
Matthew Maule? I don't know if that makes things any
simpler. What brings you to my door?"

They were all three standing inside the apartment now, and she had closed the door. With two people staring at him, Andy tried to explain. "Well, actually my uncle seemed to want to get in touch with you." Having met the young lady, he couldn't imagine that Uncle Matt could see her as a bitter enemy.

"About my grandfather, I suppose."

"That may have been it. I don't know."

She nodded wearily. "How'd you find me?"

"Not too hard. I looked on-line in the TMU student directory and there you were. Ms. Flamel."

"People who know me call me Dolly," Dolores said mechanically. She looked dubious, but after a moment she gestured her visitors to chairs. "I didn't think that directory was publicly accessible. I haven't gone to any classes yet, but I did register for the fall. Now I doubt I'll be here. Bought some clothes and books. I *wanted* to learn some things. Now . . ." Her words trailed off, in a resigned way.

"Well, it wasn't really the public version of the directory that I looked at. And 'Flamel' is an unusual name."

Her hazel eyes were fastened on him, probing, testing. "Not as unusual as Matthew Maule. With an 'e' on the end? Did you know that comes from Hawthorne?" She seemed half puzzled and half amused.

"I'm sorry?"

"Don't be sorry. The author, Nathaniel Hawthorne. Nineteenth century. In *The House of the Seven Gables*. Matthew Maule is a kind of wizard. He puts curses on people."

Somewhere in the background, Dickon made a vaguely unhappy sound. Andy said: "I didn't know that." He could feel his face turning warm, because now it seemed to him that any fool who had an uncle with that name ought to have known as much.

Dolores, or Dolly (the diminutive didn't seem to fit, somehow), appeared to relent a little. "My grandfather was a stage magician in his youth, quite a famous one actually, and he adopted the name 'Flamel' from some character way back in history. Maybe your uncle chose his name the same way. I mean he found it in an old book and just thought it sounded nice. Or does it really go back in his family?"

"I don't know," Andy had to admit.

Having given Andy something to think about, Dolly evidently decided that it was Dickon's turn. She faced him and said: "It's good you came around. We really do have to talk. Maybe you don't know it, but my grandfather died three days ago, in County Hospital. We didn't have any ready money to get him private care."

On hearing this news, Andy murmured something banal in the way of a condolence. Whether Dickon had already been sure of the facts or not, he energetically expressed his sympathy. "Oh, how very sad, my dear! And . . . and . . . I know from what your dear grandfather told me when last I saw him—goodness, that was weeks ago!—that you are sole heir to his property."

"The only property he had left, if you can call it that, was his share in your partnership, whatever that amounts to. But don't you have another partner too?"

Dickon made a slow, expansive gesture with both arms. It would have looked good on a big stage. "I grieve to inform you, Ms. Flamel, that Mr. Tamarack has also passed away." He glanced at Andy, favored him with a sad nod, then turned back to the young woman.

Andy's mind was whirling again. A few minutes ago Dickon had said that Tamarack was in Maule's apartment on Tuesday night. If that was so, his death must have been very recent, very sudden.

"But what happened to him?" Dolores wanted to know.

Dickon shrugged theatrically. "An accident. How does the quotation go? Misfortunes come not as single spies but in battalions. I am here today, my dear young lady, because you and I have important matters that we must settle between us. Matters that provide, shall we say, a silver lining to the cloud of grief, because they will be of great financial profit to you personally."

"How's that?"

"It is only right and just, Ms. Flamel, that the assets of the partnership should now be divided equally between yourself and me."

Andy was half-listening while he tried to imagine what kind of scheme Dickon might be up to. Meanwhile, the old fellow was going on to tell Dolores that in a certain house in Old Town, recently heavily damaged by fire, there still existed "certain material of great value" that her grandfather would certainly want her to have. "If you will accompany me there, to our former laboratory, I will obtain it for you. The sooner the better, I should say. At this very moment, if happily that is possible,"

"Certain material of great value?" The lady sounded dubious.

Dickon glanced over at Andy, as if Andy had just this moment intruded on a private conversation. "If I might talk to Ms. Flamel alone?"

"No," she interrupted firmly, before Andy could respond. "Never mind that, just tell me."

Thus encouraged, Andy held his ground. Dickon gave him one more unhappy look, then dropped his voice, and turned his attention back to the lady. "Gold," he pronounced softly, as if the one word might explain everything.

Andy was astonished, but somehow Dolores Flamel did not seem to be. Not really.

She looked out the window briefly, then turned back. "This gold represents my grandfather's investment? All the money he put into your partnership?"

"That is correct."

"And this gold is still just lying around, in the building where you were doing your experiments? And you want us to go over there right now and get it? It's going to be dark soon."

Dickon hastily reassured her. "That is of no concern. In fact it will make our little expedition easier—our presence will be less noticeable. Yes, it will be easier after dark."

Dolores Flamel continued to display a somewhat wary attitude toward both men, which Andy had to admit was only sensible, in her position. Still, he thought she might be warming up to him a bit. He in turn wasn't sure just yet exactly what he thought of her. But there were certainly intriguing things about her, like her clear eyes, and her forthright attitude.

On the other hand, Dolly did not seem to be warming noticeably toward Mr. Dickon. But she kept on talking to him, doggedly asking questions about the triple partnership and its odd goals; apparently her grandfather had told her very little about that before he died, except that he must have invested practically all his money in it. Andy got the impression everything Nicolas Flamel possessed must have gone into the partnership, and he had died broke as a result. If Dickon was offering the granddaughter a real chance to get a substantial part of that investment back, there was no doubt she was going to take it.

Soon Dickon, under Dolly's prodding, had begun a vague description of the experiments that he and his late partners had been conducting in the Old Town building they had occupied. Andy couldn't make much sense of it. Either technical explanations were not the old fellow's strong point, or he was being deliberately vague and confusing. Andy thought of interrupting, trying to pin him down—but hell, it wasn't his gold. It wasn't really any of his business, either.

According to Dickon, the upper floor had served him and Tamarack as living quarters for several months. Meanwhile the building's ground floor and basement had housed their laboratory, which evidently had needed a lot of space. Dickon still seemed reluctant to give coherent details, but the experiments had evidently required constant attention. "Around the clock, and around the calendar, one might say," he explained in his nervous voice.

Nicolas Flamel had also lived for some time in the Old Town building, before deciding—Dickon did not say why—he needed an apartment of his own. A couple of weeks before going into the hospital, Flamel had left the Old Town site and moved in here, in the rooms now occupied by his granddaughter.

"I think he was expecting his girlfriend to stay here with him." Dolly commented gloomily. "Her name's Miranda something. I never met her."

Evidently Dickon had now done all the explaining he was going to do. Dolly took up the story from her angle, addressing herself mostly to Andy.

"When Gramp learned how sick he was, he phoned me out in Albuquerque, New Mexico. It sounded to me like he was asking for help, really pleading for it, though he never came right out and said so. I had no money for air fare, so I jumped in my old car and got here as quick as I could."

Now she was shaking her head. "First time in my life I've ever been this far east. Chicago's a whole 'nother country, like they say in those ads about Texas."

Andy murmured something meant to be agreeable. As a child he had been taken on trips through the West a couple of times, but what he could remember of it now was mainly Disneyland.

Dolores had turned to Dickon. "You sure this Mr. Tamarack doesn't have any family, any heirs?"

"Alas, on that point I am certain. I knew him fairly well, secretive person though he was."

She continued to be wary. "I still don't understand this project that you fellows were working on. Can't you tell me in plain language what you were doing with all this gold you say you bought?"

"My dear young lady, I fear that the Great Work is of a nature to arouse suspicion when one first hears it described. But there is nothing in the least . . . wrong, about it. Nothing remotely illegal, I assure you. Remember that your grandfather, a man, as we both know, of keen intellect and honest heart, had wholeheartedly committed himself to its success."

"Nothing illegal, but you're saying we've got to keep it quiet, about dividing up the gold."

Dickon sniffed. "There are technicalities, involving the insurance. You need not concern yourself."

"I need not, except you say we should go right away and split up the assets in the dark." Dolores drew a deep breath. "Mr. Dickon, would you still have any hope of making a profit from this business, if we did not divide the assets? Or have you given up on these experiments?"

"At some time in the future, my dear young lady, I would hope to resume such efforts, taking a slightly different, ah, approach. But not now! In the immediate present, I have no doubt that the proper thing to do is to divide the assets, as you say—might I speak to you alone?" Suddenly he turned on Andy a vaguely accusatory look: *You let me think that you and she were old friends.*

"I told you, never mind about speaking to me alone," Dolores reminded him absently. She sat for a moment looking from one man to the other, then asked Andy: "Did you ever meet my grandfather?"

He shook his head. "Never saw Mr. Dickon here, either, until a few minutes ago. Well, maybe once before, in my uncle's apartment."

She shook her head doubtfully at that. But somehow Andy's relationship with Matthew Maule was scoring points for him. Dolores said: "I know my grandfather liked your uncle—if it's really the same man. He mentioned Mr. Matthew Maule to me more than once, spoke of him with great respect."

"Everybody who knows my uncle seems to respect him."

"Oh, most definitely," confirmed Dickon, nodding.

Seeming to come to a decision, Dolores said to Andy: "If we're really going to go to Old Town tonight, I'd like you to come with me. If you don't mind."

"Glad to."

Dickon swallowed. He looked unhappy. "As you wish, of course." Then he pressed on. "Dear Ms. Flamel, when the police and insurance investigators discover our alchemical laboratory, as eventually they certainly must—there is certain to be a misunderstanding. I mean a suspicion—ludicrous, of course, when one knows all the facts—but an inevitable suspicion, that whoever worked there had been manufacturing illegal drugs." Dickon looked at his hearers with grave dignity. "Which of course is utter nonsense."

"Of course," said Andy, who in the past minute or so had started to develop a definite suspicion of his own along that line.

"I can't see my grandpa doing that," Dolores protested.

"Oh, of course not, my dear young woman! No truth to that at all!" Dickon piled on reassurances.

Then he began to enlarge upon his claim that a substantial amount of raw gold was just sitting there in the burned-out building, waiting for its rightful owners to come along and take it. It was there because the process they had been trying to use required a "seeding" of gold, as it were, to produce more.

"There are already many ounces—several pounds, though I hesitate to be specific on the amount. Certainly there is enough, more than enough, to relieve any immediate financial problems that either of us might have."

"So you still say we should go there right now." Dolly still wasn't totally convinced.

Dickon nodded emphatically. "I earnestly believe that is by far the best course."

"Won't there be insurance people, as you said, looking through the place? If they haven't gone through it already, and cleaned out everything of value? Aren't there some kind of police barricades up, after the fire?"

"My understanding is that the insurance people have been delayed," said Dickon vaguely. "As for barricades, no, nothing of the kind. There are only a few ribbons. A mere formality. Anyway, as legal tenant, I have a perfect right to be in the building."

Dolores had still not entirely made up her mind. Finally she let her eyes come to rest on Andy. "I really would like to settle this if we can. Then I'll know, one way or the other, and I can get out of Chicago, the sooner the better."

"I said I'll come along, if you want me to," said Andy immediately. From the corner of his eye he saw Dickon on the verge of protesting again, but keeping quiet, settling for a silent dither. He had some kind of game in mind, but what? The old guy didn't look at all physically dangerous.

Dolores looked her gratitude at Andy. "If there turns out to be really something substantial available—I'll pay you something. I don't need to get rich, I just need to not be cheated."

Andy shook his head. "Thanks, but you don't have to pay me. I'd love to come anyway, just for the hell of it."

Dickon was not reassured. That was fine with Andy.

Meanwhile, Dolores had definitely made up her mind. "Wait for me just a minute, gentlemen, and I'll be right with you." She began to bustle around with hasty preparations. "If we're going to be messing around in the dark, I'm bringing a flashlight. I've got one somewhere. Be right back."

As soon as she was out of the room, Dickon cleared his throat and tried again. "There is really no need for you to concern yourself with this affair."

"Now there is. Because I just said I would."

The gray-haired man looked unhappy, but seemed to lack the will to argue.

Waiting with Dickon, who suddenly had nothing to say, Andy surveyed the inside of the apartment. He approached the nearest poster on the wall, and looked it over at close range.

It was dominated by the name of Nicolas Flamel, in large and garish letters. Dolly's late grandfather seemed to have had, in his youth, a name most people recognized. And there was a circus-poster image of a man who must be the magician himself, painted in the foreground, looking just the way magicians of that era thought they ought to look, complete with top hat and cutaway coat, gesturing with his magic wand.

In the background, behind the dark-clad, neatly bearded figure, showed stagy, would-be Egyptian stuff. Pyramids and snakes and men with the heads of jackals. There was a crocodile, walking upright on his two hind legs. Something about the sight jogged Andy's memory, or almost did, recalling a strange kind of dream that he'd endured recently—yes, it had been during that odd episode of sleep—if sleep was the right name for what he had experienced—when he'd crashed in front of his computer, up at Uncle Matt's.

But now he promptly forgot about the dream again. Evidently Nicolas Flamel had been some kind of stage magician, like Houdini. Meanwhile Flamel's friend, not-so-old Uncle Matt, had probably been . . . what? Andy certainly didn't know. *Some kind of a wizard.* Huh. Andy meant to have a good talk with his Dad on the subject of Uncle Matt—sometime soon, when he got a chance.

Turning around, he saw that Dickon had wandered to a nearby table, where he stood turning over the pages of a library book, whose title announced that it had to do with Egyptian art.

Egypt again. Andy wondered suddenly if Dolly too could have been having strange Egyptian dreams.

As Andy watched, Dickon picked up the book, and began to study it with every appearance of genuine interest.

Andy asked: "Is everybody in Chicago thinking of Egypt suddenly?"

"There is a venerable tradition of such interest in this city."

"Really?"

"Oh, I assure you, sir. When one considers the holdings of the Field, and the several universities, Chicago probably encompasses within its boundaries more mummies, human and animal, than any other city in the United States." Dickon paused for consideration, and then added: "Perhaps any other city in the world, excepting Cairo."

Andy was still mulling that over when Dolly reappeared, wearing a small fanny pack, and announcing that she was ready to go. In a minute the three of them had filed out into the hall, and she locked the apartment door behind her.

~ 9 ~

As they descended the stairs and emerged into the
street, Andy, peering in past the edge of the dark
glasses covering Dickon's eyes, could see the old
man suddenly squinting, as if they had come out of the
lobby into blinding glare instead of the last shaded
minutes before sunset.

Andy wondered what kind of illegal drugs might
make a man so sensitive to light. It was crazy, the things
people were willing to do to themselves in hopes of getting high; Andy himself had heard too much from his
father, and had seen too much damage among his own
contemporaries, to be seriously tempted. If, when they
got to Old Town, it looked like this business might be
taking a bad turn, he would take Dolly by the arm, and
firmly insist that he and she go elsewhere.

But maybe he was being too suspicious. He supposed
Dickon's behavior might simply be the result of some
kind of medical condition. An almost-harmless old guy
who really thought he could make gold out of lead or

whatever. But Andy wasn't going to inquire about Dickon's health. Instead, to make conversation, he asked Dolly what courses she had signed up for at the university.

Dolly explained that she had been doing (or trying to do) some hurried research on Egyptian art.

"Your grandpa planning a comeback on the stage? I was looking at your poster on the wall."

"Actually he's the one who put those posters up . . . I thought Gramp might be hoping to do a comeback. There are magicians making money out in Vegas. But what he was planning turned out to be this . . ." She gestured awkwardly. "This thing, with Dickon and Tamarack and all Gramp's money tied up in gold."

Having achieved his objective of setting Dolly on the way to Old Town, Dickon seemed in no great hurry to complete the journey. Once more trying to turn on the charm, he tried to question Andy as to whether Keogh Investigations now had his Uncle Matthew as a client.

"Don't know much about Dad's business, I'm afraid." It was Andy's standard answer whenever anyone outside the family grew curious about his father's work; and in general it was true. But the question made him wonder, and it seemed to raise new possibilities.

Dickon turned to Dolores. "Did your grandfather in his last hours have anything to say about small white statues? Or crocodile mummies?" The questions lacked urgency; he might have been asking how she liked the weather.

Dolly's tone was skeptical. "Not that I can remember. What kind of statues?"

"It is an unimportant sideline. A shipment of certain

materials that seemed to go astray." He made an extravagant gesture, dismissing the subject.

As they walked on, Dolly told Andy more about her grandfather. It sounded like she was not going to come right out and admit that Gramp had ever done anything illegal—not that she would have been likely to know about it if he had. Gramp's business had been a total mystery to Dolly, and he hadn't even tried to explain it to her until he was in the hospital. Then it was too late, for he was too sick, and even a touch delirious part of the time.

It seemed to Andy only just that Dickon should have to answer a few questions, for a change. "So, this fire that wrecked your laboratory—how'd it happen to start, anyway?"

The old man looked unhappy. "A cause has not really been determined."

"That's not how Mr. Tamarack got killed, is it? Did he die here? In the fire?"

"No." For once Dickon was quick and determined. "That was an entirely separate accident. Truly, sorrows come in battalions."

Dolores asked Andy: "Your uncle never said anything to you about my grandpa or his business?"

"No—he just sort of let on he was interested in finding someone named Flamel. The fact is, I can't remember Uncle Matt ever talking about his own business; I don't know what he does. Sometimes I get the impression that he's retired."

"But how does he spend his time?"

Scratching his head, Andy realized he didn't know that either. "Actually I was just starting to teach him how to use computers."

Dolly nodded; she seemed to approve of the image of Uncle Matt that she was forming. "It's good to see older people take an interest in things. Like learning computers, I mean."

"Uh, yeah."

Now Dickon had dropped back a little, taking an especially good long look over his shoulder.

Dolly moved a little closer to Andy, and lowered her voice. "Is Mr. Dickon really your uncle's friend?" She sounded doubtful.

"They know each other. I wouldn't want to commit myself beyond that."

Already Dickon had caught up with them again. For a few strides the three walked on in silence. Coming up with another question for Dickon, Andy asked him why he and his partners had established their lab in this area.

Dickon answered vaguely that certain necessary materials were easier to come by in Chicago than in most other places.

Gold might be one, Andy supposed—but what else? Tiring of the game, he decided not to pursue the questioning.

The version of the three partners and their mysterious enterprise that Andy was trying to piece together, listening to Dolly's questions and Dickon's short but evasive replies, didn't make much sense to him—except for the part about being unwilling to trust the insurance companies. Andy's life experience so far had left him with the impression that insurance companies were generally up to no good. So maybe there really was gold lying around, and it would make sense to get it out of the building as privately and unofficially as possible. If the old guy was trying to work some kind of con game now, Andy couldn't tell what it was. It didn't seem likely that Dickon could be making up such fantastic complications just for the chance to hit on a young woman he'd never met before.

Dolores was talking, sort of wistfully, about her abortive attempt to educate herself on the subject of ancient Egypt. It sounded to Andy like her college career was going to be over before it had got started. It hadn't been easy for a prospective freshman to sign up for any course that looked helpful.

"Of course if you're serious about it," she was saying now, "you need to start out learning ancient Greek and I guess Arabic, besides the hieroglyphics and a few other languages. But when I asked around I got the impression that most of the people who study Egypt now are real Egyptians."

"So what is it about Egypt?" Andy waved an arm. "I was just asking Dickon the same thing. Ever been there?"

"No. In my case, the only reason was because Gramp sometimes used it as a theme in his stage act. Now he's dead . . . well, there's no money for school now and no point."

Somehow Andy couldn't help thinking there had to be more than that to Dolly's sudden thirst for knowledge. For a moment he wondered if Dolly could have been having strange dreams too.

Dickon was now leading the way, but not far enough ahead to be out of earshot. They were still walking residential streets. This neighborhood looked neither very rich nor very poor, and at the moment was about as quiet as the city ever got on an early summer evening. Automobiles of every age and economic status clung jealously to almost every parking space. Many of the small front yards were thick with residential shrubbery behind their waist-high fences. The bushes were gathering deep twilight shadows, among them fireflies now and then starting to glow magic green. Here and there a homeless human body sat on a curb or shuffled along the street, pushing a grocery cart.

Most of the faces passing on the sidewalk and the street were white, but there was a sampling of what looked like every population in the world. A pack of multicolored children sped by, some jabbering into cell phones as they ran. Now, just a block ahead, there loomed a brightly lighted cross street, lined on both sides with a variety of shops. Everywhere traffic crept, horns sounded, people managed somehow to get across the streets. Smells of pizza and beer came wafting through deepening darkness, along with strains of music. Some kind of jazz. Street signs sternly warned the summer strollers against parking along this curb during snow removal.

The closer they drew to their destination, the more nervous Dickon seemed to grow, the more often he kept glancing over his shoulder.

Suddenly, as if Andy had been arguing the point with her, Dolores told him, keeping her voice low: "All right, maybe there is something crooked about this mysterious project, alchemy or whatever. But my grandpa worked hard, and earned his money honestly. If he got suckered into putting money into this, then I want to get it out."

"You were starting to tell me about his act on stage."

"He had a good act, and he worked hard at it. So if

I can get his money back somehow, in gold or however, why shouldn't I?"

Andy said: "No reason why you shouldn't." He watched Dickon looking nervously over his shoulder again; that was beginning to make Andy nervous too.

Dolly went on, as if she needed to build up her own determination: "I've been poor all my life, I don't want to be poor any more."

Andy still wasn't sure how all Dickon's talk of old statues and mummies fitted in, and if his, Andy's, own dream could have been just coincidence. It seemed there might have been some smuggling of antiquities out of Egypt, but Dolores's grandpa had died before he could profit from the deal—if he had really been in on it at all. But what did smuggling statues and mummies have to do with alchemy?

It sounded to Andy like there was almost certainly something shady going on, that Dickon and others had been bending the law, if not breaking it outright. *Was this the kind of deal that Uncle Matt might have got himself involved in? Mysterious Uncle Matt, with all those old paintings, doubtless immensely valuable, on the walls of his apartment?*

Andy didn't want to believe that of his uncle, and if it was true anyway, he didn't want to know it. He couldn't remember that Uncle Matt had any Egyptian art on display.

Joe Keogh had been an honest cop in his years on the Chicago force, and had brought up his son with the same attitude toward the world.

Dolores Flamel seemed as much in the dark about the secret project as Andy was. Suddenly he realized that his own objective had shifted since embarking on this evening stroll. Gaining information about Dolores Flamel had become less important than trying to keep her out of trouble, whatever her late relative might have been up to.

But at the same time he still wanted to learn more about her. Now he asked: "What'll you do when you get this settled? You said you wanted to get out of Chicago."

"Do I ever. I'll head west again. That's what Gramp would be doing, if he'd had the chance. In fact, he had two first-class train tickets reserved for tomorrow. He bought 'em months ago, when he still had money, thinking he and his girlfriend would be traveling home in style. Except Miranda What's-her-name up and disappeared, about the time she found out he was sick and broke."

"Train tickets, huh?"

Dolly nodded. "Amtrak. Gramp eventually got so's he was really afraid of flying—or maybe he was just angry with the airlines. He used to say they'd all declared war on their customers."

"Perfectly understandable."

"Here we are." Dickon had slowed to a halt.

Looking across the street in front of them, Andy saw that they had reached the site. The building before them had certainly suffered some fire damage, shown by black stains of smoke, and its windows and doors were boarded up. Now Dickon pointed it out to his companions, with an elegant though unnecessary two-handed gesture.

From this angle, at least, the structure surrounded by yellow tape looked almost intact.

The mental image Andy had been building up was pretty thoroughly erased. "I thought you said it was burned out."

"In fact the damage is rather greater than it appears from here. Apart from actual flames, it is amazing what havoc can be wrought by smoke and high-pressure hoses—not to mention firemen's axes." Dickon shuddered delicately. "But we may enter safely."

On the side of the building opposite the alley, the adjoining lot was vacant, and amid its rank weeds there sprouted the remnants of a foundation where some house or small store had been torn down. Whoever owned these lots, thought Andy, need not be much concerned about the loss of one more old building; the Near North Side was booming, and the land itself should have mouthwatering value.

Except for one fern-windowed grill and bar, the remainder of the block in the direction of the busy street seemed to be occupied entirely by small shops, heavy on art and assorted kinds of upscale clothing, with a sprinkling of videos and books, incense and pottery.

Gently shepherding Dolly across the street, Dickon murmured something into her ear. Andy couldn't hear what it was. In the next moment, Dickon turned his head and looked at Andy as if wishing Andy would get lost. Andy stared right back.

When they were halfway across the street, Dickon walked more slowly and altered course. Now that they were standing on the threshold of their goal, he seemed to be waffling, hesitating about going through with the promised transaction.

Now the elder man was murmuring, indecisively: "It would be a good thing if I could just see to my automobile first."

There in the mouth of the alley was what Andy supposed had to be Dickon's abandoned car. The red tape slapped across the windshield, and the metal boot on one

wheel, strongly suggested that the car was being blamed
by officialdom for not getting itself out of the way.

Andy didn't get it. "I don't know what you can do
about that. Looks like the cops have seen to it already,
put a boot on it." The steel clamp gripping one wheel was
plainly visible. The auto had been effectively immobilized.

"If you would just stand by, please," Dickon murmured. "This will take only a moment." But then again
he hesitated, seemingly until the sidewalk was clear of
nearby witnesses, as if he were fearful some passerby
might blow a whistle and call the cops when they saw
him lay hands on the marked car. What a coward,
thought Andy. Then Dickon stepped into the alley.

In a moment he was opening the trunk of his old
car, doing something inside, then closing the lid again.
Andy wondered if maybe it was the firemen's fault that
it was where it was, if they had pushed it to where it
blocked the alley, in a rush to get it out of their way.

Now Dickon, moving with unexpected quickness,
had bent over the booted wheel and with a straining
grunt was making an effort to wrench away the paralyz-
ing clamp. *He is crazy, after all,* thought Andy.

Dickon was wearing a short-sleeved sport shirt, garish in some crazy Hawaiian pattern, and the muscles in
his thin arms briefly stood out in rigid cords.

Then with a flick of his wrist he tossed aside the
heavy steel gadget, now somewhat bent out of shape.
Landing on the pavement, it sounded like something out
of an advanced weightlifter's kit.

Andy moved a little closer, unable to believe what
he thought he had just seen. "How in *hell* did you do
that?"

The gray-haired man smiled timidly. "Somehow they didn't put it on properly."

"Oh."

Now, with its wheels all free to turn, it would seem that the vehicle was ready to be driven away—but where was Dickon? A moment ago Andy had been watching him closely, and now he seemed to have vanished, like some kind of ghost, into the gathering dusky night.

Andy turned around, bewildered. "Where—?"

Dolores pointed. "He went this way. He must have gone into the building."

On the floor of the alley just beside the burned-out building, shaded from the nearest streetlight by the thick shadow of a burly wooden utility pole, Andy could make out broken pavement and a deep mud puddle, from which the water recently poured out by fire hoses had no place to drain.

Groping in heavy shadows, Andy caught up with Dolores as she rounded the building's next corner and reached what ought to have been a small backyard. This was dominated by a clump of wild and weedy trees that had sprung up in what amounted to a vacant lot. The trees were thick and bushy, growing head-high, evidently making the most of their recent watering by fire hoses, and they cast heavy shadows.

Now Dolly, practically secure from casual observation, was doing something at one of the boarded windows. If they did manage to get in, he thought, it would be very dark inside, and Dolly's flashlight was going to come in very handy.

Andy kept his voice low, though he was positive that no one was near enough to hear. "Are you sure this makes sense?"

He didn't get an answer.

~ 10 ~

A ndy supposed that Dickon might possibly have made his way into the abandoned structure as smoothly as a puff of smoke, though Andy wasn't at all sure the strange man had even been moving in that direction when he disappeared. But maybe Dolly had seen something he hadn't. Where else would the fellow have gone, after all his effort to persuade Dolly to come here with him?

Anyway, Dolly was having her difficulties trying to get in. Andy could hear her muttering low-voiced swear words as she tried to dislodge a sheet of plywood now taking the place of a recently demolished ground-level window. Probably the agent of destruction had been some fireman's axe, to judge by the savage dents and hacks around the window frame. But later, when the board-up people came around, they had not done too good a job.

Andy could dimly see his companion's small, strong hands dislodging a strip of warning tape, then prying fiercely at the edge of the plywood. He was about to offer help when something suddenly gave way, creating a foot-wide gap, leading into utter darkness.

Turning to study Andy's reaction, Dolly told him: "You don't have to come in."

"What are my choices?" But she was already gone. Mumbling bad words in turn—Dickon really couldn't have come this way, could he?—Andy climbed through the gap after her, necessarily straining to force it wider. As soon as he got through, he managed to tear his jeans on what must have been a projecting nail.

Once inside the building, they had to pause to let their eyes get used to deeper darkness. Dolores had pulled out her small flashlight, and was peppering the darkness with little bursts of illumination. Thoughtfully she was aiming the light low, not wanting a stray beam to betray their presence to people outside.

Actually this part of the structure did not seem much damaged, except that everything, floor and walls and even ceiling, looked soggy when the light hit it, and the bitter smell of smoke had saturated everything, and still retained an almost choking strength.

Touching his companion's arm, Andy whispered: "So where the hell is Dickon now? Did he really come in here?"

"He must have. He can't have gone far." But Dolores no longer sounded completely convinced.

Groping his way to a doorway, Andy put his head through, and thought he saw movement, a room away. "Dickon?" he called in a soft voice. But there was no answer, and the movement was not repeated.

When he went through the doorway, the surface beneath his feet threatened to give way. Hastily he backed up a step, muttering: "Watch out, this floor is treacherous."

Dolly, having the flashlight, naturally assumed the lead. They were in a hallway now, going in the opposite direction from Andy's doorway. In the darkness he could hear water dripping in several places, each with its own separate rhythm. Doubtless the water was coming from persistent fire-hose puddles or broken plumbing, somewhere on the second or third floor. Each drop made an echoing, almost metallic sound as it landed in the flooded basement.

Dickon had been right about the extent of the damage; once you were inside it was easy to see there had been plenty. Some of the interior walls were charred, and others were leaning crazily.

Exchanging warnings about the floor, the two explorers made their way slowly forward, Dolly still a step ahead. In another minute they had come to the edge of a kind of crater, where they stood looking down into what had been a basement. Pools of deep mud rimmed a miniature lake, created by fire hoses or broken pipes. Jaggedly splintered two-by-fours, showing where some interior walls had broken down, projected menacingly upward.

"Let's be very careful here," he murmured. It would be murderous to fall on one of those impaling stakes.

No telling how deep the water was down there; the tiny beam of Dolly's small flashlight bounced off the black and glittering surface of still water, then seemed to disappear.

Then the searching light beam found the gleam of glass. "Look at that," Dolly commented. "And that."

"The tools of alchemy, I guess. Or something." He

wished he knew just what a drug lab looked like.

Several items of strange equipment came to light—glass in strange shapes, and ceramics, and twisted metal. Odd materials and tools used by the alchemists. No wonder Dickon had thought the cops would suspect a drug lab.

"I don't see any piles of gold," Dolly whispered.

Andy was shaking his head. Was the whole business some kind of elaborate joke? "Any sign of Dickon?"

"Not since we came in. He was right ahead of me when we were just outside the building."

In another minute the two explorers had turned their backs on the gaping crater of the basement and were making their way slowly along another hall. Suddenly Dolly pointed to one side. "There—at the top of the stairs. He just moved out of sight."

Softly she called Dickon's name. But no one answered.

The stairway stood open and looked solid. A moment later, Dolly had started up, with Andy right behind. The second floor looked much like the first, rooms opening off a central hallway, all uninhabited and scant of furniture. Then back to the stairway, on and upward to the third floor.

They had just reached the top of the stairs when Andy started at the sight and sound of a large and ugly rat, doubtless here in search of his own version of treasure, scampering away.

Here on the building's uppermost floor, most of the footing was still intact. The smell of smoke was just as strong; and the ubiquitous sogginess still glistened in the little flashlight beam.

It was hard to tell just what sort of experiments the three partners might have been conducting here—maybe crocodiles and mummies, for all that Andy could tell now. The place now suggested a large and elaborate workshop rather than a dwelling. Benches had been improvised, with doors laid flat on sets of filing cabinets.

Dolly turned with a jerk. "What's that?"

The sense that they had silent company was suddenly overpowering. Andy kept his voice as low as possible. "Someone else is in here."

"Someone . . . two or three of them at least."

"If it's the cops . . ." But even as Andy whispered the words, he knew that they were wrong. Cops would be making noise and shining lights.

One of the shadowy figures was standing apart from the other two. From the little he could see in the deep gloom, none of them looked at all like Dickon.

"Let's back out of this," Andy whispered.

Moving together, they reversed their field. But it was not to be. Two more of the silent figures were now standing at the head of the stairs, effectively cutting off their retreat.

And one of them was laughing, a low, eerie sound that made the hair rise up on Andy's neck.

When Dolly flicked her flashlight upward, to illuminate their faces, both seemed to shift positions slightly, with eerie quickness, just enough to keep from being spotlighted. When she moved the beam again, they dodged again just as the beam reached them. It was like some illusion in a movie. But illusions in the real world did not laugh.

Andy cleared his throat, and did his best to sound bold and authoritative. "All right. What's going on?"

Now Andy could make out the faces of two of those confronting him. They were remarkable faces, and frightening. Their bodies were all wrapped in dark clothing, suggesting the idea of some kind of gang uniform.

Again there came a swift stir of movement, the scampering of some small animal. Then Andy blinked, unsure of what his eyes had just informed him in the bad light. One of the figures had seemed to move at lightning speed, snatched up a quivering rat—it had looked almost the size of an alley cat—tore off some portion of its body, and with an expert touch imbibed the resulting small jet of blood. The animal's shrill squeal of terror and pain cut off a moment later.

Andy heard Dolores, close beside him, reacting with a gulp and a choking sound. She clutched at his arm.

Tugging her with him, he started to retreat. But in a moment there was no place to go. Turning to face the nearest confrontation, they found themselves with their backs toward the edge of the great crater. Overhead, a sizable portion of the flat roof was entirely gone, and indirect illumination came washing in from the reflective clouds above the city. The building's upper windows had been boarded too, and only around the edges of the plywood panels could narrow spears of light lance in from the busy street outside.

No path of escape remained. "What do you want of us?" Dolly's voice was still almost steady.

At last one of their challengers spoke. A man's voice, commanding, tinged with a strange accent that Andy could not identify. "What we want is simple. We must know what your grandfather told you before he died—"

A woman's voice cut in impatiently: "He gave you a list of names, we know he did!"

"—especially everything that he told you about the little statues."

Dickon had been asking about little statues too. But

he hadn't, not that Andy could remember, said anything about any list of names.

Andy tried to bluff the nearest shadow. "Going to move out of our way, or am I going to move you?"

The only answer was a little giggle. Someone having fun.

Andy shoved one of the blockaders, sent him stumbling back. But before he could turn to deal with the other man, Andy was seized from behind, in the strongest grip that he had ever felt. Despite a furious attempt to struggle, he was held motionless.

Hoarsely he cried out Dolly's name, with some idea of urging her to run. But that was useless. The flashlight had been knocked away. Andy could see only dimly that a couple of them had grabbed Dolly too, one holding her while another rifled her pockets and her fanny pack. When she tried to scream, an effective muffling hand was clamped across her mouth.

Again Andy tried to move, but his twisted arm felt like it was on the point of breaking. The grip that held him so immobilized seemed awkward, but was enforced by a strength that felt totally unreal.

Now Dolly's little moans, and Andy's gasping breathing, were the only sounds in the dark house.

Clearly Andy's earlier impression of three or four people taking part in the prank, or ambush, had been totally wrong. He could see now that there were half a dozen of them at least. A couple seemed to be wearing ski masks—it was hard to be sure, in the gloom—and one slender woman in dark trousers had on huge silver earrings that glistened dully whenever they encountered a spark of light.

This was no chance encounter; several of them had

already called Dolores by name. Their only interest in Andy, so far at least, was to make sure he did not interfere.

But now one evidently grew curious regarding him.

"What is your name, heroic escort?" This from the fellow who was holding Andy's arms behind his back, an especially tall man in a plaid shirt.

Andy's anger was growing rapidly, so fast that it had already burned away half his fear. With it came some inner devil's prompting.

"Matthew Maule," he answered, in a loud clear voice, and was astonished at the sudden stillness that the name produced. All the snickering and whispering that had begun to grow cut off at once.

After a full ten seconds of chill silence, the tall man said: "No, you are not. But what connection have you with that name?"

Andy cursed himself for not keeping his mouth shut, or giving a straight answer. But before he was forced to speak again, Dolores let out another scream, pulling everyone's attention back to her.

Dolly's voice was shaky, but she was still managing to get out coherent words. "I don't know anything about any list of names. If you want the gold, you've got the wrong party, I don't know where it is, I never saw it. If you can find it, take it and let us go." Whoever had grabbed her was now holding her so deep in shadows that Andy could not see her at all.

"Gold?" someone in the background questioned, with a sneer. Several of the gang seemed to find that idea amusing. They seemed to be offended by the suggestion they could be distracted from their real goal by any lure as common as a fortune in gold.

One shadowy figure picked up a piece of what looked

like twisted glass—alchemical lab equipment, Andy thought—then smashed it, hurling it to the floor with a savage motion. "What did your grandfather tell you about the work he and the others were doing here? He, and noble Dickon, and unlucky Tamarack?"

But another broke in impatiently to ask: "What did he say to you regarding Sobek?"

"I don't know what you're talking a—ahh!" Someone did something that drew from her another cry of pain.

It was the woman with silver earrings who took up the interrogation now. "For the last time, where is the list of names?"

"For the last time, I don't know!" Dolly was screaming more than loud enough to be heard outside the building, but nobody seemed to care. "I don't know what the hell you're talking about!"

"Don't play dumb." Dark trousers moved closer to Dolly by a step. "That would be a serious mistake. We want the names of those who are now in possession of the statues. Who bought them, when they were being so foolishly sold as cheap, common crockery."

Dolly gasped out: "If there is any list, I don't know anything about it."

When Andy decided on one more desperate try at getting free, his captor seemed to know his intention before he had moved a muscle, and administered another jolt of pain.

When his vision cleared again, Andy finally managed to make out where Dolly was, though her figure was still almost invisible in deep gloom. Her whole shape looked pale, as if most of her clothing had been pulled off, or partially off in the search process just concluded; now she was stretched out very quietly on the floor, as if stunned or simply afraid to try to move. Having exposed and searched her body, none of her attackers seemed much interested in it. Their only concern was some secret that it might have held.

The woman's relentless voice probed on. "We know that Nicolas Flamel received, from a certain source, the information that allowed him to compile a list of names. You are his heir, his only relative. He must have somehow passed those names on to you."

Meanwhile, in the background, other voices murmured. Someone grumbled that it was too bad the shop had been burned.

Well, yes, said someone else, but we didn't do that, it was Sobek. But he didn't find what he was looking for.

Sobek again. At least that was what the name sounded like to Andy.

No, commented the previous speaker. Sobek couldn't have found what he was looking for, not here anyway. Otherwise he would not have gone on to the apartment where he killed Tamarack.

Once someone—Andy thought it was the silver-earringed woman—incongruously sneezed, marring the image of supernatural power and terror.

Dolly's pale form was moving a little now, as if she were trying to pull her clothes back on. Andy's arms were still held in an iron grip, but his mind had started to work again, spitting up one idea after another. He couldn't tell if they were all totally crazy or not. But there seemed nothing to be lost by trying out what seemed to be the best.

He spoke up in a loud voice, breaking into the monotonous interrogation. "I have money. I mean, my family does. It could be worth a lot to you to let us go."

The man who was holding him had a good laugh at that.

No one else paid the least attention. The original point of this capture, this interrogation, still held them all obsessed.

People who laughed at money were terrifying indeed. Little statues. Someone named Sobek. Above all, a supposed list of names, somehow worth killing for. Andy could not make much of any of this. But the name of Matthew Maule had had an almost magical effect, and all this resonated somehow with his strange experience in Uncle Matt's apartment.

The big man was losing patience. Suddenly Andy was being hustled forward, to the very edge of the pit. His captor had turned his head and was saying to Dolly: "You will tell us, or I will take this one apart right now!"

Andy supposed he ought to yell, but he couldn't see what difference it would make. At exactly the wrong moment there came back to him the thought of Uncle John's missing fingers. The Curse of the Southerlands, become the curse of the Keoghs, for marrying into them. He thought: *Why didn't anyone in the family ever warn me that things like this could still be happening to us? And it all had something to do with Uncle Matt.*

One of the others was murmuring something in a Latin-sounding language, something that sounded like an incantation, from which Andy could pick out only the two words: ". . . Matthew Maule . . ." For certain, a name to conjure with.

The man who was holding Andy cried: "I care nothing for Matthew Maule!" And gave his captive a great teeth-rattling shake.

Now it seemed it could not be a man at all who held

him, but some kind of Hollywood monster. The monster holding Andy was about to pitch him out from the third floor, so that in another second he would be falling helplessly right onto some of the splintered uprights at the basement level. And there was nothing to be done about it, nothing at all. He let out a helpless, warbling cry.

"Here goes your late companion, lady. One, two, three . . ."

Dolly screamed out something, just a little late. An arm of gigantic strength had actually launched Andy's helpless body into the air, and he had just screamed in terror, when another hand, entirely different but feeling just as strong, somehow came out of the air to catch him by the upper arm. The course of Andy's passage through the air was altered. His body was swept sideways in a gentle toss, that sent him rolling through darkness on a solid floor.

His momentum spun him through a final somersault and let him go. Coming out of it on knees and elbows, bruised but functional, Andy found himself looking back toward the open pit.

The scene before him was something out of a bad dream, bathed in the eerie light that washed in through the shattered roof, all of the city's lights reflecting from a cloudy sky. But in the midst of terror and ugliness, he could now see the figure of his savior. Not ten feet away from Andy, a man neatly dressed in a dark suit was crouched like an acrobat upon a narrow crossbeam that projected solidly out over the pit. The man was smiling strangely, and his face was unmistakably that of Matthew Maule.

~ 11 ~

The bulky man had recoiled slightly on seeing his victim plucked out of the air and tossed to safety. But in a moment plaid-shirt had recovered. To Matthew Maule he said in his rich voice: "I know you, old man. You have no business here tonight, and you would be well advised to leave."

Uncle Matt still crouched, motionless as a carven figure. "And I know you, or something of you—your name is Lambert. You are still in your first century, and you are wrong about my business. It is personal, and of the highest order. You have just tried to kill one who claims kinship with me."

Lambert was returning Uncle Matt's direct stare, but Andy thought that it was costing him an effort. "The Crocodile has sent you, to try to get the list of names."

"I serve no Crocodile, but only my own interests. You will release your captives. When they are safely gone, we can discourse of crocodiles—and lists of names, and treasures, if you like."

Out of the background gloom there came a woman's voice, in a tone that was almost pleading. "Make common cause with us, Vlad Tepes, against the monster."

Without taking his eyes for an instant from Uncle Matt, the big man barked at her: "Shut up, Merit!"

Matthew Maule turned his head, gazing into the shadows. Whether he took his eyes off Lambert or not seemed to be a matter of complete indifference. "I think I have no quarrel with any of you others here. Not if you release your prisoners, unharmed. Then we will talk."

The big man would not have it. "We need no help and no advice from you, old man, and I advise you to keep out of our way."

The woman, Merit, who had pleaded for cooperation, was not ready to give up. She said: "Lambert, it will be better if we abandon this effort to . . ."

Her words trailed off. Perhaps no one but Andy was listening to them.

Uncle Matt was grinning, but not at Andy. Instead he seemed to find something amusing in the presence of the bulkier man, who was sitting on the brink of the abyss only an arm's length away from Maule, and who, only moments ago, had just tried to hurl Andy to his death.

The man who had just attempted to murder Andy started to make some comment, or begin some movement, that he never finished. Matthew Maule must have judged it inappropriate, for he backhanded the fellow with a blow too fast for Andy's eyes to follow. He could only witness the effects. There was a sound like the impact of a baseball bat, and the victim's lower jaw had abruptly been detached, was hanging only from a flap of skin. Something that might very well have been a tooth sang like a bullet past Andy's head to embed itself in a solid wall behind him. A moment later the big man's body, with balance gone and all the grace knocked out of it, had gone spinning and tumbling into the wasteland of water and jagged points below.

Even before the splash, all hell broke loose. Andy's stunned senses were reporting the unbelievable. The effect of Uncle Matt's blow was as if he had thrown a rock into a hornets' nest. Half of the dark-clad gang, creatures who until now had looked like people, were taking flight, some of them going right up into the air like startled birds. In moments they were already out of sight. One or two were running to get away, and Andy heard the thud and crash of panicked human feet on wooden floors in darkness.

Others in the group were not trying to get away, but felt ready to have a shot at being Uncle Matt's opponents. They closed on him in a rush, and he in a blur of motion fought them off. What weapons might be in use was more than Andy could tell in the dim light.

Whatever their intentions, fight or flight, most of the assembly were moving faster than Andy's eyes could follow. He had the impression that momentarily the air was thick with darting, flying bodies, more movie illusions come to life.

Andy himself, still on all fours, not knowing what to do or what to think, kept edging backward, farther from the pit, until he felt his feet bump against a solid wall. Partially disoriented by his whirl through the air, he had the idea that Dolly ought to be somewhere near him, but he could not tell where.

Now on the edge of the great gap stood the woman with huge silver earrings, poised as if she wanted to fly with some of the others but was somehow held back. At the moment her gasping breath made more noise than Andy's. She had drawn a handgun from somewhere, and snapped it up for a quick shot at Uncle Matt. The muzzle flash was almost dazzling in the gloom; the pistol's noise was big in the enclosed space. Maule spun around and clutched at his own left arm.

But Uncle Matt did not fall. He had not been knocked out of action—far from it. Again his dim image in the darkness blurred. Whatever happened to the woman came upon her so swiftly that Andy could not quite see what it was, but her scream choked off as quickly as it had begun, and now she was nowhere to be seen.

Light from the smeared grayness of Chicago's night still came in where the roof was missing, and showed the struggle continuing in the pit below. Turning his head a little, Andy could look down through splintered holes in flooring, as through a window into hell. Maule's first victim, the inhumanly strong man in the plaid shirt, was still down there thrashing, his great wounds pouring dark blood into dirty water; his lower jaw appeared to be still hanging by only a flap of skin. The upthrust spear formed by one jagged, jutting two-by-four, had punctured his ribcage, so he was half-impaled upon it.

Even as Andy watched, Lambert tore himself free, and dragged himself away.

There was a fluttering and howling high above that sounded like a further evacuation. To Andy the noise evoked a vision of a flight of monstrous bats escaping from a cave. Except that some of those who fled were screaming threats, their voices seeming to mount quickly through the sky.

And now the two people wearing ski masks had come within reach of Maule's arms, down in the pit. His harsh voice carried: "You wish to be faceless? Let it be so!" And with a hand clasping the neck of each, he smashed and ground their covered heads together.

Andy was held by the scene before him, as he might have been gripped by watching a tornado. But now his instinct for survival overcame the fascination. He turned, groping and crawling in the direction where he thought Dolly ought to be. As he moved, his twisted arm still hurt, but it was functional.

There came a lull in the sounds of fighting, and it seemed the real nightmare might be over. There was dim movement just in front of him, and he murmured her name. When his hand touched her, she gave another little scream, her body lurching sideways.

"It's me, Andy. Can you stand up? Can you move?"

Dolly mumbled something. She was already doing her best to try, and had succeeded in pulling her clothing more or less back into place.

In another moment, with Andy's help, she was on her feet, saying: "I think so. What's happening? Somebody new came in, didn't they?"

A new outburst of screaming, splintering and splashing noises drowned out the rest of what she was trying to say.

"That's right. Where's the flashlight? Never mind, we're getting out." The route to retreat, straight away from the ghastly pit, though grimly dark, now appeared entirely open.

Hobbling together, Andy and Dolores quickly reached the shadowed but unobstructed hallway. Behind them, in and around the pit, still sounded a fiendish chorus of roars, bangs, slams, and sounds like splintering two-by-fours, blended with occasional outcries that seemed to issue from no human throat.

At the head of the stairway, Andy came to an abrupt halt. The way by which they had climbed to the third floor was no longer clear. A roof beam, loosened by some recent impact on the damaged structure, had fallen across the downward passage. Worse than that, a mangled body that could only be that of Lambert, his ghastly wounded enemy, was crouched directly beneath the beam, making spasmodic movements, and uttering frightening noises of pain and rage commingled.

Then abruptly the mangled body proved itself still capable of speech. The first words came in some Latin-sounding language, and they were poisonous in tone. Then in English, to Dolly: "Come, bitch, I need your blood." His words were muffled, coming through torn flesh and splintered bone, but still they sounded plain enough.

An arm in a torn plaid sleeve shot out, in a grab of startling power and swiftness for Andy's ankle. Andy dodged out of the way barely in time, so that the savage snatching movement caught only air.

The young man and young woman danced and stumbled backward, almost falling in their terror. Lambert's gurgling cries pursued them: "One day I will have your blood! Both of you!"

Abruptly the uproar behind Andy and Dolores ceased. Looking back, he got the impression that the pit, or crater, now yards away, was suddenly deserted except for the dead and possibly the wounded. But he was afraid to go back to the stair, and that part of the building offered no other way of getting out.

Dolly was crying now, fear, frustration, and anger sounding all together. Between sobs she managed to choke out some coherent words. "Maybe there's another stairway."

"There ought to be." Didn't the fire code require two in every building?

Stumbling and groping along as best he could with no flashlight, Andy turned away from the ghastly blockage, and led his stumbling companion toward where he thought the rear of the building ought to be.

Dolly stumbled again, and seemed to be having trouble walking. Andy murmured something intended as reassurance, and pressed ahead, scouting out the way. In the midst of thicker darkness, he found the passage blocked by what felt like quite an ordinary door. Some twisting of the building's frame had frozen it ajar, by only a few inches, and Andy in search of a way out now ruthlessly applied his shoulder.

The barrier suddenly gave way, and he stood staring into another room, this one relatively free of damage. The plywood covering of one window had been knocked askew, and some combination of moonlight and streetlight came pouring freely through. In the middle of the newly revealed space, a cheap bed with a stained mattress stood in comparative brightness, like part of a stage setting. On the bed two people were locked in a tight embrace. The man's dark suit now hung in shreds and rags on his pale body, as he crouched holding the woman's limp form in his arms.

At the moment of Andy's entrance, the man was bending his head sharply forward, nuzzling at the woman's neck. Beside the falling curve of his dark hair, one of her huge silver earrings glistened with a muted brightness.

In the next moment, the man abruptly raised his head, and Andy understood that his own personal nightmare was not yet over. He recognized, with the certain knowledge that comes in dreams, a face no more than half-familiar, because it was now misshapen in its lower part, distorted around the mouth by the presence of fangs that dripped and dribbled drops of gore, blood that looked black in the strange light, as they pulled free from the woman's punctured throat.

Uncle Matt's eyes were no longer really human. They seemed to be flashing green, like an animal's, with faint reflected light. They fastened their gaze on Andy's. Softly but quite audibly, Uncle Matt's distinctive voice, slightly distorted by protruding teeth, came through his bloodstained lips: "Stay with the girl, wherever she may go. Help her if you can."

And then he bent his head once more, urgently resuming the unthinkable embrace.

Andy's nightmare was only deepening, the shock redoubling. Cursed with a kind of horror he had never known before, he backed out of the room, mechanically putting one foot behind the other. He tried to pull the door shut after him—this was something Dolores must not see. He could not even try to speak. In a moment he had groped his way back to her and grabbed her by the hand.

There was another door to be discovered, on the opposite side of the hall from the one he had just closed upon the nightmare. The second door proved to lead to a second stairway.

Now, with their way out of the building seemingly clear, and no longer facing any immediate threat, Dolly was sobbing openly again. Together she and Andy blundered somehow down the stairs, only to find their way blocked at the bottom by another sheet of plywood, nailed and wedged into the exit doorway. But this barrier had been made to resist attack from outside, not from within. Again and again Andy threw his weight against it, until the thin slab suddenly crashed away, letting him fall out.

Once they had broken their way out of hell, the night air of Chicago seemed suddenly marvelously clean and pure. Andy was half-expecting to find the building already ringed with cops, drawn by the ungodly noise. But nothing of the kind had happened yet.

Four young legs ran. Hand in hand, Andy and Dolly sped limping down the alley, just past the place where Dickon's car had been parked illegally. In passing, Andy took note of the fact that now the vehicle was gone.

They did a hundred yards or so of alley at the best speed they could manage, holding hands, then slowed to a stumbling trot and turned onto a sidewalk when they emerged onto a residential cross street. Here trees were soft and lovely, the young green of June shading the street lamps. There were only the usual noises of the city. Somewhere a siren sounded, but not coming nearer, only part of the city's common background.

Dolly still walked beside him, though they were no longer holding hands. Andy's eyes kept jumping from one shadow to another, his mind seeking active reassurance that there were no dead bodies lying anywhere. No one they passed on the sidewalk was gushing blood. But he had learned in his heart that at any moment the world might again erupt in horror.

In a minute or two they had covered several blocks, and Andy could feel sure that no one was chasing them. None of the people they now encountered turned to stare. Again the couple slowed their pace. They were walking almost normally now, but still breathing heavily.

At length they stopped, in the streetlight-shadow of a huge tree, to take inventory.

Andy leaned against a comforting brick wall, built right up to the sidewalk. "Are you hurt? What were they doing to you?"

"What were they *doing*? You mean what didn't they try?" Dolly was clinging to his arm, and it seemed for a moment that she was going to go thoroughly hysterical.

"But you're not bleeding anywhere. Are you?"

"No. No, I'm not bleeding. I'm all right, nothing's broken, I can move." Rage was keeping her energy level high. "Someday I'll get those . . ."

They were both dirty, soaked in their own sweat and the clinging smell of smoke. Andy's jeans were torn, a small flap hanging open on his right thigh, over a bleeding scratch. He gave thanks for the darkness, making their condition less noticeable. He ached in more places than he could count, from being punched and bounced and twisted, but all his essential parts seemed to be working.

Andy kept looking back along the way that they had come, imagining at every moment that he would see some kind of nightmarish pursuit. But so far there was nothing.

Now they had started walking again. Without really thinking about it, he was leading the way toward his own apartment.

Catching unexpected movement from the corner of his eye, he spun around sharply. "What's that?"

This time it was Dolly who was relatively calm. "Only a dog." The large, dark animal was trotting briskly along, keeping pace with them on the other side of the street.

Another couple of blocks went by without incident—unless you counted the occasional wary looks that they received from passersby.

"Andy?" Dolly's voice had gone tiny, almost childish. Now she was hanging on his arm.

"Yeah."

"What happened back there? I mean, they were killing us. How did we get away?"

"We had help."

"They didn't just start fighting among themselves—?"

"No."

"Then who? I mean, how—?"

If he was slow to answer, she wasn't going to wonder why. Not now. "Tell you about it later."

Apparently that answer was good enough for Dolly in her current state. Presently she got out: "I'm not going to the cops." Further speech was delayed for two more gasping breaths. "Whatever Gramp was doing, I don't want to get mixed up in it."

Andy had used up all his capacity for surprise. "I think we're both already about as mixed in as anyone could be."

"Then I want to get unmixed."

"Sounds like a great idea." At the moment Andy couldn't tell if what he and Dolly were saying made any sense or not. She said things, and he answered, more or less automatically. Meanwhile, looming ever larger and brighter in his mind, like the afterimage of a flashbulb in the dark, was that last apparition, seen in that dim and quiet little room: the bloody fangs of Uncle Matt protruding from his handsome jaw, the dead or dying woman in his arms.

Gradually what Dolly was saying started to come through to Andy again. Her sudden relief at being free, and still alive, was taking the form of babbling.

". . . so, it was never really gold. I didn't think so.

That son of a bitch Dickon, he was lying. Did you hear? When I offered them gold they only laughed."

"I heard." Then Andy started violently when a nearby driver blasted his car's horn. But again it was only random noise, nothing to do with him or Dolly. "They said you had some kind of list of names."

"I do have it. I can tell you, because it almost got you killed." She made a strange sound, between a chuckle and a squeal of pain. "It's almost funny! It is funny, if it doesn't kill us both. I'll tell you about it when we have the chance."

That ought to have been a staggering answer. And it would have been, except that all the time, while he and Dolly kept on walking, there hovered in the foreground of his mind, tending to blot out everything else, a greater horror than anything Dolly had seen or felt tonight. Even greater, in its own way, this one was even greater than the fear of being almost killed—Andy had known for a long time that there were people in the world who might do that.

The picture just hung there in his awareness, refusing to be processed, refusing to make way for useful information. But when he saw a slowly cruising police car, instead of running to overtake it, pouring out a tale of kidnapping and attempted murder, he turned instinctively away.

He could see himself being arrested, certainly put under suspicion. He could have been somehow involved in whatever crazy business had been going on with Dickon and Nicolas Flamel, alchemy and gold. Maybe Uncle Matt had also been in on it from the start. Murder had been intended tonight, with Andy himself as victim, and killing had been done. But for Andy the true horror lay in what came after. . . .

He couldn't stop seeing the face of Uncle Matt, stained and disfigured with the fangs, the blood. He could neither stop seeing it, or find a way to think about it usefully. His thoughts seemed to be marching round in a dazed circle.

At last, something Dolly had told him only a few moments ago bobbed up on the surface of his thoughts. "You said you're not going to the cops."

"I'm not." Violently she shook her head, then winced as if the motion had caused pain. "I just want to get away from this fast, get far away, and then . . ." She paused. "What about you?"

Pale-faced Uncle Matt, taking a break in his blood-drinking affair with a fresh corpse, opened his unspeakable mouth to offer Andy sage advice. *Stay with the girl, wherever she may go.*

Andy said aloud: "I will."

Dolly looked round on him sharply. "What?"

He shook his head. "I mean, I agree. I don't see how I can go to the cops either."

The two of them had come now to a neighborhood playground, dark and deserted at this hour behind its locked gate and serious fences. No hiding out in there. Not that Andy wanted to hide out—he was determined to keep going. They passed a vacant lot, concealing perfect shadows for an ambush behind a looming billboard, the huge sign undergirded by a decaying latticework of lath. Gigantic figures lurched across the billboard, advertising fear and wild adventure. Something about a major motion picture, coming soon.

They passed another clump of wild bushy little trees, growing high as a man's head, beside a viaduct. Now they were skirting the embankment, part of Chicago's endless, thick-stranded spiderweb of railroad tracks. Their footsteps echoed as the sidewalk led them through a brightly lighted viaduct built up of antique limestone blocks, out on another residential street looking no different than the one they had just left.

The presence of the railroad track above them reminded Andy of something Dolly had said earlier. Amtrak tickets.

But before he could raise the subject she was talking about something else. "That man on the stairs, the one who almost grabbed us again. The way he was all torn up, he must have been dying—wasn't he?"

"I don't know. At first I thought he was totally butchered. But then, the way he moved . . . I don't know what he was."

They were no longer even walking fast, just gently strolling in their deadly weariness, when they saw another police car. This vehicle was just sitting, engine idling, waiting for the next good chance to jump into action and do some law enforcement.

Dolly's nails bit into Andy's arm. "No cops," she whispered to him through clenched teeth.

"No cops. Just keep going, don't try to duck."

As soon as they were out of sight of the police car, they changed course, moving in silent agreement. Now they had turned onto a street where there were fewer trees, and the lights shone down more brightly.

Dolly said: "We're getting out of town. Or I am, anyway. You've stuck with me, so far, and if I ever find any treasure I'll split it with you. Whatever it turns out to be."

"Treasure?" Andy repeated the word mechanically, and then forgot about it. Because only now, in the brighter light, did he notice: small, so small as hardly to be noticeable, drops of someone's blood, not their own, had spattered on them both. Already the red was drying into a dull brown. The spattering must have happened before that final scene.

"No cops," Andy echoed. He could still see the pallid, bloodstained features, the greenish, animal-like eyes looking up, sparking with a horrible energy, over the woman's savaged throat. And something had gone wrong with that man's, that stranger's teeth . . . *Matthew Maule, the wizard* . . .

"Andy!"

"What?"

"We've got through this so far. Don't go catatonic on me!"

"All right. I'm all right."

. . . something in the two horrible faces seemed transposed, as if Uncle Matt could be the dead and bleeding one, and the woman whose blood he drank was only sleeping.

He had seen Uncle Matt's fangs tear a woman's throat, seen him drink her blood. Heard the sucking, gory swallowing.

How could he possibly call the cops? How was he going to tell his father and mother what he had seen?

Dad, and Mom. And Uncle John, and all the rest of the normal, loving family.

And Uncle Matt. The world no longer fit together properly. Somehow it would have to be fixed.

Beside Andy now, Dolly in a small voice murmured: "I can't go home. Don't dare go back to my apartment. That Dickon, damn him, he was one of them, he set us up for those . . . those . . ."

He had all but forgotten about Dickon. That would never do. "You're right, he must have."

"And he knows where I live."

"But not where I do."

Get away, somehow, somewhere. Get away, just to gain time to think. *Stay with the girl,* said Uncle Matt, speaking distinctly, with practiced enunciation through his bloody fangs, *wherever she may go. Help her if you can.*

They had walked on half a dozen steps farther before Andy spoke again. "You said your grandfather left you two train tickets?"

~ 12 ~

Vlad Dracula's skirmish with the Crocodile had left him temporarily exhausted. But he had been well-rested when the fight began, and after it he recovered quickly. Once he had got his breath back (so to speak) the experience had a profoundly energizing effect. He was certain that another encounter with Sobek loomed, probably at no great distance in the future; and he knew that it promised to be the hardest struggle of his life. He was sure it would be concluded only when one of them was dead.

On Wednesday night he had several times considered spending some time in search of Dickon, who had lately been doing a very effective job in keeping out of the sight of Mr. Maule. But Maule had little hope of succeeding in a search for the elder one just now, and he spent his time in other ways instead.

* * *

On Thursday afternoon, having enjoyed a few hours of vitally important rest under the Forest Preserve wetlands, Maule emerged in man-form, under partly cloudy skies, and visited his apartment again. He listened with some hope to Andy's phone message, which had been clocked in around midday. It provided him with the name and Chicago address of a student named Dolores Flamel, who, Maule supposed, was almost certainly the "Dolly" mentioned by hospital workers. Andy gave no indication that he meant to involve himself in the situation any further, and Maule saw no reason to expect him to do so—but he felt a shadow of apprehension all the same.

Maule promised himself an excursion to County Hospital sometime on Thursday night, though he expected that by that time he would almost certainly be too late to get a look at the face of the recently deceased—a final disposal would already have been made. But an after-dark visit to the department of records might gain him access to confirming evidence, such as a postmortem photograph—in some places such likenesses were routinely kept on hand for at least a year.

But all that could wait till later. Let the dead bury the dead. After hearing Andy's message, Matthew Maule prepared to call on Dolores Flamel at dusk on Thursday.

Traveling on foot, he arrived in the vicinity of her apartment building a few minutes before sunset. He was just in time to observe a young woman walking out the front door, accompanied by an astonishing double escort.

The trio moved as if they had some definite goal in mind. Both of the men were very well-known to Matthew Maule; and he did not doubt for a moment that the young woman with them must be the very one that he was looking for.

Maule was of course startled, and delighted, to have located Dickon so fortuitously. He might have swooped down and seized the old rogue at once, except for the fact that the third member of the group was Andy Keogh. Andy's presence astonished Maule and kept him at a distance, watching carefully.

His task of shadowing was made a little easier when he observed that the three were walking steadily in the general direction of Old Town and the burned-out building, and deduced that as their probable destination. But with Dickon very much on the alert, Maule found it impossible to get close enough to hear what the three were saying to each other.

Forced to remain in man-form until the sun went down, Maule had to maneuver cautiously to keep from being detected and identified, remaining more than half a block behind the people he was following. Maule had a healthy respect for Dickon's alertness and cleverness, if none at all for his character. The old coward kept looking anxiously back over his shoulder. But of course, in his case this was only normal and expectable behavior.

As soon as the sun went down, Maule changed shape and began using alternately the forms of mist and bat. In this way he made his way gradually closer to the trio and finally managed to hear something of what Dickon was saying.

What Maule heard them discussing, regarding Egypt, alchemy, and train tickets, among other subjects, made him all the more eager to seize Dickon and force some information out of him. But at the same time it became more important to learn just how deeply Andy might be involved.

* * *

When the three people arrived at their destination, Maule, focusing his keen senses on the apparently abandoned building, soon realized that others, including several *nosferatu* and at least one breather, were waiting inside, in darkness and unnatural silence. The scene had all the earmarks of premeditated ambush.

He felt at once relieved and disappointed that the one presence in which he was most interested was not on hand. There was no sign of the great Crocodile in Old Town this evening. Maule wondered whether Sobek had yet become aware of Dolores Flamel's probable importance in the realization of his goal. Maule himself had now overheard enough to feel sure of it.

But what was Dickon's purpose in guiding the two young breathers here? Surely Dickon's keen senses had informed him of the hidden gathering in the abandoned building. It began to appear likely that he was leading his two companions deliberately into an ambush.

Maule was not at all surprised when Dickon, the unconditional coward, suddenly fled, evidently without explaining his actions to either of the breathers who had accompanied him to the scene.

The watching vampire was somewhat surprised by Dolly's daring, when the young woman made her way boldly into the building. He was not at all surprised, but more concerned, when Andy followed.

Moments later, Maule was dropping out of the gray night sky as gently as a falling leaf, settling in bat-form on the intact portion of the burned-out building's roof. From that position he was soon eavesdropping on Dolly and Andy and their captors as their ominous dialogue progressed.

He heard Lambert and the other villains badgering her to turn over the list of names, and heard in their voices how utterly convinced they were of its existence.

Twice, in the final minute or two before Maule actually intervened, he had been on the very point of doing so; but his determination to first learn all he could by listening held him back a little longer.

Of course he considered it his duty to protect young Andy Keogh; but so far the young man had suffered no real damage, and it was certainly too late now to try to keep him out of the game entirely.

It had crossed Maule's suspicious mind to wonder briefly if he himself might conceivably be the true intended victim. There could be some Machiavellian plot afoot, to draw him into a vulnerable position by threatening his nephew. But the members of the ill-favored little mob in ambush were all strangers, or near-strangers, to Vlad Tepes; Lambert's was the only name he knew. It had to be something other than personal animosity against Drakulya that had brought them here.

Crouching on his rooftop perch, poised to spring into action in a fraction of a second, he listened intently to Dolly's near-hysterical but still courageous denials, Maule could bring to bear half a millennium's experience of hearing and judging liars of all degrees of skill. Thus he found her responses not entirely convincing, while simultaneously admiring the fortitude that enabled her to give them. Whether her interrogators would reach the same conclusion, should any of them survive the night, he could not be sure. Of course he did not intend to let them have their way much longer.

At the same time he had a keen desire to learn what connection these malefactors might have, if any, with Sobek. Listening, he quickly came to the conviction that these must be the very people the Crocodile found so irritating, so much like sharp stones under his feet that he was willing to pay for their detached heads.

When the fight began, Maule made an effort to avoid destroying his opponents utterly. There were a few brief moments when he could easily have finished Lambert off. Instead he had stuck the villain in the stairway, wanting to keep him available for future reference, but somehow the miscreant had managed to wriggle free.

Maule's hope for a leisurely interval in which to interrogate Lambert was shattered when one of Lambert's damned breathing auxiliaries had surprised Maule with a pistol, and even managed to wound him with a wooden bullet. From that moment on Vlad Dracula had been forced to concentrate primarily on his own survival.

That objective was soon achieved. Very quickly the fight was over, and all who had taken part in the ambush were dead, or had run away—with the sole exception of one of the breathers, the woman who had fired the gun. In his own wounded weariness, Maule had needed her healing, strengthening blood more urgently than any information she might have been able to provide. And of course when her blood was gone, it was beyond the power of any man to force her to answer questions.

Now Maule faced a new problem, the inextricable entanglement of Andy Keogh in this desperate business. Andy, by accident coming upon his adopted uncle and his uncle's victim, had seen him raise his head from the woman's throat, had most likely got a good look at the gore actually dripping from his Uncle Matthew's engorged fangs.

At that moment, caught up in the red haze of his own needs and passions, it had been impossible for

Maule to ease the young man's shock. He had instead seized the moment to pass on what his warrior's instinct considered to be essential orders.

Hastily concluding his emergency feeding, tearing himself away from the consuming pleasure as soon as he felt that his strength had been sufficiently restored, Maule had changed to bat-form, and in a few minutes caught up with Andy and Dolores as they fled.

Twice before in his long life, Vlad Drakulya had been similarly exposed in awkward situations, stumbled upon accidentally by breathing friends who, until the moment of terrible revelation, had had no clue as to his real nature. On both occasions, the effect on the friendly relationship had been disastrous.

Just what the effect was going to be this time, Maule found it difficult to predict. When Andy told his parents (as he inevitably must tell them) what he had seen, their failure to share his shock and horror must make them seem, to Andy, to be somehow implicated as well.

Well, the problem of Andy Keogh's sensibilities was an awkward one, but still it was quite minor, compared with the current challenge of sheer survival for all concerned. It would have to be dealt with later.

Maule came down in bat-form, on a tree branch a full block ahead of the couple as they continued walking, and on the opposite side of the street. In the same instant that he slid to the ground, his cell phone and fingers regained solidity. In a moment he had tapped in the number of Joe Keogh's home phone. The two men conversed hastily, Maule moving to stay behind a tree as Andy and Dolly drew near.

Maule brought Joe up to date, then added: "If she and Andy stay together, it will greatly simplify our task of protecting them both. If they should separate, our task will become several times more difficult."

Joe's voice turned querulous. "What's this about train tickets? It's the first I've heard of that. And how did he get involved with this girl, anyway? Who is she?"

"You may take it as proven that she is the grand-daughter of my late friend—I must accept some responsibility for your son's involvement, though of course I intended nothing of the kind."

There was a long pause on the phone. At last Joe said: "We'll talk about it later."

When the latest communication was over, Maule was able to take a minor satisfaction in the fact that tonight's experience confirmed the results of certain earlier experiments he had carried out in private—it was entirely feasible to morph from one body shape to another with a cell phone in one's possession. The latest generation of such devices were compact enough to participate smoothly in the transformation that a *nosferatu* body underwent on such occasions. In this the communications hardware merely conformed to the behavior of various other small items commonly carried in a vampire's purse or pockets. It was the same, of course, for his or her shoes and other clothing. Maule was slightly disappointed, though not surprised, to find he was unable to use the technology when it existed only as part of the quantum wave-function that defined the vampire in mist-form.

Now meditating on the use of his cell phone, and the struggle he foresaw in bringing his computer knowledge up to date, Maule wondered if would-be adepts at the beginning of the twenty-first century tended to employ computers in their efforts to accomplish the Great Work.

It could be argued that loading pages of text of ancient and practically undecipherable books into one's hard drive might be the magical equivalent of actually reading them. Also, would transmitting the contents electronically, into the ocean of surrounding spacetime, be the magical equivalent of reading them aloud?

Of course it was always necessary to keep up with new technology; but he had also learned, long ago, that one had to be careful not to depend too much on the very latest inventions, which tended toward the unreliable. He could remember distinctly, as if it had happened only yesterday instead of in the middle of the nineteenth century, the first time he had sent a telegram. It was the same with his first ride in an automobile, some fifty years after that.

His current foray into the wonderland of electronics was only the latest in a long series of similar efforts. Each had been necessary in its time, but each had brought only temporary respite from the rat race of ever-accelerating change. In a sense, his long life had become a prolonged childhood. As the world around him perpetually renewed itself, it had to be repeatedly reexplored.

With Andy as his tutor, he had been concentrating on trying to get his digital cable system, described by its purveyors as state-of-the-art, to work. This included the possibility of obtaining from the cable company what was called a modem, and had led him into computers and the Internet, and explained the presence of a trustworthy young breather on the scene when the unfortunate events began to unfold. Of course that project would now have to be put on hold for the time being. Another grievance against the dastardly intruder. This one was comparatively minor, but it would not be forgotten.

At one point, Joe's silence on the phone had seemed

to question whether he, Maule, should be wasting time and effort on such matters now, given the other problems that he faced.

"But Joseph, it is necessary to keep up with change. Even, or perhaps especially, when the change is somewhat unwelcome. Looked at from one viewpoint, my life has been one long keeping-up. And now that the millennium clock has turned . . ."

"I see what you mean."

The risk that Maule's domicile might again be invaded by monsters and strange magic did not make him more sanguine about the electronic tasks he meant to accomplish when he had the chance.

Even with all intrusive magic drained and swept away, by means that Maule had learned from greater masters in the past, the new systems of technology were arcane and puzzling beyond all reasonable need. But he took comfort in the fact that the telephone, the radio, automobile and electric light, had all seemed difficult to deal with when they first appeared.

Cell phone tucked away again, he continued to follow his quarry closely, trotting streets and sidewalks for several minutes in the form of a wolfish dog, and then reverting to a bat. To his relief, he was able to detect no further immediate threat hovering over the couple. Nor, when their searching eyes happened to focus on the dog, did they betray the slightest suspicion that it was anything but an ordinary animal.

As minutes passed, and still there was no sign of his chief antagonist, Maule thought he could be certain now that Sobek was not going to put in an appearance in this neighborhood of the city tonight. Perhaps the Crocodile had chosen this time to rest, or even sleep—Maule preferred to believe that even self-proclaimed gods must rest sometime.

Drifting in mist-form, Maule was able to work his way sufficiently close to the couple to hear Dolly's confession regarding the list of names.

Maule felt somewhat better about the situation, after what he considered the brisk little skirmish in Old Town. What chiefly worried him now was that Sobek, their greatest enemy, was still free and active. Once Sobek suspected that Dolores Flamel was in possession of the list of names, then she and anyone who might share her knowledge, including Andy Keogh, must stand in terrible danger.

Maule briefly considered, and then rejected, the idea of placing Dolores and Andy, under the protection of Joe Keogh and his helpers, in the safest house or apartment that could be found in the Chicago area. Such a passive strategy ran counter to his own deepest instincts.

There were also possibilities in a certain charitable refuge, located in one of the city's grimmer neighborhoods, the branch of an organization fanatically devoted to the salvation of the poor. The director of the local chapter was a fervent and reliable friend of Matthew Maule, who had helped him deal with certain monstrous difficulties brought on by a wayward client, and would certainly shelter a couple of fugitives if Matthew Maule should ask it—but the more Maule thought about it, the less inclined he was to choose that route. It would be better, his instincts urged, if the pair could get away from Chicago altogether for a time.

The couple were now very near Andy's own apartment, and it seemed obvious that they were heading there.

Maule was airborne again, when another small form came fluttering near his own bat-body, and he tensed; but in a moment he had realized that it was only Connie.

She stayed near him while, in a few terse words, he told her something of what he had discovered about the Crocodile.

In twittering speech she wondered: "You still say this Sobek cannot be a god?"

"I still say that!"

Now their two small furry forms hung side by side upon a low-voltage power line, feeling the sixty-cycle thrum through insulated feet.

Connie attempted to offer counsel. "You say he suggested that you bring him heads? Like Lambert's for instance?"

"He did."

"Well, Vlad, possibly he would accept lesser tokens— ears, noses, something of the kind—you once told me it was so in your old breathing days, when you fought the Turk, and sent back trophies to your king."

Maule managed to make his tiny bat-voice growl. "Be assured that I will never send that monster any trophies. I will hand him no head—unless possibly his own."

Andy and Dolly were still walking quiet residential streets. In the weariness that was steadily overtaking them, each block now took a little longer than the one before.

She was saying: "And I thought my Gramp was only delirious. Well, now I know better. Crazy in his way he may have been, but not delirious. And not as crazy as his partners and their playmates."

Andy said: "We've got to decide where we're going."

Though really, to judge by the route that they were following, it seemed that decision had already been made.

She shook her head. "Not back to my place, I told you I can't go there. They know where I live, and who I am. Damn that Dickon, anyway! He set us up for that!"

"Yeah, I expect he did. So we're going to my place. They didn't know my name, or where I live." At least he could hope the survivors of the nightmare fight were still in ignorance, though crazy Dickon knew who Andy was, and who his father was as well.

Everything considered, Andy just wasn't prepared to face his parents yet.

He could also hope that the surviving villains who had fled the building would be so terrified of Uncle Matt that they might be running yet—or flying. Andy could not convince himself that he had not, less than an hour ago, seen live human bodies turn into foggy ghosts and soar up shrieking through the air.

The couple had reached a corner about equally distant from Andy's apartment and Dolly's, when she looked up to check a street sign and slowed her dragging progress to a halt. "Andy, I've got to go to my car first, and get some stuff out of the trunk. It's parked a couple blocks over this way—that was the nearest space I could find to my apartment."

In a couple of minutes they were standing in front of Dolly's old car, one in a solid curb-line of vehicles, most of them in considerably better shape than hers. She swore wearily under her breath when she saw that her right front tire had now gone flat. Then the corners of her mouth turned up. "If it ain't gonna start and it ain't gonna run, no use worrying about the tires."

Andy stood by while she pulled out keys and quickly

extracted a few things from the glove compartment and the trunk. The chief burden she took on was a heavy-looking backpack.

"Good-bye, Old Paint," she told the auto as she slammed the trunk lid down. "I leave you to the city of Chicago."

The pack did seem to weigh Dolly down somewhat, especially after the exercise they had already been through, and Andy volunteered to carry it. Dolly accepted the offer without argument.

Walking the few remaining blocks, they discussed their prospects of finding a safe refuge.

Andy was trying to think beyond the next few hours. "You were talking about train tickets. When are they good for?"

"Tomorrow. The Southwest Chief leaves from Union Station, wherever that is, about four o'clock in the afternoon. The train goes all the way to Los Angeles; I'm getting off at Albuquerque."

"I'm getting on the train with you?" His tone made it something of a question.

"After tonight, I won't say no to that. Provided we both live until tomorrow afternoon." After a pause she added: "Right now I'm not going anywhere alone."

As soon as they were inside Andy's place, with the door locked, he slumped with relief. It simplified matters that neither of his housemates had yet returned.

Before doing anything else he went through all the rooms, making sure all the windows were locked, or latched in their usual summer position of halfway open, and all the shades were down. Switching on lights as he moved, he had to look in all the closets and under all the beds. That might be irrational, but so was much else that had happened in the last few hours.

After following the couple to Andy's apartment, Maule shooed Connie away, and then examined the place as thoroughly as he could while being constrained to remain outside. He had never been invited into this particular dwelling place, and anyway he thought it would probably not be a good idea for him to confront Andy again just now.

So Maule contented himself with peering into every window of the apartment (as well as he could, while Andy was lowering the shades), listening carefully, and sniffing, metaphorically, for the psychic traces of malignant vampires, or worse. It was reassuring to be able to detect no sign that any enemy had been in the vicinity. Not even Dickon, as far as Maule could tell.

Presently, reestablished in man-form, perched in a sizable crotch twenty feet up a large tree, he got out his cell phone again.

A better means of protection might have been devised for the endangered young people, given time. But as matters actually stood, it seemed best to simply encourage her to set out on her train trip—and to arrange for Andy to go with her, if that proved feasible. Protecting the two of them would be much easier if they were together. And if the enemy did not know where to find them, that would be best of all.

Having completed his rituals of security, Andy went into the kitchen and stood looking at the apartment's one telephone where it hung on the wall. To Dolly, who had followed him, he said: "I'm going to have to call my folks—unless you want to go first? Anyone you have to call?"

The young woman shook her head. "Grandpa was all the folks I had. What're you going to tell your family?"

"First, warn them about Dickon—somehow he knew my dad's name, who he was. Second, that I'm going out of town for a while. I have to tell 'em that much."

"They'll want to know why you're going, and where . . . won't they?"

Andy just shook his head. He took down the phone, then a moment later hung it back on the wall again. He just stood there with his hand holding the receiver in place. As soon as Mom or Dad came on the line, he would have to try to tell them something about Uncle Matt, or give them some other explanation for his leaving town. He couldn't imagine what that was going to be.

Sometimes, if you delayed a little, a knotty problem was solved for you. The phone rang, with his hand still on it. When he lifted the instrument, and heard the urgency in his father's voice, he began a stumbling preamble to a revelation, but was relieved of the burden of trying to finish.

"Are you all right, son?"

"I'm fine, just a scratch or two." He didn't mention the way his twisted arm still ached, or how his hand was visibly shaking, holding the phone.

"The girl who was with you, what about her?"

"She's all right too. We were in Old Town, and— and—how did you know about her?"

Consternation showed on the face of Dolly, who was listening intently to Andy's side of the conversation. She backed away slowly, fists clenched.

The voice on the phone was so tense it sounded unfamiliar. His father said: "I've just been talking with Uncle Matt."

"Oh." The world around Andy seemed to be making less sense with every moment. "Dad, I saw—I saw him there. Where we were. He was—he—"

"Yes, I know what he was doing. He saw you too. He's just been telling me about it."

That brought Andy's half-planned revelation to a full stop. "What did he say?"

"Enough. Listen, son, this problem isn't over. You understand that? Does the girl understand that?"

"I do. She does. Some of the people who attacked us got away, and—"

"Right. Now, this is vital. Whatever Uncle Matt told you to do, you have to do it. We can trust him in this kind of thing, Andy. We not only can, we have to."

"I don't know . . ."

"I do. Look, Andy, I know all about what happened tonight, and I know *what you saw,* just before you left that place. That had to be a hell of a shock, coming on top of everything else."

"Yes. Uncle Matt . . ."

"Remember, son, I've known Uncle Matt longer than I've known you."

"Dad, I don't think you understand. He was—what I saw him doing was—"

"Drinking blood, I know, he's told me all about it." His father sounded worried, but certainly not destroyed. For him the drinking of the blood had been no earth-shaking revelation. "I wish to hell I could have kept you . . . away from this kind of thing. Too late now to worry about that. Point is, you're damned lucky he was there, and you're alive. You say Dolores Flamel is unhurt. And she's right there with you now?"

"She's okay. She's here with me." Dolores was still watching and listening, her expression frozen in silent fear and dismay, her fists still clenched. Now she drew slightly closer, and Andy tilted the receiver a little away from his ear, figuring she had a right to hear as well.

His father's voice came through clearly. "Great! The two of you have to stick together. Now, you're getting on the train with her, right? Actually the train should be ideal."

"Dad, how the hell do you know about the *train*?"

Dolores was staring at him, her expression beyond astonishment. The voice on the phone said: "Trust me, Andy, I'll explain it all later. Or I'll try. Are you with me?"

"I guess so. Dad . . ."

And his father reiterated what seemed incredible orders. "If you see Uncle Matt again, and you probably will, do exactly what he tells you. I don't want to scare you, kid, but that's your best chance of getting through this alive. Yours and the girl's."

"I'm scared enough already, we almost died back there. Dad—"

"And I realize the scariest part must have been what you saw, afterwards. Well. Sometimes he does things that seem to us—unbelievable. But . . . he knows what he's doing. Oh, one more thing: better not call home, not for a while. If the cops can tie you to what happened tonight, our phone may be tapped. It isn't yet, as far as I can tell. I'll be in touch with you."

"How, Dad?"

But the the dial tone was already buzzing in Andy's ear.

~ 13 ~

A s soon as Andy hung up the phone, Dolly seized
him by the arm. "What's your father going to
do?"

"He didn't tell me. But he knows what happened,
just about as well as we do—don't ask me how—and he
doesn't want the cops involved."

"He doesn't? Why not?"

"He didn't tell me that, either." *If Joe Keogh knew
the deadly truth regarding Uncle Matt, that could be reason enough to keep them out.* "I believe him, though."

For a few moments Dolly digested this in silence.
Then she backed up to one of the kitchen chairs and let
herself drop into it. "You said we had help getting out of
that place."

"We sure did."

"From where I was, stuck back in a corner, I couldn't
see much. I could just hear that awful . . . but it couldn't
have been your father who helped us, could it? Otherwise
you wouldn't have had to phone him."

Andy had pulled up another kitchen chair, and now he let himself sit down. His body felt like an old man's. "Actually it was my Uncle Matt who got us out." When Dolly stared at him, he added: "Yep. Nathaniel Hawthorne's wizard."

"He and who else?"

"He was the only one I saw there who was on our side. The famous Matthew Maule."

Now she looked totally lost, and who could blame her? Her voice went tiny again. "Every time someone asks you for a name, do you come up with Matthew Maule? Is that the only name you know?"

"Just the only famous one, I guess. But this time I mean it. He, my uncle, was really the one who got us out. All by himself." He paused. "I'm not sure of all the details, but I know some people got killed in the process."

"From what I saw, what I heard, I can well believe that. For one thing, I heard a shot."

"Me too. I thought it hit Uncle Matt. But I guess it didn't do him much harm." Andy closed his eyes and wearily rubbed his forehead. "Look, Dolly, maybe it'll take me ten minutes to tell you everything I know about my uncle, which isn't much. But first I'm going to take a shower, get some of the stink of that place off me. And the blood. You can shower too, we've got two bathrooms. Then we'll sit down and talk."

"I can go along with that." Painfully she heaved herself up out of her chair. Her body moved like that of an old woman, fit companion for his old man.

Dolly was badly in need of a change of clothes. Andy's own garments were all much too big, but one of his housemates was on the small side. Silently pledging restitution later, if he should manage to live that long, Andy raided the fellow's bureau and closet, finding a couple of shirts and a pair of shorts that looked as if they might fit a woman of her size.

Then Andy retreated to the shower adjoining his own room. On emerging from the bath he put on clean clothes, throwing his torn jeans in the trash. He also replaced his sandals with gym shoes, which he thought would be more suitable for traveling—and for running for his life, if it came to that again.

He even shaved, to complete the tune-up, before returning to the common room—where, a few moments later, he was brought to a stunned halt on seeing Dolly emerge from the other bathroom. As Andy had expected, she was now fully if somewhat oddly clad in borrowed garments, with her sleeves rolled up, and her hair turbaned in a towel. But under her right arm the short girl was carrying what could only be a sawed-off shotgun. Some good hand with a hacksaw had neatly amputated most of the weapon's length and a good portion of its weight. Just ahead of the wooden stock and trigger guard, twin barrels terminated abruptly in bright and slightly jagged circles.

Andy had been about to remark that he was hungry, but all thoughts of food were driven from his mind. "What the *hell* is that?"

Her eyes flared as if she had been waiting for the question. "Just what it looks like. Twelve gauge, and you better believe it's loaded. Next time those people come within reach, I'm going to be ready."

After a moment Dolly added: "I thought I ought to bring some protection, coming to the big bad city. Even before my grandpa warned me." Then she went off in a delayed reaction of near-hysterical laughter. After a moment, Andy joined in.

*   *   *

Still giggling, both of them lurching along the border of hysteria, they made their way back to the kitchen and sat down, Dolly laying the shotgun on the table's edge, in handy reach.

When the crazy laughter had played itself out, both acknowledged that they were very hungry. When Andy dug the remains of a large pizza from the freezer, it seemed indeed a gift from providence. They began a rapid progress through the find, microwaving one chunk after another.

After rapidly consuming a slice and a half, Dolly took time out for a question. "If your father wants no cops, what *is* he going to do? Just forget the whole thing?"

Andy removed a piece of anchovy from his current slice before taking his next bite. "He won't just forget it, I'm sure of that. Look, I didn't tell you this before, but my Dad is—pretty capable at this kind of thing."

"What kind of thing? You mean where people are getting killed?" Fresh alarm stirred in Dolly's voice. "What is he? 'Keogh' doesn't sound like a Mafia boss."

"No, no, nothing like that. He used to be a Chicago cop, and now he runs this little private agency. He says the most important thing that you and I can do now is to stick together, no matter what."

Dolly gulped down some water, the only drink immediately available. "Yeah, I heard some of what your father was saying on the phone. But how did he know about the train tickets?"

"That I can't imagine." Andy made a helpless gesture.

Dolly wasn't getting very far trying to come up with

answers either, but she kept at it. "All right, so much for your father. How's your mother doing?"

"Fine, as far as I know."

"Good. Now, working our way through the family, tell me about your Uncle Matt. I'm sorry I had doubts about him. He's the black sheep of the family, right? The one who comes in and kicks ass when the minor hoodlums don't follow orders?"

Andy repeated the helpless gesture.

She leaned toward him over the table, squinting. "That was *really your uncle* who came in? The same one we were talking about, my gramp's friend Matthew Maule? Him and no one else? I thought he was an old man."

Tired of repeating the same shrug, Andy just looked at her.

Dolly sank back in her chair. Absently she removed the turban-towel and rubbed her damp hair with it. As if to herself, she murmured: "I have to trust you, after you almost got yourself killed, trying to help me." She picked up the last slice of pizza and set it down again, as if her appetite had suddenly failed her. "Your uncle can deal with people like that? With—with monsters?"

"You saw. Or you heard, at least. Here we are, living proof. We walked away, didn't we? And some of the monsters didn't."

They talked some more, and Andy remarked that he couldn't remember exactly how there had come to be train tickets. Reading the timetable that Nicolas Flamel had received in the envelope with his tickets, Andy learned that Amtrak Train Number 3, the Southwest Chief, departed Chicago's Union Station daily at 3:20 P.M. The tickets, for one first-class compartment, were good as far as Albuquerque, though the train went on all the way to Los Angeles. The train was scheduled to arrive in Kansas City at 10:39 P.M., Dodge City at 6:01 the following morning, and at Albuquerque 4:20 in the afternoon—allowing for the time-zone difference, twenty-six hours after departure from Chicago.

Dolly explained that Gramp had been meaning to take his girlfriend Miranda back west with him, and he'd already bought the tickets when he got really sick. When Dolly had visited him in the hospital—her car had still been running at that point—she had started to take the tickets back to the apartment, along with some of his other personal belongings. She'd left them in the glove compartment, and tonight had thoughtfully picked them up when she had stopped to get the shotgun from the trunk.

In conclusion, Dolores sighed. "So, now you're coming with me." It sounded like she didn't know whether to be relieved or worried at the prospect.

"Unless you can convince me you've got a better idea. Look, I think we're both better off sticking together than if I hang around Chicago. Besides, like I said, my Dad knows what he's doing when it comes to this kind of stuff."

"So does your Uncle Matt. Evidently."

"Evidently. Look, Dolly, those people who grabbed us—they kept talking about little white statues, and a list of names. If you know what that was all about, I think you'd better tell me."

As if to herself, she murmured: "Gramp said I was going to need help." Then she pulled herself together and spoke more briskly. "All right, Andy: I've been trying to think this out. Either you and I are in this together or we're not. After what's happened already, I have to believe we are."

When she paused, Andy simply nodded his agreement.

"So. Yes, Gramp did tell me something." She nodded emphatically and lowered her voice, as if some enemy might be listening, just outside the window. "He said there's something very valuable—I don't know what, but it's got to be very small, maybe a diamond—concealed in one of a set of little white statues. None of which, believe me, have I ever seen. I don't even know exactly what they look like, or how big they are. I'm not even sure they exist. I tried looking for them in books about Egyptian art, but the books have been no help."

Dolores fell silent, starting at the remaining pizza fragment as if her fate somehow depended on it. Eventually Andy thought he had to prod. "Go on."

"Assuming the statues are real, what must have happened is that smugglers brought them into this country from Egypt, very illegally. I don't know what connection any of the three partners, Gramp or Dickon or Tamarack, had with that. But there must have been a connection of some kind.

"Then there was some kind of mix-up, and the statues got stolen again, by people who didn't realize that they were real antiquities. So they got sold off in some kind of auction, along with lots of really junky stuff, cheap imitations and modern copies of ancient art.

"How Gramp managed to get his hands on the list of people who finally wound up with the statues I don't know. Maybe through some kind of conjuror's trick. But he did give me a list, and that's what he said it is. None of the people on it will suspect that one of their cheap decorations has a giant diamond—or whatever—hidden in it."

"Wow. You mean you're still carrying this list on you now? I thought, the way they were searching you . . . ?"

"They didn't look in the right place. They couldn't." And Dolly raised one finger and significantly tapped her own forehead. "I was always very good at memorizing."

Andy waited, half-expecting some revelation. But it didn't come, and he wasn't going to push for it. He didn't know if he wanted to know those names or not.

After they had finished the pizza, and shared what information they could regarding their terrors and chances, real exhaustion started to set in. In a little while kitchen chairs were no longer adequate for the job of holding their bodies up.

Gallantly Andy offered to let Dolly have his own room for the night, but she declined.

He tried again. "I don't expect either of my roommates will be coming home tonight. So, you can take one of their rooms, if you like. But I can't be absolutely sure. There's a chance one of them might come in and . . ."

Dolores was shaking her head emphatically. "I'm sleeping in my clothes—excuse me, in your roommate's clothes—out on the sofa, where I can hear everything that goes on. And we're putting the chain on the door, and however many locks you've got. And moving some furniture in front of it."

Scrounging a blanket and pillow from one of the two unoccupied bedrooms, and declining Andy's offer of help, Dolores soon had built a small nest for herself on the living room sofa. The shotgun rested on the floor beside her, still within easy reach.

After overseeing these preparations, Andy groggily said good night. "I'm leaving my bedroom door open. Hope you don't jump up and shoot things in your sleep."

"I won't, less'n they're real things that need shooting."

Before crawling into bed, Andy drove his body once more through his routine of inspecting all of the apartment's windows. Utterly useless, he supposed, against the kind of creatures who had almost killed him a few hours ago. But he thought the ritual might give him some chance of getting to sleep.

His night was anything but restful. It seemed that every time he started to doze off, a rush of nameless terror brought him jerking wide awake, fists clenched, heart pounding. In the borderland of sleep, someone had just pitched him into space, and he was falling.

After that had happened for the third time, there was a variation. Andy, who had actually fallen asleep, was awakened by a scream. He was on his feet and moving for the other room before he was fully awake. In the doorway he collided with Dolly, who came running toward him, still fully dressed—hands empty of the shotgun, he saw with great relief. With the contact, she threw herself into his arms.

Her sturdy body was shaking, like her voice that babbled out her fear. This was no coy seduction game— not that he had really suspected, even for a moment, that it could be.

Her face was pressed against his shoulder. She kept saying the same thing, with minor variations, over and over: "A dream . . . oh God, a horrible nightmare!"

He patted her unfamiliar back, covered by his housemate's more or less familiar shirt, and muttered the best words he could think of. "Not surprising. There. There. It's gonna be all right."

In a minute or two the worst was over. Andy gently separated himself from his new companion, and went to pull on his jeans over the undershorts in which he usually slept. Meanwhile Dolly had turned on a light, and they sat in the kitchen again, and she told him of the terrible dream. The figure of a giant crocodile had appeared to her, speaking calmly and almost rationally, and promising her more horror.

Again he muttered something about how they had to expect bad dreams, after what they had just been through.

"No, it wasn't anything like—like what happened in Old Town. I don't know if it even had anything to do with that. I never saw this—this thing before. Something like a giant lizard, standing on its hind legs and talking. And I know it sounds funny, like something you can laugh at when you wake up. But it wasn't that way, it wasn't that way at all. Oh, God, I'm not laughing."

She paused. He thought she was looking at him strangely.

He asked: "What is it?"

"Andy, I'm going to recite the names on the list, so you can hear them. Then if something happens to me—if I don't live through the night, or something like that—"

"Dolly, no—"

"No, I mean it, I'm going to recite the names and addresses. I guess I'd advise you not to write them down. But that's up to you."

*   *   *

Five minutes later, Dolly was moving back to her nest on the sofa, and Andy started back to his room.

On the way he paused in the doorway. "Do you want me to stay with you—?"

"No. No, I just want to sleep. If I can."

At last, near sunrise, Andy, back in his own bed, managed an hour or two of troubled but still healing sleep.

He awoke to bright sunlight, and saw on his bedside clock that it was seven-thirty. He had heard names and places, but he wasn't at all sure he was going to remember everything correctly. He hadn't written anything down.

Dolores was up already, sitting at the kitchen table with dark circles under her eyes. Obviously she had fared even worse than he.

"Sorry about last night," was her greeting.

"For having a nightmare? Think nothing of it. After yesterday, we're lucky we're both not completely crazy."

"I don't suppose you've got any instant coffee. I looked in the cabinets."

"I don't suppose we do. Dolly, are you sorry you told me all that stuff? Everything on your list?"

She wasn't going to answer that. "Do we leave early for the train station, or do we wait? Where is Union Station, anyway?"

"I'm not exactly sure, but we can find it."

There was literally nothing in the house to eat for breakfast, which more or less forced them into the decision to leave early.

Anyway, he could find no particular reason to think that sitting around in the apartment would be any safer than moving about the city. All through the night, and when daylight had come round again, Andy kept waiting for a police knock on the door—of course that would not be the worst possibility. Actually it would be a big step up from the crash of one of the monsters kicking the door in.

But neither happened.

Before setting out for the Loop, Andy considered leaving a message for his parents on his own answering machine. Joe and Kate had the code to access his machine remotely. But if he left a message, anyone who came into his apartment would be able to play it too. And now his Dad would be expecting him to be on the train.

Before heading out, Andy filled a modest backpack of his own, throwing in some clothes, a razor, and a toothbrush. His pack was still lighter than Dolly's. He had a little over a hundred dollars cash in his pocket, about as much as he ever carried, and could hope to buy a few essential items while en route. He knew that if he used his credit card it could provide the police—or maybe someone worse than the police—with an easy way to trace him.

Dolores lugged her backpack, which had very little in it besides a couple of borrowed garments, plus the truncated shotgun and half a dozen extra shells, that she told Andy were loaded with buckshot.

She was adamantly determined to bring the shotgun. "I don't think they inspect your bags when you get on the train, like they do at the airport."

"You're probably right. Never heard of anyone hijacking a train. If I had a gun, I'd be carrying it too."

Dolly had with her only the few dollars she had been carrying when she left her own apartment to walk to Old Town, less than twenty-four hours ago. The ruthless searchers in the ruined building had not bothered to relieve her of that small amount of cash; they had been too fanatically intent on finding something else.

At a little after eight on Friday morning, the pair eased their way out of the apartment and, after breakfasting at one of Andy's favorite stops nearby, started to make their way downtown. Aware of how thoroughly taxi drivers recorded every passenger, Andy avoided that mode of transport. There was a subway station in fairly easy walking distance, and he headed in that direction.

She and Andy were standing together inside a crowded subway car, holding spring-loaded straps to keep from falling. At this hour the mass of commuters doing without seats on the train was almost thick enough to hold any staggering bodies upright, but Andy still liked the straps for insurance. Their train was making deafening progress through a Loop-bound tunnel, when Dolly put her lips close to his ear, and shouted against the ungodly roar: "Where does your Uncle Matt live? In case something happens and I need a rescuer again."

"He's in one of those apartment towers on north Michigan. But I don't think it would be a good idea to head for his place uninvited."

"Actually I don't think so either."

Once they had emerged from underground into the crowds and bustle on the Loop's hot pavements, he shopped with her in a bargain store on State Street, paying cash for a few necessities, including some simple summer clothes and a toothbrush.

Andy was well aware that several people had seen them leaving the scene of the Old Town slaughter, and that the Chicago police might possibly be able to identify them. But so far it seemed that no one had recognized him, or Dolores either. It didn't help that crazy Dickon knew who they were. Even if Dickon proved not to be in league with the monsters, he seemed the type who was certain to spill his guts out if he was arrested.

Joe Keogh was wondering, again, if his phone line might be tapped, and for the third time today he started to run his best electronic means of checking that. Anyone who tuned in on his talks with Maule would think they had to be conversing in some kind of code. Well, there was nothing like a day or two of worrying about vampires, and worse, to start the paranoia flaring.

At a busy downtown newsstand, Andy bought a morning paper, and Dolly read it with him as they sat at a table in a nearby coffee shop. The item of immediate interest was not hard to find: a story of a woman's body, probably a murder victim, being discovered in the burned building.

She gave Andy a newly critical look, and whispered: "If you don't want to be recognized, you could get rid of that stupid earring. That's something people notice."

"Oh. Okay." He raised a hand halfway, but did not touch the metal; it would have to wait until they had some privacy again. Removing the ring in public would only draw attention.

The newspaper article tentatively identified the dead woman, but said nothing about peculiar injuries. Nor did it mention either Andy or Dolores by name. The police were looking for two people matching their general description, but that was all. Andy's earring was not mentioned. Dickon was entirely absent from the report.

There was nothing in the paper to suggest that the police had any particular reason to be interested in the granddaughter of Nicolas Flamel, or to connect the horrors in an abandoned building with a recent tenant who had died peacefully in bed.

They walked the busy downtown streets contained within Chicago's Loop of elevated train tracks. They took shelter in a bookstore against a brisk midmorning shower, and sipped iced tea in two other restaurants, too nervous to stay still for long. Thinking of Dickon, Andy kept well clear of the public library, just in case.

Somehow the hours passed.

Union Station, built below street level into a building near the western edge of Chicago's downtown Loop, offered the elite among Amtrak passengers a comfortable semi-private lounge in which to await departure. You had to show your first-class ticket to get in. Meanwhile, coach passengers were making do in a larger and less exclusive space, furnished with many chairs and the noise of competing television sets. Andy used the privacy of the men's room to get rid of his earring.

At a little after three in the afternoon, Dolly and Andy, along with a number of others, were summoned from their comfortable seats to board their train. Most travelers carried their own baggage out of the station and through a darkened and enormous shed, uncomfortably hot and thunderous with railroad noise. Once they had climbed aboard the train it was much quieter, and cool enough, with the big diesels already murmuring to drive the air-conditioning. Attentive stewards checked tickets and gave guidance. Their passenger car was a two-story affair, with a narrow, twisty stair leading to

the upper level, where a thin corridor ran the length of
the car, and the first-class compartment reserved for Mr.
and Mrs. Flamel was waiting, one of a car-long row behind individual doors of curtained glass.

The Southwest Chief pulled out right on time. A few
minutes later, it made one brief stop in the vast sprawl
of railroad yards just west of the Loop—to pick up mail,
as the intercom announced—and by a quarter to four
was gaining speed on a smooth track through Chicago's
western suburbs.

Andy and Dolly, snugly settled into the greatest luxury Amtrak afforded, a private space hardly more than
six feet by six, were breathing a joint sigh of relief.
Whether the feeling was justified or not, they felt well
rid of the perilous city.

For several hours they were content just to sit in the
compartment with the door locked, and feel the distance
lengthening between them and the horrors of Old Town.
Not until after dark did they emerge to pay their first
visit to the dining car.

Night came hurrying from east to west, advancing
at a pace much faster than any train could move, and
presently it had engulfed them. By that time, Chicago
was hundreds of miles behind, and their train had
crossed the Mississippi into Iowa.

Pulling down the window's wide shade, Dolores murmured: "I never used to be afraid of the dark. I never
used to be afraid of falling asleep."

Somehow it had vaguely boosted Andy's fragile
sense of security to learn that all meals were included
in the first-class price. When the time came, he signed
the bill, as required, in the name of Nicolas Flamel.

Privacy at table, they soon discovered, was not the norm in dining cars. A cheerful attendant led them to a table for four, which they shared with a fiftyish couple who said they were going to visit their children in California.

After a round of self-introductions—Dolly for some reason adopted the name Miranda Flamel—the conversation limped along.

The man sitting across from Andy asked: "Been married long?"

"No, actually."

The lady sitting across from Dolly murmured with sly approval that she thought a long train ride a romantic way to begin a honeymoon. Dolly looked appropriately embarrassed, and Andy was sure he looked the same.

Soon the two of them were back in their snug compartment, with the curtained door securely locked. One of the efficient attendants had evidently been in while they were dining, for the short, built-in sofa had been converted into a lower berth, neatly made up with pillow, sheets and blankets. Its upper counterpart had been pulled out from the wall and similarly made up.

Andy puffed out breath, sitting down on the lower berth. "I think we've left them all behind."

Dolly sat in the chair. "Including your Uncle Matt?"

Andy shook his head. "All bets are off where he's concerned."

"When it comes time for nighty-night, I'm taking the upper berth," Dolly announced, in businesslike tones. "You can have the lower. Looks like you're established there."

"I'm ready for some sleep." But he did not lie down,

and after a moment he added: "All I'm taking off is my shoes." He still felt the need to be ready for anything at a moment's notice.

Presently Dolly began to nod, gripped by her natural need to sleep. She slumped and twisted in the chair, trying to keep herself awake, while Andy retained his place on one end of the lower berth and tried to comfort her.

"Talk to me, Andy, help me keep awake."

This was craziness, he thought; she was going to have to sleep sometime, and he told her so.

"Sure, all right, I admit that. But I want to get really tired first."

"Okay," he said. "If you want talk, I'll try."

He told her how he was, or had been, enrolled at TMU as a student, taking some math along with computer science and related subjects.

Conversation sputtered and lagged. Dolly decided suddenly to get up and walk about the train a little. Andy didn't want to let her go alone, and put his shoes back on.

The club car held no great attraction, and they made their swaying way to the observation car, which was no better. The walking around really didn't seem to help, and Andy feared that Dolly was well on her way to a second night of sleep-deprivation and terror. Only now, watching his companion blink and stumble, did he begin to realize how much afraid of going to sleep she really was.

Back in the compartment, she once again clung chastely to him, and pleaded: "Talk to me, Andy. Give me something else to think about."

This unnatural strain was going on too long, he thought. He was beginning to be seriously worried about her mental state.

Whenever Andy momentarily ran out of things to say, Dolly took over, talking steadily in an effort to stay awake and to distract herself. Now she was babbling about going back to her home in Albuquerque.

" 'Course it was never really my home, it was Grandpa's. There'll still be some of his stuff there I'll have to dispose of somehow. When I'm sure there's no more legal stuff to do, regarding his death.

"And if the landlord hasn't thrown all of Gramp's stuff out of the house by this time. If that's happened, we're evicted, I don't know where I'm going to stay when I get to Albuquerque."

Andy tried to be reassuring. "Not a problem. We'll work something out." He still had his own credit card with him, and he would use it if necessary, for a hotel room or whatever. Forget about trying to keep his location a secret; it seemed the cops weren't interested in finding him, not yet anyway.

Besides, his father knew where he was, which was more comforting the more he thought about it. Andy didn't mention it to his companion, but he wasn't going to be surprised if he saw his Dad waiting for them when they got off the train.

Dolly was going on again about the last conversation she'd had with her grandpa, on the day he died.

"Though on that last day I think he really was delirious about half the time. So I can't really be sure of anything he told me."

"Except the list."

She didn't answer. Outside the shaded window, outer darkness held dominion. The train swayed and rumbled through the night, dozens of wheels chattering their way over a million joinings of the rails. Stretches of rough track made the carriage lurch and sway with sudden violence, evoked new noises. Still this train was vastly quieter than the subway.

"I'm going to give it a try," Dolly decided suddenly, and climbed nimbly into the upper, where she stretched out with a kind of gasp. It sounded to Andy like she might be going right to sleep. But she had not been in her berth for more than a few minutes before she started talking in her sleep. For a time, Andy tried to listen, but it didn't make much sense.

"... crocodile ... a stone ... worth more ... more than anything ..."

He had to slide out of his berth and stand in the swaying little space. "Dolores? Dolly, wake up. You're having a bad dream."

But it seemed she was awake already. "Oh God, Andy. I don't know what I'm going to do." He thought he heard the barrel of the shotgun click on something hard as she rolled over on the narrow, padded shelf.

It was not yet quite ten o'clock, Chicago time. Dolly tried again to let her weary body sleep, and once more jerked awake babbling something more about a crocodile.

This time she sought out Andy in his swaying, narrow bunk, and clung to him fiercely. But plainly sex was still about the farthest thing from her mind—and also from his. Andy's own private nightmare was still very much with him, effectively quenching carnality.

Dolly was extremely cold, shivering despite the fact that she had wrapped herself in all the blankets she could gather.

Andy was getting worried that she was really ill. "It's not that cold in here. You got a fever?"

"It's no fever, I'm just cold."

"After what happened in Old Town—what almost happened to us—you're bound to have some kind of a reaction."

She shook her head savagely. "Not to that, to my damn dreams! And I tell you I'm freezing. Like all the cold of all the Arctic rivers in Siberia running through. Just hold me, Andy. Hold me, damn it, and don't let me go to sleep again."

He did the best he could. But before he was aware of it, she had somehow drifted off.

"A crocodile inside a statue? Then a stone in a crocodile?" Dolly's voice went up in an anguished squeal. Andy was starting to worry about the people in the adjoining compartments. "Gramp, are you going nuts on me?

"In the crate . . . six crocodiles . . . in one of them . . ."

In spite of everything, Andy too eventually drifted off, into his own bad dream, having to do with a woman with huge earrings, and fangs to match.

~ 14 ~

When Joe Keogh answered the phone in his downtown Chicago office on Friday afternoon, John Southerland was on the other end of the line, reporting from Union Station. Dolores Flamel and Andy Keogh had just boarded the Southwest Chief. It was the word Joe had been waiting for.

John added: "They were both still on the train when it pulled out. We made sure of that." Then there was a hesitation on the phone. "They won't do anything stupid, will they? Like getting off before they get to Albuquerque?"

Joe's small traveling bag was resting at his feet, all packed, ready to make a quick start as soon as he was sure about his son and the girl. "I don't know why they would. But my kid does crazy things sometimes. Or probably he wouldn't be in this mess." Reaching for another stick of chewing gum, he had half-consciously unwrapped it before he remembered that he had one in his mouth already. A moment later he had two. "See you at Meigs, soon as we both can get there."

"Right."

Descending from his office and grabbing a cab for the short trip to the small lakeshore airfield, he put his cell phone to use again, making sure to keep Kate informed as well as he could.

Meigs had been built, decades ago, on a thin tongue of filled-in land extending into the lake, broadened enough at the base to accommodate the Adler Planetarium and the 12th Street Beach. The peninsula and its single runway projected more than half a mile south along the lakefront east of McCormick Place.

It hadn't taken Joe long, thanks to certain connections, to arrange for a quick charter of the fast swept-wing jet, much smaller than a commercial airliner, whose door now stood open and ready for him and John to climb on in. The passenger compartment, comfortably furnished and sealed off by a bulkhead from the crew cabin forward, had eight uncrowded seats, only two of which were occupied this afternoon.

Minutes later the thrust of the twin engines pressed them both back in their seats with the acceleration of takeoff.

Joe thanked God that he was able to afford leasing the jet. Very rarely had he found it necessary to call on the reserve of power represented by the Southerland money; but fortunately it was there when needed. There would be no need to strain the resources of his own small company.

There were several reasons why Joe Keogh had abandoned all thought of using commercial aviation in this case. One was, of course, the sheer need for speed and efficiency. A second reason was less obvious. Having on previous occasions tried his best to defend himself against some of Maule's exotic enemies, Joe felt strongly disinclined to go another round without the aid of firearms—properly loaded ones, of course.

The regrettable necessity of sometimes carrying a gun was rendered a little easier in some of the western states, where a man—or woman—could still strap on a six-gun and cartridge belt, and walk the streets in perfect legality. Of course staying legal was about the least of his worries at the moment.

As the small chartered jet rose into the air, he got a good look at the afternoon sun glinting on some of the city's most impressive towers, including the one housing Maule's apartment, less than three miles away. If all was going according to plan, those rooms would be empty now.

The first destination of the private jet was Albuquerque, and it was there in a few hours, outracing the Southwest Chief by almost a full day.

John Southerland was dropped off in the clear sunlight of a New Mexican summer afternoon. In less than half an hour Joe's aircraft was airborne again, this time with himself as its sole passenger.

Now the small plane gave the sun a good race westward. The time was still sunlit early evening when Keogh's aircraft landed at the small but busy airfield serving California's Monterey peninsula. Joe Keogh took note of the fact that his chartered small jet, which usually drew some interest when it landed, attracted none at all at the little airport near Monterey. This, compared to other airports he had seen, was not exactly your low-rent district; a small line of similar aircraft already stood waiting on the ramp, like taxis in front of some ordinary hotel.

A glance at a railroad timetable assured him that the Southwest Chief, if still on schedule, ought at that moment to be approaching Kansas City—if Maule was proceeding on his own chosen schedule, he should be getting aboard the train quite soon.

Maule had sounded confident of making the connection—but then he almost always sounded confident. The vampire had made his own arrangements for some kind of flight west out of Chicago, and Joe didn't know the details, or particularly want to know them. He had no doubt that after dark the man he knew as Matthew Maule could easily enough board any grounded aircraft, guarded or unguarded, that happened to be scheduled for a flight in some convenient direction. Efforts to maintain security were all virtually meaningless where Uncle Matt was concerned.

One difficulty that might slow him down a bit was that in June, at the latitude of Chicago, empowering night came late to vampires. If forced by circumstances to depart before sunset, Maule might have been compelled to buy a ticket.

On the ground in the mild California evening, Joe made arrangements for the plane to be held in readiness. Then he got himself and his small traveling bag into a rented vehicle, consulted a necessary map, and started to drive the winding roads of the peninsula toward the coastal village of Carmel.

Carmel, on the southern coast of the peninsula, seemed to have won a resounding victory in the war on poverty, but was a little short of parking spaces. The address that Joe Keogh wanted turned out to be that of a small house, on a lot overgrown with trees and shrubs and flowers, in varieties that Joe had never seen anywhere but California, within smell of the ocean. It ought to be an easy walk to the beach, though Joe hadn't actually seen the water yet. Only the well-to-do lived in houses like this one—or like any of the others on the narrow, almost countrified street, on the fringe of what here passed for a downtown district.

If there were only a minimum of sidewalks, it was certainly not because the population could not afford them. They tended to park their Mercedes and Jaguars where the sidewalks would have been, had there been any room for sidewalks beside the narrow roads, under the overhanging, exotic-looking trees and shrubs.

Joe managed to park his modest rental vehicle only about a block from the address he wanted, got out of the car and stretched his legs. The sun was down now, and mellow streetlights had come on. It wasn't raining, and didn't really look like it was going to rain, but the sky before sunset had been faintly tinged with gray, and there was a heaviness in the air that smelled and felt like seawater.

The building he now approached on foot was of one story, and only modest size. It seemed to have its living quarters in the rear, while the front had been somewhat remodeled to house one of the many local upscale antique shops on one of the side streets just off Ocean Avenue.

Foot traffic here on the fringe of the business district was fairly brisk. It was the time of day when you might expect some retailers to close, but Joe saw to his relief that the door of the shop was standing open.

Most of the building's front, remodeled for business purposes, was taken up by a broad window. The window's protective steel cagework had been mostly rolled aside, allowing the eye of the tourist access to a somewhat exotic display. Gazing into it, Joe had the feeling that this time he had hit paydirt. If his eyes were not tricking his hopeful imagination, there were not just one but two small plaster statues on display, each portraying a somewhat crocodilish figure standing upright on its hind legs. As far as he could tell, they matched Maule's rather detailed description exactly, and were absolutely identical. They stood facing each other across a display of trinkets, curios, and oddments, most of which were probably assessed at vastly greater worth.

Neither of the statues bore a visible price tag, but then nothing else in the window did either.

Two statues, out of a diminished number that still remained unbroken. The odds ought to be very good indeed that one of the pair before him held the grand prize.

Joe drew a deep breath, and tried without much success for a moment of calm, of something as close as he could get to meditation. Then he went into the shop.

The interior was crowded with a wild assortment of stuff, everything from clocks to stuffed animals, as seemed appropriate for this kind of business. The lighting, mostly from small, pink-shaded lamps, could have been better. In the rear, a curtained doorway led off to what must be living quarters.

The man behind the small and antique counter was alone in the shop, and his black T-shirt and large size did not fit Joe's preconceived image of an antique dealer. Tattoos on his massive forearms rather suggested the renegade biker.

But he spoke up courteously enough. "Can I help you?"

It took Joe perhaps half a minute to feel absolutely sure, but then he did. This fellow was no vampire.

Joe had already decided that in this case there was no use being coy, pretending at first to be interested in some other object. He said: "The pair of little white statues in the window. They look interesting."

The man appeared suddenly to take a keener interest in his customer. "Was kind of hoping somebody might recognize 'em."

Moving slowly, the owner went to get one of the statues out of the display, and with a faint smile held it up for Joe's inspection. But he made no move to hand the statue over.

Still carrying it, he moved back behind his counter. "Actually, I picked 'em up more for decoration than anything else. Strange little buggers, and at first I didn't think they were worth much."

"And now you do?"

The man was going to get around to that in his own way. "This one I'm holding is slightly damaged—see the little chip here in the back?"

Joe said: "I didn't notice." Down near the feet, a little spot of something dark was showing through the white. "You think that makes it more valuable?"

The man was smiling faintly. "Had it on my mantelpiece back in the living quarters, trying to decide what to make of it, and the cat knocked it off. It fell on the fire irons and chipped. Ever meet a clumsy cat? Maybe this one knew what it was doing."

The animal, massive and dark-furred, seemed to come from nowhere, and hopped up on the counter even as it was being talked about. As Joe watched, it gave the dark spot on the statue's surface one curious sniff, and then turned away disdainfully.

"Does look like it might have some history behind it," Joe remarked.

"Maybe you could tell me something about that."

"How would I know?"

"You could tell me that too. See, when the little chip flaked off, some interesting contents came into view." And the man in the black T-shirt went on to explain to Joe how he, aware that something very unusual had been revealed, but not at all sure what, had poked at it very carefully and had at last taken a small sample of the organic-seeming material now visible inside.

Joe felt compelled to make some comment. "That a fact?"

"Fact. Right now that sample is at a lab at one of California's famous universities. You don't need to know which one."

"I don't see why I'd need to know that, no."

"I expect I'll get a report in a day or two, should provide me with some evidence of what I've got. Until I can figure out what the something is, I didn't want to take any chances. You from around here, by the way?"

"No, actually."

"Let me guess. The way you sound—Chicago?"

"I've been there."

"Yeah. Well, how much would you give me for one of these?" He placed the tip of a huge finger precisely on the statue's head.

"A thousand dollars," Joe promptly offered. He thought that starting any higher than that would be sure to set off an alarm in the other's suspicious brain. At best the deal would certainly be delayed.

"Apiece?"

Joe tried to project signals of an inward struggle, of

a man being forced to the limit of his budget. "Eight hundred apiece."

The biker behind the counter was somewhat overweight, but the hands he spread out looked strong enough to tear up a Chicago phone book.

"When a tough guy from Chicago comes offering a thousand bucks for my little thing here—that makes me think I better wait a little, until I can figure out just why he thinks it's worth that much."

Joe gave an indifferent shrug. "I like its looks. And I wouldn't count on someone coming in tomorrow with a better offer—how long have you had them here?"

The man didn't answer that.

"All right, a thousand each." Joe let his shoulders sag. "But that's the absolute limit."

The man was smiling faintly, very slightly shaking his head. "I'm about to close up for the night. We can both think the situation over. Wouldn't want to make a deal that left either of us unhappy. I'm open again at nine in the morning, if you want to come back."

Joe backed away a step or two. "Might do that. Anywhere around here that a tough guy from Chicago might be able to get a hotel room?"

"My name, by the way, is Turner." The shop owner reached into one of his pockets, and there followed an exchange of business cards.

Then Turner helpfully described a couple of possibilities for his potential customer.

Between gasoline prices and the fear of power outages, the tourist season was a little slow, and Joe had no trouble finding a guest cottage. This was the simplest accommodation readily available, surrounded by a fantastic floral display of bushes. He paid a high cash price in advance, and signed for the bed with a name not legally his own, but which matched that on the business cards he was currently carrying, and for which he could have produced additional documentation on demand. On this occasion no one demanded anything.

A restaurant chosen at random from a handful within walking distance served the visitor a tasty dinner—also paid for in cash—for which he had little appetite. After dinner he turned in early for some much-needed sleep. The biker wasn't going anywhere tonight, not when he hoped to find out more about his treasure in the morning. But Turner would probably not be getting much sleep, either. Joe set his mental alarm clock for 5:00 A.M. local time, which meant 7:00 in Chicago.

When Joe returned to the antique shop just a little after sunrise on Saturday morning, freshly shaved and showered, and munching a jelly doughnut picked up on the way, he studied the place carefully as he approached. Again he had parked a block away. The sign on the front door showed the place was definitely CLOSED. The steel cagework had been deployed over the window glass, but Joe could see in well enough to determine that neither statue was any longer on display.

At the moment, streets and sidewalks were practically empty of strolling or jogging people or moving cars. Going to one side of the building, sliding around and through a heavy growth of exotic bushes, advancing one step at a time with great care, he discovered that the back door had been forced open, with little splinters of raw wood showing around the lock, and then reclosed, but not quite tightly. Whatever alarm system might have been attached must have been disabled.

A little whimper of sound was coming from somewhere inside. Joe's first impression was that it might be coming from an unhappy cat. From there, the possibilities went downhill.

He thought of knocking on the door frame, but then he decided not. The sun was well up now, and he was ready to take a chance.

The battered door swung open in almost perfect silence upon well-oiled hinges, revealing a small and simple kitchen. From farther inside the living quarters came additional sounds, a little cheerful whistling, and then a repeat of the mewing, like a suffering cat.

Joe Keogh needed something like a full minute to advance some twelve or fifteen feet inside the house, traversing the tiny kitchen and a short angle of hallway. Just ahead, a hanging curtain blocked a doorway. With the curtain where it was, Joe still couldn't see anything of importance, but with every step he advanced he could hear a little better.

When he got within an arm's length of the curtain, he could see around its edge to get a fair view of the room beyond.

He owned a nice home, about two thousand miles away in suburban Chicago, and for several minutes now a part of him had been wishing that he had stayed there. Now the urgency in the wishing ramped up sharply. As usual, Joe Keogh recognized a vampire when he took the trouble to look at one carefully.

A *nosferatu* visitor, one who happened to have something very wrong with his head, but could still manage a little cheerful whistling, was standing over the man in the black T-shirt. The latter was stretched out on a table, which now and then creaked under his weight, and something had been done to him to keep his massive limbs from moving. Right now something that looked even worse was being done to him as well. The vampire was bending over him, sampling blood like vintage wine, meanwhile slowly peeling his scalp from his living head, like taking the skin off an orange.

He who feasted on Mr. Turner was a big man too, maybe not quite as big as Turner himself, but Joe had no doubt that this one was perhaps an order of magnitude stronger.

For the last half minute Joe had been moving his right hand slowly, concentrating on complete silence in the effort to get his revolver out of his shoulder holster.

Now the vampire turned his head a little, affording Joe a better look at the horrible injury that had left the predator with no teeth to speak of, forcing him to forgo biting in his quest for blood. About half the lower jaw was missing, the great wound sheathed in repulsive scar tissue and raw scabs. Knowing something of the *nosferatu*, Joe could imagine that it was halfway through the process of growing back, from one side to the other. No teeth were visible, except for the broken stump of one of his two main fangs, the eyeteeth of his upper jaw. The stump looked too stubby to be of much use, though at the moment it was bluntly swollen.

Maule had described a vampire, Lambert, who had come to look like that, since saying and doing things displeasing to Uncle Matt. At the moment Lambert looked not much better off than his victim, except that the fresh blood around what was left of Lambert's mouth was not his own.

It would all have to do with the little statues, of course, and where were they? No sooner had Joe thought that than he saw them. There they were, or what was left of them, rather, a thick scattering of white chips and larger fragments on a sideboard at the far side of the small parlor, under a pink-shaded lamp. The top of the sideboard seemed to have been swept clear of other objects, to make a kind of workbench, and some blackish organic stuff was scattered with the white chips.

Meanwhile, some part of Joe's suspicious mind kept telling him how very strange it was that he could have worked his way as close as this to a *nosferatu* without his presence being detected—but suddenly an explanation suggested itself: Lambert's massive head injuries might well have affected his hearing.

Right now other matters were claiming Lambert's full attention. Streams of Turner's blood were simply running down on the table, being wasted. He continued to make peculiar noises while he was being peeled, but none of his noises was loud enough to be heard out on the street. Joe could only suppose, watching from as remote a psychic position as he could manage, that the vampire had done something to Turner, maybe to his throat, that prevented any serious outcry.

Now at last Joe had his pistol out. The extraction had taken just a fraction of a minute longer because of the four inches of cylindrical silencer on the end of the stubby revolver barrel.

Lambert may have heard that last, comparatively rapid movement, for suddenly he lifted his head and looked through the gap beside the curtain, directly at Joe.

With the back of his left hand, Joe pushed the curtain completely open. To Lambert he said quietly: "You did your best to kill my son."

Lambert's eyebrows went up. Of course he would know about wooden bullets. And now, though caught off-guard in daylight, he was good at dodging them—but in his half-crippled condition he wasn't quite good enough. Joe's first shot, making only a vicious little spit of sound, just grazed the vampire's turning, dodging torso. The second missed its target altogether, as Lambert faked a flight through the doorway leading to the shop, then spun around instead to charge.

That was a mistake. The third shot split Lambert's breastbone, the wooden impact sending him crashing back and down, shattering and crushing antiques. Joe stepped in through the curtained doorway, took calculated aim at the writhing figure on the floor, and put a fourth little slug of *lignum vitae,* so heavy it wouldn't float in water, right through the *nosferatu* head.

That finished him off. Joe had been half-expecting Lambert's body to disappear almost at once, as was the way with elder vampires, but evidently Lambert was too young to go that route. Therefore the Carmel cops would sooner or later find his body, or some remainder of it anyway, and take an interest in his killing. So Joe would do well to get rid of the pistol—but not just yet. He decided that he'd better reload instead.

What was left of Turner had been knocked off the table in the flurry of action, and when Joe bent over him he could see that what was left of the man's life had now run out. Keeping his feet out of a puddle of blood, Joe turned to the sideboard and ran his gaze over the debris of the statues in the light of the pink lamp. Only white chips and what looked like mud.

A moment later, Joe was kneeling beside the remains of Lambert, forcing himself to go quickly through the vampire corpse's pockets. There was nothing like a magic gemstone to be found.

He had straightened up again, and was about to

start the process of reloading his revolver, when a faint sound came from the rear of the building. Someone—or something—was trying the broken rear door. Was opening it and coming slowly in.

There was only one other way out. Joe moved with deliberate speed to get himself through the other curtained doorway, leading out into the shop. There he was delayed for a full second, by the mortal certainty that if he opened the shop door leading out to the sidewalk, all kinds of alarms were going to go off.

As he looked back through a slit of curtain into the room he had just left, his blood turned cold inside his veins. The figure that had just entered the little parlor from the rear looked a lot more like a crocodile, walking on its hind legs, than it did a man.

Sobek. Joe came near whispering the name aloud. The thing was not hurrying, but careless of what noise it made. It took in the parlor with one sweeping look, then went straight to the sideboard, where it briefly studied the remains of two crushed statues, obviously finding in the litter nothing of great interest.

In the next moment Sobek turned, and his inhuman yellow eyes brushed Joe. The man cringed, certain that he had been noticed. But it was as if the monster had no interest in the accidental presence of another human being.

A dead vampire, however, was quite another matter. Sobek effortlessly picked up Lambert's slowly shriveling body and began to eat him, approaching the meal in gourmet style.

Forgetting about alarms, Joe grabbed the gnarled antique knob of the shop's front door, at the same moment holstering his revolver. A moment later he was out on the sidewalk, walking briskly in the lovely California morning.

Some ten minutes later, there was movement on a beach on the fringe of Carmel's residential area, where huge gray twisted logs of driftwood lay stacked in bizarre shapes.

The Crocodile had come out of the water here, shortly before dawn, leaving a slight trail as he crawled up the beach, a trail that abruptly changed from slide marks in sand to a set of prints made by the shod feet of a manlike walker on two legs.

Now, having accomplished the same transformation in reverse, he was going back into the water again.

A young man in formal evening dress, tie undone and reeling with the effects of an all-night drug binge, regarded the apparition with more amusement than terror. "Hey, buddy, you got the wrong coast. This ain't Florida."

The Crocodile gave him one yellow-eyed look over its scaly shoulder, but returned no answer as it slid into the gentle surf.

~ 15 ~

*I*n Illinois, the train had stopped at Naperville and Mendota, Princeton and Galesburg, before rumbling on into darkness at Fort Madison, Iowa, on the west bank of the Mississippi. A little before eleven o'clock, local time in yet another state, the Southwest Chief slowed again. This time the darkness outside the car dissolved in a bright glare of artificial light.

Andy checked his watch. "This has to be Kansas City. Should we get out and stretch our legs?" He thought they might as well, they sure as hell weren't sleeping.

"Okay." Dolly sounded resigned but not unwilling. "Sorry I'm keeping you awake."

"Forget it."

Putting on their shoes, they descended to pace the open concrete platform. The night was warm, somewhat sticky with humidity. Swarms of wanton insects assaulted electric lights on poles. At this hour, very few other passengers had decided to get up and stretch their legs. Most of those who did were looking for some relief from their long ordeal in single seats in coach.

"Andy, I don't feel like—what's the matter?"

He took her by the arm and pulled her to a spot on the platform where there was no one near. "Thought I just saw something—that darted under the train. Like there was something, someone, moving right under our car." It was too dark under the train for anyone to see much of anything, but he could tell that there hardly seemed room for a human being.

Quickly Dolly bent to look. None of the few other people near at hand seemed to be paying the least attention to their goings-on.

Now Andy heard strange sounds that seemed to emanate from right beneath the train: a scrape of something hard in gravel, a muffled outcry from what might well have been a human throat. His imagination, well-stocked of late with images of horror, immediately presented him with several gory scenarios, each worse than the one before.

No one else on the platform was looking under the train. No one appeared to be hearing or seeing anything bizarre.

He bent once more, trying hopelessly to see, then straightened up. "I'm not going to crawl under and look." He took Dolly's arm in a firm grip. "Let's get back on."

Reboarding, they passed a sleepy-looking trainman on watch at the door. When they were well inside the car, she whispered: "Andy. There was someone under there. There was, I swear it."

"I know." He was wondering how much more her nerves could take. Or his.

*   *   *

Shortly after eleven, the Southwest Chief pulled out of Kansas City, only a few minutes behind schedule.

Andy wasn't sure whether there had actually been anyone under the train or not, or what might have happened to them. But a few minutes in the open air seemed to have done Dolly some good. She seemed to have recovered some energy and alertness, and no longer wanted to be held.

"Andy, I'm still afraid to sleep. Don't know when I'll have another chance to take a shower, so I'm going to try it now." The coffin-sized subcompartment containing the shower did double duty as a private toilet, and so far they had used it only in the latter function.

"Maybe I can wash some of this fuzz out of my brain," she added. Then, absently, as if it did not really matter: "I trust you to close your eyes when necessary."

"Sure." He thought the only difficulty he might have with his eyes would be in trying to keep them open.

She opened the narrow door to the tiny plumbing module and surveyed the interior, eyeing the nozzle overhead beside the shielded light, and the drain in the floor. "Looks just about like the shower in my mom's old RV. Close down the potty lid and pull the chain for water."

"Okay."

"I have to leave my towel out here, 'cause there's not going to be a dry spot inside this iron maiden. My shotgun's under the covers in the upper berth, just in case you need it."

"Right." Andy nodded soberly; the possibility still seemed all too real. So far Dolly had managed to keep the weapon out of sight of the sleeping-car attendants, putting it back in her bag whenever she left the compartment.

* * *

Now Andy took a peek around the edge of the lowered window shade. Looking out into the night from the lighted compartment, it was impossible to see anything but darkness anyway. A moment later, the muffled noise of water running in the shower blended with the endless roaring murmur of the train.

Cutting through these sounds almost immediately came a sharp tap on the door to the corridor. Andy got up, decided he had better leave the shotgun where it was, and twitched the curtain cautiously aside from the door's glass panel. Uncle Matt was standing in the narrow passage, neatly dressed in what looked like a new suit, not quite so dark as the one that had been torn to shreds in Old Town. No monstrous abnormalities protruded from his handsome mouth. His clean-shaven lips and chin were free of stains, and had nothing in the least abnormal in their shape.

He spoke just loudly enough for Andy to hear him above the rumbling of the train. "May I come in?"

It was as if some part of Andy's mind had been expecting this visitation, and he did not hesitate. "Yes, of course." He opened the door, at the same time edging his body sideways, making room for the other to enter the tiny compartment.

Uncle Matthew Maule came in, looking the same as ever—but no, at a second look, not quite the same. He was now older, with a touch of gray in the dark hair, carrying the appearance of a vigorous man of sixty.

"You look . . ."

"More mature than you have known me." Uncle Matt nodded. "Yes. Well, at this age I shall be more convincing to Ms. Flamel as a friend of her grandfather. Which indeed I was."

For a brief moment Andy considered firing questions having to do with disguise or makeup. But that subject was relatively unimportant, and he let it go. There was a different kind of stumbling block to be got over first.

"Dolly's in the shower," he informed their visitor.

"Yes, I heard the water start. I wanted the chance to talk with you alone. After that, there are important things that I must say to both of you."

Andy nodded his agreement. "Sit down, Uncle Matt."

Maule briefly delayed that move. Evidently he had somehow already become aware of the shotgun inside the backpack resting in the upper berth. He slid the weapon briefly out of its wrappings, regarding it with what seemed cheerful approval before he put it back.

Then Maule bowed his acceptance, folded the upper berth partially up, where it would be out of the way of anyone who sat upon the lower, then planted himself gracefully in the single chair. Andy took the foot of the lower berth. The two men were facing each other, both next to the huge, completely shaded window.

Andy said: "I have to thank you for saving our lives."

"You are most welcome." A slight pause. "Young Andrew, I am curious. I would like to know why you gave the miscreants my name, when they asked for yours."

"You heard that? You had that place bugged, somehow?"

"No, not bugged. I was nearby. Close enough to hear directly."

Andy just looked at him, waiting for more explanation. When it was not immediately forthcoming, he pounded a fist gently on the armrest. "Why did I tell those slime-bags I was Matthew Maule? I don't know, it just popped into my head." He paused briefly. "You want to know the truth? By then your name had begun to sound to me like some kind of magic incantation. I mean the way that crazy Dickon reacted to it, and so did Dolly. She told me 'Matthew Maule' is a wizard's name."

"Not altogether inappropriate. But perhaps it is time I adopted a new one." The dark eyes were twinkling faintly with something that Andy took for amusement.

The car swayed viciously, rounding a slight turn. The whole train rattled and roared. Inside the compartment the ongoing noise was not really very loud, but there were moments when the side-to-side vibration could threaten to throw you from your seat.

Uncle Matt sat at his ease, attentive, waiting. After a moment, Andy said: "Before we left Chicago, I talked with my father on the phone."

"I am aware of that."

"It seems you know just about everything."

Maule shook his graying head. "Far from it, I assure you."

"Whatever. Dad told me to follow any orders you might give."

"And that astonished you."

"It did."

"Very fresh in your mind, even as you were speaking with your father, was that last image you had of me. Only moments before you saw me I had killed a woman—and several men—and you saw me drink her blood."

Andy's throat felt very tight. "That's right."

Uncle Matthew nodded slowly. He did not seem to be uncomfortable with the way the discussion was going. He had turned very serious, now that they were getting to the point, but gave no indication of anything like shame or guilt. He was taking his time to frame his next statement, not at a loss for words but choosing them with extreme care.

Gently he pulled one edge of the window shade very slightly aside, and when he spoke again he was looking out the window into darkness. "I have truly enjoyed trains. Remind me to tell you, sometime, about my first train ride. I was sealed inside a box. Larger than your standard coffin, but even smaller than this." He looked around the little first-class compartment with a trace of disapproval. "Boxes were not, of course, a part of the regular passenger accommodations, which were quite roomy."

Carefully he restored the shade to its proper position, and once more faced Andy. "Over the last two decades I have come to respect your father, as a man of considerable practical wisdom."

"I've always thought of Dad that way." Andy wasn't sure if this talk could get anywhere, or even where he wanted it to go. But he had to try. "You stand very high in his estimation. But when I saw you Thursday night . . . Dad didn't even sound surprised when I told him. And now you admit it."

"Let us say I acknowledge the fact. 'Admit' implies wrongdoing."

Andy made a small sound, not quite a word.

Maule went on, unperturbed. "Since before you were born, your father and mother have known of the essential ways in which I differ from ordinary men. They have accepted me as I am. So have your Uncle John and his dear Angie. The rest of your family knows nothing of those differences—no more than you have known, up till now."

Andy was stubbornly shaking his head. He was groping for answers, hoping to find some way through the horror, or around it. "Right, my Dad vouches for you. He says you've done more for us, for the family, than I can ever imagine. I believe that, though I don't know all the details. But I can't believe my mother and father have ever seen what I—"

Maule interrupted, harshly. "Your parents and I were bound together by ties of blood, and more than blood, before you were conceived. It is a complicated story, too much so to tell you now, but when you hear it someday you will find it shocking. Kate and Joseph fear me, sometimes, but they love me too. Whatever your father may have told you about me is quite true."

"All he's really told me on that subject is I should follow your orders."

"And will you do so?"

"I can't remember the last time my folks gave me any real bad advice. And whatever else you did, back there in Chicago, you saved our lives."

In a sudden lightening of mood, Uncle Matt smiled at Andy and reached with a long arm to clap him firmly on the shoulder. "Then be of good cheer. Speak openly of me to your parents, when you have the chance to talk to them in private, and tell them I say they should do the same. They will have astounding revelations for you, now that you are in on the great secret."

Seeing that Andy still sat as if frozen, Maule went on relentlessly. "The truth is that the blood of animals serves me very well for sustenance—most of the time. In war, a man takes what he needs from a defeated enemy. Were I not a hemophiliac in the literal meaning of the word, a lover of blood, did I not share in the nature of the *nosferatu*, you would not have been alive at that point to see anything. Instead it is virtually certain that the woman I killed, or one of her companions, would have been drinking your blood instead—and that of Dolores Flamel."

It took Andy a long time to answer. Finally he asked: "The nature of the what?"

"It will be easier to explain if I first give a short demonstration. I prefer to do that only once, so I will wait till Ms. Flamel has rejoined us."

Vaguely Andy was aware that several moments ago the water had ceased running in the shower—it was barely possible to hear the difference, under the steady roar of railroad passage.

The door to the combination cubicle opened a few inches, and a bare and pinkish arm came groping out. "Towel!" a muffled voice commanded.

It was Uncle Matt's hand that put the towel into Dolly's blindly grasping fingers, which immediately withdrew. Then he resumed his talk with Andy.

"It is natural that what you saw has not only changed your opinion of me, but of your parents also. Since they have known all along what I am, you can no longer view them in quite the same light as before. In fact, your entire view of the world has changed."

Maule leaned forward a little. All traces of amusement had disappeared. "You are a considerably more grown-up young man than you were only a few days ago. But know this, Andrew Keogh: What you saw me do on the field of battle was not done in frivolity, nor as some sacrament of evil. Nor does it mean I am insane."

The door to the combination stall had opened again, and Dolly's face, above towel-wrapped shoulders, had emerged, wearing an expression of surprise. "You're Uncle Matt. You've got to be. I'd ask you to hand me in my clothes, but I can't dress in here, there's not enough room to raise my elbows. You guys are going to have to clear out for a minute so I can use the compartment."

"But naturally." Uncle Matthew stood and gave Dolly's exposed head and neck a piercing look. After a slight shake of his head, he managed a courtly bow. In another moment he and Andy were standing out in the corridor, where they waited silently. At this hour of the night they had the narrow, swaying passage entirely to themselves.

Andy said to the man beside him: "I haven't told her everything I saw."

~ 16 ~

*E*vidently Dolly was still very much afraid of being left alone, or else she was simply very curious. Well before Andy had really expected her to reappear, she was at the door of the compartment, fully clothed, to summon them back in.

The garments she was wearing now had been hastily purchased just before departure from Chicago, and they were a better fit and more becoming than the male garb borrowed from Andy's housemate. She promptly installed herself in the single seat, facing forward, leaving the lower berth for the men. Maule sat on the end by the window, directly facing Dolly, who seemed prepared for serious discussion.

After a brief exchange of banalities, she got down to cases.

"Andy tells me that we owe you thanks, for saving our lives back there in Chicago. Sorry I didn't thank you right away. I couldn't see much of what was going on."

Maule offered a slight, seated bow. "I was delighted to be able to be of assistance."

Dolly nodded slowly. "Just what kind of business are you in, Mr. Maule?"

Amusement touched his thin lips. "My usual reply, these days, is that I am a consultant in the field of conflict resolution."

"But that's not the real answer?"

"I might also describe my work in terms of stress management."

Dolly shrugged and abandoned that approach. "I guess you knew my grandfather pretty well."

Maule nodded. "I did—decades ago, in Europe—and I truly mourn his passing. Also I regret I had no chance to see him again before he died."

"I didn't see you getting on the train at Chicago, Mr. Maule. Or should I call you Uncle Matt?"

"As you please; this is no time for formality, as I am sure you must realize. I flew to Kansas City and boarded the train there."

"Then you saw what happened when we were on the platform? Like something was happening under the train?"

"Ah, yes." Uncle Matt's face took on a pinched look, as if it pained him to think about it.

Andy interrupted to put in: "You flew to Kansas City just to catch up with us?"

"An interesting place. Ah, but Chicago . . . Chicago is truly fascinating, is it not? On my first visit, I too found it somewhat bewildering. One of the great cities of the world. Though like many another metropolis, it encompasses within its borders much that is crude, and, sad to say, much that is truly dangerous. Difficult for a sensitive soul to deal with, or even to understand."

Andy pushed ahead. "Uncle Matt, we want to know the whole story. How you helped us in Old Town, what that whole scene was all about. I know some people got killed there, but they were ready to kill us, so . . . I also know that some of them got away." Andy hesitated; let Matthew Maule be the one to raise the subject of drinking blood, if he felt up to explaining that.

When Maule said nothing, Andy added: "Also, just who the hell is Mr. Dickon? If you can tell us that. I think we have it coming. You got us out of a real deadly mess, and we're grateful, but . . ."

Andy's tone grew more aggressive. "But didn't I get tangled up in all this in the first place just by being in your apartment? Didn't something really strange happen there on Tuesday night?"

Uncle Matt was nodding slowly. " 'Strange' is not an adequate description. Something unheard of in my experience, and that is saying . . . saying very much. More than you can realize. A man named Tamarack was killed, by a truly incredible intruder. You are correct, both of you have a right to know what has put you in such danger. Therefore I will tell you what I can.

"In return, you will both tell me all that you know pertaining to this affair. Including the matter of little statues." His black eyes burned at Dolly. "Most importantly, if I am going to take part in this search, I must know all that you know regarding the location of the prize."

Dolly was nodding silently.

Maule went on. "I think you understand that undertaking a long journey has not removed you from the path of danger?"

"I understand that."

Maule looked at her closely. "I see you do. The secret

you retained even under the threat of torture, you have already divulged—I know the list of names, as you gave them to Andy. No, he has not betrayed you. My skill at eavesdropping goes well beyond what you may imagine to be possible."

Dolly looked at Andy, then back at Maule. She was obviously afraid.

Andy moved closer, and reached out to take her hand.

After a moment, Maule went on, in gentler tones: "If there is any additional secret you still retain, you would be well advised to tell me now. I wish to help you, and your very survival is still at stake."

Still Dolly did not seem entirely convinced. She murmured something that might have been a denial she still had any secret knowledge. She gently disengaged her hand from Andy's.

Maule was content to let the matter rest for the moment. "But before we go any farther, a little background. A minute ago I was recalling my first train ride. You will be astonished to learn that it took place in eighteen ninety-one."

The two young people looked at each other, then back at the older man. "Nineteen eighty-one?" Andy suggested.

"No, I gave the date correctly. Well over a century ago. In that same year I also rode the Orient Express. A vehicle of memorable luxury."

Somewhere in the distance, a train whistle made its lonely sound.

It was now time for a demonstration of the more fantastic aspects of reality. And Maule found this easy to accomplish after dark in the small compartment, where three passengers were all necessarily so close to each other as to be on the verge of touching. A short course, with demonstrations of shape-changing, disappearance into thin air, and of strength. Andy, using the full strength of his two arms, discovered that he could not twist one of Maule's fingers against the older man's will.

When the show was over, Maule's stunned companions were involuntarily leaning back in their seats, as if they wanted to get away from him, but knew that they could not.

He said to them: "Now I must solemnly warn you both that the powers I have demonstrated will be shared not only by the coward Dickon, but by certain others who will be much more ruthless about using them."

He looked at Andy. "I believe that the man who almost killed you in Chicago is still alive, despite what happened to him there. His name, you will recall, is Lambert, and he is very dangerous. Also, I think he will not be alone. I found one of his associates beneath the train in the station at Kansas City."

Maule switched his gaze to Dolly. "Your situation is, if anything, more dangerous than Andy's. Lambert wants to wring from you every secret that you possess. He will have effective ways of doing that, and afterward he will want to drink your blood. Keep the shade of this window closed, from sunset to sunrise. If you should see at night a face outside the moving window, looking in, be assured that you are probably not dreaming.

"Above all, allow no strangers, no matter how innocent in appearance, to enter this compartment."

Andy said in a subdued voice: "The attendants come in, sometimes."

"If they are genuine, they will be able to enter without an invitation. So far that has been the case, I take it? Very well."

And after that, the demonstration was capped by the brief appearance, right there in the compartment, of the dog that had come trotting after the two fugitives on a Chicago street.

Then the dog was gone, and Uncle Matt sat smiling at them again.

After that followed a full minute of numbed silence. The spell was broken by Dolly's half-dazed comment: "And I thought my gramp was a cool magician!"

Maule nodded gently. "He was indeed a foremost practitioner in his field—as I am in mine. But the two are, as you must now realize, not at all the same." He was staring at Dolly now, and without pause he went on: "You cannot sleep, can you? Tell me what it is that makes you dread to sleep."

"It's dreams." Dolly's voice was suddenly a child's. "They're killing me."

"No, they shall not kill you. We must not let that happen. Allow me, please."

Bending forward, Maule briefly examined her throat. "Excellent, it seems you are unmarked by those who might have sought to drink your blood. Now, let your right hand rest here, in mine. Young Andrew, you may remain in the compartment. But grant us a minute or two of silence."

Andy watched, fascinated. Maule said nothing more, just looked at Dolly. At first, her eyes stayed locked on his. But in fifteen seconds, she was sound asleep in her comfortable chair, her head tilted just slightly on one side.

A week ago Andy would have been certain there was some trickery, or that he himself had been somehow dosed with an hallucinatory drug. But that was a week ago, and he had changed, along with the world around him.

Maule released the girl's hand, which fell softly to her lap, and sat back in his chair. As if to himself, he murmured: "There is one much worse—much worse—than Lambert, who has also become your enemy. But it would be pointless now to worry you with that."

Switching his gaze to Andy, he said quietly: "Now we may talk again."

Suddenly remembering something, Andy said: "Back there in Old Town, I thought I saw Dickon just pry a boot off the wheel of his car. With his bare hands."

Uncle Matt gravely inclined his head. "It is quite possible, for a *Homo dirus* of his age and strength." He looked keenly at Andy. "You must realize, he can be deadly dangerous in his fits of panic. He has them frequently."

"It'll be fine with me if I never see him again."

"And with me also. Possibly neither of us ever will. But it would be foolish to count on that."

Presently Maule restored the upper berth to its proper position, then lifted Dolly's sleeping figure gently into it, while Andy hastily scooped baggage out of the way.

Having seen that she remained in restful sleep, Uncle Matt took his leave. "I shall not be far away. Cry out if you need help."

He left the compartment without opening the locked door. He simply stood in front of it, favored his hosts with a slight bow, and disappeared.

* * *

Dolly slept on for some time, and Andy, stretching out in the lower berth, let himself sink into oblivion, secure in the knowledge that somewhere nearby, Uncle Matt was standing watch.

—and then Andy was suddenly awake again. Maybe it had been some sharp lurch of the rolling car that roused him. Certainly the train was still in motion, speeding through deep darkness. Impulsively Andy reached for the window shade and twitched it aside an inch or two, gazing into empty blackness.

Then for one shocking moment the blackness was no longer empty. A pale face loomed up, suspended in mid-air, close beside the window. The forehead was tilted toward the engine, as if the owner of the face might be swimming or flying, keeping up with the speeding train. It was certainly not the countenance of Uncle Matt. It was beardless and Andy thought it was a woman's, and its eyes were looking at him. It was gone before he could capture any further details.

The sight jerked Andy wide awake, but the shock left him uncertain—had he been dreaming, only a moment earlier?

He let the shade fall back, and went to sleep again. There was nothing else he could do.

In the morning his memory of the night's apparition already seemed unreal, and he was more than half convinced that it had been a dream. Andy took his turn in the tiny shower, and when the train's intercom announced that breakfast was served, he and Dolly headed promptly for the dining car.

This time they were seated with a different couple, but perhaps word about the newlyweds had got around.

No one seemed surprised that the youthful pair should look a trifle haggard when they showed up for breakfast. Andy did his best to respond to cheerful smiles.

When their tablemates had finished early and departed, Dolly asked in a low voice: "Where's Uncle Matt now?"

Andy swallowed coffee. He thought it was probably good coffee, but he couldn't really tell. "God knows. I'm scared to try to think about it. On the train somewhere, I guess. I'll bet we won't see him unless he wants us to."

The couple passed Saturday morning almost entirely inside their compartment, now restored to its day-time mode—they had been warned.

Lunch in the dining car began uneventfully—but a moment after they were seated, an attendant escorted Uncle Matt to their table, making a party of three.

Andy wondered, but did not ask, if Maule had somehow been able to wangle his own compartment on the train. Their protector was on hand, and that was all that seemed to matter at the moment.

Rolling wheels and chatter made the dining car noisy enough to allow them to converse in privacy. Uncle Matt ordered a sandwich, then gently explained to Dolly that he did so only for the sake of appearances. She should not be surprised when he ate nothing.

Dolly responded with a feeble smile. "Uncle Matt, nothing about you is going to surprise me any more. But you're all right?"

"I am in excellent condition. And you—?"

"Okay, I guess."

"As well as can be expected." He paused. "In a way, it worries me that Sobek does not seem to be pursuing you."

"That he does *not*—? ... but you say that Sobek is the one who sends me dreams."

Maule nodded. Now he had put on a pair of dark glasses, against the sun threatening to come in the window. "Oh, that he is not aboard the train and attempting to devour us is of course good in itself. What concerns me is the strong implication that he is content to wait, to send his dreams and bide his time...." He paused, having been struck by a sudden thought. "I wonder, now, if he is even conscious of all the dreams his mind transmits to others?"

That possibility sent Uncle Matt into a brief period of introspection. But presently he roused again. "Of course, a partial explanation may lie in the fact that the monster finds it comparatively difficult to move across country. It seems unlikely that he will find any magical false door in the right place to afford him a quick passage."

"What is he doing, then?"

"He is seeking the same treasure that your grandfather wanted you to have, and that those creatures in Chicago would have killed you to possess. He is also sending you visions of great horror. Our enemy derives amusement from inflicting pain—and he may rely on these dreams to accomplish some more practical purpose too. Perhaps, in some sense, he fears you—or fears some knowledge that you have."

Andy cleared his throat. "Speaking of visions, I saw something funny last night. Later I thought I must have been dreaming, but I don't know."

Maule listened with obvious concern as Andy described the apparition, then pressed him to give a better description of the face. But the young man could add nothing helpful.

His face somber, the older man turned back to Dolly. "And now, I believe there is something of importance that you wish to tell me."

She nodded. "Amazing, how much more human I feel after a few hours of sleep."

She paused, sighed. "Uncle Matt, it's like I said to Andy once, either you and I are in this together or we're not. After what's happened already, I have to believe we are. And if something, well, happens to Andy and me, maybe you can get some good out of it."

It seemed to Andy that some revelation was on the point of bursting out, yet again Dolly hesitated. "You know, I'm still not completely sure that Gramp just wasn't a little crazy. It's that damn list of names and addresses again."

"Your last secret has something to do with the list?"

The young woman nodded. "What it is, is that there's one statue that the list doesn't mention."

Andy got a sinking feeling in his gut, but he noted that Uncle Matt did not look terribly surprised at the revelation.

Dolly was going on: "The last thing Gramp said to me, before he died, was that he had kept one statue for himself. He did it just on a hunch, before he really knew how important they were going to turn out to be."

"And where is this statue now?"

"In Albuquerque, I guess. I hope. Still in our house there, probably, I don't know where else Gramp could have hidden it. I've been meaning to go and look for it soon as I got off the train. Now I want both of you to come with me, if you'll do that."

Having finally, as it seemed, unburdened herself of her last bit of secret knowledge, Dolly sank back in her chair looking relieved. A minute later she picked up the sandwich she had been toying with and took a healthy bite.

Slightly more than a full day had passed since the couple had boarded their sleeping car in Chicago. Now the train had at last emerged from the winding mountain passes of northern New Mexico, had made a last preliminary stop at Lamy, and was pulling into Albuquerque practically on schedule. The window shade of their compartment had been up since early morning, and the afternoon outside looked fine and hot.

From Albuquerque it would be only a short journey by car to Santa Fe, and Uncle Matthew, squinting out the window into the waiting ordeal of sunshine, vividly remembered a previous adventure in that old city.

"At the time I was keenly interested in the whereabouts of a certain painting." He sighed, and his current companions looked at him without understanding.

Gritting his teeth—at the moment his upper canines felt like they were shrinking, as if in anticipation of the solar pain to come—Maule put on the dark glasses and broad-brimmed hat that these days made part of his essential luggage, along with a small plastic bag of his native earth.

Having somehow retrieved his valise from its chosen hiding place, he disembarked in the teeth of the punishing, blazing sun, among American Indians who waited patiently to sell him rugs and pottery.

~ 17 ~

Andy was only slightly surprised to see John
Southerland, in blue jeans, hiking boots, and a
checkered shirt, waiting for them on the open
platform when their party descended from the train.

He noted that his Uncle John, for some reason, was
carrying some kind of unopened umbrella or parasol, and
that his face wore a look of concern as he immediately
approached Uncle Matt with this object in hand. But
Maule thrust the umbrella aside with an impatient gesture before John could get it open. Then Uncle Matt,
with the rest of the party trotting to keep up, made his
way quickly down off the platform, through a gateway
in a fence, and past a small gauntlet of sellers of artifacts, to a graveled parking lot beside the small and
timeworn railroad station. In the parking lot a large-
sized SUV was waiting, and someone inside the vehicle
opened a door for Uncle Matt as he approached.

Moments later they were all inside, arranging themselves quickly, as if they might have rehearsed this

boarding, in the three rows of seats. Dolly had never met John Southerland or Joe Keogh, who occupied the driver's seat, and quick introductions were performed.

Andy was not surprised at all to discover that it was his father who had opened the door from inside. Joe Keogh, established in the driver's seat, was still wearing his sport coat, unbuttoned. He looked somewhat haggard, though he had shaved recently. Father and son exchanged a look meant to convey mutual reassurance.

Dolly, at a word from Maule, now passed on to John and Joe the content of her grandfather's last words—how old Nicolas claimed to have hidden one of the statues somewhere in or near his Albuquerque house.

The news brought a sharp question from Joe Keogh. "If that's true, why didn't he tell you about it earlier, before he went to Chicago? Or when he phoned to ask you to come?"

Her chin lifted. "I've wondered about that. Only reason I can think of is that maybe Gramp didn't entirely trust me either. Then later when he knew he was dying . . . he just figured I was all he had."

In the silence that followed, Andy managed to get in a greeting to his father. "Glad to see you here, Dad. How's it going?"

"Could be worse. Just flew into Albuquerque about an hour ago." Joe Keogh shifted his gaze to Maule. "I'll fill in the details later, but there were two more statues in one shop in Carmel. I saw both of 'em smashed, and both were empty, except for little crocodile mummies." He paused. "I also got a good look at your Crocodile, and it was kind of a near thing. I don't see how he could have failed to see me. I suppose he just didn't think I was worth noticing."

Uncle Matt nodded slowly. "Sobek."

"Couldn't have been anyone—anything—else. Matched your description."

"To ignore you, or any other human, would be consistent with what I have seen of his behavior. Indeed, you must tell me the details, and soon."

Immediately on climbing into the front passenger seat of the cavernous vehicle, Maule had pulled shut his door, putting a barrier of steel and tinted glass between himself and the high desert sun. Relaxing with a sigh, he turned to find his left elbow in close proximity to the shaft of a familiar, long wooden spear. The full length of the weapon extended from between the two front seats to somewhere in the rear of the cabin. Gratefully he rested his hand on the hard wood, feeling its faded but still reassuring power.

"Better get buckled in, Uncle Matt?" John made it practically a question.

"Yes, to be sure." More buckles were snapping in the capacious rear of the cabin, as Andy and Dolly settled themselves in.

Maule looked to his left and added: "My compliments to you, Joseph, as a master of logistics."

"You're welcome." The vehicle was already in motion, making a preliminary turning movement. "Would you rather wait until dark to do this?"

Maule shook his head. "The thought is tempting, but we had better not delay."

The SUV had been waiting with the coolers on, so the interior was already comfortable. Now the radio had come on too, and a calm voice informed them that the current temperature in Albuquerque was ninety-five degrees, humidity fourteen percent.

Joe Keogh turned his head to the rear seat. "Where to, Ms. Flamel?"

"My friends call me Dolly. Head north to Central—that's just a few blocks—then take us west. I'll give you directions as we go. We'll turn north before we cross the river. Gramp's place is in the north valley."

"Close to the river?" Maule asked thoughtfully.

"Yes, maybe a quarter of a mile. Why?"

Uncle Matt just shook his head uncertainly.

Joe Keogh had finished giving Maule a more detailed report of the events in California, which the vampire received in brooding silence. The others, who had overheard, were digesting the grim facts without comment. Now Joe was studying the world around him as he drove.

He understood that belting on a gun was still generally legal in New Mexico, but so far Joe hadn't actually seen anyone availing themselves of the opportunity. He thought his own concealed weapon was very probably against the law, but he would have to take his chances. After what had happened in Carmel he was not going to go unarmed.

Soon they had turned north, leaving the modestly congested downtown area behind, moving in four lanes of busy traffic. Thunderheads were massing in the west, and a shapeless cloud had draped itself across the crest of the mile-high mountains just to the east.

The north valley turned out to be a picturesque place, viewed from a winding highway now diminished to two lanes. By this time they were well clear of anything that could be called a city. Both sides of the road displayed a full variety of housing, from handyman special shacks to substantial country estates; horses observed the passing traffic from behind pasture fences, some of the fences solid and decorative, others falling down. Signs promised vineyards, apple orchards, and tribal casinos.

When a few more miles had gone by, Dolly was leaning forward in her seat. "We're almost at our turnoff. Take this lane coming up on the left."

The lane was unpaved and narrow, running almost straight for a quarter of a mile, between banks of burgeoning summer vegetation. A narrow bridge carried the drive over a venerable irrigation ditch.

There was a slight turn near the end, and a house came into view, a one-story frame dwelling, considerably in need of paint. There were no vehicles parked anywhere nearby. "Here we are. Oh, oh. Something's happened."

One of the windows in the old building's modest front was broken, providing a view into dim emptiness.

Conveniently for Maule, tall cottonwoods screened most of the afternoon sun from the immediate vicinity of the house. Joe Keogh pulled up in the shade.

Dolly murmured: "I guess it's not too surprising. The place has been standing vacant for weeks, ever since I drove off to Chicago."

Maule was first out of the vehicle, then carefully maneuvered his spear out through its rear hatch. The other four arranged themselves carefully behind him, and approached the building warily.

Maule gave his spear a little shake. "Dolly, you must grant me permission to enter. Then you will please allow me to go in first."

"Well, yeah. Sure, of course. Go ahead." After a moment she murmured to herself: "I'm bringing in my shotgun."

Stepping quickly up to the front door, Maule listened

and then pulled it open with his left hand, spear ready in his right. The thought crossed the mind of Andy, watching, that the long shaft would be unhandy in a tight space. Moving forward with the others, he joined a single file that followed Uncle Matt inside.

The interior might almost have been that of any small house on the verge of poverty, anywhere in the United States, except that the walls tended to display old stage posters rather than sports or religious art.

Dolly touched Andy's arm and pointed to one of these. "That was Gramp. He loved that old carny kind of stuff."

More remarkable was the casual but extensive ruin of furniture and contents. Drawers everywhere had been pulled out and their contents strewn about, closets and cupboards emptied. Already Maule had propped his spear in a corner, and was muttering what sounded like swear words in some exotic language. It appeared that he was ready to abandon hope of finding any small white statues here, or anything else that might be of help.

Dolly had set her shotgun down again. As she moved from room to room she was increasingly disturbed by the mess. "Oh my God! Look at this!"

"The landlord certainly didn't do this," Andy observed.

"Landlord lives out of town. I'm sure he doesn't know about it yet. He'll have a cat-fit when he does."

They were standing in the vandalized kitchen. Maule patted her shoulder. "That is the least of our problems, I assure you, and easily solved. Now I would like to make sure of the vandals' identity. Perhaps they were some surviving friends of the late Mr. Lambert. Or . . ."

"Maybe it was Sobek," Joe Keogh offered. "Could have been here before he visited Carmel. This place could have been torn up yesterday, or the day before."

Maule nodded; there was a distant look on his face, that of a man listening intently.

Moments later, the others heard it too: the sound of a small car pulling up in front of the house. When Andy moved that way to look out a window, he could see it was a late model with heavily tinted windows. It stopped very close to the SUV, as if determined to seek the shade as well. Now a young woman was getting out.

"Connie. She's alone." John's voice sounded only slightly surprised.

A moment later the newcomer was tapping briskly at the front door. Maule's voice spoke the necessary invitation.

When Connie took off her sunglasses she still looked wide-eyed and innocent, though less prim and ladylike than she had in Chicago. She was wearing a different outfit now, but this one was just as stylish and the pants were just as tight. Her bright red toenails were hidden now in low-heeled shoes that still managed to avoid looking practical. The dark curly hair had been somehow differently arranged, and the heavy silver earrings were no longer to be seen. Her perfume was no less entrancing, though different from the fragrance Andy could remember.

Her eyes lit up as soon as her gaze fell on him. "Ah, there you are, young Andee! I must apologize for hovering outside your window late at night—the window of your little room aboard the train." She looked at Dolly. "And my apologies to you, my dear, as well." Back to Andy again. "Ah, but I regret I did not have the chance to get to know you, back in Chicago. I can hope you have not utterly forgotten me?"

"I don't see how I could have done that," Andy heard

himself saying. "But I just don't remember clearly."

"Ah, how sad, to feel myself forgotten!"

Her smiling eyes swept on around the group—rested for a moment on the silent Maule, warily making sure he was not really angry with her—and came to rest on Joe. Now she brightened again. "Ah, it is the very dangerous Mr. Keogh!"

He nodded, gravely. "Please, call me Joe, or Joseph. Why dangerous?"

"Mr. Keogh—oh I beg pardon, Joseph!—but you are becoming something of a legend among certain clans and families of the *nosferatu*."

"Really?"

"Oh yes. I think no breather who now walks the earth has killed as many of us as you have." Connie pouted prettily. "I am almost afraid to be in the same room with you myself."

And I with you, Joe thought to himself. Aloud, he performed a tersely formal introduction between Connie and Dolores Flamel.

Presently a renewed search effort was under way, with Connie, at a nod from Maule, allowed to take part. She threw herself into the task, searching as energetically if not as efficiently as Uncle Matt himself.

A quarter of an hour later, when every room of the house had been examined in detail with no result, Maule gathered his helpers in the ruined parlor.

John Southerland broke the glum silence. "If one of the statues was here, whoever tore the place apart like this must have found it."

Maule was shaking his head. "Not necessarily. If one of our enemies has indeed gained control of the Philosopher's Stone, then I believe we would already have convincing evidence of the fact, in the form of a noticeable change, and not for the better, in the nature of the world."

The room was very silent. All Maule's companions were listening intently, watching him.

His voice was less somber as he went on. "If that has happened, then it would seem that the game is over, and we have lost—but be of good cheer. All that I can see, and hear, and feel, tells me that the game is not quite over yet."

Now his manner became brisk. "As I see it, there remain three possibilities." He looked keenly at Dolly. "The first is, that no statue was ever hidden here—a young woman was somehow deceived by the ravings of a dying man."

Dolly was shaking her head, as Maule turned to regard his other colleagues. "Second possibility: a statue was hidden here, our enemy discovered it. Of course Sobek smashed it at once, hoping for treasure inside—but he found none. In that case the white plaster fragments should still be visible, in or near the house. But so far none of us—hey?—have observed any such debris."

The others nodded agreement. Maule sighed, and spoke more slowly. "A third possibility remains: that a statue was indeed hidden in or near this house, hidden by one of the most cunning stage conjurors of the twentieth century—and hidden so well that the intruder in his arrogance, haste, or confusion failed to discover it."

The vampire's compelling gaze came back to Dolly. "Now, my dear—you have lived here, and know the house, the grounds, quite well. And you know your grandfather. Think carefully, and tell us what you think."

The young woman stared at Maule for a full ten seconds before answering. "You know what the first idea is that comes to me? I remember there's a hole, just about the right size, in the trunk of a tree, in that little patch of woods just behind the house."

Maule nodded briskly. "Go and look into the hollow tree. Take someone with you. Meanwhile the rest of us will examine the house yet again, slowly and carefully this time."

Dolly shot Andy a questioning look. He nodded.

The grass in what had once been the backyard had long since gone dead and yellow for lack of watering. Farther back, there stretched an expanse of earth now supporting only a few tough weeds, that doubtless at some other time, and for some other occupant, could have been a vegetable garden. Defunct grapevines were still crucified on scaffolds of dried-out poles. At the far end of the former garden stood, or squatted, a miniature religious shrine, a knee-high grotto of wood and adobe, holding a small figure of the Virgin.

"You see a lot of things like that around here," Dolly observed as she walked past with Andy. "It's a pretty Spanish state."

The hollow tree she had set out to find was farther back, surrounded by a dozen or so other trees, in a scrap of woods some fifty yards behind the house.

Weaving among thin trunks and thick ones, tramping on tough weeds, Dolly found the cavity in a dead tree just as she had remembered it, and reached inside. Her grasping fingers pulled out dried leaves, but nothing else. She muttered bad words; Andy heartily agreed.

In a moment the couple were on their way back to join the others, recrossing the dry, untended garden.

"Can't think of any other place," she muttered. "Of

course if you want to hide something, you can always dig . . ."

Andy had just put a consoling hand upon her shoulder, when her words died away. Dolly turned her head to one side, and stopped in her tracks.

In the next instant she was running, leaping over the parched earth, toward the religious shrine. It looked as if it had been in place for decades, built by the landlord or some other tenant, years before Flamel had moved into the house. The image of the Virgin, blue-gowned, white-faced, and crowned with gold, was a little over a foot tall, partly sheltered from the elements in a small recess of wood and deteriorating adobe brick.

Dolly tore the little statue from its niche and held it up. A light blue robe, covering most of the figure's surface, had been smoothly painted over white plaster, and gold paint dabbed around the head skillfully suggested a radiant crown. From a few yards away everyone who looked at it would see a commonplace religious statue.

But surely no Virgin had ever confronted her votaries with a face like this one.

"Not the statue that was here before! That's my gramp!" she screamed in her excitement, thrusting her discovery high in the air. "If you want to hide something, put it in plain sight!"

Dolly's friends and helpers, Maule running in the lead, came hurrying to see what had provoked the screams. Only Connie remained hovering near the house, under a shade tree.

The strange little figure stood on two small feet on a narrow plaster base. The arms, or forelimbs, swathed in concealing drapery, hung straight at the sides. The face unpleasantly combined a pug nose with a long jaw and a suggestion of large teeth.

Maule's dark eyes were uncovered under his broad hat-brim, and for the moment he seemed oblivious to the glaring sun. "Yes," he muttered. "Yes, certainly. Stripped of its paint, this would be practically identical to the statue broken in Chicago."

Dolly was looking at her adviser questioningly. "Then we smash it open?"

"It would be pointless to delay. And certainly the honor of discovery should be yours."

Dolly dropped the statue on the sunbaked soil, then looked about for a rock of handy size. There were several within reach and she grabbed one up. "Here goes."

It took three blows to satisfactorily shatter the whole length of the figure. Eager hands and eyes then probed minutely through the resulting white chips and dark organic mess. But there was nothing to be found, nothing at all that might suggest a gem.

Within a minute, feverish excitement had faded to cold disappointment. Maule had dropped to his hands and knees, joining in the search, but now he raised eyes blazing with anger and frustration.

Glumly the party retreated to the shade before the house, where Connie stood waiting for them in graceful gloom.

Once more it fell to Maule to sum up their situation.

"We now know of one statue that was not on the list compiled by Nicolas Flamel.

"I have a suspicion that is growing stronger by the hour—that the famous, or notorious, list is not as all-important as we originally thought."

Dolly cleared her throat. "You mean maybe the Stone was never inside any of the statues?"

"The possibility cannot be totally ruled out. But I had other matters in mind. One statue smashed in Chi-

cago, a second and third in Carmel, and now a fourth—
that was not on the list—in Albuquerque. All of them
devoid of treasure.

"In the dream, as several of us have seen it, there
are six statues drying in the workshop of the crocodile
god. What I am saying now is that we cannot be sure of
numbers or locations.

"Tamarack, one of the three partners, had a statue
with him when he was murdered in Chicago. A second
partner, Nicolas Flamel, contrived to keep a statue for
himself and hid it here.

"There was, of course, a third partner. What ought
we to assume about him?"

Maule and Joe looked at each other, but it was Andy
who spoke the name aloud.

~ 18 ~

Joe Keogh was fielding an incoming call on his cell phone, and everyone stopped to listen. Joe was mostly listening too, just putting in a few words now and then.

At last he pocketed his phone and looked around. "Most of you people already know, my agency has working arrangements with certain others around the country. Dolly, I passed along to some of them the two remaining addresses on your list, having scratched off Chicago and Carmel, and asked that they be carefully checked out. One, in Salt Lake City, is a real antique shop, the other, in Reno, more like a secondhand store—but according to their owners, neither place has ever bought, received, or ordered a statue of the kind we're looking for."

Maule asked: "How sure can we be?"

"Reasonably sure, I'd say. Don't know why the shop owners would lie about it. If they thought they'd caught hold of something valuable they'd want to cash in." Joe

gave everyone a moment to think that over, then raised
his hand. "There's more. My people have located one
statue, that from its description has to be one of our original six, in a museum in Cairo—I should say, it was
there until about a month ago, when it was smashed to
pieces in a mysterious accident. So it looks like there
were only five that ever actually made it to this country."

There was a little silence, while the crew digested
this. Then Maule removed his broad-brimmed hat and
rubbed his pale forehead. "It would seem that the usefulness of the list is at an end. We can now be reasonably
certain that there is now one statue left, and only one.
And it is not at any of the listed addresses."

"Then what do we do?" Dolly demanded.

Uncle Matthew looked around, meeting the eyes of
each of his associates in turn. "We must locate the monster. Find out where he is going, what he is up to. We
do not know where the last statue is, but I think Sobek
will be able to track it down."

Joe said: "We can assume that he was here, trashing
this house, not too long ago. He may still be near."

"Or he may not. One thing the Crocodile does *not*
seem to be doing is following us, though he may believe
that we are trying to run away."

"How do we locate him?"

"There are ways. Here is a token that ought to help."
Reaching into his watch pocket, Maule drew out the single scale from Sobek's hide, the horny little wafer that
he had picked up on the bank of the Sauk. This he displayed on his white palm. "I have good hopes of success,
since one among us is already in mental contact with the
Crocodile."

"You mean me," said Dolly.

"I do."

"What is that thing?"

Everyone listened in awe while Maule gave a brief account of his skirmish on the riverbank, back in Illinois. To Andy the scale looked like nothing so much as a giant's thumbnail, hard and translucent, leaf-shaped at its thinner end, knobby at what seemed to be its base.

Uncle Matt was not given to wasting time. Two minutes later, Dolly had been established in the most comfortable chair available, in the center of the littered living room, whose doors and windows now stood open to let a little breeze blow through. Perching near her on another chair, Maule had given her the scale to hold, making sure that the fingers of her right hand were clenched firmly around it.

Dolly was as good a hypnotic subject here as she had been in the railroad car. In less than a minute she had fallen into a light trance, and was giving her anxious listeners a report on the Crocodile's location. "Yes, I see . . . I feel . . . he is in water. It's flowing, but quiet . . . he's moving against the current."

Maule asked gently: "He is crossing a stream?" Everyone else was watching in attentive silence.

A frown. "No . . . not crossing. But moving steadily along. Upstream all the time, against the current . . . swimming most of the time . . . sometimes crawling . . . staying under water."

"That is very interesting. I am reminded of something I noticed in Chicago. Early Tuesday morning, while waiting for you, Joseph, to arrive at my apartment. A rippling in the quiet water of the Chicago River, at the side of a lone canoe."

*   *   *

Maule asked a few more questions, gently, but it seemed that at the moment Dolly could discover no more useful information. After bringing her easily out of her trance, Uncle Matt looked about him thoughtfully. Then he fixed his gaze on Connie.

He spoke to her in such an amiable voice that she gave him an especially wary look. "Do you have any idea at all, my dear, of where it might be possible to find our old acquaintance, Dickon? Some brighter hope, perhaps, than the roof of the Chicago public library? You might know better than I whether that venue should be ruled out?"

"Dear Vlad, it would be hard to say," she began hesitantly. When Maule stared at her, she hastily added: "Maybe something will come to me."

"Let us hope it does. But that task may take some time, for your quarry is clever and elusive. So before you devote yourself entirely to finding him, I would be pleased if you would gather samples of water from all streams within two hundred miles of where we are—in this desert region, that cannot be too formidable a task, for one who is able to go flying about by night, as swiftly and purposefully as you. I need not tell you to use small, clean glass or plastic bottles of some kind, and label them all carefully. When I have them it will be easier to determine the monster's true location."

Connie murmured, and protested prettily, but Andy thought she did not really find the assignment that much of a problem.

Maule added: "And need I caution you not to approach the Crocodile?"

Connie almost whimpered. Her feelings were hurt, that dear Vlad could have so poor an opinion of her intelligence. She meant, she said, to remain inside Flamel's house till after sunset, then promptly undertake her assigned tasks. There would be no use her trying to start before dark anyway.

There was no reason for any of the others to linger in the vicinity. Before leaving, Dolly grabbed a few items of clothing from the shambles of what had been her room, and made sure her shotgun was snugly packed aboard the SUV. Moments later the vehicle, with everyone but Connie aboard and John Southerland at the wheel, pulled out and headed for the highway, its destination Albuquerque International Airport.

Just as they were getting back on the highway, Joe Keogh wondered aloud whether Maule really ought to trust Connie.

Maule said that despite her flightiness, he had confidence that she would not actively betray him. "Besides that, if I give her nothing to do, she will think up her own ways of trying to be helpful. And that could be disastrous."

Uncle Matt was sitting beside Dolly now, and lightly hypnotized her once more as they rode. She readily reestablished the mental contact with Sobek—he was still in the water somewhere. "Muddy water, it seems to me." But she could not tell what he might be thinking—supposing he was having thoughts.

Having discovered a road map in one of the convenience pockets of the SUV, Maule held it out flat and open on the spread fingers of his hand. "Dolly, I want you to indicate to me which river Sobek is in now. You can point it out to me on the map."

Her right hand continued to clutch the monster's detached scale. But her left hand rose slowly in the air, and then descended, forefinger pointing. Her work-shortened fingernail came to rest upon one small blue line. Her eyes had stayed closed, and it seemed that whatever was guiding her finger could not be her conscious mind.

"So!" Maule was well-satisfied. "It is the Rio Grande. We may not need any of the water samples Connie is supposed to be gathering ... which is probably just as well.

"Upstream, you say, so he is evidently ascending the river, moving purposefully toward its source. Somewhere in that direction must lie the final statue. Our goal must be to follow him."

Joe Keogh thought that Maule looked and sounded disgustingly cheerful, for a vampire setting out in pursuit of a monster who enjoyed capturing and eating vampires. And Joe was wondering, silently so far, just what Maule thought they were going to do if they ever managed to catch up.

As they headed back to the city Joe worked his phone. Calling ahead to his people at the airport, he directed that their plane be made ready to fly within a few hours.

"I'll tell you later exactly where ... yes, I know you need to file a flight plan. We'll work something out. And we'll need to set up some reliable air-to-ground communication."

The party split up at the airport, John Southerland boarding the plane along with his brother-in-law. Joe had had a long hard day, beginning very early in Carmel, and planned on catching some sleep in the air.

Before the SUV left the airport, Keogh's associates on the ground had installed an ultramodern communi-

cations device on the console between the two front
seats. And before heading out of the city again, Andy and
Dolly stopped for massive hamburgers, fries, and coffee,
while Maule caught a pre-sunset nap in the back of the
SUV.

Within an hour the SUV was heading north again, this
time taking Interstate 25, heading out of the city toward
Santa Fe, some sixty miles to the north. Within a few
miles, the interstate diverged from the course of the Rio
Grande, and they were plunged into a strange, stark
landscape. At intervals around the far horizon there
loomed distant mountains, and the cumulonimbus pil-
lars of distant thunderstorms.

Andy was driving now, while Maule talked with
Dolly, telling her that the dreams Sobek was sending,
cruel as they were, might be turned to her own advantage. By maintaining the contact Sobek had established,
they could follow their great enemy to the great prize
that must be his goal.

Under mesmeric influence, Dolly once more made contact with the Crocodile. "He's still going north." Dolly's
eyes were closed, as she murmured: "I can't see anything
really, but I can feel it. There is water all around him
still."

During the night Sobek left the Rio Grande, but
within minutes after doing so he had entered some other
stream. For some reason the Crocodile evidently preferred to remain in water as much as possible, as he
continued in the same general direction.

The sun had gone down, and the Santa Fe turnoffs had
been left well behind. Maule was driving now, cruising

the four-lane Interstate, the highway climbing in gentle curves through mountains that only he could see clearly in the night.

The two breathers aboard were trying to get some normal sleep, but Dolly was soon awakened by her recurrent nightmare.

When Maule questioned her gently she swore she could not remember much about the dream.

"Except it had something to do with Egypt—and it scared the . . . can you help me? You've got to help me, Uncle Matt. These dreams are wearing me down." She gave a little gasp. "Do you suppose he knows I'm anywhere around when I go—go spying on him?"

"I doubt that."

"So why am I getting these—these . . . ?"

"At some level, perhaps unconscious, Sobek may be aware, and is inflicting these visions as a defense. Or . . ."

The vampire fell silent, suddenly lost in thought.

"Or what?" asked Andy, now awake in the rear seat.

"I was about to say, they might even be interpreted as a cry for help."

"A cry for *help*? From the Crocodile?"

Uncle Matt only shook his head. Dolly had been sleeping in the right front seat, and now his pale hand stroked her forehead. He said: "I will give you as much protection as I can, without jeopardizing the contact. It is a dangerous burden for you to bear; but we must maintain the contact. Like many another burden, it is best disposed of by carrying it willingly."

Dawn on Sunday morning found the SUV cruising deeply into southern Colorado. Maule was an extremely skillful and practically tireless driver, particularly by night. He allowed Andy and Dolores to share most of the long summer daylight hours between them, while he huddled in the backseat, or between the backseat and the middle, curled up oddly on a dark plastic garment bag that crunched and crackled strangely when he moved.

Sunday wore on. Waking at intervals, every hour or so during the day, Maule put Dolly into trance. Generally she reported that Sobek was still in water, though not in the same stream, and still moving north. Only once did she make contact with the monster as he was moving on dry land. "He seems to be walking on two legs now, like a man . . . but I think he's only going a short distance . . . now he's coming to another stream—can't see it very clearly . . ."

"Let me get out the map again, said Uncle Matt." Fortunately, here in the West the streams were comparatively few, and comparatively small.

Two or three times during the day, Joe Keogh in his aircraft made wireless contact with the party in Maule's SUV. Joe's plane had landed early Sunday morning at an airfield near Colorado Springs, and he and John were waiting there for further word from Uncle Matt on Sobek's whereabouts.

Andy said to Maule: "We're going to need another map."

"At least one more. At our next stop for fuel we will obtain as many as we can."

Traffic thickened and slowed as the SUV drew near Denver, came near stopping as the highway dragged them painfully through the city's congested heart. By Sunday afternoon the earthbound pursuers had made several stops for fuel and food. Maule met his own needs in his own way—at dusk on Sunday evening, in the woods beside a highway rest area well north of Denver, Andy watched the vampire catch a rabbit. Maule, standing a few yards away and with his back to the others, seemed to have somehow hypnotized the small animal into jumping into his hands. Quickly he raised it to his mouth. Only a few seconds later, the small, drained body was tossed away.

The blood-drinking Andy had witnessed in Chicago came back to him strongly, sharp and clear. With a sigh of relief, he saw that Dolly was looking in the other direction, and had evidently noticed nothing disturbing.

At dawn on Monday it was once more Uncle Matthew's turn to sleep, curled on his handy bag of powdered native earth, nestled between the second and third seats of the SUV. There well-shadowed floor space offered a small nest where a lean man could sleep comfortably on his back with his knees bent, and a blanket or tarp thrown over him and his thin crackling cushion of magic earth.

"Hope we don't get stopped for anything," Andy wished aloud. He could all too easily picture their guardian being rushed to the hospital by the first cop who saw him in his present state. What he had trouble picturing was what might happen after that.

Dolly agreed. She also wondered aloud what the cops might make of the great spear, which still extended through the cabin, back to front. And that in turn reminded her of her shotgun, which she supposed was sure to one day get her into trouble—if only she could live so long.

After mentioning her concerns to Andy, she suggested: "We could say we're on our way to some kind of fantasy convention. Trade show? Don't people have those kind of things?"

"I think we're on our way to a fantastic gathering, all right."

Later on Monday morning, with Andy driving, and Dolly in a trance, Maule was talking to them both. "I am sure the great beast still has the power to transport himself from one place to another by any of several modes of magic—but for the most part, he does not want to do so. By using rivers, he avoids what he must perceive as the difficulties and inconveniences of traveling overland . . . also, I believe he has several times employed some form of magic to carry him swiftly and invisibly from one stream to another. Where is he now?"

Dolly's small finger, nothing at all magical in its appearance, found the new blue line on the map. Wordlessly she frowned.

Through the remainder of Monday, and into Monday night, they traced their enemy's route. Overall the Crocodile's progress was taking him almost directly north from Albuquerque, and by now he had come nearly a thousand miles. Sometimes upstream, sometimes downstream, but in general always north. He had visited the South Platte, the Missouri, the Bighorn.

Looking at the road map, Dolly supposed that driving up to Montana from Albuquerque would have taken something like two days. But as long as the monster remained in the water he moved at a slow pace, only a few miles an hour, much slower than highway traffic.

On the other hand, he kept going day and night, stopping only infrequently. Sobek seemed to need no sleep, and very little rest. And in going from one stream to another he could move at magical velocity.

The SUV, thought Andy, could easily have raced ahead of their enemy—if only they knew where he was going. As it was, they made frequent stops, and endured long waits. Joe Keogh's airplane had left Colorado Springs, but it was spending much more time on the ground, at one small airport or another, than it was in the air.

The sun came up on Tuesday morning, and Andy realized that a week had gone by since the adventure started.

Another day went by. It was on Wednesday, after several days of steady, tireless swimming and crawling for the Crocodile, and of driving or flying-and-resting by his pursuers, when Maule confirmed, questioning the hypnotized Dolly, that his enemy had now entered the Yellowstone, after leaving the Missouri River at a spot near Buford, North Dakota.

Andy was struck by a new concern. "What if he goes on into Canada? Can Joe fly over into Canadian airspace?"

"I can, if he cannot. But your father is looking into that. Wherever Sobek goes, we must pursue."

Now Dolly was sleeping no more than half an hour at a time, usually taking Maule's favorite spot when he was not there, between the second and third seats of the SUV. She stayed awake no longer than two hours between her tortured naps.

~ 19 ~

J oe had radioed his intention to land at the Billings
airport, and suggested that the hunters ought to
get together in that city for a face-to-face conference.

Maule was agreeable. He and his fellow passengers
in the SUV had now passed Custer's last battlefield, and
were keeping up with the flow of interstate traffic at
eighty miles an hour. Billings was only a few miles
ahead.

On landing in Montana, Joe found himself reminded of
Carmel—simply because this place was just so completely different. He had heard that Billings was the
largest city in the state, with a population of around one
hundred thousand, and it looked about as mundane and
workaday as any city could be. There was an aging and
moderately congested central area, with a strong beginning of modern sprawl taking shape to the west and
south. A rim of rock nearly as sharp as a stairstep, per-

haps two hundred feet in height, ran east and west across the northern part of the city. Logan Airport perched atop this shelf, while along the very rim a row of the city's most luxurious homes were sitting like spectators on a balcony.

The SUV had arrived in the city at about the same time, and Maule's party had taken several rooms in a downtown hotel.

Within the hour they were joined there by Joe and John.

When Joe Keogh discovered that his son and Dolly were sharing a room, he gave his son a look.

Andy shot back: "By this time, it would feel strange if Dolly and I didn't share a room."

"Getting married sometime soon?"

The young man's anger flared. "Dad, we're in two beds. We're not sleeping together—staying together and trying to sleep would be more like it. After this last week, sleep is about all I can think of when I see a bed."

His father grunted something that sounded about half-sympathetic, and turned away.

In truth, Dolly was beginning to seem to Andy something like a sister. The thoughts that came disturbing him when he lay down to sleep were actually of Connie, whose image in his mind combined a perfect woman's body with all the exotic mystery of Uncle Matt. . . .

In the grayness just before dawn, Connie reported in again to Maule, tapping on the outside of his window on the tenth floor of the hotel. When he let her in, she said that she was glad they had at last found reasonably comfortable quarters.

In elegantly gloved hands Connie was carrying two small, mismatched glass bottles, each about one-third full. Hesitantly she began to report on her assigned mission of gathering water samples—it seemed obvious that she had managed to botch it up, and in fact was not sure from which source either bottle had been filled.

Uncle Matt heard all of this with no surprise. Brushing aside Connie's rambling excuses, he told her to forget about taking an inventory of rivers, and devote herself in earnest to finding Dickon.

She brightened somewhat, setting down her two bottles with exaggerated care. "I can try that, Mr. Maule. You understand that I make no promise of—"

"I want no promise, I want results. You seem to have no trouble in finding *me* wherever I go."

Connie hesitated. "Certainly you are very angry with Dickon now."

"I surely am. But if you are trying to save him, set your mind at ease; the wretch seems so good at punishing himself that I hesitate to interfere. Tell him this: I will forgo the satisfaction of revenge, if he will give me information. I want to know all that he knows of the last statue, the Stone, and the Crocodile."

Dawn had not yet broken when Connie was on her way again.

Dolly's first report after sunrise indicated the Crocodile was still progressing upstream along the Yellowstone, now within a few miles of Billings, and steadily approaching the city from the east.

Sobek had determined that his long trek across the continent would soon be ended. Now and then, sometimes by day and sometimes by night, he emerged from one stream or another long enough to find food in the form of a cow or steer or sheep.

In one case, an antelope, taken by surprise on the otherwise deserted bank of the South Platte, had not been swift enough to escape his open, lunging jaws.

Now and then, in the vastness of open country well west of the Mississippi, he observed a human, or sometimes two or three. Not wanting to be distracted, he generally took precautions so they should not see him. He considered feeding on one or more of them, but he preferred to wait until he could satisfy his special fondness for vampire blood. The fact that vampires were so rare made them all the more desirable. It was a special craving that the Crocodile meant to fully satisfy quite soon.

Sobek had come to rest in a deep pool in the cold mountain stream, pausing there because he was finding it increasingly difficult to know which way to move. His magic had brought him very near to the last statue, but its presence seemed to blanket a whole circle of a quarter of a mile or so in diameter. Once he had moved within that circle, he had to wait a long time to know which way to move next.

By now the Crocodile had given up his efforts to attract Dolly to him—she had become largely irrelevant, now that his private magic was leading him infallibly to the only Crocodile image that had not yet been destroyed, and so must inevitably contain the prize.

Yet he had not entirely forgotten the young woman— and now he could sense dimly that she was not far away, and in fact very near to the great prize.

Sobek could not remember how much time had passed since he had last had sexual relations with either beast or human. At certain dim and remote periods in the past he had frequently tried both, female crocodiles as well as women, but had failed to experience much real satisfaction either way.

Of course he understood the reason for the failure. It was simply that his true mate would have to be a goddess, and no lesser being could truly satisfy him. It bothered him, sometimes, that in his worldwide wanderings he had never encountered another example of divinity. Not even in old Egypt, where their numbers had been almost uncountable. Perhaps when he had taken possession of the Stone he would return there, to the land of his birth, and this time his fellow deities would not avoid him.

There were moments when he imagined himself using Dolly in that way, and then devouring her afterward. But he still could not quite decide whether that course of action would afford him the most pleasure or not. The truth was that, for either kind of union, the Crocodile much preferred the flesh of vampires over that of breathing humans, and she was not a vampire. For a time the Crocodile had toyed with the idea of somehow arranging for her to become a vampire—and then he would devour her, deriving maximum pleasure from the taste of her *nosferatu* flesh. Such an outcome would take some time and effort to arrange, of course, but the result ought to be well worth the wait.

He was still serenely confident, though not absolutely certain, that none of his enemies had yet located the all-important treasure. Had they managed to do that, they might even feel themselves strong enough to attack him.

He cared little whether they attacked him or not, but he doubted that they would. Except for the *nosferatu* called Vlad Tepes, they would be too much in awe of him to try to use it against him. Tepes worked on a different level than the others—but probably, after the little skirmish they had fought in Illinois, even he would be overawed.

The thought of Tepes made the Crocodile once more aware of a persistent sore spot on his shoulder, where several days ago the vampire's spearpoint had torn away one of his lovely scales. At the time, Sobek had hardly noticed the small wound, but it was slow to heal, and sometimes itched and burned.

The longer the small wound bothered him, the greater a punishment he decided to impose upon the one who had inflicted it.

He, Sobek, was, after all, a god, and all the rest of them were only human. He could almost find it in his divine heart to pity them.

The morning's second report from Dolly, still flat on her back in the hotel, snug but exhausted, gave convincing evidence that the monster's destination was not in Billings, but somewhere farther west. Sobek had continued to follow the Yellowstone upstream right through the city. The monster's course took him within half a mile of where his enemies were staying, but either he did not realize that they were there, or did not care.

Maule grunted. "If he passed through the city without being noticed, the water must be deep enough to hide his ugly shape. Or else he has used some cloaking magic."

Maule and Joe Keogh agreed there was no point in rushing the pursuit. Sobek was still moving, and might continue to do so for days. At this hour breakfast, for those who ordinarily ate breakfast, seemed in order.

About an hour later, Dolly offered another mesmeric

report: "... wait a minute, here's a change. Now he's out of the water again ... his magic carries him ... but never mind, he's not coming this way. ..."

"Out of the water and going where?"

Dolly's short frame tensed, and then relaxed. "He's in another stream."

Examining the latest map that Maule had spread on the bed beneath her groping fingers, he read the tiny print beside the fine blue line on which her pointing fingernail came down.

"Rock Creek," he muttered. "Unmemorable and unoriginal as a name."

"Maybe," said Dolly, opening her eyes, "whoever named it was feeling tired." She let her lids sag closed again.

Sensations of tiredness were of no interest to Uncle Matt. "Now, should he continue to ascend Rock Creek—where will that lead him?"

Andy said, looking at the map: "The Beartooth Mountains, it looks like, if he goes on another fifty miles or so. But before he gets that far ..." The map showed a small dot, and a small name, close against the foothills of the Beartooth Range. "A town called Red Lodge."

From its location, and the thread of winding highway that passed through, Red Lodge looked like it might do as a kind of rear summer entrance to Yellowstone National Park. Just west of Red Lodge, said the fine print on the map, the highway was closed during the winter months.

Maule now decided that he should take advantage of a hotel room's availability to get some sleep.

"It is well to be rested when going into battle. I shall be up again well before sunset." He took his spear into his room before he closed the door.

* * *

An alarm was sounding stridently in the darkened caverns of his mind. The vividness of the dream he had just experienced set what had just happened apart from natural vampire-sleep. But this time no hypnotic compulsion had been imposed upon him by anyone—or anything.

Someone was shaking him. "Uncle Matt? Wake up, Uncle Matt. You're dreaming."

Maule groaned and stirred. He was lying on his back in a bed in an early twenty-first-century hotel, and he recognized the face of Andy Keogh looming over him. It had been the Egyptian dream again, and as usual very vivid.

"You let out a yell that time, Uncle Matt. We thought there was something wrong."

Again he had inhabited the body of the skilled and daring thief, had passively shared the rascal's desperate and scrambling flight, running through strange streets, inhaling strange smells, under a sun and sky of glaring heat.

Again the blackly shadowed doorway loomed before the hounded fugitive. Maule had no doubt where he was—he had entered the local Temple of the Crocodile, a sprawling and rambling house raised to the glory of the great god Sobek. But this time, Maule noticed something new and different as he went running into the temple—there was an inscription over the doorway, and, in the way of dreams, he had no trouble reading the hieroglyphics. It was one of the traditional verses, in which many of that time and place found comfort:

You live again, you revive always, you have become young again, you are young again, and forever.

So it had seemed to Vlad Drakulya, as he remembered now, more than five centuries ago, on his own first coming forth from his own tomb.

Large statue-images, crocodile heads carved of pale limestone and pink granite looked down on the intruder with what seemed glaring disapproval.

Inside the Temple of the Crocodile it was very dark, by contrast with the sunbaked street. The fugitive had to pause, to give his sun-dazzled eyes a moment to start adapting to the gloom.

When his vision cleared, he saw that he had entered a part of the sprawling complex in which small images were made, to be sold later in the temple and on the street to Sobek's devotees. As in every earlier version of the dream, he saw that six newly molded plaster images were present in this broad passage, three on one side, two on the other, on waist-high tables of stone.

But this time a new detail had been added. Maule got a fleeting look at the treasure he was carrying, when the thief took his loot briefly from his mouth, examined it momentarily, then put it back again. The stolen object had the appearance of a giant ruby, and this was obviously no ordinary gem. The weight of it was almost as startling as its beauty.

The small Stone lay so heavy in his dream hands that it pulled them down. While it lay in his palm, it sent forth one coruscating flash of light. A startling, knife-sharp flash of red that brightened the dark passage, a sudden sunrise within the little rock.

. . . *and Maule recalled that he had seen that flash before, or something very like it, in recent waking life.* And again there came that wavering in its appearance, a momentary reversal of light and dark. A glassy flash within the little rock, as if it were a tiny window to some new universe, and in that universe there rose a sun that had never before been seen by mortal eyes.

For the merest instant the burden in the dreamer's palm took on the aspect of a red scarab, and for that instant gave him the sensation that it was scrambling in his hand, trying to get away. Tiny claws, like a child's fingernails, were scraping at his palm. . . .

". . . and at that point the vision faded." Maule had slept fully dressed, a soldier on the battlefield. Now he was sitting up in his hotel bed, recounting his latest dream to a ring of anxious faces. "And the Stone he carried in his mouth felt as cold as ice. What significance ought we to read in that? Ice, simple water ice, was one form of mineral that was never to be seen in ancient Egypt. Therefore it would have been much more rare in pharaoh's court than diamonds.

"But this ice did not melt. By now, the thief's tongue, the roof of his mouth, were numb with cold.

"He might have thought of trying to hide his loot by swallowing it, but it was simply too big to allow that. He might have tucked it into the simple loincloth that was his only garment, but he did not—maybe that had proved an unreliable pocket in the past."

"What happened then?"

"The dream broke off at that point."

Andy's young face looked worn and tired, but at the moment its expression was of relief.

"You were kind of yelling, Uncle Matt. It scared me. I didn't know . . ."

Swinging his legs out of the hotel bed, Maule stood up. Even for one immune to fear, nightmares could be—unpleasant. "The monster may not yet realize I am immune to fear. I wonder if he is? Probably not." The thought gave Uncle Matthew something to smile about.

Andy, watching, felt a shiver go down his spine.

An hour or so after noon, Dolly reported that the monster had stopped moving, though he was still submerged in Rock Creek.

"What is he doing?" Maule sounded as patiently implacable as ever.

"Just waiting . . . I think. I don't know, he's never acted like this since I've been following him. Is he hungry? Is he tired, angry? I don't know, I can never tell."

To land at the small airport nearest to Red Lodge would be sure to draw unwelcome attention. After a brief discussion it was decided that it would be better to leave the plane in Billings, with the pilot standing by to bring it on if and when Joe called for it. The drive from Billings to Red Lodge was a short one, with good highways all the way, and it seemed that it should only take about an hour.

With Maule's approval, Joe Keogh also rented an additional vehicle, a smaller four-wheel-drive, to complement the SUV, and give the party greater maneuverability.

It was John Southerland, starting to gather his few belongings, preparing to resume the chase, who asked wearily: "How long can this go on?"

Maule's response was quick, and flinty. "Until Sobek is dead—or I am."

It was midafternoon, and the five of them were checking out of the hotel. Dolly's latest report, obtained just before she left her room, told them that Sobek had still not moved.

"You know," she said at last, "I still don't understand

a thing about this alchemy. I never heard of it until Gramp started on this craziness."

Maule sighed. "I admit I have some knowledge of its theories and its jargon. One of the fruits of a misspent youth."

"Then just what is this Philosopher's Stone?"

Joe Keogh put in: "I second the question. Trying to turn lead into gold—isn't that the game?"

"Indeed it is. Though the devotees of alchemy will tell you that such materialistic achievements are beside the point, mere details in their search for spiritual enlightenment."

"Learning to make gold out of lead sounds like just the kind of enlightenment that would appeal to most people."

"Indeed it is, Joseph. Wealth is an addictive drug, and gold can bring on the obsession in its most virulent form."

Maule was grimly silent for a moment. "I can personally vouch for one thing—our great enemy believes very strongly in the treasure, its power and reality. Sobek is utterly determined to have the Stone."

Joe sounded weary. "So, he believes in it. Trouble is, we know he's crazy. *But*—all right, maybe he knows more about the subject than we do—it'd be hard to know any less. And that's another problem: almost everything we think we know comes from this collective dream that some of us keep having."

"Our knowledge of the statues," Maule pointed out, "came also from the dream, and they have turned out to be real."

"Yeah. Well, anything or anybody that survived from ancient Egypt . . ." Joe's voice trailed off as a thought struck him. "Were there *nosferatu* back in those days?"

Uncle Matt mulled the question over for a moment before answering. "I shall tell you a true and verifiable story, and when you have heard it, you may judge that matter for yourself.

"In 1952, archaeologists digging beneath an unfinished pyramid at Saqqara uncovered the tomb of the Third Dynasty king, Horus Sekhemkhet.

"Like the tombs of many other pharaohs, the burial chamber had been doubly and triply sealed. But unlike almost all the others, the seals were still unbroken after three thousand years. So it was with the sarcophagus itself. The investigators glowed with anticipation—for once the less academic looters had not been before them. But when the sarcophagus was opened, it proved to be empty—as empty as my own tomb is at the moment."

~ 20 ~

Dickon might be good at hiding, but there were certain things that Connie was very good at too. And one of them was finding what had been hidden.

When Connie knocked on Dickon's door, there was at first no answer. But she persisted. Kept knocking, right hand, left hand, using both sets of little knuckles. She walked back and forth on the little wooden porch, tried without success to peer in through the little window, where she tapped briskly on the glass.

Well over two hundred years had passed since she had taken part in anything like an actual battle, and she had done the best she could to dress herself for the occasion, borrowing clothes in a way that would have upset the righteous Mr. Maule if he had known about it. Even so, the best Connie had been able to come up with was a set of almost-military camouflage fatigues, complete with a soft, matching hat. She thought the boots were truly ugly, but what else could one do? Anyway, the state of women's fashion in 2001 was deplorable, and probably no one would think her appearance especially odd.

The small cabin was solidly built of logs, and looked to be some decades old. The slanted roof looked solid too, but the place had a generally uninhabited appearance. No real road came near its door, only a kind of double track whose rank growth of weeds showed how little traffic passed this way. Not many people would ever set eyes on this little, abandoned-looking house, and none who did would have any reason to believe that it contained anything worth stealing.

Even on the brightest days, the sun would have little to do with Dickon's house. It nestled in a mixed grove of evergreens and aspens, trees pressing close on every side, so that you might walk by within a hundred feet of the little building and never see it.

Now she was listening, her ear pressed against the door. The nearby creek kept up its steady, tumbling roar, but the inside of the cabin was quiet as the grave. Indeed, Connie had known some graves that were practically pandemonium compared to this.

In another moment, giving way to restless impatience, she had started walking completely around the cabin. There could be no more than two rooms inside at the most, she thought. In the rear wall was a back door, tightly closed, narrow and solid, no more inviting than the door in front. Twenty yards or so behind the cabin, almost lost among trees, stood a tiny building that must be, or have been, the outhouse. Connie shuddered delicately—eat and eliminate, eat and eliminate, the lives of breathers were so messy!

But Maule had entrusted her with important business, and she would not allow herself to be distracted. The cabin windows were all small, and each was solidly covered, inside its dusty but intact glass, with a plain interior curtain. It was practically impossible for anyone outside to see in. None of the windows were open in the summery warmth—not that Connie, lacking an invitation, would have been able to sneak in anyway.

For some time now, for longer than she could clearly remember, she had been hearing rumors, in certain circles where she moved and the elegant Mr. Maule did not, that Dickon owned some kind of retreat, perhaps better called a hideout, somewhere in the northern Rockies. She hadn't wanted to admit to Maule that she knew that much—he would be very angry to learn that she had been withholding any information.

But when she checked out the rumor, it proved to be correct.

For Dickon, the sight and sound of Connie in broad daylight, dancing about on nervous feet outside his door, trilling her usual cheery nonsense at him, came as a devastating shock.

Less than half an hour to go to sunset, and he had just awakened from a troubled daylight sleep.

Connie was obviously not in the least troubled by any doubts that he might not be here. After walking completely around his house she started calling to him, in an old and melodious language, saying she knew very well he was inside. "You might as well come to the door, dear Dickie, and speak to me as if you were civilized."

Muttering obscenities in several languages, realizing it was hopeless to pretend he was not home, Dickon gave up and called an answer to her through the door.

Before he would talk of anything else, he extracted a promise that she would not tell Maule or Sobek where he was.

She gave the pledge so lightly and cheerfully that he could have no hope at all that she might mean it. "You could invite me in, you know. I could bring in one or two of these rabbits or squirrels that seem to be everywhere out here, and we could have a drink. You have nothing to worry about, dear Dickon. Why should I want to harm you?"

"I don't know! Why does anyone want to harm anyone? Please go away."

"If you won't let me in, then I must continue to talk to you through the door."

"Why?"

"Because."

"*Why?*"

"Because I have an important question for you."

Dickon got his in first. "Does Vlad Tepes know where I am?"

"No, I'm sure he doesn't. He was asking me if I knew."

"Please, Constanzia, please! You must not tell him!" Dickon raved on, assuring Connie that he was willing to do anything, anything, to square himself with Dracula. "Though of course, after what has happened, that cannot be possible."

"Oh, I don't know. He said that when I found you, I should tell you that all he wanted from you was information. Whatever harm you may have done has been forgiven."

Dickon could not believe that for a moment. "Whatever has befallen his young—young nephew—it is not my fault!" Dickon proclaimed his innocence with righteous fervor—by now he had talked himself into believing he was innocent.

"Oh, the young man? The son of Joseph Keogh? He

was perfectly healthy when I saw him last. That was only—only a couple of days ago." Connie didn't want to say she had spoken with Andy within the last few hours.

"Really? He's unhurt?" Dickon desperately wanted to believe that. "Oh, that is good news. Are you telling me the truth?"

Connie was suddenly indignant. "Little Andy is all right, I tell you, but no thanks to you. Do you now consider, Dickon, that you may bear any responsibility for endangering the young man's life?"

"I, responsible? I tried to tell our beloved Mr. Maule, truly I did, that the creature endeavoring to kill me was deadly dangerous. But he—he . . ." He let it die away.

Connie had absolutely no fear of Dickon, knowing what a coward he was. If he did let her in, she meant to box his ears. "Were you not in the habit of crying wolf at every puppy, he might have believed you then."

Dickon made a wordless sound of misery.

"Dickon? What are you going to do now?"

"I don't know! How can I know?" Dickon was in an agony of indecision, which, as Connie had observed, was quite a common state—she supposed it went with being always fearful.

Connie now told him about the statue smashed in the house of Nicolas Flamel, down south in New Mexico. "Do you realize how your trusted partner was trying to cheat you? You know that Mr. Maule is someone you can trust."

"Shocking," said Dickon, absorbing the news about the image fragmented in Albuquerque, and found to be devoid of any prize. "That is truly shocking."

And he meant it too. Even as he spoke, he was staring at an object resting on his floor—actually one edge was on the floor, while another was leaning at an angle against one of the thick log posts that supported the one-room cabin's exposed roof beams. The object was a FedEx shipping box, received here almost a month ago but still tightly sealed. Since Dickon's return to the cabin a few days ago, he had looked at the package often, even as he was looking at it now. But the recipient of this swift shipment had yet to touch it.

No need to open the box to find out what was inside—Dickon knew that perfectly well, for he had shipped the package to himself, under the name in which he owned the cabin. He had left a note tacked to the door, directing that all deliveries should simply be set inside. When the truck actually approached, Dickon had heard it coming in the distance, and went out, leaving his door unlocked. And when it arrived, he had been watching carefully from behind some trees only a few yards away, making sure the box was safely delivered.

Now that he had heard the fate of Flamel's statue, Dickon knew that his own must be the last unbroken copy. And he could be virtually certain that it contained the prize.

The evidence was now clear that each of his late partners had independently taken a similar step, reserving a single copy of the statue for himself. That, of course, had been before any of them had quite realized that the little figures were much more than simply magical aids that might be helpful in creating the Stone. In fact, the Stone had already been created, thousands of years ago, and actually lay hidden inside one of the figures. Sobek, the dreamer and sender of dreams, already gifted with divine power, had been the first to grasp that point. . . .

Each of Dickon's partners had intended to work secretly with his stealthily obtained statue, in hope of gaining the secret of the Stone all for himself. Dickon himself had done the same. And now Flamel and Tamarack were both dead, their statues smashed and worthless.

For once, it seemed, the goddess of fortune, whoever that might be, had smiled on Dickon. Unless Sobek and all the others were completely deluded about the way the great gem had been hidden, the treasure was now here, in Dickon's hands the moment he reached out for it. Power even beyond what Sobek wielded, power that Dickon could scarcely imagine, lay on the floor of his rude cabin waiting for him, for anyone, to simply open the package.

But so far, even before he had been absolutely sure of what the package must contain, Dickon had been too afraid to open it, too timid even to hold the statue in his hands.

The truth was, he feared the power of the Stone in his own hands almost as much as he dreaded to think of it in the hands of any other.

Now, Connie. Did she suspect he had a statue here in his cabin? Quite possibly. Almost certainly, in fact. Could she somehow even *know* he did?

Dickon couldn't tell.

Of course he had locked the package in his cabin when he went back to Chicago. Then when he had returned here, only a few days ago, it was with considerable relief that he found the box still waiting for him just as he had left it, unopened, untouched, undiscovered by any of his enemies. After Sobek had nearly killed him in Chicago, Dickon had gone to earth here in his secret place. Hunting in the woods at night provided all the mammalian blood he needed. Under the worn wood floorboards lay a substantial store of the black earth of

Dickon's native Britain. Like the statue, it had taken him some time and trouble and ingenuity to get the necessary soil conveyed here in small parcels.

But the sensation of relief did not last long—for Dickon pleasant feelings never did. Out of his ghostly throng of chronic worries, a new dread always came pushing forward, ready to dominate his existence.

Possibly Connie did not guess that the Stone was here, but the Crocodile was a thousand times more cunning than she. Dickon could not shake his apprehension that Sobek had somehow discovered his secret stronghold, that the monster had learned the prize was here, and was on his way to claim it at this very moment.

As a god, the Crocodile needed no help from lesser beings.

Connie had now completed her slow walk all around his house, and was back on his porch, where she seemed to be trying to peer in through the keyhole—of course he had made sure that was covered.

But her sweet voice could get in. "Do you know what your trouble is, Dickon? If you think that everything in the whole world is just too frightening to think about, then you have to spend your life just trying not to think about one thing after another."

He wasn't going to try to sort that out. "What is Maule doing now? What do you know of Sobek?"

"What would you expect? The two of them are contending to see who can get control of the Philosopher's Stone." She sighed and sounded mournful. "I think dear Mr. Maule would be better off if he could allow himself to show a little fear."

Dickon's worst fears, or one set of them anyway, were thus confirmed. Sooner or later Maule and the monster were probably both going to show up at his door. Trying to be logical, he told himself fiercely that the Stone itself, once he held it in his hand, would probably reveal to him the means of using it. It would grant him such power that he would need to be afraid of nothing and of no one. Ah, by all the gods, to be free of fear, utterly free of fear at last . . .

But even the prospect of courage and freedom carried its own anxiety. Any ordinary human, breathing or unbreathing, who possessed such a treasure must stand in terror of losing it. And Dickon had been so terribly frightened for so long, his soul so soaked and saturated in terror, that fear now occupied the core of his being.

Clinging to the inside of his front door, pressing his mouth almost against the wood, he whispered: "Connie? It is terrible. If I were suddenly to cease to be afraid . . . I don't know *who I would be,* then."

The contempt in Connie's voice was plain, even through the thickness of the door: "I see now you are afraid of becoming brave. And that is the worst cowardice of all."

"Are you never afraid? Or are you like *him,* the great—great—"

"No, I am not much like Vlad Drakulya—he is one of a kind. I am afraid of some things. Many things, I suppose. The Crocodile, for one. I wish he would not send us all these ugly dreams. Do you get them too?"

"Yes, oh yes. The scene in ancient Egypt. The five little statues. Then the thief runs on, eventually out into the hot sun again . . ."

Connie was not listening, she was airing her own complaints. She knew that as a *nosferatu* she stood in much greater danger than any breather of being eaten by the great Crocodile, more or less alive.

Trying to keep himself from thinking about that, Dickon soon interrupted, tremulously posing a question: "Tell me, with regard to this great contest between Maule and Sobek—how are they going about trying to find the statue? How will either one of them discover where it is?"

"Oh, how should I know? They each have their magic, I suppose."

From Billings the small convoy of two vehicles headed west on Interstate 90, in the direction of Butte. Andy was driving the SUV, with Maule, once more wearing hat and sunglasses, seated beside him, and Dolly in the next row back. The conversation had taken a turn back to the strange events with which the adventure had begun.

Andy was saying to Uncle Matt. "As far as I can remember—I was working on your stuff there and I just fell asleep. Really crashed, right in my chair."

Maule nodded. "As I did, in mine. But in each case the crash, as you call it, was by no means accidental."

"I thought we were both just tired. But . . ."

Maule was shaking his head. "Death passed us by, quite closely, on that night." And, with Dolly listening wide-eyed from the next seat back, he went on to relate the basic facts regarding the murder of Tamarack.

After the fantastic events of the past few days, Andy was prepared to believe the story.

"So by the time Dad got to your place—and I woke up—there was this murder victim lying in a bedroom down the hall?"

"There was indeed. And both you and I were fortunate not to share his fate. Do you remember anything else about that evening and that night, anything at all?"

Andy shrugged his shoulders, as best he could, keeping his hands on the wheel.

After only a few miles on the Interstate, they reached their turnoff, at a place called Laurel. Now they were on the two-lane Beartooth Highway, which over the next few dozen miles made repeated crossings of winding streams. Andy saw signs identifying first the Yellowstone River, and then Rock Creek. His father, driving the other vehicle, came on the radio to comment on the fact.

Maule had hitched around in his seat and was once more hypnotizing Dolly, who reported that the Crocodile's movements had become shorter and slower, more and more erratic.

Uncle Matthew nodded slowly. "The most likely interpretation is that he is very near his goal."

After passing a few small settlements the little convoy had come to Red Lodge, which looked to have about two thousand people in it, small houses surrounding a one-street business district about six blocks long. Rock Creek ran right through town. There were several promising hotels, and a few shops selling antiques and curios, including one whose sign offered good deals on buffalo skulls, wholesale and retail.

"It could be in one of these shops," Joe commented.

Maule had his doubts. "Possibly, but I think not. Our enemy has already progressed upstream from the town."

Joe decided it would be a good idea to have some facilities lined up, in case they wound up spending the night here. The neatest-looking hotel was right on Main Street, and fortunately had a sufficient number of rooms available.

*   *   *

All his life Vlad Drakulya had trusted his instincts when in great peril—and following that course had kept him alive for more than five centuries. Now his instincts told him that a final battle was coming soon, perhaps within a few hours. He could feel it like an impending storm.

The shadows of the summer afternoon were lengthening. Andy and his dad were strolling the short Red Lodge business district, having sworn to Maule that they would stray no farther than a block from their hotel. Both men marveled to see a pickup truck yield the right of way to a mere pedestrian.

Andy saw pepper spray prominently displayed on sale in a local store, labeled as bear repellent. Talking to the storekeeper, Andy learned it was a common belief among the citizens of Red Lodge that on cold nights in spring and fall, bears came into town. And not the common, backwoods-variety black bears either: these were grizzlies. Or so the story went.

Tonight, thought Andy, there might well be something even stranger than a grizzly prowling. Looking wistfully at the pepper spray, he tried to imagine that it might be of help.

After hearing the latest report from Dolly, of slow but seemingly purposeful movement by the Crocodile, Maule quickly but unhurriedly gathered his troops. In a few minutes, they were in their vehicles again, following the narrow highway west out of Red Lodge. This time Maule was at the wheel of the larger SUV, while Joe followed, driving the smaller one.

After a few miles, with the serious foothills of the Beartooth Range beginning to bulk around the road, Uncle Matt called for a conference, and turned off on an unpaved lane.

After briefly conferring with the vehicles parked side by side, Maule dispatched Joe and John in their Jeep to take a position about a mile ahead. There, according to their most recently acquired road map, the lightly traveled lane that they were on once more came close to a bend in the creek.

Maule pointed with a dangerous-looking fingernail. "The monster is now in the creek somewhere between here and there, and when you are in position, we will have him between us. I mean to approach him, slowly, from this direction, and challenge him—I think I can wait no longer. Which way he will move next, if he moves at all, I do not know. But I will have my phone—though I may turn it off if I believe I am near the enemy. If you see him, in the stream or on land, call me instantly."

As soon as Joe and John had driven off, Maule moved the SUV a little distance, then parked it offroad in a quiet place. Then he got out, withdrawing the spear from its resting place in the middle of the cabin.

He told Andy and Dolly that he was going to leave them for a time. "The best way to protect you now, and to protect the rest of the world, is by eliminating the source of danger."

Andy gestured with his empty hands. "What do we do?"

"I cannot give you precise orders, for I do not know what may happen. Probably you will do best to remain in or near the vehicle, and drive quickly away if immediate danger threatens. Of course the radio may be of some benefit." Maule turned and glided noiselessly away, spear balanced in his hand.

"Protect yourself," Dolly called quietly after him.

Maule raised his spear in a silent wave of acknowledgment, and vanished into the shadows between tall trees.

Andy and Dolly were left alone. They had nothing to do at the moment but wait, taking in the beginnings of a sunset show. Clouds in the west concealed the sun, but night had not yet fallen.

There was still plenty of daylight to see the lone figure, certainly not Uncle Matthew, that came walking toward them out of the woods.

"Who in the hell is that . . . Connie?" Andy heard his own voice go high with the release of tension. It was the camouflage suit and combat boots Connie was wearing that made her hard to recognize. Now he rolled down his window.

Moving briskly up on the driver's side of the SUV, Connie acknowledged Dolly's presence with a nod of greeting. But when she spoke she seemed to be talking only to Andy. "I have something to show you, young man. I have promised someone, very solemnly, that I will never show it to Mr. Maule—" A smile, a tiny, wicked giggle. "—but of course if *you* should show it to your uncle sometime soon, that will not be my fault, will it?"

He moved awkwardly in the driver's seat, wondering what was she talking about.

"No, do not start your engine. And leave the headlights off. Dear Andee, you should come with me on foot, this way, for just a moment. The young lady will excuse us."

Andy looked at his companion, who shook her head in puzzlement. He sighed, and opened his door. "Be right back," he told Dolly.

"I'll stay in the truck and keep an ear on the radio." Then she raised her shotgun, hacked-off barrels high. "Want to borrow this?"

"No, you keep it."

With Dolly waiting alone in the SUV a hundred feet or so away, out of sight behind some trees and brush, Andy and Connie were for the moment utterly alone. From somewhere along the bottom of the wooded slope in front of them came the muted roar of Rock Creek, dealing with the boulders and outcroppings that ever tried to hold it back. Twilight was definitely approaching.

"What is it you want to show me?"

Connie folded her pretty hands, almost as if in prayer. "Ahh, Andee, the true answer to that question is that I would like to show you the ways of love. You may think you know something of those ways, dear young man, but in truth you have no idea."

And with a smile unlike any he had ever seen before, she reached out and patted him on the cheek. "Has dear Uncle Matthew been telling you things about me? Has he warned you against me, how terrible I am because I am like him? They call us the 'undead,' you know. But what is one to make of such a word? What can this 'undead' mean, except we are not dead, and still alive? Aren't you just as much undead as me?"

Andy swallowed. He wanted very much to take this woman in his arms, combat fatigues and all, and see what happened next. Maybe someday.

Connie laughed softly. "Are you worried of what dear Vlad will think, if you and I make love? Ah, I can only hope that he is still alive when that time comes. He understands, my dear. Only if you were somehow cruel or unpleasant to me would he be upset—and I am sure you will never be cruel."

For a moment, the vampire looked almost the perfect type of helpless maiden. "You don't think he could be *jealous,* do you? You must understand that he and I have gone beyond being jealous of each other. He takes lovers, as I do. What persists between the two of us is certainly love, if that word means anything at all. And the love between us is still very strong—stronger than you can imagine. But it no longer depends on—what is the preferred way of putting it, nowadays?—no longer depends on the exchange of any bodily fluids. That has been impossible for us for many years, since both of us are *nosferatu.* So you need not worry that your uncle will be jealous."

"I haven't really been worrying about that. Maybe I'd better get back to the—"

When Andy made a halfhearted effort to pull away, Connie caught his sleeve with her little hand and effortlessly pulled him back. "But another time we will talk of what is in our hearts. What I must show you is something else altogether. Come here. Come here!"

She tugged him a few yards farther, so that they stood together, looking down over tiers of treetops, surveying a long, irregular slope in fading daylight. She put one arm round Andy's waist, and pointed with the other. "There. Behold what I must show you, a little house."

Andy looked. Perhaps a quarter of a mile away stood a log cabin, with a shingled roof, almost entirely swallowed up in trees.

"It is owned by the man you know as Dickon." Connie sighed. "I believe he uses it to keep things in, to hide things he does not wish to have discovered. I have never been invited into that cabin, and I never will be. So, it is impossible for me to enter. Dear Vlad would also be kept out, if he were here. However much dear Uncle Matthew huffed and puffed, and threatened to blow down the walls, against him they would stand. But of course you and your lovely Dolly can go in, my dear."

"Why should we do that?"

"I think it very likely that the answer we are all looking for is to be found inside that little house. I have known Dickon for more centuries than you would believe, and I know his voice. When I talked to him he was hiding something, something he desperately wanted to keep secret."

~ 21 ~

A ndy and Dolly had left the SUV, dark and locked, behind them. They were walking together now, looking for the faint descending footpath Connie had told him would lead down to the lane, and eventually to the cabin she had said was Dickon's. Dolly was carrying her shotgun, but all Andy had in hand was the little flashlight, and he was trying out its beam. Around them the shades of dusk were thickening by the moment.

Connie had disappeared, after offering some last words of advice, cautioning them both that there was no time to lose if they wanted to get their hands on the Philosopher's Stone.

Naturally Andy had put in a radio call to his father and uncle. Joe and John were still waiting in their vehicle where Maule had posted them, about a mile away. Joe had been able to offer his son only some tentative advice. He was not ready to accept anything Connie said as gospel, but he thought Andy and Dolly might as well investigate the cabin if they wanted to. Meanwhile the two men were staying where they were for the time being.

Both parties had attempted to reach Maule by cell phone, but got no response.

"Uncle Matt said he might turn his phone off," Dolly reminded her companion.

"Yeah. And Connie told me she was going to try to find him. Maybe she will. We don't know where he is, and I don't want to just go yelling in the woods."

"That would probably not be wise."

By the time Dolly and Andy had advanced a hundred yards, moving tentatively along what might or might not be a trail, the flashlight's help was welcome in the thickening gloom. The woods were quiet, except for the steady murmur of the stream at the foot of the long slope, growing louder as they gradually approached it.

Presently Dolly asked, in a near-whisper: "Did Connie say if there was anyone in this cabin?"

"She didn't actually say, and I kind of assumed there wasn't. She just said she's pretty sure the Stone is there, and it's impossible for her to get at it. Look, she may be flaky, even for a *nosferatu,* but she's not going to betray Uncle Matt. He told us that himself. I don't think she'll do anything that would get herself into real trouble with him."

"I can understand that. I wouldn't either."

Sobek, at the beginning of his long trek north from New Mexico, had given no thought at all to the temperature of the water through which he moved. But gradually he realized that the farther north he went upon this continent, the colder the streams flowed. If this continued, it might eventually bring on an uncomfortable slowing of his mental and physical activity. If that happened, he would want to change his mode of travel.

The last stream that Sobek ascended was comparatively narrow, and so shallow in most places that he no longer could remain completely submerged. It was also colder than any other stream he had encountered on his way north, and grew still more frigid as he ascended it. Also its flow was very swift, so he had to exert some effort to make headway. These were only minor inconveniences for the Crocodile, and he still preferred to follow the watercourse rather than make his way overland, or employ the energy-draining magic that would bring him much closer to his goal without the need to traverse the space between.

How inconveniently the world had been designed, that it was not provided with a really adequate number of false doors! He meant to raise the point when he met some of his fellow deities. . . .

It was a bothersome point, to which he frequently returned in his private speculations . . . it was very strange, yes, truly extraordinary when he thought about it, that over a span of thousands of years, he had never met any other gods or goddesses at all.

On the other hand, he sometimes had trouble believing that thousands of years had really passed, since the epoch of his earliest memories. They were of a time in the ancient Temple of Sobek, the scene of the dream that never ceased. That was where and when his thronging worshipers had first gathered round him to offer him their prayers, their sacrifice. . . .

Certain rooms in the great house of memory were pleasant to return to. But most of that sprawling man-

sion was not an agreeable place in which to dwell, and
Sobek generally found the present and future more congenial.

Right now his thoughts had taken a turn toward the
nosferatu known as Dickon. He could tell that at the moment the cowardly and comparatively old one was not
far away. That very soon he should actually be in sight,
and that he was somewhere near the prize.

Muttering bubbles under water, Sobek said to himself: "The flesh of the *nosferatu* has in it a special tang
of predation, that I find quite enjoyable. But even more
than Dickon, I expect I shall enjoy the one who has been
known as Tepes. It seems to me that he is not far distant,
either."

Sobek had already decided that Tepes would prove
hopelessly unreliable as a servant. It was as well that
he had not wasted any time trying to carry out that plan.

The Crocodile was well aware, when he bothered to
think about it, that a number of his enemies were closing
in on him. But the fact did not perturb him in the least.
He was almost wholly absorbed in the fact that he had
nearly reached his goal.

Meanwhile, Sobek's days-old spear-wound itched
and burned, despite the constant laving in cold rushing
water. But right now he had little time to spare for the
contemplation of revenge. A glorious certainty was developing in his mind. His magic, informed by his divine
wisdom, was succeeding, as he had never doubted that
it would. He now knew the location of the one remaining
statue, and the precious treasure it must contain. It was
possible that some of his enemies and rivals might know
the secret too. But what those inferior beings might
think or do could hardly make any difference in the inevitable outcome.

The Crocodile moved upstream a few more yards, then brought the front half of his body up out of the surging waters of Rock Creek, the better to look around.

Daylight was fading swiftly, the sun already hidden behind the wooded flanks of a nearby hill. There was a kind of building, constructed out of logs, only a few yards upslope from the stream.

There. Almost certainly in there.

By now Maule had left the young people and the SUV a couple of hundred yards behind, well out of his sight atop a wooded slope. He could sense that he was within an approximately equal distance of his foe, somewhere ahead. But Sobek had not yet begun his final move to seize the Stone, and Maule still did not know just where it was. So he would wait a little longer. In more than five hundred years he had learned something about how to be patient.

This near his enemy, after days of striving for close mental contact with the Crocodile, Maule no longer needed Dolly or any other medium to maintain the linkage. What he sensed of the monster now told him he still had nothing to do but wait.

Nervelessly he settled himself for his last pre-combat meditation. He would conserve his energy while preparing for what would doubtless be his greatest fight. Setting his back against a tree, he slowly lowered himself into a sitting position. His eyes were closed, mind and muscles almost totally relaxed, his spear balanced in his lap. He told himself that as soon as the Crocodile moved, he would awaken instantly.

Maule's mind retreated from full consciousness, entering a state that was not like normal daytime sleep. Nor did it even bear much resemblance to common hypnotic trance. Yet it was a withdrawal deep enough to accommodate one more version of the Dream—a dream that this time was very interestingly prolonged. . . .

. . . this time Maule's mind melded with that of the running jewel thief just as the latter once more began to run, leaving behind him the room where molded plaster statues dried. Now, still gasping with the exertion of his flight, the frantic youth darted into another part of the darkened temple complex. In this next chamber a bad smell hung in the air, a faint stink reminiscent of the pestilential atmosphere in the House of the Dead, where human corpses were made ready for the long journey into eternity.

But here in Sobek's temple the preparation tables were much too small for human bodies. Quickly Maule realized that only baby crocodiles were being mummified within these rooms. In fact a number of small reptiles, already slain and gutted, were lying about in various stages of preparation.

With sounds of pursuit once more fresh behind him, the thief ran on again, reeling with weariness. Abruptly reemerging into brilliant sun, he stumbled to a halt, body near exhaustion with the heat and strain. He had come out of dimness into a long, broad, unshaded courtyard, bounded on three sides by doorless walls. A central pool of water, also long and broad, flanked on both sides by reeds and water lilies, shimmered in dazzling sunglare. Suddenly the runner's foot slipped on the flat polished stone of the poolside pavement, and he teetered for an instant on the brink of falling in.

Along the sides of the courtyard, tall palms offered scanty spots of shade, but no concealment. The far end of the pool was carved from native rock, the near end bounded by an artificial, sloping beach of tile.

The angry shouts behind him were closing in, sounding a new note of triumph, as if the hunters knew they had him trapped. There was no possible hiding place in sight—except the pool itself, should it prove deep enough. Near the far end, lily pads and blossoming stalks of tall papyrus might offer concealment enough for a man's head, or at least his nose, projecting above the water.

Advancing hastily, the thief lowered himself as quietly as he could into the sacred pool, trying not to raise waves that would betray him when his pursuers burst into the courtyard, as surely they must at any moment.

The water proved just deep enough for him to stand in, up to his neck. Half wading, half swimming with motions of his submerged arms, he was two thirds of the way to the possible shelter of the lily pads when something stirred in the depths ahead of him.

Stirred and then rose, erupting majestically through the mirrorlike calm.

A grinning crocodile head, rimmed with a picket fence of teeth, confronted the intruder, reminding him with great force just whose temple it was in which he trespassed.

The eyes atop the head were huge, all black and yellow. They hypnotized with terror, swiftly growing bigger as the huge beast lunged. . . .

. . . the dreaming Maule could feel it all, though dimly and at second hand. Every detail of the last moments of the young thief's human life. The muscles of his thin body still worn and aching from the long flight, the great jaws clamped upon his leg. The burning cold and heaviness still inside his mouth, as he tried to cry out and began to drown. . . .

The burning cold. Inside his mouth.

. . . still *inside his mouth*.

One small detail that changed the world.

As Maule's latest dream experience shattered into fragments, shards that faded quickly to grim memories, he sat up straight with his back against the tree. Other pieces, those of a puzzle, were falling into place. Eyes wide open, he said aloud into the fading twilight of the woods: "I know now where the Stone is hidden."

By the time he had finished speaking, he was on his feet, spear gripped in one hand, fingering his cell phone with the other. But he did not turn on the instrument. It would be a waste of time, he thought, to try to explain about the Stone to his allies at a distance.

Much better to talk the matter over with Sobek himself. He rather looked forward to being able to do that.

Minutes later, walking briskly toward the place where he expected to discover his enemy, he found himself approaching a small cabin. The cabin had the look and feel of being long unoccupied, and he knew that this was not the place he wanted, that the monster was still hundreds of yards ahead. But a notice had been posted on the door of this dwelling, and Maule detoured a couple of steps to read the jovial warning:

THIS HOUSE PROTECTED BY
SKINNER TAXIDERMY

Smiling lightly with appreciation, Maule found himself for some reason thinking again of Dickon. He wondered just how the elder vampire might look stuffed and mounted. Not the old fool's whole wretched body, of course. Probably only his head, fixed on a plaque of some dark wood, and displayed high on a wall, like the head of the moose that he had noticed in a tavern on the main street in Red Lodge. There was a certain satisfaction in the image.

But tonight he must devote himself to grim and earnest business. Tonight Vlad Drakulya was very likely going to die the true death, to fall before the Crocodile's power—but he was not dead yet. And now he knew something that could make all the difference. Switching on his cell phone, he gave orders to Joe and John to drive back in his direction. Explanations could wait till later.

For a while after establishing his secret hideout, Dickon had been able to tell himself that here in this private sanctuary, far from cities and crowds, he could feel secure—that no breather or *nosferatu* in the entire world had the least suspicion of where he was. His nearest neighbor's cabin was hundreds of yards distant, and that neighbor seemed never to be in residence at the same time Dickon was. Rarely had any of his neighbors seen him, and his mundane, day-to-day appearance was so ordinary that they would have paid him little attention if they did. He was certainly not the only recluse dwelling on the fringe of the Montana wilderness.

Whatever sense of security he had managed to achieve was utterly destroyed when Connie showed up on his doorstep.

Still pondering her recent visit, Dickon had now abandoned himself to a habit he had when he believed himself to be quite alone: that of talking to himself aloud.

After nervously making sure, for the thousandth or ten-thousandth time, that all of the cabin's doors and windows were securely closed, and every portal locked, he finally hurled himself, with an air of desperation, at the shipping container and with vampirish strength tore its outer packaging into shreds.

Soon his unsteady hands had freed the small white statue from its inner wrappings. His fingers trembled as he stroked the smooth and white and ancient surface, now beginning to be somewhat discolored by reason of sheer age.

A faint whining and squeaking sound, compounded of terror and desperation, emerged from deep in Dickon's unbreathing throat. *Now, do it now,* he urged himself. *Put an end to the centuries of sniveling, suffering, hiding from your own shadow.*

But all his urging accomplished nothing. He could force himself to the brink of action, but could not make the final effort. What if the miracle truly happened, he broke the statue and the Stone fell into his hands? What if the highest dreams of all the hunters, the adepts and inepts down through the centuries, were realized in him?

He could not escape the craven certainty that Sobek, the god, would instantly be aware of what had happened. And quite soon fearless Maule would also know, and presently all the others who were true adepts. From that moment, he, Dickon, would be marked as a being of great, transcendent power, the envy and target of every inhuman power and genuine wizard in the world.

Then all of them, no doubt including powerful beings of whom Dickon had never heard—all would come after him to take the Stone away, and to punish him, annihilate him, for his presumption in trying to make himself the first and greatest of them all.

Of course if he had the Stone, it ought to grant him overwhelming power—if only he, the lucky one, knew how to use it. Aye, that could be the rub, right there.

Dickon's lurid imagination was now running at full speed, and not to be denied. Probably the first to arrive here to corner him in his pitiful, useless refuge would be Sobek, and the Crocodile would not be coming to offer his congratulations.

Other powers would probably be close behind the Crocodile in the race for power. Who would emerge victorious from the melee? Not Vlad Drakulya, who was, after all, only a man. Who but Sobek, Sobek the god.

"And—and supposing, on the other hand, Maule should find me before Sobek does? What will he do to me? Ah, gods and saints and demons, help me! Maule understands by now that it was I who guided his chosen nephew nearly to his death—ah, Vlad Tepes, why was I not content to remain loyal to you?"

Dickon's imagination presented the sound of Drakulya's voice, of the footstep of Mr. Matthew Maule just outside the cabin door. Almost gibbering in terror, Dickon started, jumped at nothing.

He cursed the day when he had decided to reserve one statue for his own private research. But it was here now, and chance had decreed that it should be the one to hold the prize.

And the vivid images of what Vlad Drakulya might do to him were just as terrifying as any picture of the Crocodile that his fears could paint. In the case of Drakulya, Dickon's memory presented him with several grisly examples, standing out as remarkable even in the bloodsoaked annals of world history. That vision was enough to send him reeling, almost fainting, into near-paralysis.

*   *   *

Andy and Dolly had now almost reached the cabin's door. He was sure this was the small house Connie had pointed out to him from a quarter of a mile away.

At the last moment Dolly asked in a low whisper: "What if the monster's in there?"

He shook his head. "Connie may be dippy, but she's not the one who's been trying to get us killed—I don't know whether to be glad she disappeared, or not."

"Better knock before we try the door," Dolly advised. Having no effective way to conceal the shotgun, she was now carrying it in her right hand, the foreshortened barrels down. It seemed to her that if they should encounter any normal people on this walk, it might at least be a little less noticeable that way.

"Sure." And Andy, turning off his little flashlight, raised his right fist and knocked. The full darkness of night had not yet quite established itself. From somewhere back in the woods came a soft sound that he imagined might be the calling of an owl.

The vampire inside, lost in tortured introspection, had not heard his visitors approach. At the sound of a knock, he almost dropped the statue in his astonishment. Moments later, someone tried the door. He recognized his callers by their whispering voices, and was stunned with surprise. This was partially alleviated when he realized that Connie must have directed these children here.

Fatalistically Dickon moved to discover whether Maule had come with them. Quickly he pushed the statue and its torn wrappings under a pile of spare clothing, then stepped warily to the door and opened it.

From the startled reaction of his visitors, it was plain they had not really expected to find anyone at home. Hastily Dickon inspected the night behind the two young breathers, then stepped aside, and curtly motioned them in. He was anxious to find out if they had yet told Maule where he could be found.

As soon as they had crossed his threshold, Dickon shoved Andy out of the way and pulled the door tightly shut again. The darkness inside the cabin was absolute, except for the thin beam of Andy's little flashlight.

"Leave the door open!" Dolly ordered sharply. She wasn't pointing with her shotgun—not quite yet.

"When you are ready to leave," the old man said, calmly settling a wooden bar across the door. If Dickon had even noticed the shotgun, he gave no sign. He sounded more forceful now than she had ever heard him, and he was smiling. It seemed a harmless smile, on the face of a harmless old man—but his little shove had sent Andy staggering.

Sobek felt a divine pride in his divine magic. He was greatly pleased with how smoothly and inexorably it was now conducting him to his goal. He could feel that he was closing in upon the treasure, though the pinpointing of its exact location still eluded him. Certainly the Stone was now much closer than a quarter of a mile—yes, very much closer indeed.

Joe Keogh had been on the point of starting his engine, Maule or no Maule, and heading back to see what was happening to his son, when the call came from Uncle Matt, advising him to do just that.

"Good. This was turning into some kind of a damn snipe hunt."

With John Southerland muttering beside him, he eased the vehicle into gear and moved out slowly, using his headlights only occasionally as he drove along the bumpy, overgrown lane in the direction of the place where Maule had said the action would be taking place.

If anything that looked remotely like a crocodile should materialize out of the night in front of him, he decided that he was going to try to run it down.

Dickon had pressed his visitors to tell him whatever they knew concerning the whereabouts of Mr. Maule, and they had told him shortly that they knew nothing. It was very easy to believe that they were lying.

Andy was keeping the beam of his flashlight turned mainly in Dickon's direction, but every now and then he jerked it briefly aside, illuminating one of the single room's far corners. There was very little to be seen. Near the center of the single room stood an old cast-iron wood-stove, its metal chimney climbing through a protective metal patch built into the roof. Near the stove, a crude box held a little firewood. Against the far wall lay a disorderly pile of what looked like surplus clothing. That was about it.

There was also a narrow back door, as heavily locked and barred as the door in front.

Clearing his throat, Andy announced: "I was told that the Philosopher's Stone is in this cabin."

"Who told you such a lie as that?" Dickon's voice was going shrill. "Who? It was the witch-bitch known as Connie, was it not?"

"You were pretty good at telling lies yourself, last time we talked. Is the thing in here or not?"

Now Andy had turned his flashlight beam directly on the box of kindling wood, trying to peer into its depths.

"Put out that light!" Dickon snarled, and took a quick step forward, suddenly menacing.

Andy had never forgotten the easy strength with which this little man had torn loose a steel boot from an automobile's tire. Keeping the flashlight turned on Dickon, Andy reached into the box and grabbed up the only choice of weapon he had available, a wooden stick with somewhat pointed, jagged ends.

Dolly had leveled her shotgun. When Dickon turned and took a menacing step in her direction, she fired one barrel, the charge spreading murderously wide. Metal shot stung the vampire, drawing no blood, doing no true harm. But more shot, striking close beside him, blasted a storm of splinters from one of the timber posts supporting the cabin roof. Dickon's face and arms were suddenly pocked with blood as the wooden fragments gouged his flesh.

Letting out a scream of pain and terror, he threw up his arms, crossing them over his face, and staggered back.

A moment later, he had disappeared.

"Where in hell'd he go?"

"Vampire tricks. Never mind him, where's the Stone?"

Seizing the wood-box, Andy with a great heave turned it upside down, dumping out a trove of wood, and a scampering mouse, but nothing else.

Meanwhile Dolly was kicking, scattering the pile of assorted clothing, much of it winter gear. Here were paper wrappings that had been buried, and—

"Andy!"

He turned swiftly, the flashlight's beam quickly centering on an object of startling white.

Dolly was just reaching for the statue, when the heavy front door, the one that Dickon had just rebarred, burst in with a great crash.

The incredible shape of the monster, a crocodile walking on two legs, filled the doorway.

Dickon suddenly reappeared, still in human shape and marked with his own blood, groveling on the floor and screaming.

Dolly's reaching hand had just touched the great prize when Sobek's huge reptilian paw knocked her hand away and snatched it up.

Andy fumbling at the back door—only for a fraction of a second, but it seemed like months—lifted the heavy wooden bar and hurled it aside. Somehow bolts and catches yielded. Dolly was with him, turning, firing her second barrel into the cabin's darkness. The flaring blast from the shortened gun barrel showed her the Crocodile's heavy paw raising the small white statue in triumph. It seemed that Sobek minded shotgun pellets no more than confetti.

In the next instant, Andy had the back door open. Both breathing humans seemed to squeeze through the narrow aperture at the same time.

Moving quickly toward the cabin from in front, Maule observed the escape of the two young people with relief and satisfaction. A moment later he had stepped up on the porch, spear ready in his hand. Without pausing he swiftly moved inside, through the gaping hole where Sobek had already demolished the front door.

Dickon, cringing and bleeding on the floor, looked up at him with unbelieving eyes.

Maule gave the coward one of his warmest smiles. "Have you forgotten, old one? Not many days ago you gave me a blanket invitation, never to be revoked—I can enter any dwelling you may ever own."

As Dickon shriveled, Vlad Drakulya shifted his gaze to Sobek, who stood before him on two stubby, reptilian legs, holding the last statue up in one greenish and malformed hand.

The Crocodile turned toward Maule a gaze of perfect arrogance. "It is too late now, Tepes, for you to surrender on favorable terms. Now I have caught you."

Maule shook his head. He was standing straight upright, spear balanced in his right hand, point toward Sobek.

Dolores Flamel and Andy, running for their lives, heading uphill to where they had left the SUV, could see the lights and hear the engine of the smaller vehicle in which Joe and John were approaching.

Dickon, peering up between his fingers like a child, could see that Maule was still smiling, but now in a way that suggested sadness. Maule said to the Crocodile: "I told you when we last met that you might catch me—and then wish that you had caught the plague instead."

Sobek as usual did not seem to be listening. Tauntingly he held up the statue, as if perhaps he expected Maule to make a grab for it. Sobek rubbed it with his reptilian fingers. "I can feel that the Stone is very near."

Dracula nodded slightly. "Oh, yes. Very near to you indeed. But it has taken you a long time to realize the fact."

"I mean to kill you slowly, Tepes."

Maule nodded. "Before you try, I intend to tell you a story. But perhaps you are already familiar with this tale—I am told it is commonly repeated from one end of Africa to the other."

"I have nothing to do with stories."

"But I would like you to hear this one. It has to do with a crocodile, one famed for his strength and cunning and ambition, which even excelled the remarkable attributes enjoyed by most of his race—your race.

"It is instructive—as Cousin Sherlock used to say—to contemplate the artistry of this great predator. How, when some land-based animal approached the water to drink, the crocodile lunged up out of concealment to grab its victim by a foreleg. Then, with a single, overpowering, twisting surge of strength, pulled its unfortunate captive into the water, broke its bones, and held it under until it had drowned."

Sobek, Maule noted, was listening now, as if despite himself. He even seemed to be enjoying the story. It was as if no one had ever told him a story before.

Smoothly the narrator went on: "On one memorable occasion, our noble crocodile appeared to have transcended the achievements of all others of its race. He gave the impression of setting forth to conquer new worlds, because he was observed by many to have attained a position high in the branches of a thorn tree, yards inland from the water and many feet above the ground.

"Every climbing and flying creature for a mile around came to perch in the nearby treetops and admire this accomplishment. But alas, your namesake was already uncomfortable at such an elevation, and soon discomfort was too weak a word to describe what he was feeling. Before an hour had gone by the vultures were pecking at his eyes."

Sobek was still listening, but it was plain that he no longer found the story entertaining.

Maule went on: "Some were ready to credit that

crocodile with divine powers, but the true explanation was somewhat more mundane."

A growl.

Maule shifted his position. "Before you try to kill me slowly, you must let me deliver what I believe is called the punch line. You see, the last thirsty animal he grabbed by a foreleg had turned out to be an elephant."

~ 22 ~

"You tell an amusing story, Tepes. But what has it to do with me?"

"More than you might think. Perhaps, like you, your namesake had come to believe he was a god. He dared to bite the elephant, only because he had forgotten who he really was."

Sobek's voice and bearing were those of an emperor. He said: "I *am* a god. If I have forgotten anything in these three thousand years, it is only because I have chosen to forget."

Maule shook his head. "Memory does not become more reliable as the years turn into centuries, and the centuries add up. I am a mere youth compared to you, but even I . . . there are things I have forgotten. The farther back one gazes along the path of history, the thicker grow the mists of time. At some point they tend to swallow up the truth."

Deliberately the Crocodile turned a little aside, as if it were trying to ignore its enemy. Once more it centered its attention on the little statue in its great green hands.

Maule prodded sharply: "Are you afraid to listen to me, monster? Can you really think back to the day when those clever Egyptian adepts created this version of the Stone, then had it stolen from them? Your name was not Sobek on that day, was it?"

After waiting briefly for an answer that did not come, Maule went on: "Probably you truly do not remember what your name was. Nor does it matter, I suppose. But you were no more a god then than you are now."

Dracula's voice sank low on the next words. "You began that incredible day as a human being—though a human of the most contemptible type. You were the thief."

"What?" For once the Crocodile was fairly startled, and swung round on Maule again. "What insanity is this?"

Maule calmly shook his head. "You were the robber, the two-legged child of the streets."

Sobek was growing angry. "A damned lie! Who has told you such a tale?"

"It was your own dream, your endless, ongoing dream that we were cursed to watch, that told me part of it. Another part came from something I saw in you—a certain flash of light—at our first meeting."

Connie was standing at a little distance from the cabin, close enough for her *nosferatu* ears to hear what was being said inside. Joe and John, their weapons drawn, were slowly rolling closer in their four-wheel drive.

Dolly was trying to convince herself to run back up-hill to the SUV, in search of shells to reload her shotgun. "I had some, somewhere—"

"Never mind, it won't help." Andy had stopped running when she stopped, and was now edging back toward the cabin. Now and then he could hear the rumble of Sobek's voice coming from inside, but was still too far away to hear Uncle Matt's.

Maule was going on: "But you were also something even lower than a thief, if that is possible. You were a nearly brainless beast, whose blood ran cold, who crawled in slime. And you still are."

Sobek was holding the statue close to his body now, as if to keep his trembling hands from dropping it. He moved a step nearer his antagonist. "I will kill you, Tepes. Kill you slowly."

Maule shrugged. "Soon or late, the true death comes to everyone."

Then he raised his spear. "Break your statue," he advised. "You will find it empty, as empty as all the others. The Stone was never in any of them."

"You are insane!"

"Not I. The Philosopher's Stone lies buried in your monstrous heart, where it has been for three thousand years. What lesser power could possibly have made you what you are?"

For a second it seemed that the Crocodile had been paralyzed. Then its great hands crushed the statue, letting the remnants dribble away in a stream of white chips and black organic residue. In another moment Sobek was down on all fours on the cabin floor, unbelieving, searching the debris for a prize that was not there.

Dracula's spear-thrust came at him too quickly for a breather's eye to follow. Swift as it was, it still was parried by the rapid movement of a thick forelimb. Bellowing hoarsely, the monster sprang up from the floor into a charge.

In the next moment, the spinning bodies of Crocodile and vampire, grappling for advantage, had burst outdoors, crashing right through the sturdy wall beside the ruined doorway. Thick logs were jarred loose, and a large section of the wall came crashing down. Maule had one shoulder jammed up under his enemy's lower jaw, keeping his body too close for the Crocodile to bite.

The Crocodile's hide shone dull green in the Jeep's headlights, making a big target, and Joe leapt from the driver's seat to fire round after round. This time he had loaded steel-jacketed lead, not wood, and so had no fear of hitting the vampire by mistake.

He heard the sharp sound of metal impact on the monster's scales, blending with the crack of his revolver. But the green shape bellowed and fought as fiercely as before, showing no sign of damage.

Beside him, John had pulled out an automatic pistol and opened up his own barrage, with no more noticeable effect on Sobek.

The struggling combatants had now rolled down the short slope below the cabin, into the rushing waters of Rock Creek, knocking down small trees and bushes in the process.

John and Joe had emptied their weapons, and were pausing to reload. Not that it seemed like it was going to do much good.

"Lead's no better than paperwads," Joe gasped.

"Next time we try depleted uranium."

No sooner had the fighters fallen into the creek than they surged out again, Sobek roaring and bellowing in his rage.

Maule had been forced to drop his spear at the start

of the wrestling match, back near the cabin. Now he changed abruptly to wolf-form, breaking free of his opponent in the process. In a burst of four-legged speed he bounded over the stream, and dashed up the slope, at the top regaining his human form, to snatch up his weapon in both hands.

The great Crocodile had recrossed the stream bed also, and now he lowered his belly to the ground and charged again, making startling uphill speed on his four stubby legs.

Several breathers' voices cried out unnecessary warnings. Instead of trying to avoid the charge, Dracula screamed out a war cry and lunged forward with his long spear leveled like a lance, aiming for the monster's open mouth.

In their first encounter, back in Illinois, his enemy had adroitly dodged this thrust, and the spear had only torn a few scales from his shoulder. Now the monster snapped his jaws shut at the last moment, and twisted to one side; but this time Maule's second reaction was quicker than before. With a sound like a crowbar pounded on an anvil, the spear-point glanced from a row of teeth, to tear open a small wound at the corner of the mouth.

A fraction of a heartbeat later, the great jaws snapped sideways with blurring speed, to close with a ringing clang on nothing but damp air, as the man dodged neatly away.

The sparring and maneuvering went on, moving closer to the cabin and then away from it again, working up and down the slope. Maule's breathing allies kept hovering anxiously, unable to do anything to help, trying to stay close without getting run over. Dolly had abandoned all thought of running for more shells, and was gripping her shotgun in two hands like a club. Still she wisely was not trying to get close enough to use it.

John and Joe, back at their vehicle, argued whether they should turn off the headlights or not. Let it be, they decided; if Maule wanted less light, he could shout an order.

In the end, it seemed to make no difference.

Sobek must have been shaken by Maule's revelation, shaken even more by his failure to crush the vampire quickly, and by the sting of a new wound. One side of his great cheekless mouth was steadily leaking blood, of a bright unnatural red.

"You are a liar, Tepes!" he roared madly. "Your story is all lies, vicious and childish lies!"

Then, belatedly, an idea struck him. Swiftly he grabbed up a fallen log from the forest floor, broke off some awkward branches, and turned to use the weapon of wood against the vampire.

Dracula brandished his spear, which now in the headlights' gleam showed the blood of the monster on its tip. With it he parried blows from Sobek's enormous bludgeon. Each impact bent the slender shaft of Merlin's spear, sometimes almost double, but it did not break.

The clumsy log-club caught on other trees, first rebounding awkwardly, then breaking. Whirling the remnant round his head, at last hurling it away in mad frustration, Sobek surprised the watchers by trying to summon help.

His voice went up in a long, inhuman howl. "Rally to me! Rally to your god, my followers!"

The great sound vanished without an echo, was absorbed into the dark surrounding woods. Answer came there none—only the crushing realization that his many worshipers existed almost solely in his imagination.

Sobek moved uncertainly. Vlad Tepes relentlessly advanced.

Once more, the Crocodile sprang, with incredible speed. Somehow he got past the spear's bloodied point.

There was a renewed clash, the fighters grappling again, sliding down into the stream. Rock Creek ran shallow almost everywhere, though its swirls concealed the occasional unexpected pool. But it was in most places swift and violent, particularly along this steep descent.

Suddenly it seemed that Sobek was winning, that he had Maule pinned at a disadvantage between rocks in the rushing torrent.

Trying to aid the struggling vampire, Andy went splashing into the furious flow, to find he had all he could do just to keep his feet. John, next in, lost his footing and was suddenly swept away, drenched and pounded on rocks by the frigid, rushing current. Desperately he clawed for a grip, felt rocks and tree roots slide past his grasping fingers.

At last he managed to grab something solid, and pulled himself out, gasping, on the shore.

Andy was there beside him, and now Joe Keogh, who had tried to come to his aid. All three of them were bruised and battered, partly stunned, splashing in the creek.

. . . then they looked up in shock, to see the bodies of monster and vampire, locked in combat, come rolling down on them.

The three men tried to scatter, then were knocked aside like toys as the brawl went rolling past them.

Maybe, thought Joe, he should have brought along an axe. And then a saner thought: *I'm much too old for this.*

Dolly, weeping in frustration, had picked up a rock the size of her head, and was trying to balance it for an accurate throw when Sobek once more came near. John Southerland, too, had got out on the bank and was looking for more rocks to throw.

And over and beneath all other sounds, the endless roaring of the stream.

Again and again the Vampire and Crocodile went splashing into the stream, again and again they emerged from the water to go rampaging through the woods.

There were moments when the Crocodile's eyes, the whole upper portion of its face, were warped into a sickening semblance of humanity, above the great jutting snout with its glut of teeth.

Maule had lost his spear again, regained it, and kept trying to get in a killing thrust. It was only a faint residue of Merlin's power that still charged the spear, like the last lightning of a departing storm; and Maule could only pray that there would be enough for one more thrust.

Connie, hovering near the cabin, watching from a distance, was now holding a shrieking Dickon by the hair to keep him from escaping. She screamed advice to Vlad Tepes to get away, run for his life while he still could.

Dickon's eyes were closed, his fingers in his ears, and he was shuddering.

Dolly threw another rock and watched it miss, then added more bloodthirsty encouragement. "Get him, Matt! Tear out his bloody guts!"

* * *

And, suddenly, Maule's spear was broken.

An instant later, the Crocodile's lashing tail struck him a hard blow, knocking him into a crevice between two rocks at the top of another stretch of rapids that almost made a waterfall. Joe winced, then stumbled forward again, sloshing in wet clothes, trying to grab pieces of the spear before they could be washed away.

But it was Andy, younger and faster, who grabbed up a splintered fragment of the shaft, and saw that it had the spearhead on one end. In another moment he had scrambled close enough to the combatants to try, ineffectually, to jab the green hide with the spear-point. Before he could try again, Maule's white hand deftly reached to take his weapon back.

The fighters had now stalled in the stream, on the brink of a minor waterfall. Below them ran swift rapids, studded with sharp-edged rocks.

It seemed that the monster had managed to get the vampire wedged into a crevice between rocks. Maule was gripping one foreleg of the Crocodile, keeping himself too close under its jaw for it to get in a killing bite.

Sobek cried out again, this time in some language too old for even Maule to understand. But his meaning sounded plainly in his agony—he was bellowing again, this time in despair, for help from a universe that could have none to give.

The end came suddenly, just as the huge jaws opened to grab Maule's body in their crushing, rending grip, or to tear his arm off at the shoulder. Instead, the broken spear-shaft went straight down the Crocodile's throat, with all the strength of one of Maule's long arms behind it.

The point of hardened wood, informed and blessed by Merlin's power, went stabbing, probing on through softness, until it reached the center of the great, writhing body.

There was an explosion of light as Maule withdrew his arm, and he was flung aside, to land half in the creek, half out of it.

For just a moment, both banks of the stream, and the woods that clothed them, were filled with a pulsing, crimson glare.

The glare was centered upon Sobek. In the center of that pulsating outline, at the moment when the Crocodile died, a small lump of something that resembled scarlet ice, a burning coal surrounded by a layer of crystal, became briefly visible to everyone.

There came another dazzling explosion of light.

To some of those who watched, it seemed for one nearly blinding moment that their enemy's body had been converted to mere frozen water.

But a moment after that, the Crocodile had utterly disappeared. Where he had been, there lay only a most peculiar artifact; a twisted remnant of Sobek, retaining something of his shape, though of somewhat lesser size. The color of it gleamed pure gold.

Throwing down another useless stone, Dolly came dashing forward. Others were running also, but she was first to reach Maule's fallen body. Murmuring anxious words that Andy could not quite hear, she started to pull the fallen vampire from the rushing stream.

Uncle Matt stirred as she threw her arms around him. Now he was sitting up straight, and his eyes were open, glinting with triumph through exhaustion. Catching Joe Keogh's eye, he nodded in the direction of something over the treetops, and in a weak voice muttered: "The god of war is with us, Joseph."

Joe turned and looked. Low in the southern sky, Mars burned as red and bright as he had ever seen it.

~ 23 ~

*H*alf an hour after the battle, injuries had been salved and bandaged—fortunately none were severe enough to require treatment beyond first aid. And rest and food had already begun their job of restoration.

Dolly's treasure, in the form that all its seekers had imagined, had proven to be an illusion. The dream had evaporated—but in its place a new prize had appeared, this one all the greater because of its reality.

Both vehicles had been driven closer to what was left of Dickon's cabin—no one could remember seeing Dickon anywhere since well before the climax of the fight.

Connie observed: "Perhaps this time the old one has really taken shelter on the roof of the Chicago public library—on the theory of that being the last place where anyone will look for him."

Maule's dark eyes glittered. "Bah. If he ever comes within my reach again, I will crush him like an insect.

But search for him? I have better uses for my time. Life is too short to spend it hunting for mosquitoes." A pause. "Or for any ordinary treasure."

The headlights on both vehicles had been turned off; the darkness in the woods was far from absolute, and there were flashlights enough for breathers to see all they had to see. The survivors of the fight, breathing and unbreathing, were half-expecting that someone else would have taken note of all the racket, and would be coming to investigate. Joe Keogh had been mentally at work, trying to get ready some kind of cover story. But now he supposed that the nearest other human might be a mile or more away, and had never even heard the noise. Dickon had chosen the location of his hideout well in terms of isolation. No outsiders had been attracted by the noise of gunshots and breaking logs.

All that was left of Sobek was indeed a lump of solid gold—the Philosopher's Stone, at the moment of its destruction, had fulfilled its legendary power of converting ordinary matter to the noble metal. Joe thought that "trophy" was an awkward and inappropriate word to describe the grotesque, bright yellow lump, almost the size of a full-grown crocodile, and retaining something of the creature's shape—which was all that remained of the great god Sobek. But right now he could not think of a better word, so maybe "trophy" would have to do.

After making sure that no one minded, Joe took a couple of flash pictures of the thing. Someday, maybe, he would secretly show them to his grandchildren.

The combined strength of two vampires—one of them admittedly exhausted—was needed to wrestle the mortal remains of the Crocodile into a dense thicket, over which Connie recited a simple spell that she promised would make it hard for anyone to see. She had suggested a deep pool in the creek as a temporary hiding place, but quickly abandoned that idea when some practical breather pointed out that, come the dawn, some eager fisherman might possibly appear on the banks of Rock Creek and begin to probe its depths with line and hook.

Everyone who still had energy to move went over the site of Sobek's demise, closely examining the ground for any surviving trace of the Philosopher's Stone. But there was nothing to be found.

When the broader site of the conflict had been inspected, various tire marks erased, and ejected cartridge shells picked up, all were ready to adjourn to their waiting hotel rooms.

Having regained the security of a hotel room back in Red Lodge, Maule uncharacteristically slept through most of the remainder of the night. But he was awake and moving on the following morning, up early enough to join his breathing companions for what they considered a late breakfast. He had already enjoyed what amounted to his morning meal, and had been greatly refreshed and strengthened thereby.

On rousing from a deep, and thankfully dreamless, sleep, he first packed away his plastic bag of native earth, then moved to adjust the elegant window curtains of his room to shut out a maximum amount of sunlight. Then with thoughtful attention he observed that his companion of the last few hours was still asleep, in the far half of the double bed. Bending close over Dolly, tucking the cover up round her bare shoulders, he glanced, with tender concern, at the pair of tiny red spots that their union had left upon her throat. They were so small, he noted with approval, that it was highly unlikely any-one else would notice them. Nor should the young lady be troubled with any lasting aftereffects.

In a few hours Maule intended to return to bed, alone, and enjoy a delicious daylight trance. But he did not want to miss the breakfast conference with all of his loyal associates.

Their hotel, a solid brick construction right on the main street of Red Lodge, had proven to be an unex-pected oasis of urban comfort and even luxury. Moving about in the process of showering and dressing, he found that a condensed, fax edition of the *New York Times* had been thoughtfully slid under the door. The marvels of modern electronics! Pleasurably he allowed his thoughts to return to his own plans for a web site.

After dressing, and making sure that Dolores Fla-mel was awake and would soon be up, Maule made his relaxed way downstairs.

He found most of the others already at table, in the dining room just off the tiny lobby. To a quiet chorus of greetings he acknowledged having slept well.

Refusing an offered menu, he took a chair beside Andy, who said that he had slept well too. "First time in more than a week I had a room to myself."

"Indeed, there are times when that is much to be desired."

After breakfast, the entire party retreated from the din-ing room to the privacy of the suite rented in John South-erland's name. It was necessary to reach a quick decision on several matters, notably what disposition should be made of the golden Crocodile, which all agreed ought to be theirs by right of conquest. "It would be hard to imag-ine who else could have a right to it."

It was promptly decided that the great trophy should be cut or broken into chunks of manageable size, on the spot where it lay hidden in the woods. From there the pieces would be transported directly, in two vehicles, to the Billings airport, where Joe Keogh's aircraft waited.

Maule cleared his throat politely. "If I may suggest—?"

If Uncle Matt wanted to put forward a suggestion, everyone was going to fall silent and listen carefully.

"In Chicago, where the necessary technology should be available, I suggest that the pieces be melted down, poured into ingots, weighed, and sold, then the money divided into equal shares."

After a moment he added: "I am assuming that we each desire to have a share?" Then, in response to unanimously surprised looks, he explained: "Gold is, after all, the deadliest metal. I wonder if, over the centuries, despite its rarity, gold has not destroyed more human lives than steel blades or leaden bullets."

With discussion of the treasure out of the way, at least one of Maule's allies found the climax of last night's events hard to believe.

Andy spoke up, in a slow, determined voice. "There were some things that happened last night that I don't understand. Maybe I never will, maybe I just don't have to know. But before we all shut up about this, and none of us ever speaks of it again—hey?—I'd like to have one shot at getting matters straight in my own mind."

"Proceed," Maule said agreeably. "Now is the time."

"Well—he really had the Philosopher's Stone inside him, for the past three thousand years? And how did you know that?"

"He really did. I doubt that those alchemists in ancient Thebes—I must admit that they were truly adepts—understood the magnitude of their accomplishment. Or perhaps they were stunned into a fatal carelessness. For somehow, before they could even begin to reap the benefits of their achievement, it was taken from them.

"The dream we shared—and which has now ceased to trouble us—was accurate in its essentials. The wretch who stole the priceless treasure really was carrying it in his mouth when he ran into the temple of Sobek. He really did stumble to a halt in the dark passage where six virtually identical statues, still wet from the mold, stood drying on two shelves.

"And that is where we were deceived. Over the course of centuries, Sobek somehow convinced himself that the thief—with whom he did not identify himself— had hidden the Stone in one of the statues. As long as he did not know where the Stone really was, he need not face the truth about his own identity."

"So, the thief never really put it in any statue. Instead, he—?"

"He ran on, with the great gem still in his mouth, into the next room of the temple. And from there on into the courtyard of the crocodile pool . . . where he was devoured, but did *not* die.

"Instead, he underwent a monstrous transformation. When the fangs of the sacred crocodile closed on his helpless body, he was still carrying his loot, still feeling the coldness and the weight of it inside his mouth."

"And the crocodile—I suppose it was only a natural crocodile then—?"

"Precisely. And it ingested the Philosopher's Stone, along with most of the thief's head, in his first or second bite. A few more gulps sufficed to devour the thief's entire body, or most of it. But it is with his brain that we are chiefly concerned here. The human brain, and the magic Stone, both inside his luckless head.

"Imagine, if you will, chunks of raw human flesh, billions upon billions of human cells. The vast majority of them were still totally alive, only moments after being swallowed into the belly of the beast—and this sample of live humanity was suddenly brought, at the same time as the crocodile's own flesh, into contact with the transcendent power of the Stone.

"The angry men who came bursting into the courtyard moments later, desperate to recover their priceless Stone, were stopped in their tracks.

"What emerged from the pool to greet them was no longer a mere beast, and it was something at once much greater and much less than a human thief, and very different from the crocodile who had lived in the water.

"Priests and guards and laborers all fell back in fear and trembling. A new kind of being, one that they had never seen before, now walked—or crawled—among them.

"Perhaps it stood before them on two legs. Almost certainly it spoke to them—though what its first words were may not be easy to imagine. They were humans, bound by the conventions and the knowledge of their time and place. What choice had they but to fall down and worship this monstrous, talking apparition from the sacred pool? It was they who, by worshiping the Crocodile, first convinced him that he was Sobek the god.

"What the Stone would have made of the crocodile's body alone is difficult to say. Perhaps the result would still have been a memorable monster—on the other hand, the treasure of the ages might have remained inert, and passed through the creature's gut like so much gravel.

"But human lives are unlike any others. They have a special quality."

Andy was nodding. "Then human deaths must be different too."

"Indeed they are. And this one was, I must suppose—unique. When he who had been a human thief regained awareness of himself and his condition, he much preferred to believe he was a god, rather than face the fact that he had also been a mindless animal."

Maule's audience were motionless, listening.

"Consider. How did the creature who called himself Sobek acquire that name? How did he become so unshakably convinced of his own divinity? Ancient Egyptians confronted with this huge, monstrous crocodile would never have doubted it to be the god Sobek in the flesh. They must have called the creature by that name as they fell down to worship.

"In that time and place were many gods, and many who wanted to believe in them. Those who had driven and harried the thief to his doom probably just assumed that the god had appeared and devoured him.

"And after a time—perhaps that part of the process required a long time—the idea that he had ever been less than a god would become unthinkable.

"And why not? His new powers transcended anything he had imagined in his few years of brutish life.

"Only by the overwhelming magic of the Stone could a human body and brain be melded with those of a crocodile—I suppose no other power on earth could have accomplished such a feat.

"Both his human memory and his crocodile memory

were effectively destroyed—the human memory surviving only as part of the subconscious—only as a source of dreams.

"Perhaps there were moments when his purely human consciousness struggled to reassert itself. He might then have briefly considered himself a dead man, a spirit on his way to the Egyptian underworld, to undergo judgment. It might have been then that he discovered the usefulness of the false doors—everyone knew they were basically intended to enable the departed to revisit their old world in spirit, to partake of the offerings placed inside their tombs.

"At some point, some of his worshipers must have dared to ask their god what had happened to the Stone—and that he could not tell them. What he still retained of the thief's memories no longer seemed to Sobek like his own—they were too full of fear, and flight, and weakness. And the thief had never understood that what he stole was anything more than a fine gem.

"What he did not realize was that it was now somewhere in the center of his own reptilian body. Where it remained, until I struck it with a spear whose point was fortified with Merlin's magic. I hoped to win the battle with that thrust, but the golden bonus came as something of a surprise. Perhaps it should not have done; the main attribute of the Stone, in its legendary appearances, is its power to transform whatever surrounds it into gold."

After several seconds of silence, Dolly asked: "But—that was thousands of years ago—what was Sobek doing all that time?"

"It is possible that his powers allowed him to travel extensively through time. His experience of duration might have been very different from ours. For him, perhaps, the theft of the gem took place only a few months ago, or only a few days."

Dolly was gazing at Uncle Matt with awe. "How did you manage to figure all this out?"

And Connie muttered, with an air of mockery: "Your cousin Sherlock would be proud." Everyone had noticed that Connie was looking much more cheerful this morning, and in fact had been up early to do some shopping in Red Lodge. Her camouflage suit was gone, replaced by an outfit she evidently considered much more stylish.

Maule ignored her mention of Cousin Sherlock. "In my last dream I learned that the thief was carrying something hard and solid, cold and heavy, in his mouth, in the last moments of his human life."

Joe Keogh shook his head doubtfully. "It would seem too much to swallow—"

"It was. And so might the story. But it is true."

In another hour Maule and his five helpers, with both of the *nosferatu* heavily shaded against the morning sun, were gathered again in the forest, standing over their incredible trophy where it lay hidden in the thicket. This time they had brought with them suitable tools for cutting up soft metal.

Maule strongly urged that the treasure be divided equally, without trying to estimate the various contributions to victory of the several members of the club.

Dolly agreed to that. "It's not the treasure Gramp thought he was leaving me. I don't see how I could rightly claim more than one share for myself."

Joe Keogh, who was making it a point to notice certain things this morning, saw that when bright morning sunlight fell on Dolly's throat a certain way, two small red dots showed up quite plainly. He also noticed that this morning Dolly had a special way of looking at Uncle Matthew—nothing too overt, just a fierce glance now and then.

Well, that was all right with Joe. He would have been very upset if red dots had shown up on Andy's throat as well. But there were none, and he and Connie were paying each other no special attention.

Connie was fluttering her eyelids delicately at Uncle Matthew. "I was a good girl, was I not?"

"So far, your behavior in this matter has been—acceptable. You shall have a share."

"Dear Vlad, you are so generous."

When Dolores Flamel looked at the estimate of a full share's value someone had jotted down, her eyes widened and she said: "My God, this is more than even . . . well, no, it isn't more than Dickon told me I'd be getting—oops, shouldn't have mentioned that fella's name. But this is real. Good lord!" Evidently struck by a new and disconcerting thought, she fell abruptly silent.

Andy asked: "What's wrong, Dolly?"

"Looks like for once in my life I may have to pay income tax."

Maule hummed a small sound of amusement. "I myself have found that unavoidable. The subspecies *Homo dirus,* also called the 'undead,' has only a few members— but if the category of 'untaxed' exists at all, its numbers must be much smaller, approximating zero.

"If you would strive to hold financial damage to a minimum, there are in Chicago many expert counselors.

I know one in particular who should look with favor upon any friend of mine. Her fee should be quite reasonable."

"That's one lady I'm going to want to talk to."

The phone in John Southerland's hotel suite was ringing.

At the moment, Maule was alone in the front room of the suite, looking broodingly out the window through a chink between drawn drapes, and wondering if he ought to try to sleep again. Actually he felt well rested, well healed of the cuts and bruises he had suffered in the fight, and generally content. A moment later, John's voice sounded from somewhere in the remoter recesses of the apartment. "Could you answer that, please, Uncle Matt?"

"Of course." Maule roused himself from contemplation. He lifted the receiver and by way of greeting pronounced the number of the room.

The childish voice on the other end sounded somewhat disconcerted: "Daddy?"

Maule's attention was abruptly recalled from exotic speculations about the web. He cleared his throat. "This is Matthew Maule, and I trust I am not your father. What is your name?"

A pause. Then: "My father is John Southerland."

"Ah. I surmised as much. Your father will soon be available." Maule hesitated awkwardly. Conversing with children had never come easily to him. At last he repeated: "And what is your name?"

When he heard the answer, he frowned, and repeated it, as if not quite certain of what course to take. "Your name is Andrew V. Southerland?"

"That's right," came the treble over the line. "Andrew after my grandfather and my uncle."

Grasping at a conversational straw, Maule ventured: "And what does the middle initial stand for?"

"Vlad. Isn't that a goofy one?"

Driving the SUV toward the Billings airport, with a fortune in gold aboard, wrapped in small packages, Maule told Joe that he looked forward to being able to get back to trying to develop his web site—though he was coming round to the idea that a further period of study and contemplation might be in order before the site could actually be established.

Joe suggested diplomatically that Andy might not be helping his Uncle Matt this time. "When I called Kate last night, she kind of put in a special request along that line."

"That is understandable." Maule was not surprised. "Yes, understandable."

"Oh, and of course she sends her love. Her congratulations."

Maule nodded.

Andy said, from the backseat: "Give Mom a little time to cool off, Uncle Matt. In a while she'll come around. Especially if you went and talked to her."

"We shall see."

While they were helping load the packaged gold aboard the aircraft, Andy asked Dolores, almost casually: "Going to be staying in Chicago? I mean after we get this gold thing divided up?"

"I don't know."

Andy had noted, but did not mention, the two small red spots. "He's a pretty neat guy, my Uncle Matt. Taken all in all, quite a man, as I think someone in Shakespeare says."

*   *   *

As far as Joe Keogh could find out, by means of a few cautious and long-distance calls, asking carefully crafted questions in the right places, the Chicago police had never caught on that they ought to be looking for Andy Keogh and Dolores Flamel. Going home ought to be safe enough.

Joe felt sure that the current situation, reports of mysterious death and destruction scattered across the country, with Matthew Maule lurking just out of sight in the background, would definitely ring a bell with Charley Snider—if Charley ever heard about it. But, thankfully, the homicide captain had retired years ago.

Sooner or later some hunter or hiker or snowmobiler in the Montana woods would stumble over signs of remarkable conflict, such as the half-wrecked cabin and the broken trees. Well, at least this time there were no bodies of unbreathing breathers to be found.

Dolores Flamel had taken the seat right next to Andy on his father's plane. They had climbed to altitude and leveled off, jets droning smoothly, pushing them to Chicago.

"It was good being with you, Andy," she said sincerely. "I mean, I don't see how I ever could have got through all that alive without you. Let alone come out of it a rich girl, like it looks I'm going to be."

"It was good being with you too. Don't know anyone I'd rather"—he felt a twisted giggle coming—"fight monsters with."

She smiled. "Got a girlfriend, Andy?"

"One or two. Nothing special, yet. They'll never—"

He had to break off, shaking his head. "They'll never hear anything about this."

Dolly nodded sagely. "I'm not going to be talking 'bout it much, either." She drew breath. "I was wondering—would you be upset if I kind of took over your job?"

"My job?"

"With Uncle Matt. Teaching him what to do with his computer."

Andy was shaking his head again.

Dolly smiled. "I know a little bit about the web. I guess maybe I could show him a thing or two."